Dennis McCort - **A Kafkaesque Memoir**

Dennis McCort

A Kafkaesque Memoir

Confessions from the Analytic Couch

PalmArtPress
Berlin

Bibliografische Information der Deutschen Nationalbibliothek
Die Deutsche Nationalbibliothek verzeichnet diese Publikation in der Deutschen Nationalbibliografie; detaillierte bibliografische Daten sind im Internet über http://www.dnb.de abrufbar.

ISBN: 978-3-941524-94-1

First Edition, 2017

Publisher: Catharine J. Nicely
Pfalzburger Str. 69
10719 Berlin, Germany

www.palmartpress.com

Printed in Germany

Table of Contents

PART THREE: TRANSFORMATION

Foreword

To be sure, there can be no literal endpoint in analysis, since self-realization is a process susceptible of endless deepening. Nevertheless, I can say in a provisional sense that Dennis McCort is one of only three analysands I have known in my practice who have gone "all the way." That is to say, he is now in a position from which he can manage his own "case," chart his own path, enjoy his own process of growth. This very book, the story of his nine-year analysis with me, is perhaps the first manifestation of such enjoyment, the first flowering of a strongly individuated consciousness. Indeed, I told him that the experience of writing this memoir, which took place over roughly the final year of his analysis, would become, in effect, a kind of meta-analysis, an enrichment and consolidation of our original journey together. In reproducing his analysis in these pages, he has, one might say, done it again on his own—reexamined the dreams, sharpened the insights, more fully assimilated the psychic unfolding he has realized himself to be. And told a gripping tale into the bargain! Though he always waves me off when I say this, I have by now come to regard him as more a colleague than a patient or analysand.

It is, I think, impossible to overstate the magnitude of the accomplishment this book represents. Unlike most narratives of psychoanalyses I have read, what we have here is no mere collage of subjective impressions or truncated description of a particular phase of the analytic process (say, the "dawn of insight" or the "grand finale"). It is, rather, a brave and, I believe, brilliantly successful attempt to recreate in a straight- forward, realistic style the entire span of the process from its faltering beginnings, through its long, dark years of pin-balling anxiety and tedium to its final emergence into the bright sunlight of self-mastery. Dennis McCort's analytic story has unfolded over the first decade of the new millennium, and I would like to view it as a hopeful microcosm of a similarly benign destiny in store for our presently benighted culture. As Carl Jung never tired of telling us, facing one's own demons with honesty, and therefore also courage, is an absolute *sine qua non* for the health of a society no less than an individual. May the story told in these pages help to lead the way.

There is another, self-evident, feature of this book that puts it into an elite class. I refer to the fact that the analytic tale is here told, not by the analyst, which is usually the case (e.g., Robert Lindner's classic *The Fifty-Minute* hour or Vamik Voltan's *What Do You Get When You Cross a Dandelion with a Rose?*) but by the patient himself. It is entirely his own story, told exclusively from his own point of view, without so much as a single correction, editorial emendation or "friendly suggestion" from yours truly. In my five or six readings of the manuscript, I am proud to say I gamely resisted any impulse to read as an editor, rather respecting my patient's right to exercise the same absolute control over his material as the many analysts who have enjoyed such control in their own accounts. So here the shoe is on the other foot, the tables turned, and I am glad of it. This book belongs to analysand McCort alone, perceptions and misperceptions, charms and warts, such as they may be. I can only assure the reader that I have come across very few of the latter in either category. What one reads in these pages is as close to the psychospiritual drama that took place between us over a nine-year period as my memory is able to attest.

Dennis McCort's book tells the story of what it means to traverse both phases of Jungian analytical psychotherapy, the Freudian monologue (the resolving of the core conflict within the personal unconscious) as well as the Jungian dialogue (the confronting, encountering and integrating of archetypal aspects of the collective unconscious). In his account the triumphs of the individuation process, coming mainly in the third part, read like narrations of a series of little "kenshos." I know of no other book about "being in therapy" that does this and, generally speaking, no other book that approaches this one in its presentation of the depth of the therapeutic experience. Reading it has been nothing less than a mutative experience for me. I know it will be that for others as well.

Charles Purper, Ph.D.
Syracuse, New York
May, 2010

Preface

I am an ordinary man who, to all outward appearances, has lived an ordinary life. I was born into a solid, God-fearing middle-class family, enjoyed the good will of relatives and friends as I grew up, attended excellent schools and universities, had a rewarding career as a professor at a major university and am now savoring the creative leisure of retirement, which has made it possible for me to write this book. As enviable as such a life may seem to some, there is little about it that would rate space in a newspaper. I did once hit a 330-foot home run as a Little Leaguer; that got about two inches in the next day's *Jersey Journal.* I've written three books, which, however, have been read by no more than a handful of scholars and now sit on a lonely shelf in my study next to books just as lonely written by friends. Before age sixty, I had to be rushed to a hospital only once, for a seven-year-old leg broken by the bumper of a car I never saw coming, which means there are no grave threats to life and limb in my past of which I can boast. During the draft-board years of my youth, my student deferment kept me out of Vietnam, so I have no war stories to tell. While I generally enjoyed the approving nods of my colleagues and students as a professor (that is, unless I'm deluding myself), I never fulfilled my pipedream of reaching the "rock star" echelon of academe, the rarefied air breathed by, say, a Doris Kearns Goodwin or a Carl Sagan or even a Jacques Barzun.

Nevertheless, I do believe I've drunk well and deeply of life's heady ale, so much so that I am presumptuous enough to think my tale worth telling others. It is a tale that has all the elements of a good story: conflict, suspense, farce, "quietly desperate" doldrums, struggle, triumph. The thing with me is, almost all the drama has played out on the inside, in the relatively private worlds of psyche and spirit; and so, in my effort to find a generic category for my story, I find myself resorting to the ungainly adjective, "psychospiritual," a word that has yet to assume its rightful place in Websters, which would be between "psychosomatic" and "psychosurgery." This, then, is a psychospiritual memoir. More specifically, it is a memoir tracing the arc of a nine-year psychoanalysis I undertook with Dr. Charles Purper, a certified analyst who also happened to be theologically trained, in Syracuse, New York, from 2000 to 2009.

My analysis with "Dr. P.," as I've come to call him, was the culmination of a series of discouraging attempts to assuage recurring bouts of anxiety and depression that had plagued me throughout adulthood. Even in the summer of 2000 as I dialed his number for the first time, after picking his name at random from the Syracuse Yellow Pages, I certainly had no plan for long-term psychotherapy in mind, particularly of the psychodynamic sort; I'd already tried that several times, found it wanting (to put it kindly) and no longer had any emotional or intellectual stomach for it. I'd also tried Logotherapy, Primal Therapy, Zen, Avatar and a bunch of other self-styled panaceas, with similarly disappointing results. All I wanted from this Yellow-Page Svengali, "Dr. Charles Purper, hypnotherapy," was a quick fix for my increasingly debilitating phobia centering on interstate highway driving. I needed to drive to Boston to give my daughter, who had recently graduated from college, a hand moving into a new apartment and didn't want to have to "sneak" my way there using back roads. Nearing sixty by then, I'd more or less given up youthful idealized fantasies of personal transformation, resigned myself to taking my neurosis with me to the grave and sought from the mental health complex no more than support for "holding actions" against "guerilla symptoms"—a phobia here, an obsession there.

But I'm getting ahead of myself. I began with the intention to persuade the reader that this life of mine, in which "nothing much has happened," and the writing of a book about it, have been well worth the effort. For that I must take the reader back to the day on which the notion of such a book first suggested itself. A little over two years ago, having just retired from forty years of service to my university, I was having lunch with a friend and colleague in the German Department, Gerd Schneider, who had retired two years before me. Gerd had just written, in German, an absorbing memoir of his years of struggle with grinding poverty growing up in war-time and post-war Berlin[1] and we were discussing the feasibility of my translating it into English. Suddenly, over dessert, he said to me, "Dennis, why don't *you* write an autobiography?" Certain he was ribbing me for my placid American life that had never known war, I replied, "Oh sure, Gerd, why not; after all, I've led the kind of life biographers salivate over, haven't I—you know, the epic backdrop of post-war New Jersey and the compelling struggle of my family to save up enough for that first TV set. Now there's a story!" He laughed and waved me off, saying, "No, no, I don't mean an autobiography like mine, an external history; I mean an *internal* history: write the history of your *inner* life." At first I dismissed the idea, but over the next few months this casual suggestion of my friend just kept surfacing in my mind, more or less in the form of a series of questions I at first didn't especially want to entertain: Why not? Isn't it true that my inner life has been, by far, the dimension of greater interest? The private misery? The many failed, yet curious, even fascinating, efforts to deal with that misery, right up to and including my analysis with Dr. P. (which by that time was well into its seventh year)?

But finally I thought, seeking a way to banish the idea, even if I seriously considered it, no one really wanted to read an entire book about someone else's *inner* life, unless that book were written by, say, an Augustine or a Rousseau or a Flaubert.[2] It would be just too claustrophobically private, too, well, . . . "inner." And that's when it hit me: the analysis itself would be the ideal format for writing a predominantly inner autobiography since all the private features, the things within, that fill an analytic session— the memories, the feelings, the intuitions, inklings and moods—were, inevitably, grounded in external life events, relationships and social fields without which nothing could be told. The analysis gave me the formula, the framework, within which to narrate the interplay of dominant internal and recessive external that was my life. And since the analysis, as made up of my weekly conversations with Dr. P., provided, all by itself, the plot line of a dramatically unfolding relationship, that between doctor and patient, on which to hang this dialectical interplay, I could pick and choose which particular events from my external life to tell about: naturally they would be the ones of which I told *him*, the interesting ones steeped in conflict, longing and regret, and I needn't fear being burdened with a tedious birth-to-old age chronology.

On the contrary, I need only tell as much of my outer life as was necessary to cast light on my inner life, and that in no particular order, or rather in the random order of analytic free association. Viewed from this angle, the outer life would have the charm rather of a mosaic than a linear sequence, a jigsaw pieced together by the heart and mind of the teller as revealed to the listener.

That settled it. I would write my confessions, the confessions of my analytic "sins," in the original Germanic sense of that word as the "sunderings" or "cleavages" in my soul. I would write them for the entertainment, edification and possibly even instruction of those like me who found themselves psychospiritually at sea. Alas, no sooner did I commit to the idea than I found myself facing the dilemma of every memoirist: how to account for the long trail of quoted conversation begun many years before the time of writing (not to mention the subtle play of gesture, attitude and body language animating that conversation). If critics rolled their eyes over Frank McCourt's "total recall of dialogue overheard from the crib!",[3] what would be their reaction to me for implying I had an eidetic memory of my own psychoanalysis. Moreover, in my own case the problem was compounded by the very nature of analysis as "the talking cure"; conversation was just about all there was to it, whether Freudian monologue or Jungian dialogue.

I don't know how the reader feels about Carl Jung's principle of synchronicity,[4] but let me relate here an incident that surely speaks in its favor. During the time I was fretting over this problem of the limits of memory with respect to my "memoir," I picked up Somerset Maugham's autobiographical novel,

The Razor's Edge, a book I'd been meaning to read since retiring and was now finally getting around to. As I opened the cover and began to read, I was astonished to find the solution to my problem right there on the first page. It is contained in the attitude Maugham takes at the outset of his own spiritual "memoir":

> I do not pretend that the conversations I have recorded can be regarded as verbatim reports. I never kept notes of what was said on this or the other occasion, but I have a good memory for what concerns me, and though I have put these conversations in my own words they faithfully represent, I believe, what was said. . . . I have done this for the same reasons as the historians have, to give liveliness and verisimilitude to scenes that would have been ineffective if they had been merely recounted. I want to be read and I think I am justified in doing what I can to make my book readable. The intelligent reader will easily see for himself where I have used this artifice, and he is at perfect liberty to reject it.[5]

He is also at perfect liberty, as far as I'm concerned, to regard my book as a first-person novel, one that happens to be highly autobiographical. In fact, as far as the events of my life occurring outside the treatment room are concerned, the book is, for reasons of discretion, at least as much novel as memoir. In the end, I am, like Maugham, less concerned with questions of genre or cognitive limits or even factual accuracy than with the importance of telling a good story, a story, one hopes, that might in some small way contribute to the reader's quality of life.

There is, I hasten to add, one part of this story of my analysis that is emphatically not an amalgam of memory, reconstruction and invention, and that is its core, the dreams. The twenty-seven dreams set in italics that head up the chapters, along with a score of others interpolated within them, are recounted from a combination of clear memory and notes made, in most cases, in the morning upon waking. These notes, scribbled on slips of paper many of which also contain my spontaneous associations to and thoughts about the dream in question, are dated in most cases, though not all. Such dream-dating, which I began years before I ever thought of writing this book, has been of enormous help to me in my efforts to reconstruct the long chronological arc of the analysis. I truly believe I could never have written anything even ironically justifying the term "memoir" without it.

Nor was the dating of dream notes the only happy accident aiding me in my reconstruction of personal history. The reader will be amused to learn that, during the years of analysis and without giving it a thought, I developed the habit of tossing these slips of paper, upon returning home with them from a session, into a desk drawer and forgetting about them. Imagine my overflow of gratitude years later when, having decided to write the book, I opened the desk drawer and immediately realized the pile of note papers was already arranged for me in nearly perfect reverse chronological sequence, with the most recent dream on top. Thank God the fact struck me before I could scoop up the papers, including the undated ones, and spread them out randomly all over my desk! I'm sure Dr. P. would insist this was a great gift from the gods of synchronicity.

I described my dreams above as "the core" of the analysis, and this is no exaggeration. Though I have no wish to put words in Dr. P.'s mouth (yes, I know, an entire book of such words follows!), I'm confident he would agree with Freud's description of dreams as "the royal road to the unconscious." Over time and little by little, our persistent ruminations over the themes and images of these dreams revealed what the "money" issues were in my psychopathology and, in so doing, suggested new, more effective ways of looking at old problems. The dreams also charted the phases of the analysis as it unfolded and supplied clues to important shifts in psychic structures as these occurred, as, for example, when "Judge Loophole" in chapter 17 morphs into "General Slacker" in chapter 23. Although I didn't have a dream to report to the "dream master" (as I was fond of calling him) every week, I usually showed up with at least one, often two, and on occasion even three. By my best estimate we analyzed well over four hundred dreams in the course of the nine years, of which the twenty-seven that lead off the chapters here are among the most important and interesting. At the very least, these twenty-seven can be said to provide an accurate map of my analytic journey.

No matter how many aids to memory the memoirist may call upon, memory itself remains a most subtle and slippery thing. The line between reflection and reconstruction can be impossible to locate; often there is simply no telling where one leaves off and the other begins. This vaguely unnerving state of affairs was brought home to me in astonishing fashion on a few occasions when Dr. P., having reviewed this or that part of the manuscript as I was writing it, would say to me something such as, “Yes, I remember our discussion of that; you wrote it up pretty close to the way it went,” and I would be embarrassed to admit, “You’re kidding! I was sure I was reconstructing that—I have absolutely no memory of it!” Slowly I became aware of this interplay of recollection and reconstruction as a dialectical principle guiding my writing. This, it turns out, is quite appropriate since the dialectical nature of truth is one of the book’s leading ideas.

The great German poet, Goethe, an idol of mine as a teacher and student of German literature, titled his own autobiography, *Dichtung und Wahrheit*, or *Poetry and Truth.* He avoided any genre term connoting facticity, such as “autobiography,” “life history” or “memoir.” Yet the book is full of facts: names, relationships, dates, places, events of both personal and general history. I believe Goethe’s title, doubtless carefully chosen, reflects his insight that the truest truth of a life is its poetry, which may or may not adhere strictly to the facts. He might have titled it *Poetry* or *Truth,* had he wished to emphasize the deep identity rather than the superficial contrast of these two opposites. There must be a truth that is somehow not the opposite of falsehood. Maybe that truth is *Dichtung.* I offer this book as my *Dichtung,* hence also my *Wahrheit.*

To be sure, a writer needs his muse, but he also needs his models, writers he admires, to inspire him. When I wrote as a scholar, I always kept the noble pen of William James before my mind’s eye, whose supreme clarity and elegance of style were, all by themselves, sufficient reason for me to read him. Now, as a memoirist, I raise that eye to the lofty sphere of St. Augustine’s *Confessions* for its profundity of spirit, to Rousseau’s *Confessions* for its matchless courage of self-disclosure and to Frank McCourt's *Angela's Ashes* for the seductive charm of its Irish tongue. Just a mote of magic dust for my own book from the dust jacket of each of these masterworks would more than content me.

Finally, there is one other writer who must not go unmentioned here, even though, having never written a "Confessions," he is, strictly speaking, not a model, and that is the Czech-German master, Franz Kafka. Yet even if Kafka had "confessed," it would still be misleading for me to identify him as a model for myself. The German word for model, *Vorbild*, literally means "pre-" or "pre-existent image," a sense emphasizing the essential otherness of the person or thing inspiring emulation, and the fact is, I've never felt any separation between Kafka and myself, not even in college days when I first read *The Metamorphosis* and felt at once transfixed by all that strangeness that—strangest of all—felt so familiar. The uncanny aptness of Kafka's existential tropes, images and situations for charting the labyrinth of my interior life will, I hope, become manifest in the pages to follow. For me Kafka is whatever one calls a model after it has been absorbed into one's being. It was the least I could do to share the title of this book with him.

Introduction

I never bargained for what was to come, that day in late September of 2000 when I first walked into Charles Purper's consulting room. But the next nine years would tell the tale. He was a portly man, probably in his late forties, cordial and soft-spoken. He offered me a choice between chair and sofa. I sat down in the chair facing him and we began.

"What brings you here, Mr. McCort?"

"Well, I'm having trouble driving on the interstate, especially in the left lane."

"What sort of trouble do you mean?"

"I sometimes get panicky feelings when I'm in the fast lane, a kind of claustrophobia, I think, a feeling of being stuck there whenever cars are next to me in the right lane. We're all there going at high speeds and it freaks me out that I can't get off even if I want to. The cars and especially the eighteen-wheelers to my right are blocking me. I feel totally hemmed in and begin to panic."

"Why don't you just stay in the right lane, so that you always have the option to pull over?"

"Well, actually that does work to some extent, but I resent not having the freedom to use the left lane if I want to—I guess I've got a phobia."

Dr. Purper seemed to consider this, neither confirming nor rejecting my self-diagnosis. After a moment he told me that many simple phobias could be treated rather handily through hypnosis. I told him that was what I was there for and we agreed to try it.

On my next visit he had me take a comfortable sitting position on his sofa and proceeded to induce trance. He had me close my eyes and imagine myself going down a flight of stairs, step by step, each step taking me deeper into the hypnotic state. When I reached the bottom, he gently suggested all sorts of reasons why interstate driving need cause me no concern, the basic idea being that I was in control. He brought me back up the stairs and soon I was out the door and on the interstate doing 70 mph., feeling no pain. The placebo lasted a week or two and I wound up back in the doctor's office wanting to know why.

"I said *simple* phobias can be effectively treated with hypnosis, that is, those brought on by recent trauma, say, the death of a loved one or some other acute stress, but usually not those symptomatic of some underlying pathology of long standing."

"Why do I sense we're heading towards the issue of psychoanalysis here?" I asked in the drollest professorial tone I could muster. "If in fact we are, I don't want to hear about it. You'll recall I only came here for the quick-fix hypnosis."

"You certainly seem to have a strong opinion on the subject of analysis," he said with a wry grin, smoothing his dark goatee with an index finger. "How did you come by it?"

"Through three bouts with three different therapists, all three into depth psychology, which netted me absolutely zero in terms of the improvement of my mental health."

"Ouch! Sounds like you've been burned."

"Well, at least you're giving me the benefit of the doubt, which I appreciate—but that's no reason for me to reconsider my verdict on psychoanalysis."

"No, it certainly isn't," Dr. Purper granted, looking thoughtfully out the window. He pondered this as he cast a brief gaze upon the brilliant fall foliage. “But since we’re at it, why don’t you tell me a little about yourself—you know, the usual vital statistics?”

My initial inner response, totally knee-jerk, was “Oh no, here we go again,” but something about “vital statistics” made it seem as if he were teaming up with me in what would be for both of us a perfunctory exercise—the Grand Introduction—and willing to share the mild tedium of it with me. This disposed me favorably towards him. I decided he’d at least earned a one-paragraph plot summary of my personal history.

“Well, I was born at a very early age,” I intoned with narrative solemnity and then immediately apologized. “Sorry, I’ve waited years for a chance to drop that line into a serious conversation. I guess, to be honest, it’s just a way to express my frustration at having to go down this path yet again. And for what?!”

“Mr. McCort, I get that you’re down on psychotherapy, psychoanalysis in particular. Believe me, many people who’ve come to me over the years [‘Over the years’? He didn’t look nearly old enough to be saying that] have shared your disillusioned view, and it *is* an issue we’ll take up in due course … Or better yet, maybe we should start there, since the issue of therapy itself is obviously very much on your mind.”

“That’s fine with me,” I wasted no time replying, “and if you don’t mind, I’ll get right to it. My problem with psychoanalysis, and with the whole idea of depth psychology, is that I just don’t believe it—or better yet, believe *in* it—anymore. The whole business strikes me as much more faith than science, really. The unconscious, repression, the shaping influence of early childhood experience—the whole Freudian ball of wax—its day has come and gone. It owned the twentieth century, but, looking at the world these days and our own society in particular, can you honestly say we're any better off for it? I've read that even Freud himself wasn't particularly interested in the therapeutic effectiveness of his own ideas—only their scientific validation (though I fail to see how you can have one without the other)."

Dr. Purper gestured as if to offer clarification on this point, but it was already too late for interjections. I was on a roll, with the right target for my frustration trapped in a chair ten feet directly in front of me. I hammered on.

"We need a new approach for a new century, not that there haven't been a thousand approaches already between Freud and today on a therapy smorgasbord ranging from orthodox psychoanalysis to Skinner's rat box to SSRIs that make you feel no pain. You know, from the subjective to the objective. Even the idea of 'a new approach' is probably dinosaur thinking; I should probably say 'an entirely new paradigm, a metamorphosis of perception, a fresh *Weltanschauung*, with a new psychology as merely one of its "fruits," so to speak.'"

I suddenly became aware of the sermonizing tone of my own voice, disagreeable as it was, and simultaneously of the rapt seriousness of Dr. Purper's gaze. Instinctively I shut up so as to give him room to get into it.

"I can see your disillusionment with Freud is based on more than just personal therapeutic experience," he observed, relaxing slightly into a more comfortable position.

"Yes, it is," I hastened to confirm. "I've probably read some fifty or sixty books by and about Freud, Jung and the other members of the early circle—Rank, Reik, Ernest Jones, etc.

I've thought about the issues and explored them with my students in many of my German lit. courses up on the hill. In fact, the unconscious—its meaning, its status, its cultural sources and such—is probably the dominant theme of my scholarship over my entire career."

I was now presenting my credentials to speak with authority on the subject. I wanted to establish myself as, at the very least, a worthy partner in a relationship of equals (assuming, that is, there was to *be* any relationship). In my fantasy, I could even envision myself as a *primus inter pares*. I was determined to have no more of the bottom-dog patient (euphemized as "client") status in which my previous therapists had straitjacketed me, knowingly or not. Of course, I didn't quite recognize it then, but all of this maneuvering on my part was an effort to take out my anger on Dr. Purper over the failures of my previous therapists. I wanted to rub his nose in those failures, and in general, in the failure of the profession he represented. I also wanted him to know that I was fully aware of this abject failure, and possibly even more aware than he of the reasons for it. That might even elevate me to "top dog" (to complete the Fritz Perls metaphor) in our nascent relationship. Needless to say, I was also totally oblivious to the contradiction that my very presence here, as a patient sorely in need of help, deafeningly announced.

Suddenly I felt the need to pee, but immediately suppressed it, calculating that I could hold it till the end of the hour. I would not give him the satisfaction of knowing the stress the interview was putting me under.

I went on. "Or maybe I should say 'the dominant theme over the *first half* of my career,' until about the mid-eighties, when I made two profound personal discoveries which, together, turned everything topsy-turvy."

"Oh? And what were they?" asked the good doctor, with what seemed like genuine interest.

"One was postmodernism and the other was Zen, and I honestly can't remember which happened first," I answered as I sent my mind back to those heady days, to summon up a picture that would in some measure recreate for him what I believed to be my experience of losing the blinders. My recall was briefly interrupted by the sound of the front door of the house slamming shut on its heavy spring. Dr. Purper shared the building with a chiropractor who occupied the downstairs premises. I envied what I imagined to be the patient who had just come in for his bi-monthly spinal adjustment. Five or ten minutes under the strong yet gentle hands of Dr. Farinelli and he'd leave feeling great, every time. "Whichever it was, one fired up the other in a great synergy. The basic insight of both, which hit me like a thunderbolt, was that the ego, the individual self, the person—whatever you want to call it—was unreal. It just didn't exist! This meant that *I* didn't exist the way I thought I did—that I wasn't who, better yet *what*, I thought I was."

Dr. P. nodded thoughtfully, which meant either that he was carefully weighing what I had just told him or that he was confirming to himself I was a madman. So I felt somewhat reassured when he finally said, "I take it you understand that you're using the term 'ego' in the Buddhist sense of self-image, and not in the Freudian sense of a mediating function between inner and outer worlds?"

"Yes, I certainly do—that's the only way I ever use the word. For me it means the internal image someone has of himself as a discrete, conscious entity, but an entity, it turns out, that is nowhere to be found. It's an image with which each of us identifies that has no model in reality the image is *of*. (Excuse the awkward preposition, but it makes my point). The Freudian 'Ich' or ego, on the other hand, is of no use to me in my thinking. As far as I'm concerned, its only function is to separate the sane from the insane, and issues of sanity are not my cup of tea.

"But to get back to my story, to my discovery of this great hoax of ego (in the Buddhist sense): it's not as if I wasn't acquainted with such ideas and their variations from my study of literature, philosophy, religion and such, for practically my entire mature intellectual life. But, you see, there it was always merely ideas, theories—interesting, even exciting stuff, to a student of the humanities, but basically all just maps of the territory, and, as such, of very limited value. Now I began to feel that I was, however gropingly, tentatively, beginning to set foot on the *territory itself*. Looking back, I can remember the awe I felt on discovering that it was of the nature of these two disciplines, Zen and postmodernism, to deliver a blow to consciousness that could jolt a person, in spite of himself, from map to territory, theory to experience."

I saw nothing in the doctor's demeanor to indicate that he wanted to interject anything, so I soldiered on.

"Postmodernism, or poststructuralism, or deconstruction—or any number of other equally uninformative labels—took a long time to get to me. It had been making trouble on campuses at least as far back as the early seventies, especially in university English departments where some version of it was being used as a way of reading literature, to the consternation of older traditionalist professors who, I think, feared its revolutionary implications. But, snuggled away in the docile, unimaginative foreign language department as I was, it was at that time all pretty much like a war being fought on the other side of the planet to me. That is, until I began sniffing around Zen, circa 1983—for totally unrelated personal reasons. As I began to learn about the Buddhist doctrine of *anatta* or no-self, the few little nuggets of postmodernist wisdom I had picked up by osmosis—such as the death of the author, or the fact that 'there is nothing outside the text'—began to light up in me like Christmas tree ornaments.

"Anyway, to bring it all back to psychoanalysis and my loss of faith in it, this new view of the unreality of the ego, of its essential emptiness, that postmodernism and Zen had shown me—not just in theory but—and I can't stress this enough—in practice, that is, through the meditative consciousness—left me convinced that dynamic psychotherapy amounted to no more than tinkering with a chimera, with the delusion of individual selfhood. And what could possibly be the point of that? Even if you manage to 'improve' the content of a delusion, it's still a delusion, isn't it? Far better to attack the real problem: the *belief* in an ego in the first place, the belief in ourselves as separate beings, a belief that, as Buddhism teaches, is the source of all human suffering."

"Beliefs in general, I take it, belong to the 'map' half of the map/territory dichotomy you made a moment ago. But tell me, how long did it take you to reach this insight in your Zen practice?" Dr. Purper asked.

"It's hard to say, there was no one dramatic moment, though the process certainly wasn't lacking in drama to me, tremendous psychospiritual drama, with many gratifying little epiphanies along the way. Once, the day after a weekend Zen retreat, with two or three years of sitting [6] under my belt, just walking to class across the Syracuse campus, I suddenly felt—and saw—lightning flash just above the central quad, even though I knew it couldn't have anything to do with the weather. I knew the flash had somehow come from me, and it charged my whole being with an indescribable exaltation. At the same time, I sensed this instantaneous identity with everything around me, the chapel, the grass, the nearby physics building, as if the whole world were my body, and that anything that happened in the world were the *willed* movement of my own body. I don't mean my ordinary will, of course—this was an entirely different force, somehow both gentle and omnipotent, and it was totally new to me. I was in awe.

"But anyway, I had many other experiences of this kind, the vast majority far less 'Pauline,' over the course of the nine-plus years I practiced Zen."

"Oh I see, you're no longer practicing."

"No, I'm not. It's been several years, maybe seven or eight, since I've sat *zazen*. There are several reasons why I stopped. Suffice it to say for now, toward the end of those years of sitting, I began to get headaches. They increased in frequency and intensity until I was forced to conclude it had to do with *zazen*. I'd eliminated all other likely causes. So I stopped.

"Well, you know," Dr. P. ventured, with an air of casualness that put me on my guard, "there are monks who spend their whole adult lives meditating and just hang in there and work their way through these dry and sometimes painful periods. You know, the 'inner dessert' phase the meditation manuals speak of, St. Ignatius, St. John of the Cross, and so on. It's all part of the rocky ascent up the spiritual mountain."

This stung and angered me. The man thinks I'm a spiritual wuss! "Listen," I shot back, "nine years and change on the *zafu* is not exactly a warm-and-fuzzy weekend retreat. I poured myself into Zen with everything I had. Call me a dharma drop-out if you like, but don't think I dropped out easily. Those headaches went on for years."

Again I heard the downstairs door slam shut. Lucky man—he was in and out, back mended, while I sat here squirming in uncertainty.

"Mr. McCort, I don't mean to imply you weren't a dedicated Zen student. I was just pointing out that 'the Way', as Zen people call it, is fraught with difficulty for anyone who takes it seriously. It's to be expected. But then, I guess with nine years of sitting, that's not something you need to hear from me … I did actually do some sitting myself, some years ago."

"I thought as much, from your comments," I nodded.

"Yes, I sat with Philip Kapleau at the Rochester Zen Center, so I don't speak of Zen entirely as an outsider."

"That's good to hear," I said, "because I don't see how I could possibly get anywhere with a therapist whose empirical outlook caused him to be dismissive of spiritual concerns, or worse, to regard them as mere 'defenses.'"

"Have no fear on that score," the doctor assured me. "Although I no longer practice Zen as such, I do still meditate, and my therapeutic orientation, as you'll come to see if we stay together, leaves plenty of room for the spiritual; in fact, I would even say my practice is grounded in the spiritual. Which doesn't mean, by the way, that I don't believe it's possible for someone to use religion as a psychological defense. Obviously, *anything* is grist for the mill of neurosis.

"But anyway, before time runs out, I would like to get back to that autobiographical synopsis you promised me earlier in the hour."

"Ah that ... Of course. Well, I was born into a lower middle-class Catholic family in Hoboken, New Jersey, on September 26, 1941, which makes me fifty-nine. My father, Edward, worked as a rate clerk in the traffic departments of various trucking companies in Jersey, most notably Roadway Express, located in the town of Kearney. I think he spent about fifteen years there. You've probably seen their humongous orange and blue sixteen-wheelers on the interstate," I surmised.

"Traffic departments?" Dr. P. asked quizzically.

"Yes," I explained. "All trucking companies have so-called 'traffic departments' whose function it is to calculate the cost of shipping whatever-it-is from point A to point B. This can become very complicated, with shipping regulations varying from state to state, and even in different areas within a state. So a rate clerk is a highly trained office worker. All of which is to say that my Dad was a pretty smart guy. He was very good in math and loved to read."

"I guess you could say," Dr. P. added, "that he was the one in control—commercial control at least—of all those humongous sixteen-wheelers crowding the interstates."

For the second time in the session I was taken aback, this time profoundly. Dr. P. didn't even need to refer to the phobic complaint of highway trucks I presented at the top of the first hour. Just the word "crowding" in his ostensibly casual remark was enough to get me to make the connection on my own.

I was as impressed with his skill in this as I was with the insight itself. He did it in a way that left me no ground for knee-jerk protestations, or as he might put it, denial. I was deftly maneuvered into considering the viability of a symbolic connection between my Dad and those massive highway trucks.

I knew he could see I was impressed by this insight, that I was made thoughtful by it. Part of me resented his ability to see this deeply into me so quickly, if indeed that is what he was doing, for I had my doubts, but another part was flushed with honest admiration for what was, at the very least, acute observation. Not wishing to betray this to him, however, I pushed on with my story. "My mother was a housewife who never got beyond the eighth grade. She was a shy, anxious woman and generally took a passive, even defensive attitude towards life; she was dutiful and kept a good house. Her religious faith was her indispensable bulwark against 'the slings and arrows' [Damn it, I thought, there I go again, validating his assertion of religion as a possible defense mechanism. Of course, I'd often considered Mom from that angle, but I didn't want *him* doing it, and before I'd even 'introduced' her. Then I suddenly realized he hadn't said a word.] She was loved by all who knew her and generally thought of as a woman of simple yet deep faith who was moved by that faith to help anyone in need. She was self-effacing, at times to the point of saintliness.

"Then there's my sister, Iris, four years younger. Iris and I were pretty close growing up, though I must admit I teased her way too much. I wouldn't call her an 'afterthought child'—certainly my parents loved her—but I always felt, you know, that I was the apple of my Mom's eye. I think Iris sensed that—how could she not?—and it's left her as an adult with this refractory anger she's never been quite able to shake. Still, as far as I can see, she functions well and has a nice life, while I struggle with my phobias and sometimes barely manage to function at all. So I don't see how being treated as 'Number 1' by Mom did me much good."

"Being the doted-on firstborn can have its own liabilities," the doctor opined. "Whether that's the case here remains to be seen, of course."

"Yeah, I guess," I said absently, suddenly feeling an urge towards brevity and concision. I wanted to fast-forward through the rest of the bio and wrap it up, so I could get out of there and enjoy the same freedom that Dr. Farinelli's patient was almost certainly taking for granted. "We lived in Hoboken, which in those days was a grimy industrial city, the port across from Manhattan where the immigrants arrived. I grew up amidst factories that made everything from Tootsie Rolls to slide rules. The city had great low-end Italian restaurants and bread bakeries; it also produced Frank Sinatra—in fact, my mother, who as a girl lived three houses down from the Sinatras, baby-sat little Francesco a few times. (I'm not sure that story's not just my mother's little urban legend.) There were also a lot of sandlots in Hoboken for baseball, and I guess I got to know just about every guy in the city who played the game to any extent. Good Catholics that we were, I went to Catholic schools from first grade through college, spending eight years with the nuns and then another eight with the Jesuits. For graduate school, I went to Johns Hopkins to study German—I had an aptitude for foreign languages—finally breaking out of that claustrophobic religious ghetto, though I didn't see it that way at the time. My years at Hopkins included a year 'of study'"—as I said these words,

I made digital quotation marks—"in Germany, 1964-65, at the University of Tübingen in the southwest. Two important things came out of my year abroad, neither having anything to do with academic life: I saw a lot of Europe and I finally lost my virginity. At twenty-three, can you believe? My only consolation was that I had a Jewish friend over there, an American exchange student like me, who lost it even later than I did.

"The rest is a rather banal history: I went to Syracuse in 1968, at 28, joined the German-department faculty, most of whose members personally repelled me right from the get-go. So, of course, I stayed there and endured for the next thirty plus years."

"But why ... ?" Dr. P. made to interject, but I saved him the bother. "Oh, I suppose *you,* as a Buddhist-friendly psychologist, might say, once you got to know me better, that it involved some deep masochistic need to suffer, to burn off karma for sins known and unknown. (An old friend of mine once put it to me the American way: 'Denny, you just don't know how to live.') But there's an equally important reason that's far less exotic, though my friend might consider it rationalizing: I got married and had two kids, and that at a time when the academic job market was well into a career-long nose dive, and that, I guess, pretty much sealed my fate."

Dr. Purper looked at me steadily and without expression, apparently using the moment to take it all in. Perhaps because I'd given him more than he felt inclined to summarize, he selected one facet of my story for comment: "Eight years with the Jesuits, eh? I can empathize. I did eight myself, four at the University of Scranton."

Suddenly all my impatience to make an exit drained out of me, replaced by a feeling of warmth as the doctor shared something that was not merely personal, but parallel to my own development. I felt as if I'd just downed a double shot of Jack. It was not just the particular fact that he too had been molded by the Jebbies, but the clear implication that he had, just like me, been dragged up through the entire Catholic indoctrination program: the profound alienation from the body, the sexual guilt, the threat of eternal punishment, the Russian roulette game of dying outside the state of grace, and so on. He knew about youthful Catholic misery, not from that vantage point of vague puzzlement that non-Catholics always seemed to take, as if they were bemused by the bizarre behavior of another species, but through identity—he'd been there in the same trenches.

I felt grateful, for the moment at least, for having found a therapist who, on first meeting, already knew a fair amount about me from the inside, who had this invaluable knowledge-through-identity. All my previous therapists had been "alien-species observers" in this respect. My gratitude moved me to add a detail about my life with the Jesuits. "The Jebbies do generally live up to their reputation as good educators, good teachers, I guess; still, of all the priests and scholastics who taught me at St. Peter's Prep, or College for that matter, only one stands out in memory as a man of intellectual depth who truly cared about the welfare of his students. Father Raymond York, S.J., taught us Greek with brilliance, and élan, and humor. He knew how to bring the ancient culture to life for young boys. Of course, he was helped in this just a little by Homer's mythic imagination: what kid could resist a giant cyclops with one eye smack in the middle of his head, or a hero who shoots an arrow through the holes in twenty-four ax heads (is it twenty-four?)? York and Homer, the dynamic duo! He made us sing the dactylic lines of *The Odyssey* to the tune of 'Stars and Stripes Forever': you know, 'ANdra moi ENnepeh, MOUsa, …' and so on. It fit perfectly and made it easier for us to memorize large chunks of the epic.

"Anyway, one day not long before graduation, Fr. York calls me up to his desk during class—the other kids were doing a writing assignment—and asks me what I had in mind for a career. I told him I was thinking of teaching. He put the ever-present balled-up hanky to his mouth for a moment of reflection and said to me, 'Teach in black.' Yep, that's right, 'Teach in black,' he said, intoning the words as if they were some sort of sacred Jesuit mantra. If you're going to teach, you ought to teach as a priest since both are really more vocations than careers. One is *called* to do either, and all such calls come from the same source, and so on. Anyway, that's how I read what he said. I pretended to consider it, but inwardly I was already shrinking away, since the one thing I knew for sure regarding my future was that it would not exclude sex. (Please, I was a naïve seventeen-year-old!) Putting the same certainty negatively, I knew I could never wade across the river of sexual guilt I was already in over 'self-abuse' to the redemptive shore of the priesthood. I didn't have that kind of heroic renunciatory strength. I suppose the irony is that I have, in a sense, taught in black—just not the way York intended it.

"For whatever it's worth to you as a psychoanalyst, I might mention that, every few years, Fr. York would have what people in those days called a 'nervous breakdown.' He'd just start babbling incoherently, and they'd come and take him away and you wouldn't see him for a few weeks. Then one morning he'd pop up in class again and pick up where he left off. He had no self-consciousness about his own instability; in fact, he even joked about it, about how the doctors would discuss 'his case' and spout their medical jargon in front of him, totally unaware that, as a Greek scholar, he grasped just about everything they were saying. Electro-en-cephalo-gram, and so forth. As for us kids, we loved him all the more for his deep imperfections; somehow they only added to his mystique. I think we understood intuitively that a man of his depth could not be conventional in the way our other teachers were."

As I made this last remark, it occurred to me Dr. Purper might read it as a patient's "apologia pro" mental illness, an attempt to romanticize and mythicize emotional suffering as, in some cases at least, heroic, a kind of perverse gift, rather then just miserable. Another defense mechanism, with a bit of self-aggrandizement thrown in. Whether he did or not, I don't know. What I do know is that I was resentfully projecting all sorts of therapist-stereotypic ideas onto him in our early days together and that I hadn't the slightest notion of how astonishingly broad and encompassing—indeed accommodating—his worldview was. If I could really have listened to him that first day with any keenness, I would have recognized as much in his generous response to the Fr. York story: "Jung had a lot to say about what you might call 'divine madness,' that is, genuine inspiration that so moves a person that he behaves in ways that could only be described by others as 'crazy'. St. Francis of Assisi dancing naked in the town square or Meister Eckhart punctuating his sermons with patches of schizophrenese or 'word salad.' I'm not saying your Fr. York was one of these, but who knows? …"

I sensed it was time to finish, but suddenly a question for the good doctor arose in me and took hold of me with such urgency that it rendered me momentarily mute. I couldn't even consider saving it for next week. Inhaling deeply, I asked, "So Dr. Purper, I realize I'm putting my head in the lion's mouth by asking you this, but how come my great liberating insight into the non-existence of the ego, the individual self, hasn't liberated me? This is supposedly the fruit, so to speak, of my long Zen practice. If I've truly seen through the delusion of my own existence as a separate individual, a discrete consciousness—and I'm convinced I have—why am I still the same old fearful, depressed bastard I've always been? How profound could these so-called spiritual discoveries have been if they've left me with the same emotional sack of rocks?"

Some deep intuition told me he would not take the low road here and give me some "I told you so" type of answer exalting the superiority of psychoanalysis to Buddhism, or religion in general, and therefore, ultimately, the superiority of the scientific-materialistic to the idealistic (in the German sense) worldview. My peripheral attention, the small preconscious part of me unencumbered by anxiety, must have sensed him as a man who, however he might answer this one important question I'd put to him in the hour, would say something consoling, whether because he was a man with heart or because, basically seeing the world as I did, he could tell me something enlightening about my own worldview I didn't know. His answer, while not exactly enlightening, did not disappoint me either, and gave some cause for hope: "Maybe we can find out together, and find out more as well about those sixteen-wheelers. Next time you come, bring a nice dream with you."

A *nice* dream, no less. I felt, not unpleasantly, like a bagel delivery boy. Bring a nice dream already, with lox and cream cheese. As I got up to leave, my thoughts turned reflexively to the question of a common restroom in the building, that is, until I realized that, oddly enough, I didn't have to go anymore.

PART ONE: CONFESSION

(1) October 2000: The Concave Mountain

It's nighttime. I'm standing at the edge of a high ridge, somewhere just outside the city limits of Montreal. I can look over the entire city from this spot, see all its bridges and towers and twinkling lights. Somehow I'm also able to see my wife, Dottie, facing me from a corresponding spot all the way over on the other side of town, as if the ridge encompassed the city in a more or less circular shape and she were at the opposite end of the diameter. Don't ask how I can see her from so far away; it must be one of those tricks dreams use to telescope distance. Anyway, the problem is that she and I are literally separated by the city, which is ironic since Montreal is where we spent our honeymoon. How do I get to her, or she to me? Or can we meet in the middle? It's obviously more than a problem of logistics. Then, as I look more closely, I see that the topography of the city resembles a gigantic chessboard, only without the squares, but with the board bent like an ordinary chessboard into two halves, the crease bisecting the city between us in concave fashion. So, to get to her, I'd have to descend my half of the "city board" and climb up her half, till I finally came to her. It seems daunting.

Finishing my recital with a mystified shake of the head, I let myself feel the cool air being blown my way by a nearby floor fan set up just beneath the window. It was an unusually warm early Fall day. I looked out the window at the treetops bordering the building's parking lot. They were totally motionless; it was easy to imagine them listening intently to my dream tale.

"So, what are your thoughts about the dream?"

"What are *my* thoughts? Aren't *you* supposed to be the dream master here? I'd much rather hear what *you* make of it," I answered, unwilling to suppress just the barest trace of a sneer. My good will towards the doctor had evaporated in the intervening week and I was ready for bear again, therapist-bear.

"All in good time, Herr Professor, all in good time," he soothed, parrying my remarks with a mild jibe of his own. "It's important to hear from you first, to get the dreamer's own impressions and associations while they're pristine, so to speak, untainted, uninfluenced by the therapist's 'professional' views."

Who could argue with that? Sounding so reasonable to me as it did, it diminished my itch for an argument. It also put the ball back in my court and heightened my self-consciousness. I had no idea what to make of the dream and was afraid of saying something stupid. If he'd give me ten minutes, maybe I could work something out, but to have to wing it like this …

Almost as if he were reading my thoughts, he came to my rescue, casually inviting me to "Just start talking and don't worry about it. You don't even necessarily have to talk about the dream itself. Sooner or later, what's on your mind and on the dream's mind, so to speak, will come out in any case. I'm not asking you to interpret the dream; just bring up whatever occurs to you or whatever you want to. We're merely having a conversation, no more no less.

"But how can you possibly know that?" I asked with obvious skepticism, and just as I put the question, I recalled Freud's well-known method of free association, which encouraged the patient to express anything and everything that popped into his head, no matter how embarrassing or ridiculous or seemingly irrelevant. The good doctor must be using some version of this, I reasoned, and I anticipated with pleasure this first opportunity of the hour for an intellectual attack, the more so since I'd been nursing a deep animus against the principle of free association itself (it offended my "humanistic sensibilities") ever since I first heard it enunciated way back in my undergraduate psych courses. "The way you put it, it sounds just like free association, one of the sillier misnomers of psychoanalysis: after all, if the unconscious is forging the links in the chain of associations, what's 'free' about it? Don't tell me it's still possible to subscribe to this gloomy deterministic view of Freud's of the mind as a machine: no choice, no discrimination over what it puts out, anymore than a nineteenth-century steam engine could avoid belching smoke into the air. I can't accept that no matter what I say here, or anywhere else for that matter, its form and content are determined by antecedent causes totally hidden from me and therefore beyond my control. How then am I any different, essentially, from that steam engine? That might've been fine for Victorian-age scientistic thinking, but we're in a new age now and the bloom is long off that rose."

I must confess I felt a certain smart-ass pleasure in getting off that volley, but it was hollow since I didn't really believe a word I'd said. I'd long ago come to the conclusion that the determinism/free-will debate was, at bottom, fueled by a false dichotomy. I had no idea why I felt this; it was just some inchoate inkling that manifested itself every once in a while in meditation. It seemed to have something to do with a vague sense that the two positions were valid antagonists only on the "stage of ideas" and not in the far subtler realm of nature or consciousness, whatever those two things were.

At any rate, Dr. Purper once again seemed to divine my inner disposition, this time one of intellectual insincerity, and reacted to it with amused tolerance: "The vagaries of the debate over free will are the agenda for a meeting of the Friday afternoon philosophers' club, and don't really concern us here, at least not for now. We may have cause to take up the issue at some time in the distant future, but I think this particular hour would be much better spent discussing your dream." The man would not be baited. I was beginning to realize his perspicacity was rare, his intelligence powerful indeed. This dawning awareness filled me with a strange mixture of intimidation, awe and excitement.

So it was with the oddly grateful sense that I might finally have met someone who could help me get out of my own way that I responded, "Yeah, back to Montreal by night. I don't know … The one thing about Montreal that leaps to mind is that Dottie—my wife—and I honeymooned there in August of '73. Though that certainly wasn't my first time there; I'd been there twice before that, I think, with my family, once to visit the World's Fair in 1967 and even some years before that, we passed through the city on our way home from Quebec City where we'd visited the shrine of Saint Anne de Beaupré. That little 'Catholic vacation' would've been my mother's doing. I can still remember touring the shrine and climbing up all those wooden steps on my knees reciting the rosary in broken French or something. 'The family that prays together …' Can you imagine anything more fun for a teenager on his summer vacation than kneeing your way up a hundred cathedral steps while reciting the rosary? It gives new meaning to 'tedium,' like so much of the mind-numbing repetition that passes for Catholic ritual.

"One funny incident—funny mainly in retrospect, of course—happened when we were trying to find our way out of Montreal on the trip back. My father was driving and I was riding shotgun, which meant I was responsible for navigating, and, having no city map, was doing a pretty lousy job of it. I could see my Dad was getting increasingly uptight about being lost in the city, which did not surprise me at all, as he always got nervous when he couldn't find his way in a car, and, being a man, of course, his difficulty covering up his anxiety made him angry, and he'd have no choice but to dump that anger on the rest of us, not in a clean explosion that might've dissipated it, mind you, but in a scowl of suppression and a pulsating red strawberry that would form right between his eyes. The air in the car was thick with foreboding. I saw a passerby heading towards us on the right sidewalk and urged my father to pull over so we could ask for directions out of town. But as we pulled over, it occurred to one of us, my Mom I think, that we'd probably need to ask our question in French. This caused my sister's eyebrows to rise sharply, as she was the only one among us who had any French: exactly two years in high school. I could feel that this transaction was foredoomed and shuddered inwardly over the consequences for my father's mood. I rolled my window down so that Iris could stick her head out of it from the back seat and put her question to the stranger as clearly as possible. I could hear her mumbling to herself behind me, frantically trying to rouse the French that had been in deep slumber within her all summer. Finally the moment of truth: 'Pardon, monsieur, si'l vous plait, ou est …' That was as much as she got out before the guy cut her off with, 'Sorry, lady, I'm from Brooklyn, I don't speak no French,' and shuffled off. Even my father, as livid as he was in that moment, couldn't suppress a wry smile."

I have no doubt at all that Dr. P. enjoyed my little Montreal anecdote as he laughed heartily and popped a phrase or two in his own studied Brooklyn accent, something like: "Whaddya wan' from me, lady, … fuhgeddabowdit!" (He liked doing regional accents, as I would learn over time.) Yet, at the same time, I thought I detected in him a sort of second brain that was sharply focused on what I was saying and how I was saying it for any psychological revelations that might percolate up. It would take me a long time to get a clear sense of this double-focus intelligence of his for the simple reason that his first brain, which was involved in the story for its amusement value, was absolutely sincere. I never felt, as I had with other therapists, that he was just feigning ordinary interest in our conversation to mask a cold, clinical focus on my pathology. Somehow he was able to operate in a genuine way on both levels; the nearest analogy I can think of would be a virtuoso pianist who is able to play two, three or even four distinct melodies of one of Bach's Goldberg Variations in simultaneous counterpoint. By some magic of "multiplex" consciousness no melody gets slighted. (Once, when the great Horowitz was asked how it was possible to concentrate on four melodies at once with only one mind, he merely dangled his ten gigantic fingers before the interviewer and wiggled them, implying that the mind or thought had little to do with it. I wonder if Dr. Purper would have said something similar if asked.)

In any case, I know now that his clinical brain was fully functional during my story. Once the laughter over the incident had waned, he cocked his head a bit and said, "I wonder if you notice anything of psychological interest in this little tale that you no doubt meant simply as an aside, or as a prelude to the 'important' Montreal association you were heading for, which is, of course, your honeymoon."

I thought for a moment and shook my head, saying, "Not really, outside of how well the story illustrates my Dad's style of anger, always just under the surface, ready to explode, but rarely doing so."

"Yes, certainly, but think of the context, the background for the anger in this scene. If father's anger—or rather its threat—is the 'figure' here, what's the 'ground?'"

"Well, it would have to be the city, Montreal," I said, "or … no wait, it's the car, the situation of our being lost in the car, trying to get our bearings as we drive along. It's scary because Dad's literally scared by not knowing where he is, and being scared always made him angry."

"Barely suppressed fear and anger on the road," Dr. P. summarized, "sounds as if you may have unconsciously taken those painful feelings of his into yourself and then learned to project them onto those 'big bad' sixteen-wheelers that frighten you on the interstate. What do you think?"

"I've heard of phobias that even animals 'learn' from one another," I ventured. "My wife had two dogs growing up at home. The older dog always shook with fear on July 4th from all the fireworks explosions going off in the street. Eventually, the younger dog learned to do the same, even though in its first few years, it took no particular notice of the fireworks."

"Now, I'm not saying it's all as simple as that, that your driving phobia is nothing more than an unconsciously learned stimulus/response pattern," he cautioned, "not at all, but I think we may have unraveled at least one important strand in the psychic quilt," he concluded with an air of confidence and self-satisfaction.

For my part, I was still much too wary and cynical just to concede this, even though in my heart of hearts I hoped he was right, for I longed for the kind of insight that would finally heal. "I'll admit you make an interesting and compelling connection," I said, "but for me the proof has to be in the pudding. How comfortable will I feel next time I drive the interstate?"

"Well, I guess we'll see," is all he had to offer. "but let's get back to Montreal and your honeymoon there."

"Yes, of course. I thoroughly enjoyed our week in Montreal, and I'm sure Dottie did too. We ate in some of the best restaurants in North America. In fact, by the end of our stay, we couldn't stand another bite of *haute cuisine,* and walked around looking for an ordinary burger joint. It's funny, whenever we tell other people about our honeymoon, it sounds as if we did nothing in Montreal but eat one lavish meal after another, as if our honeymoon was only about food, with sex being an entirely secondary appetite."

"Was it?" Dr. P. asked.

"Well … , we'd been living together for months already before we got married. That's what people did in those days. It was 1973, remember, still the emancipated era of the counterculture. So sex for us no longer had the mystery of uncharted territory. We did have sex on our honeymoon, of course, but I must confess that our memories of that week coalesce more around food, around fancy menus without prices and waiters who knew when to approach your table and when not to (unlike in some countries I could mention)."

"Well, Montreal is certainly a gourmand's paradise," Dr. P. interjected. "I've been there several times myself and I suppose you could even say I have the evidence to show for it," he joked, caressing his bourgeoning paunch with two bear-claw-sized hands. He looked so uncomfortable sitting there in his suit and tie, the analyst's "uniform" totally unsuited to his girth. "But dining out can't be the only thing you did on your honeymoon, can it? What about all those hours in between meals?"

"Well, we did the usual touristy things, walked up and down Catherine St., explored the famous underground shopping center, went up and down the mountain, and so on. But these typical tourist-type activities all tend to pale in my memory. What sticks out are the curious little odds and ends, like the downtown carriage horse wearing a Depends diaper or the nutjob you run into on a tour bus or in a bar … There was this one character, who was it, a Mr. Lamarque or Lamont, Lamont I think, who ran the pension we stayed in on Mountain Street. A true French romantic, the perfect foil for a young honeymooning couple. He had to be in his late seventies at least, having outlived his wife after a long marriage, so he was this sort of self-appointed expert in matters of domestic bliss, and needed no prodding to give advice to newlyweds. He charmed Dottie and me utterly and we hung on his every word. So one afternoon, as we're coming down the hallway steps from our apartment on our way out, he happens to be slowly making his way upstairs, a tall, thin, white-haired stick-figure of a man with horn-rimmed glasses. He's cradling four or five rolls of toilet paper in the crook of his left arm and holding a sixth in his right hand, which he's also using to steady himself on the banister, obviously on his way up to replenish his guests' supply. Of course, as soon as he spots us, he resumes his running monologue on male-female relations, this time waxing poetic and rhapsodic in his thick French accent on the glories of *l' amour:* 'Ah, eez zere anyting so beautifool as ze lav between a man and a wooman?' and so on. By this time, he's about five steps above us, so he stops, slowly turns around and continues making his point, now with his right hand off the banister and held upright, waving the roll of t.p. almost in our faces to emphasize his point. Dottie and I looked at each other, struggling mightily to keep straight faces. As we closed the outer door behind us, I said to Dot out of the corner of my mouth, in mock-secrecy, 'That's not the prop I would've used,' and we both went week-kneed with convulsions."

Dr. P smiled as he savored my t.p. image, and then offered this: "It's obvious you've really enjoyed relating these anecdotes about your honeymoon, and, of course, the truest free association happens precisely when you're deeply 'into' the telling, so to speak, when you become an off-the-cuff raconteur of your own life. That said, allow me an observation on your associative links here: you went from relating a memory of how food overshadowed sex on your honeymoon in Montreal to a funny story of how a dowdy old man inadvertently linked sex to feces. What do you … ?"

"Wait a minute, hold on here," I protested. "You can't be seriously implying that my anecdotes show that I, consciously or unconsciously, believe that sex is distasteful or even dirty, can you? Because the fact is I don't believe anything of the kind."

"I don't know what they show, if anything," Dr. P. retorted. "We're just getting started here and, as I said, I'm only offering an observation. It's my job, as a more objective yet sympathetic point of view, so to speak, to mirror to you things your own defenses may be keeping you from seeing. Whether my observations are 'true' or not, only time will tell."

"Yeah, that's just the problem with psychoanalysis and depth psychology in general," I said in a voice flushed with scorn. (At last I'd found an opening for my next sally.) "'Truth' in the analytic sense is an absurdly problematic concept, isn't it? Its very indeterminateness makes it a tool analysts easily use to unfair advantage. It's like the impossibility of proving a negative. There's no way I could ever 'prove' to anybody that you *don't* have the goods on me with your sex-shit connection, is there? And it all sounds so smart, so clever, so symbolically resonant. How could it not be so? So then, over time, its 'truth' does not so much become revealed, as you said before, as believed in, which is a different sort of truth entirely, isn't it? Inasmuch as our beliefs do have power over us, this belief in a sex-shit connection I've acquired about myself from 'analysis' does, over time, come to shape the 'truth' I believe I've discovered about myself. And that in turn becomes an issue, grist for the mill, so to speak, for further analysis, for analysis 'terminable or interminable.' It's a beautiful set-up, I must say."

"I won't even attempt to argue with your logic, Herr Professor, except to note the anger—justified no doubt—that's obviously driving it. All I can say is you're here, so some part of you *wants* to be here, and we're trying this out. So we might as well give it a go, and on its own terms, so that if it doesn't work out, it won't be because one or both of us sabotaged it. Can we see eye to eye at least that far?"

"Yeesss, we can," I said grudgingly. Again, bait not taken. How could I wage my personal crusade against the depth-psychological establishment if my foe refused to take up the gauntlet? His strategy seemed to be to let me vent my spleen against him as a symbolic target, probably because I needed to, but to carefully avoid engaging my arguments, such engagement being from his point of view a waste of time, not to mention seriously detrimental to the analysis, if in fact it were being fueled by his own countertransference (i.e., psychological issues of his own that I had succeeded in evoking).

"What about this chessboard image in the dream?" he asked. "It's certainly an arresting one."

"Well, it's not a chessboard *per se*, remember, it's just shaped like one ..."

"Yes, but it's not just the image itself that's revealing but what the image suggests to you in recollection. So I wouldn't necessarily discount the idea of chess or a chess match."

"Right, right," I scoffed, "that's part of this analytical pan-determinism of yours that allows you to set up any parameters you like in constituting the field of interpretation. If I were to say right now, in exasperation, 'Why not throw in the kitchen sink,' you'd no doubt be mentally off to the races in search of tie-ins between sinks and sexual psychopathology, no?"

"I thought we'd consigned the free-will/determinism debate to the philosophers a while ago. Meanwhile, the *board*, chess or no ... ?"

" … Well, I think I'm at the southern point of the ridge, facing north, with Dottie at the northern point facing me. We're separated—on our honeymoon no less!—and I need to get to her, and the only way is to descend this 'chessboard,' or half of it at least, into the dark pit of the city—somehow Montreal has caved in, in this artificially symmetrical way, as if it were a huge nocturnal V-shape that I have to traverse."

"What about the letter 'V'?" Dr. P. asked. "Mean anything to you?"

"It could mean so many things," I muttered, at a loss. "Wait a minute, though," I said suddenly, interrupting myself. "Not 'V' but 'U,' which is similar. Both picture the theme of descent followed by ascent, crucifixion and resurrection. There's a book by Northrup Frye, the Canadian literary scholar. What's it called … ah, oh yeah, *The Great Code: The Bible and Literature.*[7] It argues that the Bible itself has a U-shape tracing essentially the three-part myth of Paradise Lost: Eden or innocence, the Fall from grace and, finally, resurrection or redemption. That's the signature myth I've used my whole career to teach German romanticism to S.U. students: naïve awareness (the Garden), the descent into the darkened consciousness of history (exile), and enlightenment or total consciousness, or god consciousness, or whatever one wants to call it. It's almost as if the V-shaped chessboard were an image of my personal myth in some sense," I said, almost to myself, my voice trailing off.

"'He descended into hell. On the third day He rose again from the dead. He ascended into heaven, seated at the right hand of the Father. From thence He shall come to judge the living and the dead.'" Dr. P. intoned the words as if they'd been chiseled into his memory, his voice deep, resonant, sacerdotal.

"That's right, that's the idea," I assented. "But you speak those words with such *gravitas,* as if they meant something to you, as if they were more than the vestigial promptings of some grammar-school nun. I thought you were a Freudian, a strict religious reductionist; you know, … the oceanic feeling is baloney, nothing but the father imago cast against the sky, and all that. Don't tell me there's some Jung in you too, some appreciation of myth, some sense of the transcendent, the spiritual … ?"

"Isn't it interesting," the doctor speculated, "how you seem to have entirely forgotten my mentioning last week of having sat *zazen* with Roshi Kapleau and of having a therapeutic practice grounded in the spiritual? How selective our memories can become when we have an axe to grind … Anyway, as I see it, Freud went far, Jung went further, much further," Dr. P. said. "Sure there's some Jung in me, and more than a bit, along with some Melanie Klein, Harry Stack Sullivan, Eric Erikson, Carl Rogers, Robert Langs, A. N. Whitehead, David Chalmers, and a whole bunch of others—not to mention the active ingredient, Charles Purper."

I felt chastened. He'd caught me *in flagrante delictu,* so to speak, exposed as the unwitting conjurer of a straw dog: the image of "the godless empiricist psychoanalyst" I needed to attack. In my embarrassment all I could say was, "It looks as if labeling you is going to be a challenge."

"Why waste effort on it?" he said. "The labels game will only distract you from the work, the process that's already begun to unfold here, which is in any case unique to each patient, even while following certain predictable stages. Besides, I have no absolute commitment to any theory or expert. I am above all a pragmatist: I use whatever works.

"As for your religious take on the chessboard image in your dream, it rings true to me. Since Northrup Frye is (or was?) a Canadian, it's consistent with the logic of the unconscious that the dream would use a variation on his symbol of the Fall from Grace, the 'U,' to represent a Canadian city as a descent into Hell. But here's the thing: even though the dream evokes memories of your honeymoon in Montreal way back in the 1970's, the fact remains that you had the dream only a few days ago—probably in unconscious response to my suggestion at the end of our first hour that you 'bring me a nice dream'—so it stands to reason that its significance is decidedly contemporary. It's saying something about your life right now; it may well be saying something about the work we've now begun together, maybe a kind of alert, in Jung's sense of the vatic or prophetic dream, that what you've decided to undertake here is not going to be easy, that you may well have to descend into a kind of Hell, a kind of Dark Night of the Soul, what we would call today—much less poetically—a depression. But, one hopes, only in order to come up the other side of it and find, waiting for you there on the precipice, your soul mate. Maybe your dream promises, if you can respond to the challenge of honest self-inquiry an analysis poses, a second honeymoon, a second Montreal, far richer and more fulfilling than the first, since you'll then enjoy the freedom that deep self-knowledge brings."

I just sat there, letting his words waft over me like the breeze from the fan, savoring the vision, both heroic and idyllic, they so powerfully conjured. I needed that vision for motivation, and I'm sure he knew it. Within seconds, however, I was assailed by the demons of doubt. Was I up for this?

Did I really want to open the Pandora's box of analysis? What if I can't face what pops out and then can't get whatever it is back into the box? What if … ?

I inhaled slowly, deeply, finally responding with a tongue-in-cheek jibe that ill-concealed my admiration: "I thought analysts hid behind their patients and limited their feedback to an occasional 'hmm' during a session."

"That's the classical psychoanalyst. As for me, I'm a talker. Don't get me started. And by the way, feel free to lie on the couch over there. The option is yours, … starting next week, that is. Our time is up," the good doctor smiled.

(2) February 2001: Frankenstein in the Forest

It's an overcast morning on the old farm in Treadwell. Dark clouds are rolling in. My cousin Alice and I are making our way up a gently graded field, heading away from the rear of the farmhouse. We're on a berry-picking expedition. Alice can't be more than six or seven, with me a year younger. This is the farthest I've ever gone from the house without a grown-up and I'm feeling the thrill of adventure. When we reach the top of the field, the land flattens out and becomes crowded with trees and shrubbery. This is the uncultivated extension of our farmland and gives me the feeling of going into the wild. I've been told there's a fence marking the outer boundary of the property deeper in the woods, and the idea of actually going that far is exhilarating.

As we head off into the woods, something prompts us to stop, turn around and look back at where we've just come from. From this vantage point the house is hidden from view and we can see no farther back than the crest of the grade we've just left behind. Suddenly a stark figure appears on the crest, apparently in pursuit of us. It's my Mom. She doesn't speak but just stands there glaring at me, looking slim in her housedress. It's a feral glare that shoots out from beneath a dark, fierce brow that I can only describe as Frankensteinian. It roots me to the spot and pierces me with horror. She's young, agile, inescapable. Standing there, perhaps darkly savoring the moment, she stands between me and home, me and safety. But how can that be? She is *home, isn't she?*

"I'm guessing this is not a recent dream."

"That's right. Actually, it's the earliest dream I can remember ever having. I probably had it at around the age I am in the dream, five or six, a time when we were living on a farm near Treadwell, New York, a few miles from Oneonta. My Dad hated office work and wanted to give farming a try, so he hooked up with my Uncle Fred from Brooklyn and they went in together on this farm upstate, hoping to make a go of it. They had about twenty-five milking cows, Guernseys, and grew alfalfa, which they harvested with two workhorses I was very fond of named Dick and Fred. Dick was white and lazy, Fred was black and a workaholic. Unfortunately, things didn't work out and we were back in the city, in Hoboken, in, oh, less than two years, I think."

All I could see through the office window were a few snowflakes not quite piercing the gloomy gray of another Syracuse February. It was a good day to huddle inside and do analysis.

"It must have taken great courage for your father to pull up stakes like that and chart a radically new course, what with a young family to support and so on," Dr. Purper ventured.

"Courage or desperation. Actually, I don't think I've ever considered it from the point of view of *his* motives before. But I do know he was ready to do just about anything to get out of working nights."

"What do you think prompted you to begin today with this early dream?" he asked in an avuncular tone, sitting there like some kindly, well-fed guru.

I was caught short a little by the abrupt change of subject. Even though I'd been seeing the doctor for a few months now,

I still wasn't used to this way he had—surely a deliberate technique—of suddenly shifting levels of awareness from whatever 'story' I was telling to my motives for telling it. "Oh, I'm sorry, it wasn't clear to me that only current dreams were fair game …"

"No, no, on the contrary, all dreams are fair game," he hastened to assure me. "In fact, anything on your mind is fair game, dreams old and new, real-life incidents, stories, anecdotes, the latest novel, any kind of narrative at all, historical or fictive—whatever comes up. There's this analyst, Robert Langs, who is convinced that the unconscious communicates through any and all of these forms. Deep down, all stories are really *your* story. That's the point of view we take here."

"God, it all sounds so claustrophobic!" I groaned. "Anything I say, do, or fart is just one more string being pulled by the grand puppet master, Signór Unconscious. I've been coming here for, what, four months now and I still bristle at your dreary brand of determinism. I suppose that, except for a handful of elite 'self-realized' individuals like yourself, we, the great unwashed, are condemned to live out our lives as the response half of an internal stimulus-response mechanism."

"I thought we'd agreed at the beginning to leave philosophical issues aside—"

"Yeah, yeah, I know, but how can I be expected to open up to someone who holds a view of the world, and certainly a view of human nature, I abhor? I'm wondering why I'm even here."

"All right, since this philosophical issue is becoming an impediment to the process, it becomes itself a psychological issue warranting examination. So let's look at it."

"But I don't want to examine it *psychologically*," I said with exasperation, "as if it were just some wrinkle in my psychopathology. There's the shiftiness of the psychoanalyst right there, making sure the argument stays within his own backyard! I want to examine it *philosophically*, as a valid issue on its own terms."

"Fine, let's do that," Dr. P. conceded.

I was taken aback. I felt like the Social Democrats in Germany after the Kaiser abdicated at the end of World War I. Finally they had power. Now what?

I tried to gather my thoughts. "Actually, strictly speaking, it's not even a philosophical issue—it's spiritual and has everything to do with the fact that we have theories or worldviews at all, of *any* stripe or hue or ideology, and how these symbolic or language-based 'eyeglasses' distort the world as it is rather than clarifying it. The mere fact that we're arguing right here over the distinction between 'psychological' and 'philosophical' shows the profound extent to which we've sundered the world into categories. What does the world care whether we regard it psychologically, philosophically, or paleontologically? But we don't see the world, we see only our categories, our maps of the world. Then we commit to some categories—true over false or good over evil—while rejecting others, and suffer the consequences. But, as Krishnamurti says, the world is always simply the 'what-is' in any given moment, categories and thought be damned.

"Anyway, that's why I'm having so much trouble warming up to your viewpoint. I have seen 'the-world-as-it-is'; in the course of nine years of Zen practice and some seven years post-Zen, I've had many glimpses of it, some of them quite deep, and I know to my own certainty that even the loftiest, most brilliant, most sublime interpretation of the world is beside the point. And how is that, you ask? I'll tell you how. Because any view, theory or interpretation presumes to be *about* something other than itself: point of view and thing viewed, and alas, this very presumptive starting point is the Original Sin, the movement of mind that 'splits the atom,' that sunders itself from the world and the world itself into the 'ten thousand' pairs of opposites we then proceed to struggle with all our lives.

"Well, I'm pushing sixty and I'm tired of the struggle, dog tired, which means I'm probably not a good customer for the snake oil you're selling."

From the look of stony intensity on Dr. Purper's face, I knew I'd finally engaged him—on *my* turf: "But surely you're not advocating intellectual nihilism, a return to some Rousseauean ideal of soft primitivism. Where would civilization be without the intellect?"

"One might well ask where it is *with* it," I said somewhat smugly. "But no, of course not, that would be absurd. What I *am* advocating is inquiry into a dimension of consciousness, which, once realized, would allow us to keep the intellect and the knowledge it yields in their proper place and out of trouble: that would be the domain of technology, the domain of things that can and should be measured and manipulated, like the temperature at which water boils—a useful thing to know. But the intellect will never, under its own power, answer man's deepest questions or fulfill his deepest needs. And the longer we go on thinking it will, the longer we will suffer."

"So this dimension of mind, of consciousness, you speak

of, would it allow or empower us to—as you put it—'see the world as it is'?"

"Yes."

"You say you've experienced it. Can you say more about it?"

"Ah, well, there's precisely the rub," I sighed. "You see, anything I said would necessarily be a consequence of that splitting of the atom I mentioned earlier, fated to conceal more than it revealed. This Mind (capital 'M') is, so to speak, 'upstream' of all language and thought. Still, one must speak! ... Sometimes a great poet can be a bridge to it, since her or his use of language can go beyond its representative function, which entangles us in the pairs of opposites, you know, sign versus referent, etc. So when a seer like Blake urges you to 'see the world in a grain of sand' or his German counterpart, Novalis, insists you 'Go deep inside yourself—there or nowhere is the entire world,' just suppose these guys are not simply bandying mystical metaphors but actually intending what they say in the most literal sense! How could the world be in a grain of sand, or in yourself? That would turn the laws of space, size and distance inside out, wouldn't it? ... Well, that's how radical the perspective offered by this deeper dimension of consciousness is. Sound scary? Sure it does, that is, until you get a taste of it, a whiff of its perfume, and you realize immediately that that's your home, your true home.

"But you mentioned spending time on the *zafu* yourself, so I'm sure you have more than a vague idea of what I'm getting at."

"Yes," Dr. P. nodded, "I just wanted to hear what *you* had to say about it. And I must say, much of what you said reminds me of Carl Jung and the goal of his analytic psychotherapy, which he calls 'individuation,' and sometimes 'self-realization.' I think Jung was trying to work out a Western path to the same psychospiritual emancipation—the same Enlightenment—that the Eastern wisdom traditions cherish. He didn't think we were spiritually evolved enough in the West to make safe and profitable use of Eastern practices. You know, it's said that Jung died with a book about Zen on his bedside table."

"Comforting," I said, resuming my smug tone. I didn't want him ingratiating himself with me by pointing out this overlapping in what I'd thought were our irreconcilably opposed points of view. But the thing that really bothered me was that I had no idea why. Certainly it would be in my interest to be able to regard the doctor as a kindred spirit. "Well," I continued in a tone that was a good deal more conciliatory than I actually felt, "I suppose it's possible I closed the book on you a bit hastily. You do seem able to entertain views of the world generally thought to be at loggerheads—science and religion, psychoanalysis and metaphysics. My inability to pigeonhole you is beginning to feel … uh, strangely bracing."

"Thank you," Dr. P. said with mock-superiority, "I'll take that as a compliment, especially since I think it's the first one you've given me." Then he went on in a serious tone: "You know, in spite of ourselves, and all of this sparing—indeed, maybe even because of it—I think we're getting to know one another a little better. So I'll tip my hand to you a little bit, give you a quick glimpse into my therapist's bag of tricks: the fact is, you and I have to dither around for a while, maybe even a long time, on this relative level we live on, the level of science, analysis, the level of ordinary subject/object experience, the level of awareness on which most human beings live most of their lives, and we have to dither there long enough to clear away whatever psychopathology is in the way of our letting go of our attachment to the deepest, most refractory pair of opposites into which our binarizing minds have sliced up the world. I'm talking about the polarity between self and other. Not until we've managed that—no mean feat, believe me—will we be ready to take a flying leap into the great ocean of Being, or Freedom, or Reality, or Enlightenment, or Self-realization, or whatever you want to call it. In other words, we work within this delusive world of polarities—the world of good/evil, true/false, analysis/religion, even, with a nod to the deconstructionists, identity and difference—long enough to undermine our psychological attachment to any of the poles and finally break free into the unitive world. Only by getting our feet wet in that breathtaking world of Oneness, and beginning to see how it fits together seamlessly with this relative world of toil and moil we already know only too well, can we expect to know any peace and happiness worth a damn. We use the trap of delusion, the trap of the polarizing mind, to get out of the trap. The trap itself becomes its own principle of liberation. Once out, we leave the trap behind, just as the Buddha tells us to leave the raft—of spiritual practice—behind once we've reached the desired shore.

"So, maybe now you can understand that I'm not being coldly indifferent to you, or analytically aloof to your heart's concerns, when I decline your 'invitations' to philosophical, or even spiritual, debate. You see, ultimately I don't 'believe' in beliefs, or positions, or points of view—not even my own!—I'm only concerned to observe how these operate in my patients, so that I can help them to see the same, and so seeing, drop them all like vipers. Like Nietzsche, I'm looking for a 'transvaluation of values,' of all particular values, into Value itself, which is just another synonym to add to the list mentioned earlier of terms for the *summum bonum*. That's where the real action is …

"God, I've said too much," Dr. P. checked himself, but his self-satisfied tone gave the lie to this. "But since we're about it, just let me round all this off by saying that it'll be clear to you now why it doesn't bother me in the slightest that you have profound doubts about the validity of analysis. Such doubts, too, are merely beliefs, and I can work with *any* beliefs. (Remember, the upside of beliefs is that they are things which, when examined in the right way, will get us out of the trap.) It would only bother me if you let your doubts persuade you to drop out. But even that would only mean you weren't quite ready yet for this journey. Maybe in a couple of years. I'm not going anywhere," he finished cheerfully, then adding, "But time grows short and there's a dream to consider."

Naturally, it would take time for me to process all he'd said, and there was still the matter of those deep, lingering resentments of mine towards psychotherapy, but for now at least I was enjoying a sense of mounting delight that maybe, just maybe, I had found a true companion on the path, a fellow wayfarer who could help me—and maybe even I him—to go deeply into the Mystery.

"Yes, the dream," I said. "That dream has been with me my whole life, casting a pall over everything. And is it any wonder? I've got my mother menacing me like Frankenstein's bride, cutting me off from home when she should be the very embodiment of Home. I'm sure the dream reflects how I was struggling at that age, five or six, to cope with a serious depression that came over her then. It apparently was a postpartum reaction to having my sister, and it was certainly a tough way for Iris to start out too. When I look at family photos from that period on the farm, my mother's facial expressions are like so many variations on that Frankensteinian dream mask. I'm told she spent about a year pretty much just sitting in a chair, staring out the window. She was alone, with no one—and no pharmacopeia—to help her really. My father, aunt and uncle were too busy trying to make a go of the farm and I was too little to be of help.

"I don't recall very much of that time, but I do remember developing these ritualistic bodily habits that annoyed the hell out of my mother, like sniffing. I had this habit of sniffing all the time, as if I just couldn't get my nasal passages clear enough. Every once in a while Mom would snap at me, 'Will you please stop that!', and I'd say, 'Okay, Mom, I promise not to do it again, if you'll just let me take one last big sniff,' which I would do and then proceed to hold out for two minutes before the repetition compulsion would kick back in, and we'd go round again. It was miserable. I must've felt really trapped with her."

"You did what you could to make life tolerable, like negotiate with her: 'Only one more time,' and so on," Dr. Purper reasoned. "I'm sure you can see how mother's illness, her depression, filled you with the most intense contradictory feelings of love and fear, attraction and repulsion, a profound internal tug-of-war. Certainly the dream is fraught with painful contradiction: there stands Mom, the source of any child's comfort and security, a lethal obstacle to that very comfort and security. Your sense of abandonment must've been horrific."

"'Abandonment,'" I repeated. "Just as you say the word, I'm reminded of something relevant my sister told me about life with Mom even earlier, before the farming misadventure. Iris told me Mom once confessed to her that she (Mom) liked to take me shopping with her when I was three or four. She'd take me into a department store, say Grant's or Woolworth's, and, as soon as I'd get distracted, she'd hide behind a counter or partition and wait for me to notice she was gone. Of course, as soon as I did, I'd burst into tears, which would be her cue to pop out, run up to me and take me in her arms. She told Iris she loved the feeling of being needed by me in this raw, brutal way. Naturally, when she revealed this to Iris decades later, she was filled with remorse. I think she sensed clearly how much of my fearfulness of life as an adult—traveling phobias, sticking close to home even in youth—came out of those earliest years of feeling trapped with, and at the same time abandoned by, a mother who desperately needed help herself."

What had been snowflakes at the start of the hour were presently bourgeoning into a thick, heavy squall outside. We had whiteout. I had to grimace to myself as it occurred to me what a perfect backdrop the weather was to my theme of feeling trapped.

"Yes, that's how the chain of pathology grows, link by link, generation by generation," the good doctor mused. "The ancient Greeks mythologized it, for example, Sophocles in his *Electra,* which makes much of this tragic curse on the house of Atreus. Of course, for the ancients the tragic-curse-mongers were the gods, whereas we moderns have internalized the gods in the form of psychoneurosis. Sometimes I'm not sure which paradigm works better …

"Well, I must admit you've had a fair amount to overcome. You had some pretty tough breaks from the get-go: a mother virtually paralyzed by depression and a father who had to work nights and so couldn't provide much more than financial support.

I'd like to go back for a moment to the idea of mother as both home and a barrier to home, which the dream dramatizes so starkly. Do you think that theme could have any relevance to your life today, I mean, quite apart from the lingering effects from childhood, which are, of course, profound?"

"I'm not sure I follow … " I said, wagging my head.

"What I'm doing here," the doctor said slowly and emphatically, "is going back to the question I put to you earlier, shortly after your narration of the dream."

"You mean, what moved me to tell this old dream?"

"Yes."

"Gee, I don't know," I said, perplexed. "It's been on my mind lately; in fact, I'd say I've been thinking about it on and off since I began coming here."

"Exactly. Why do you think that is?"

"Are you implying my unconscious has been trying to tell me something?"

"You better believe it!"

"Oh come now, a call from underground that's been getting nothing but a busy signal from me? How romantic can this analysis get?"

"Please, Herr Professor, can the sarcasm and indulge me for a moment. Think about it," he said invitingly, coaxingly.

"Why might the memory of such a dream keep popping into your head since we began here?"

"Well," I speculated, "your question, which any lawyer will tell you is a leading one, implies that the dream, or at least the memory of it, is meant to tell me something about *you,* or about our relationship."

"Yes, and what could that be?"

"Surely not that you're some kind of Frankenstein, a lethal threat to me and my security."

"Really? Are you sure?" the doctor plied me, with just the barest mischievous smile.

"But the dream's all about my Mom and me, and the beginning of my life," I objected. "Obviously you're nowhere in sight."

"Au contraire," he scolded mildly, "You know all about compacted meanings in dreams, what Freud called 'overdetermination.' Any dream is about more things than we can count, and old dreams accumulate new meanings as we recall them later in life. Their compactness is their genius, a genius even the greatest poets can only marvel at. And consider this: any dream that lingers in the mind the way yours has, is certainly about something important going on in your life *at the moment.* Wouldn't you say that's a fair characterization of our relationship?"

"Let me get this straight," I said, "you're telling me the dream is warning me about some danger in our relationship?"

"Of course it is! Don't you think there's any danger in what we're undertaking here, the dismantling of lifelong psychological defenses, the bringing to light of feelings and experiences that may cause you deep pain—if not worse? You don't think that's risky?—Well, your unconscious certainly does and it's been trying to alert you to the fact. Now, don't misunderstand, it's not saying, 'Get away from Frankenstein [i.e., evil *moi*] and run home before he traps you in the forest primeval, the *Urwald,* of the psyche!' Not at all. It's saying, 'Take heart, you're in for a perilous journey, one on which you'll be confronting some emotional monsters'—you'll recall a dream we explored earlier that pictured it all as a dark descent into 'the concave mountain.' 'But keep in mind that there's support and companionship along the way [your cousin Alice, the 'good *moi*,' if you will], and that your courage and perseverance will ultimately bear fruit: you will fill your berry basket with ambrosia, the fruit of the gods.'"

Just for a second I let myself bask in his ambrosial vision. Then, "I guess in pushing, or at least nudging me to explore those areas of the psyche I've put 'off limits,' i.e., repressed, you are in a real sense cutting me off from home, aren't you?"

"Certainly," he affirmed, "the 'home' of your old and comfortable defenses, a make-shift home you began constructing around the time you first dreamt this dream, a home it's now time for you to leave, or shall we say, analytically deconstruct. You can't find your true home until you abandon your false one."

"That's funny," I said, "back in my card-carrying Zen days in the late 80's, my teacher, Eido Roshi, would often make that very point with a story about Rinzai, the great Chinese master during the Tang dynasty. It's said that Rinzai would constantly bellow at his students: 'Not one of you has come before me, having completely left home!', which, of course, was his way of saying that no one, or at least damn few, take the leap into Zen or Enlightenment without first having to be pried loose from an armor of protective psychological defenses, the 'home' they have always known. It's just impossible to start out from a posture of total honesty, before oneself or before others—which should not be surprising, I suppose. If we could, we'd all be enlightened from the get-go."

"And people like me would be out of business," Dr. P. quipped. "But, invoking your romantic myth of Paradise Lost, you might look at it this way: We *are* all enlightened from the get-go; we're *born* enlightened—you know the Zen koan[8] about your pre-parental face—but inevitably the cloud of forgetfulness and ignorance descends upon us—it's called 'life'—and we spend the rest of our days struggling to get back there, to climb up the greased right-hand side of the "U" of history, our own life-history, and regain Paradise."

"That's all I need now, my analyst teaching me my own area of literary specialization. The ultimate indignity," I sighed.

"No extra charge—and anyway, it's not teaching, just reminding. But listen, speaking of being reminded, I'm reminded myself of something I've been meaning to bring up for a while. It has to do with the matter of defensive styles. It'll come as no surprise to you to be told that yours is intellectual. You intellectualize your experiences, your feelings. You sublimate the real, the actual, up into your head as the 'theoretical' and thereby keep it once removed, as it were. Now, this style has certainly stood you in good stead throughout your life, protecting you the way the elaborate social rituals of primitive peoples protect them from the real and imagined terrors of nature. It's provided you with a good life, an interesting, rewarding career, the pleasures of scholarship, and so on. On the other hand, this style is particularly 'devious' in that it makes 'understanding' itself a barrier to the real, and hence to freedom, since freedom can only be found within the real. And this applies, in a dialectical way, to positive as well as negative experience: your elaborate thought processes will protect you from the deepest emotional pain, but also bar you from the most exquisite joys. Compare your current aesthetic response to Elgar's *Enigma Variations,* one of your favorite compositions, to the way you'll respond to that piece a few years from now, after we've done some real work here and you're no longer either able or willing to keep 'meaning,' or rather 'meaningfulness,' confined to discrete works of music or art or literature, when Meaning (capital 'M') just rolls unto your feet from every one of the ten thousand directions, as the Buddhists are fond of saying. In other words, when it's drained out of your head back down into your being."

I wanted to interrupt him with a barrage of questions and clarifications, but thought better of it. Right now it was better just to listen.

"But that's not all of what I'm getting at either," he continued. "The other part of it has to do with me, with the fact that intellectualization also happens to be my own style of defense. This makes the countertransference, which an analyst must never lose sight of, a fiendishly subtle and seductive aspect of our relationship for me. I must watch myself very carefully in our sessions, that I don't get lured into your 'philosophical' or 'metaphysical' arguments, which could easily happen since the fact is that I share many of your intellectual interests and passions (notwithstanding what I said before about my 'not believing in beliefs.' There are different interests for different levels of self; and beliefs, though no longer believed in, can nevertheless remain intellectually appealing). But that said, you mustn't think you seduced me into a debate earlier in the hour when we got into it over determinism and the limitations of theory—on the contrary, I was responding to your expression of genuine anguish over the claustrophobia of theory, of forever having to look out at the world through its iron bars. You were feeling the pain caused by your own defensive style and I acknowledged that. Being an intellectualizer myself, I share all the liabilities, all the misery, of that style. As the kids say, I know where you're coming from. What's so difficult for me is recognizing the difference in myself between a response that's genuine, whatever that means, and one coming out of my own unacknowledged need—and knowing where the line is between these two …

"But that, as they say, is a whole 'nother analysis … Time's up."

As I heard the door click shut behind me on leaving the building, I suddenly realized the sun was shining. How could that be? Oh, of course, I was in Syracuse.

(3) May 2001: The Cobra under the Boardwalk

It's nighttime somewhere at the Jersey shore, maybe Belmar or Seaside Heights. The problem is, I'm underneath the boardwalk that runs alongside the ocean beach. Down here it's much darker than above—inky black. I can hear occasional strollers passing by overhead, sense some semblance of nightlife—snatches of conversation, laughter, cars whizzing by, but it's got nothing to do with me. I'm stuck here below, more or less walled in by the darkness and by the mounds of sand all around me. There's no clear exit. And to my horror, poised opposite me, peering right at me, from maybe six feet away, is the scariest looking cobra you've ever seen. We're stuck together in this cramped space, the snake upright, taut, maybe just waiting for the slightest false move on my part to lunge at me with those fangs. I can see the snake as if by its own inner light, for it sheds no light around us.

"Chilling," he said.

"That's putting it mildly," I quickly seconded. "I've had many nightmares in my life about being threatened by poisonous snakes, not to mention other nasty creatures and critters, but this one tops them all for stark, naked terror. How could anyone afflicted with such dreams *not* be claustrophobic?"

"I have no doubt the dream relates to your claustrophobia—your problem with elevators, tunnels, bridges and so forth—among other important issues, so I'm eager to hear what you make of it. Whether it ties in with the complaint that originally brought you here, your anxiety over driving on the interstate, remains to be seen. Anyway … " he said, gesturing for me to continue.

"Well, this is another one of those dreams that I originally had many years ago, in this case in the early 70's, but that popped back into my mind a couple of weeks ago and keeps popping."

"As you know by now, this probably indicates that something happened recently that caused that old dream to resurface. Whatever it was, it's apparently still going on, or at least its consequences are. Any idea what it might be?" the doctor asked.

I knew only too well what it was and had come to today's session bent on discussing nothing else. What had happened was that a fierce depression had descended on me like a sudden summer derecho. One evening at home, after returning with my wife and foreign exchange student from an S.U. basketball game, it just swooped in on me like some airborne predator and began battering me with horrendous internal violence. I was not only in pain, but profoundly disoriented and scared witless. Lying awake in bed that night, I even began to fear going mad and could actually see with my inner eye some fiery abyss of insanity beckoning to me. I'd had a few bouts of depression before this, the first one occurring when I was twenty, and so was no stranger to that malady's cruel onset, but this was the first depression I'd known that could accurately be described as an attack: sudden, powerful, relentless.

I'd been doing okay in the weeks leading up to it. At least I wasn't miserable; my anxiety was down, my interest in work was up—which is not to say I was any more convinced than ever that my visits to Dr. P. were having any effect, one way or the other. My skepticism regarding analysis, and depth psychology in general, had been hard-won, and I wasn't giving it up without some soul-rocking revelation to the contrary. Then, all of a sudden, WHAM!!! I was shipped off to hell and spent the next two-plus weeks prior to this session in survival mode. The only way I could teach my classes was by gathering what little energy I had and focusing it with rigid exclusivity on the present moment, student by student, idea by idea, detail by detail. Paradoxically, by the end of a class hour when I took mental inventory, I'd find myself in a condition approaching samadhi, a state of intense concentration that was in some ways pleasurable, since it enabled me to direct my attention at anything with a laser-like focus. Of course, once I relaxed my mind I would be overcome within minutes by mental exhaustion, and of course the depression, which would force me to try to avoid even routine conversation.

Only my years of Zen meditation made it possible for me to concentrate in this way when I needed to and so muddle through each day. To this day I thank the Buddha for what Zen taught me about navigating one's mind through the minefields of one's own inner chaos. Still, by the time my head hit the pillow at night, I was mentally gassed. What exacerbated the situation was that, at the very time my depression hit, Dr. Purper was forced to take to his bed for a few weeks, laid low by a bout of bronchial pneumonia, made worse no doubt by his smoking. Consequently, except for a brief phone call, I was virtually without his support during the onset and first weeks of the depression. This both scared me and pissed me off. "Where the fuck does he get off abandoning me at this of all times!"

was the anger part of it, more or less. Of course, in such moments I would conveniently overlook my staunch conviction that there was nothing he could do for me in any case.

Even more exasperating was his facile—or so it seemed to me at the time—response to my account of these inner events when I finally got to tell him about them in this particular session, after hungrily accepting his invitation to speculate about the surfacing of the old cobra dream: "Looks like we're right on schedule," he said with obvious self-satisfaction. "Don't tell me you weren't expecting this," he asked, noticing my scowl.

"Well, it's certainly no secret to you," I huffed in wounded indignation, "that I'm deeply skeptical about analysis, about what we're doing here. From the very beginning I've been on a sharp lookout for any internal sign that might confirm its validity and prove me wrong—a sudden insight, a revelatory dream, any kind of seismic change or indication of healing. What I wasn't expecting was that 'revelation' to come in the form of a crushing depression! What am I to make of it? Is this analysis, with its endless sifting through painful memories and experiences, in fact making everything worse by its relentless focus on the negative?"

"First off," he said in a mild, empathic tone, "I want to apologize to you for my illness and long absence. True, there was nothing I could do about the horrendous timing; it seems almost a perverse synchonicity that our respective illnesses began together, my bronchitis and your depression. Of course, none of that has made these days any easier for you to bear. But maybe this perspective that I want to offer you will help a little: as I said a moment ago, it looks like we're right on schedule, and that's a good thing. This is what your sudden depression signals to me."

My impulse, barely restrained, was to leap across the gap between us, grab onto his throat and squeeze for handing me such patent bullshit. "Right on schedule," indeed! And would a flying leap into the infamous suicide gorge on the Cornell campus be right on schedule as well? Looking out the solitary window of the room, my eyes took in the sunlight dappling the rich green foliage of the trees bordering the parking lot. Yielding momentarily to self-pity, I grimaced over the irony of "poor me" in a vortex of depression amidst the new verdant life of the season. Hadn't I read somewhere that the incidence of depression actually increases in the warm, sunny seasons? Not the statistic one would wish to help validate from personal experience.

Taking a deep breath, I steeled myself to hear what I was sure would be another therapeutic rationalization. "You'll recall the prediction, or should I say 'prophecy,' symbolically expressed in the very first dream we analyzed back in October of last year: you must descend the chessboard to its nadir before ascending the other side to Dottie. Well, you're in descent—or, in clinical terms, depression. I understand very well that even the knowledge that a depression is a necessary part of a journey ultimately leading to transcendence or liberation isn't much consolation when you're bogged down in it, but you must learn to have faith in these quasi oracular utterances of the deep unconscious. They will sustain you when the going gets rough, as will I to the best of my ability."

Damn him, I thought, he has this uncanny ability to defuse my anger with his silver tongue. How can I stay pissed at anyone able to cast my misery in such mythic-heroic terms? Anyone with any poetry in his soul might almost wish for such a noble depression—almost.

"You know, I was pushing you pretty hard in the sessions before the hiatus," he went on, "probing and poking at those calcified intellectual defenses of yours. I'm sure a consequence of that was the release of this depression that was no doubt lurking just underneath. Since you have to face it anyway, you might as well do it now. I think you're ready. The sooner you take it on, the sooner you'll process it and get through it. As I said, I read your misery as a sign of progress, and, again, sorry about the rotten timing with my illness."

"But what if you're wrong?" I asked emotionally and with insistence. "Here I am, reduced to clinging for life to some mythic-therapeutic scenario, a glorified so-called 'Hero's Journey' a la Joseph Campbell, that I'm not even sure I can believe in! It's one thing to warm vicariously to Campbell's stirring evocation of these myths with Bill Moyers on TV, from the comfort of an easy chair, but quite another suddenly to find yourself in the midst of the fray itself, wondering what the hell hit you—"

"—Ah, but you see, now you know 'what the hell hit you,'" the good doctor hastened to interject. "A myth has hit you, and now you're being called upon to enact that myth, to realize it in your own life, for your own sake and, in some mysterious way we can't understand, for the sake of the world. 'He descended into hell. The third day He rose again from the dead. He ascended into heaven . . .' The dialectical principle that there is no resurrection without crucifixion is not just a religious truth; it is a living—and fundamental—psychological truth as well.

We must undergo the pain, the self-mortification, of analysis—or something like it—and suffer the death of the old self if we would hope to know the birth of the new.

"Now, granted it would be better, easier, for you if you believed in this mythic scenario wholeheartedly, for obvious reasons. But, being the skeptical head case you are, let me suggest that, for the time being, you merely act *as if* you believed in it as a way of 'trying it out.' 'Fake it until you make it'—you know, the old Al Anon mantra. As time goes by, the wisdom of the myth—its inner psychology—will become evident to you, and all the conflict and frustration caused by your skepticism will vanish."

"Well, actually, despite my complaining, the myth of the Hero's Journey is not such a truth-stretch for me as you seem to think it is. As I've said here before, meditation has shown me the validity of dialectical logic, and I am convinced that the opposites— pleasure/pain, true/false, good/evil, etc.—do meet somewhere deep within psychospiritual reality. But to feel as if I'm betting my sanity, my very life, on that truth …"

He looked at me sympathetically, a look I instantly absorbed like balsam, for I had confided in no one else since my misery began.

"There's something else," I said tentatively.

"What do you mean?"

"My depression is not vague, it's not a generalized blanket of pain without specific content. It came, or rather struck, in the form of a 'problem,' an 'issue.'"

"I see. Well, let's hear about it."

I gathered myself for a few seconds and began: "This issue has a history … Way back in my bachelor days, around

1970, I met a girl from Staten Island named Nicole. We were both students in a summer psychology course I was taking at my undergraduate college. She was a petite Italian brunette, very attractive, with long, flowing, dark hair and a way of walking—a way of carrying herself—that was somehow both erotic and 'proper' at the same time. It's hard to describe—let's just say it caught my attention. She was taking the class to fulfill a requirement for her teaching certificate; she wanted to teach emotionally disturbed children, just like my sister Iris.

"Anyway, we started dating and before long we became intimate. The sex was wonderful, and frequent, and we had some great times together, going to summer theater in Manhattan and having no trouble finding interesting things to talk about. I began thinking of her in terms of a permanent relationship—if not marriage, then at least shacking up as a prelude to it. Remember, those were the heady days of the tail end of the counterculture, 'b.a.' (before AIDS), when experimenting in sexual behavior and male-female living arrangements was *de rigueur*. I was lonely as a twenty-nine-year-old bachelor living in Syracuse, a married community if ever there was one. It was time for me to find a mate.

"So, everything was going swimmingly for most of that summer—until one weekend which we spent together at the Jersey shore. We were staying over Saturday night at a motel—I think it was in Point Pleasant. It must've been around four a.m. and we were sleeping. Suddenly I hear a low groan coming from Nicole. I turned to her and asked what was wrong, but her only response was a continued groan. I switched on the lamp and asked again, but she just moaned and groaned and then began babbling more or less incoherently. I grew worried and started considering what, if anything, I should do. She didn't seem in any physical pain; it was more a kind of subdued hysteria, some emotional upset that was slowly mounting in intensity. I sat next to her on the bed trying to soothe and calm her, without much success. Then she began complaining that she was hungry and thirsty and would I please go out and get her such and such. I tried to reason with her that it was four a.m. and nothing was open, that we could grab an early breakfast in a few hours, and wouldn't a bottle of juice or soda from the motel vending machine do for now, and so on. But she was implacable and started accusing me of being insensitive to her needs, saying what a disappointment I was to her and how the whole relationship was just another illusion gone bust. After about an hour, her upset seemed to have run its course and we were able to get a few more hours of sleep. When we woke up, I was naturally expecting some sort of explanation from her, something ... but she didn't even mention it—not a word, as if it had never happened!

"Long story short, my relationship with Nicole died with that incident, at least from my end. I decided I had enough emotional problems of my own and just couldn't afford to take on someone else's. Besides, I could no longer regard her in the same glowing, optimistic light. Something dark and sinister had shown itself, something she'd managed to carefully conceal for the first few months, and it repelled me."

"Of course it did," the doctor said. "When a man is 'shopping' for a wife, he naturally finds such profound emotional liability lethal. Time to move on."

"Which, of course, is what I did, though not immediately. At the time I wasn't quite ready to throw in the towel, so we continued to see each other, less and less often, and I even invited her up to Syracuse for a weekend that Fall. But it felt more like an epilog, a wake even, than a living thing—even the sex, which had always been good, was now beginning to feel perfunctory, and it all just petered out after that visit (no pun, I swear!).

"But you know, looking back, I think Nicole was probably as ready to end it as I was, whether she knew it or not. The drifting apart was mutual; she never called to ask me why I wasn't calling. I suppose it's even possible she staged that episode of semi-hysteria in the motel as a way to begin wriggling out of the relationship. Who knows?"

"Quite possible," Doctor P. agreed.

"But, my good doctor," I said airily and shifting position, as if to signal him that I was finally coming to the "issue," "all of that is prelude to what happened next. Some months later—in fact, it was over the Christmas holidays when I was down in New Jersey visiting my family—I ran into a mutual friend, a girl who'd been in that summer psych course with Nicole and me, at a mall in Jersey City, and she happened to mention to me just in passing that Nicole was seeing someone and that it might be serious. I thought to myself, my God, the ex's corpse isn't even cold yet and the widow's already on to the next one. But then this mutual friend said something that would change my life forever: 'She's confided to me that she's pregnant and that she and Neal, her fiancé, are planning a wedding.'—The girl went on for several minutes telling me about Neal and the preparations he and Nicole were making, but I didn't hear a word of it. I could only nod at appropriate intervals, swept up as I was in the whirlwind of frantic thinking that was pouring out of the simple mental math I'd just done: of course it could be mine. But how could I possibly know for sure without having a detailed conversation with Nicole?—

"... So, screwing up my courage, I called her a few days later and quickly found my worst fears confirmed. Yes, it was mine, she confessed—the chronology of her intimacy with Neal left no doubt. I had no reason to doubt her on this: she had nothing to gain by lying and even preferred to keep it from me, and would have, had our mutual friend not spoken out of turn. She said that she thanked God for Neal, who knew all about it, loved her unconditionally and was more than willing to begin married life with a ready-made family. Finally, coming to the most awkward part of it, speaking slowly and with hesitation, she said she knew by the end of summer, and knew I knew, that our relationship was winding down and had no future. Several weeks later, when it was clear she was pregnant and she was already seeing Neal, she knew without a doubt what she had to do: level with him, hope for the best and leave me out of it.

"When I asked her if she didn't think I had a right to know, she replied with the utmost pragmatism, 'Listen, Dennis, we both know you wouldn't have wanted any part of this scenario—all things considered, this was—and *is*—the best solution for all concerned.' And you know something, Dr. Purper, she was right, and I felt she was right, deep within, when she said those words to me. I had no wish to take on fatherhood at that point in my life; it would've been an enormous complication, especially considering that I'd already ended the relationship with Nicole internally—I mean, in my heart. Still, something inside me would not let me simply agree with her, wish her the best and hang up. I kept asking her if she didn't want financial support, if there wasn't something I could do, and so on. But she just kept waving me off, saying that Neal was doing all right, better than that, in fact, and that the best thing was for us to go our separate ways, no hard feelings either way. In any case, that was what she wanted.

"So finally, yielding to her clear-headedness, I said goodbye, hung up and thought that was the end of it ... Oh how wrong I was! I soon found myself depressed and obsessing about the whole business. I just couldn't get it off my mind. Had I done the right thing? Should I have insisted on maintaining some tie to her and the child? But wouldn't such insistence have gone against her wishes? Wasn't it right to let *her* dictate the course of events? And besides, I really didn't want to be connected to them, did I? Wouldn't I just be acting compulsively out of guilt, and did guilt ever do anyone any good in the long run? And on and on—

"These and a hundred other questions kept turning over in my mind, and the longer and deeper I thought about it all, the less able I found I was to reach closure on any of it. It seemed to take on a life of its own, becoming some sort of obsessional juggernaut. Like any 'good' obsession, it began crowding and eventually commandeering my field of consciousness at the most inconvenient times, demanding my attention, like when I'd be teaching or in the middle of ordinary conversations with colleagues or friends—even on the phone. It was greedy for my attention and rarely left me in peace, the irony being that the more I gave in and entertained the 'Problem'—for capital-P 'Problem' was what it had grown into—the more it mocked me by removing peace of mind ever further from me and demanding ever greater attention. It was insatiable.

"After a few weeks of this misery, I began having nightmares very much like the cobra dream I came in here with today. Eventually I realized that, for the sake of my sanity, I had to find a way to protect myself, to shield my exhausted mind at least provisionally, from what seemed like an endless struggle. In time I stumbled on the strategy of making 'deals' with the juggernaut (yes, 'deals!'): I would promise to entertain it on a given date, say, one week from then, agreeing to give it my full attention for a certain period of time, in return for being allowed to live free of it till then. Strangely, it agreed, though somewhat grudgingly since it would usually hang around the outskirts of my awareness, just waiting to 'collect' on its end of the bargain. But then, when it came time for me to 'pay up,' I would pull a fast one and renegotiate the terms of the deal, this time for *two* weeks from then, and again it would seem to agree. (It was powerful but not very bright! I realized it could be manipulated like a sort of gullible bully.) And on and on it went like that, with the periods between negotiations getting longer and longer, until, at some indeterminate point, the juggernaut slipped down into the nether regions of consciousness.

"Every so often as the years went by, it would show up again and roar in protest, sometimes mightily, sometimes feebly, but each time I would simply dust off the same strategy and use it again. I think I was always half aware that what I was doing was really just a stopgap measure, designed to put the problem on hold, to bracket it, so that I could get on with my life, at least to some extent, until such time as I could work out a real solution, whatever that might be. But over time, I guess the stopgap turned into the solution itself. But it was never a satisfying one; it could never protect me from a subtle sense of dread that lay at the heart of even the most uplifting periods of my life …"

"Did you ever feel moved to contact her, to see the child?" Dr. P. asked.

"Oh, every now and then through the years I would feel an impulse to call, but at the same time I'd also feel … blocked, impeded, by what I knew were her firm wishes against it. If she really wanted to hear from me, she would've let me know. Besides, I had no way of knowing what complications my sudden appearance might bring into the child's life … That phone call, by the way, was the last contact I ever had with Nicole."

"What about Dottie? Does she know of all this?"

"Oh, of course. This is not the kind of thing you can keep from a partner you love deeply. She's never been anything less than sympathetic and supportive—wonderfully so, I would say. And I'm profoundly grateful to her for it. Had she taken any kind of critical or adversarial stance, it certainly would've made the whole business a lot harder for me."

Dr. P. breathed deeply, audibly, and looked high up on the wall behind me, as if searching for something. "… You have my sympathy for your long suffering," he said finally, lingering in an empathic gaze, "… but I'm afraid it makes perfect sense. The 'cobra of dread,' the dreadful cobra, has stalked you through all the years of this half-repressed emotional trauma, and it will stay right there, poised under the boardwalk of consciousness, until it's brought up into the light and tamed; and we tame it by coming to understand what it's made of, by learning what ingredients, psycho*log*ical ingredients, go into its deadly venom. And we can start right now with the little time we have left by looking carefully at the dream."

By now I knew well that "we" meant "me" and that I was being asked to free-associate to the dream. This time I was more than ready: having made myself into an amateur depth psychologist over the years in a largely futile effort to help myself, I had subjected the cobra dream to all sorts of Freudian theory about sex, guilt and punishment, and these I now unleashed on the one person I could regard without question as an appreciative audience. On and on I went about serpentine phallic symbols and vicious *Bisse* or "bites of conscience," as German has it (*Gewissensbisse*), in contrast to our milder "pangs" in English, and how the dream so neatly blended the two antagonists of sex and reprisal, or id and superego, into that one self-luminous image of the cobra. Then I extrapolated to the theme of parents and church and how they, wittingly or not, became so deeply interwoven in my life in the formation of a sense of responsibility that had hardened over time from reasonable into dangerously scrupulous, in other words, the draconian superego phase of the cobra.

I lingered on the subject of my father, whom I described as long-suffering, a man carrying a lifelong cross in the form of a job he hated to make sure his family never went without food, clothing and shelter. And look at me, taking the easy way out, not even having to pay child support, free even of the responsibility to know the appearance of a child of my own loins. I told of the smothering blanket of shame such thoughts had always thrown over me, that this shame was the most inescapable, claustrophobic feeling of all, the deepest and most toxic *Biss* of the cobra of conscience: the knowledge that I, with my superior material means, had utterly failed to live up to what was, in its way, my oppressed father's heroic standard.

Then I turned to summing up my mother's role in this history as one of fear and loathing. She loathed sex and feared it and had learned to cloak her anxieties in a stony silence. Sex was always the naked elephant in the room in our family. There was never any discussion of it, and any conversation relating to the body was limited strictly to its sartorial or medical needs. A joke or quip about sex, say by a comedian on TV, might be laughed at, but the laughter would always be followed by a squeamish disconnect, never a follow-up joke or remark by one of us. The vast difference in the breezy, enjoyable way my wife's family talked and joked about sex was a real eye-opener for me.

As for the dream vis-à-vis the Catholic church, I explained what I thought was a subtle distinction to the doctor, that, whereas my conscious feelings about the problem clustered around shame, falling short of a parental ideal and so on, my *un*conscious feelings, at least as reflected in dreams, had much more to do with a primitive kind of guilt over illicit sexual behavior per se, as if the sexual act itself, more than its social consequences, were the reprehensible part of it—in other words, everything twisted and perverse I'd ever absorbed from the Baltimore catechism in school regarding the sixth commandment and from the Jesuits (not all, but many) with their Augustinian body-hating mentality. This was the cobra in all its shining ambiguity: its proud phallic posture and its fanged threat to transgression, poised to strike either way.

Head resting on the palm of his hand, Dr. Purper had been listening intently, almost without blinking, it seemed.

Then, upon inhaling, he said, "Well, you see the dream as expressing the conflict between sexual behavior, with and without consequences, and conscience, and clearly there's little to take issue with there; I'm sure you're right on. The point I would make is one of emphasis, I mean, that the pole of conscience in the sex-conscience polarity is clearly dominant (as indeed it was in the history you just narrated to me); the whole feel of the dream is one of suffocating terror, with nary a wisp of id pleasure. If the cobra is a phallus, it seems clear that the phallus is there to be punished and not to enjoy itself."

How could I not agree? The dream was after all a nightmare, not exactly a stage for sexual indulgence.

"Yes," I said, "It's obvious I'm dreaming with my conscience here."

"That's an interesting way to put it."

"It's not my own expression," I said, "It comes from one of my favorite German—actually Swiss—writers, Conrad Ferdinand Meyer. He wrote this historical tale about the Thirty Years War called 'Gustav Adolf's Page,' in which a fan, a kind of seventeenth-century groupie, of the Swedish king named Gustel dons a uniform and disguises her gender to get into the army and close to her hero. She becomes his personal assistant, with him 24/7, attending to his every need, separated from him even in sleep by only a tent canvas near the battlefield. Describing a dream she has one night, in which she's pursued on horseback by an angry king, the narrator says 'Gustel träumte mit dem Gewissen,' that is, 'Gustel dreamed with her conscience.' The dream expresses fear of punishment for illicit sexual desire, just like mine—though in Gustel's case it's quasi Oedipal. I remember reading in the literature on Meyer that Freud himself said he learned something about this class of so-called superego dreams from this tale of Meyer's. That impressed me."

"Undoubtedly a key source for your unconscious in fashioning your own dream," Dr. Purper affirmed. "And yet, with all its anxiety, I don't necessarily want to read the dream as unequivocally dark and sinister either." In response to my quizzical expression, he explained, "What I mean is, the cobra, and the serpent in general, has a rich lore in Western cultural symbology, one that goes far deeper than the rather simplistic Freudian isomorphism between snake and penis. Here is where I find Jung much more helpful, in that he leaves far greater room for the interpretation of dream symbols in terms not just of the dreamer's personal history but the history of his culture—in particular his religious culture—as well. I'm not just talking here about the sectarian commitment the dreamer might have but the general religious-cultural atmosphere he's born into and breathes his whole life, whether committed or not. In this deep cultural sense, we're *all* religious, every one of us.

"Anyway, getting back to the dream in this wider context, ... just as the cobra here can be read as embodying—literally—sexual potency, albeit in a recessive mode, that is, held in abeyance by the fanged superego, it also carries other meanings in this same minor key that may be more to your liking. Serpents are wonderfully ambiguous symbols in many ancient mythologies—the serpent wound around the staff carried by the healer Asclepius, the so-called caduceus, for example, has become the symbol of modern medicine, the idea being that any chemical from nature, including snake venom, can either heal or kill, depending entirely on how it's used. Similarly, the cobra in your dream can mean either sexual expression or repression, depending on the 'balance of power,' so to speak, in your psychic economy. The psyche is a dynamic, living system—'dynamic' in the sense that its power is distributed in such a way as to constitute a field of entirely interdependent tensions; how much power a given 'player,' say, the phallic cobra, has within the system depends on how much all the other players have. If energy shifts in one part, it simultaneously shifts in all other parts as well, to some degree. The implication of all this relativity is to me very optimistic: it is that the psyche is originally, intrinsically, organically whole and that its sundering into parts (or subsystems) that thereafter jockey for power is simply the normal course of internal events in a human life. If that's the case, then it's a small leap to the conclusion that this 'internecine warfare' is at bottom a struggle to restore that lost wholeness, a struggle that can be profoundly mitigated by psychotherapy. That makes the therapist a kind of priest, a *sacerdos,* as Jung might put it, who mediates the patient/disciple's bumpy return trip to wholeness, helping her or him up that slippery right-hand side of the 'U'—if you'll forgive my re-invoking Northrup Frye's biblical paradigm."

"I just love it when you wax religious-philosophical," I said in the drollest tone I could muster, fully aware of its failure to mask my sincere admiration for the doctor's passionate vision. And I couldn't resist throwing in my own two cents, especially since they were an association spontaneously produced by his words: "I was intrigued by what you said about the way cultures mythologize the antithetical powers contained within even something as intuitively harmful as venom. I wonder if you've read or heard about the philosopher Jacques Derrida's famous disquisition on the Greek word, *pharmakon.*[9]

He says that Plato uses the word in the *Phaedrus* to mean 'poison,' but that the word also carries the directly opposite meaning of 'remedy.' Derrida's point is that words (and language generally) are inherently unstable and will never, despite our best efforts to control them, mean simply 'this' or 'that.' They're forever shifting in what they signify, depending on social circumstances. The term Derrida coined for this is *différance,* in the sense, I think, that words are always 'differing' in what they mean. But I believe he also uses the term in another sense (appropriately enough!), to express the idea that any given meaning of a word manifests itself in consciousness only by virtue of 'deferring' or putting off other meanings, in other words, by a kind of repression. So the meanings of a given word enter and exit the stage of the mind more or less separately and at different times, depending on which one is holding all the others off in the wings at any one time. (It reminds me a little of the old experiment in Gestalt psychology in which you look at a picture that, in one moment, resembles a flower vase and, in the next, two profiles facing each other.[10] Which of the two you see depends entirely on which is currently 'repressing' the other in consciousness.)

"It seems to me this is very close to what you were just saying about images in dreams, which I suppose could be called 'dream-words,' the vocabulary or *lingua franca* of dreams. The conscience cobra in my dream is rigidly repressing the phallic cobra, and our work here is to 'loosen up' the relationship enough to let each one begin to flow into and out of the other with some grace and freedom. The work, then, is to 'unstick' the system where it is stuck, thus bringing greater harmony to the whole.

“Maybe this is also what that other French oracle, Jacques Lacan, means when he says that ‘the unconscious is structured like a language,’ though I must admit I’ve given up all hope of ever understanding him. Still, the point is that, paradoxically, it is this very elusiveness, this dynamic, shifting quality of the meaning of words—or dream images—that is so clearly telling us something we don’t want to hear, namely, that we shouldn’t even be trying to control it or ‘figure it out’ in any one-sided, once-and-for-all way, since these are systems whose inner laws clearly transcend any move the rational ego might make to hold them still in its own partisan interest. The tail cannot wag the dog. What we need to do, I think, is put our egos aside (no mean task, I grant) and just let those signs, be they word or image, speak to us directly in all their multivalence. This calls for a deeper ear.”

“The ear of a poet, maybe,” Dr. P added, smiling. “I kind of like the idea of my job-description as ‘poet maker,’ though I admit it has no rhyme or reason.”

And with this unpardonable quip he mercifully ended the session.

(4) November 2001: She Stoops to Conquer

I'm facing the tenement house I grew up in, located at 610 Grand St, Hoboken, New Jersey. But I'm not embodied—I'm just a witnessing presence, a pair of eyes, so to speak. Seated on the middle step of the stoop fronting the house, maybe ten feet directly in front of me, is my cousin Nicky. She's wearing pedal pushers and a blouse, as she usually did as a teen, and is sitting sideways on the step with her right leg extended along its surface and her left bent and supporting her on the step below. So she's sitting at a right angle to me, facing left, showing me her profile, arms folded. My vantage point has me looking slightly up at her, such that, if I had a body, I'd be about two feet tall.

Meanwhile, to the right of all this, "stage right" as it were, some twenty-five feet away, are my mother and my Aunt Mabel, standing together and whispering to each other—probably gossiping. They seem concerned about a dark baby carriage nearby, behind which "a second 'me,'" this one embodied, is hiding by crouching down behind its hood. The "point-of-view" me is looking right at the back of the crouching me, from maybe five feet behind. They can't see crouching me (nor, obviously, "point-of-view" me), but I can see them. Presumably there's a baby in the carriage, but I'm too low to see it from either of my positions.

"So, let's have at it," the good doctor began with a touch of gusto, just enough to stoke the embers of anger in me. At this point, a little over a year into the analysis, I was feeling more skeptical than ever that what I was doing was worthwhile. Quite the contrary, my depression had deepened over the summer and fall months and, on top of that, I was plagued by doubt, in the form of feelings that this so-called therapy was either totally ineffectual or harmful in and of itself. (Dr. Purper's assurances that my depression was a necessary phase in a long-term process of growth, the 'crisis of fever' before healing, were by now totally lost on me.) To add insult to injury, and literally so, I'd just been through a draconian ordeal at the university, culminating in my promotion to full professor. It seems the college committee's initial straw vote had gone against me, eight to seven, the reason being, as I heard through the grapevine, that I was thought to be "professionally disengaged," meaning, I think, that I wasn't attending enough professional conferences and presenting enough papers. (Never mind that the university offered its faculty no more than a pittance to defray expenses for such activity.) In any case, a wonderful colleague, Professor David Miller of the religion department, represented me to the committee, making the case for the quality of my scholarship, with which he was quite familiar, and apparently persuading the nay-saying members to rethink their positions, since the final vote went unanimously in my favor. It was, however, with more relief than happiness that I received the news. The whole affair had been so long and tedious and fraught with niggling resentment that the very idea of professorial rank had become to me ... well, rank.

So it was only after making some effort, on this raw November afternoon, to put aside strong feelings of antipathy that I was able to respond to the good Doctor's challenge. "Mm—," I said, "this is another old dream from the 70's that's been on my mind a lot lately, probably more 'bitter fruit' from my depression—which, by the way, has become extremely draining the last few weeks. All I want to do is sleep."

"… Maybe you should consider going on an antidepressant—an SSRI like Prozac or Paxil," Dr. P. suggested.

"I need something to give me energy, that's for sure. I feel exhausted when I come here, hardly able to muster the necessary focus."

"I would say that clearly indicates the need for medication. There's a psychiatrist I know nearby who literally wrote the book on psychiatric drugs. Let me do some checking and get back to you."

"Thanks, I really appreciate it."

"Not at all, analysis takes considerable energy and focus—we can't have you zoning out on the process. And even if you go on something, that doesn't mean you'll stay on it; it might be just for a while … Meanwhile back to the dream."

"Yeah … obviously this dream, like other old ones we've looked at, is all about the pregnancy and its repercussions, only this one introduces a new 'character' in the person of my cousin Nicky."

"Interesting. Tell me about Nicky," Dr. P. requested, settling into his chair as if in anticipation of a good story.

"Nicky and her family lived just around the corner from the tenement house I grew up in at 610 Grand St.," I said. "She was very pretty, a buxom brunette with this lush wavy hair, but a real tomboy teen who liked to hang out with our gang, playing poker with us for comic books, playing stoop ball and other boys' games. The thing is, she was a couple of years older and I was attracted to her—in fact, she ignited my sexual awakening when I hit about twelve, wearing those tight peddle pushers she liked, just like the ones in the dream. Of course, I never made a move on her, because I was totally ignorant of such matters. The thimbleful of knowledge I had about sex came to me from two opposed sources: the lurid world of boys' talk about breasts and hard-ons (hards-on?) and the finger-waving warning to 'leave it alone,' care of Holy Mother the Church.

"But Nicky's connection to the dream has more directly to do, I'm sure, with the fact that she got herself pregnant in her late teens. I don't know any of the circumstances, just that she gave the baby away. And I only know about her pregnancy at all because I overheard my Mom and my Aunt Mabel, who lived upstairs from us, talking about it one day when I was in another room and they probably thought I couldn't hear. That's just like the image of them in the dream gossiping about the baby carriage, with me listening in from my 'hide-out' behind it."

"Sometimes dreams are very transparent, leaving little to the interpreting imagination," the good doctor opined. "But there's so much more there; it's a very rich dream, so please go on."

"Well, it seems just as obvious to me that Nicky isn't merely herself in the dream, she's also *me*, in a sense, or at least a stand-in (or should I say 'sit-in') or proxy for me. In fact, she's a perfect blend of Nicole and me, a two-in-one: the tomboy cousin (i.e., 'my boyish blood' or me) with the same name as my old girlfriend, an interesting difference being that no one ever called Nicky 'Nicole.' It's a kind of androgyny, isn't it?" I asked.

"Absolutely," he replied. "Androgeny is a central feature of the anima archetype[11] in Jung—and in Hermann Hesse, his novelist disciple, by the way. Actually, all archetypes are bipolar, the anima sexually so—it's feminine for a man and masculine (called the 'anim*us*') for a woman. In a man it stands for his unconscious feminine side, and even for the dark, mysterious 'feminine' unconscious as a whole, which a man must learn to listen to if he is to become whole himself. And while I'm not sure I'd go so far as to say that Nicky in the dream is meant to be understood as an archetype, I certainly grant your accurate reading of the clues as pointers to androgyny."

"But I think she *is* an archetype."

"Why?"

"—because I have this funny feeling that I'm supposed to find out or learn something from her," I said with urgency, "something deep and important I'm just not getting on my own. Don't archetypes appear in dreams *de profundis,* so to speak, in times of crisis when we need their help?" He nodded. "There's something in her bearing, in her posture there on the stoop, that's meant to communicate something vital to me, even though she doesn't say a word. I need to know what it is."

"Well, what do you think it is," he asked.

"I don't know, I've looked at that image in my mind for so long … her just sitting there turned to the side, and the feeling I usually get is that she's coldly spurning me or ignoring me. I just don't know … if she's trying to tell me that I should be ashamed over what I did or didn't do for the child, I certainly don't need her to know that—"

"Ex*act*ly," Dr. P. cut in, "You're doing a great job with that all by yourself. So maybe that's *not* what you're meant to learn from her."

Dr. P said this with such conviction that I felt a slight

internal charge of inspiration to explore "dream Nicky" once again, this time with four eyes. "The dream has several striking images," I said, gently trying to imagine myself into it, "but what always arrests my attention first is that disembodied point of view, staring up at Nicky …"

"Go on," he said in a softly encouraging tone, "take your time."

"She's above me, but only by a couple of feet. As I said, she's sitting in the middle of the stoop, turned away from me, maybe five feet above the sidewalk, while bodiless me is about two feet high, looking up at her … Oh my God, a *baby* is about two feet high!—Does that mean we have a three-in-one here? I'm myself, Nicole and the baby all wrapped up in one?"

"Slow down, we're just exploring here—no hard-and-fast conclusions," he cautioned.

"Well anyway, it's her higher—'superior'—position that always gets me. Somehow those few vertical feet between us seem important, much more important than the ten horizontal. . . . "

"You say 'superior,' as if to qualify 'higher,'" Dr.P. pointed out. "Why do you think that is?"

"Well, if she's an archetype, then she's certainly superior, isn't she?"

"Yes, but that's a Psych 101 textbook speaking. What I'm asking is, what is there specific to the situation in the dream that makes her 'superior' to you?"

"I don't know … maybe it's her attitude, that aloofness that's expressed in her posture, arms folded, turned away from … me …" And that's when the flash of insight struck: "Wait a minute, why am I assuming she's turned away from *me*?

Why shouldn't I assume she's turned away from my Mom and my Aunt, who are directly behind her. Why shouldn't I see her as having turned her back on *them,* which means, of course, on their point of view, on their gossipy bourgeois attitude towards her having a baby out of wedlock and then giving it up? Nicky is showing her superiority to their censure … her independence, which is pretty much the kind of person she is in life. She's always marched to her own drummer. That's what she's trying to teach me, isn't it?" I asked Dr. P.—rhetorically, for I didn't really need his confirmation. What had just come out of me just felt so right. Still, his broad smile showed he was with me all the way on this one.

The power of this modest discovery, this unassuming insight, stunned me. All I had done was correct a 'small error' in the way I was viewing Nicky's turned back: it wasn't a rejection of me (a mistaken assumption generated by my excessive self-criticism); on the contrary, it was teaching me, demonstrating to me, a more mature attitude of independence from 'public opinion,' even—or especially—when that public is the intimate one of family, an attitude deep within me that my harsh conscience had always blocked. Nicky, with her back turned to the family's narrow arbiters of morality, was trying to inject some balance into my perspective.

I felt so elated over this insight that I was sure I had "gotten" the therapy and that I would be a card-carrying ex-neurotic within a few weeks—if indeed I wasn't already. And while I was soon to be disabused of such naïve exuberance, what I had learned in that moment nevertheless *was* important as a "live demonstration" of the way insight actually can bring about change in therapy—only it must do so over and over and over again, like steps in a process that is, by its nature, slow and cumulative, like neurosis itself, its flipside. Nor is the "payoff" moment usually so dramatic as it was in this particular instance. Nor did my "breakthrough" miraculously clear up my depression, though it did lift for a few days in the afterglow of this session. It would take about eight to ten weeks of Paxil to do that.

I would also learn over time that even flashing insights that set off the bells and whistles like the one of that day would not obliterate once and for all my skepticism of the validity of the analytic process, since such skepticism was an essential part of my defense system and could only be dismantled gradually like the neurosis it reinforced. "In the first half of life we 'mantle' ourselves with neurosis," as Dr. P. often loved to say, indulging his addiction to wordplay, "and in the second half we *dis*mantle." On an especially punny day he would add, "People come to me deeply disgruntled, but those who stick it out here leave totally gruntled."

I was certainly feeling gruntled as I sat there, basking in the glow of that insight, and was ready to call it a day, but the good Doctor protested, "Hold on now, we're not quite done here. You're a little too easily satisfied. Remember, there are two 'you's' in the dream, and we've only talked about one. Let's go on."

"I guess there's not much mystery about the other, embodied, me," I snickered. "That's me trying to hide from 'public opinion,' from the moral scorn of mother and aunt. I'm hiding my shame over having this child and then reneging on my responsibility to it—even hiding, in some sense, *behind* my own child, using my inability—or refusal—to see into the carriage as a shield from him/her. That would be the distance, emotional and geographical, I've put between us. Crouching down could also mean 'stooping pretty low'—a dream pun."

"Yes, that's awfully harsh self-criticism, isn't it," he noted. "But now, put that self-critical interpretation into the larger context of 'the other me' who is learning from the wisdom of the 'superior' anima deep within—Nicky on the stoop ..."

I thought a moment and then almost shouted, "—Of course, the disembodied me—that would be the deeper 'spirit' me—is witnessing two things, two quite different things, from a position sort of in between the other two 'players,' Nicky and family: on the one hand, I'm seeing objectively the abject misery I'm causing myself through my overly rigid conscience, my fear of offending the harsh standards of responsibility I was raised with—how, to paraphrase the bard, it makes a coward of me, causing me to hide—and, on the other, I'm taking in a new, more mature posture of independence, embodied in the cool, cross-armed, back-turning Nicky. Her cool attitude, 'higher up' as she is, represents her stable superiority to the chaotic forces of emotional conflict down on 'street level' where crouching me is ... Something for me to aspire to ..."

"*Not* just aspire to," the Doctor objected, "—something you're already participating in, already embodying, even as we speak! 'Aspiring to it' casts it away into the future. Don't wait, do it—or rather *be* it now, right now as it's being offered to you," he insisted. "The cool attitude here is the one you originally took when you hung up that phone on Nicole for the last time so long ago but then quickly repressed, the attitude that says, 'All in all, this is the least worst outcome of an unfortunate situation. Therefore, so be it.' Dream Nicky's cool posture embodies that attitude, as apparently do both Nicole and your cousin in life, judging at least from the way you represent them."

I looked down at my shoes, needing a moment to take it all in. Sensing this, Dr. P. fell briefly silent, and then went on: "I'd like to step back for a moment to make a point about how important it is to look at dreams—or any other aspect of one's self-concept, for that matter—with the aid of eyes other than one's own. We've already seen that demonstrated here at least once in this hour: recall how earlier you expressed your long-held view of Nicky's 'turned back' as a rejection of you: 'the feeling I always get is that she's ashamed of me ...' or something to that effect. But then I sort of cajoled you into taking a fresh look at it, and it wasn't long before you 'saw the light,' so to speak. Just a little jolt from me was all it took. Just a little nudge and all of a sudden decades of conditioning yawned. But would you have ever given yourself such a nudge, that is, out of the deep groove of habit, of a rigidly conditioned self-critical point of view? ... And notice this: once you were able to bring a new focus on 'the turned back' in this way, it bore immediate fruit: your disembodied self in the dream wasn't a reprehensible attempt to 'remove' yourself even further from the moral drama going on at the right, which is probably how you would've viewed it yesterday; rather it was your 'spiritual self,' as you put it, learning what the dream was teaching. By the same token, the broader, more reasonable perspective you've gained reveals your inability to see the baby hidden in the carriage as more likely a reflection of the simple fact that you've never seen him than it is an indication of any craven hiding or denial on your part. The hiding makes sense only in relation to the judgmental family 'stage right' … So you see how your defenses, which you created early on to protect yourself when you had no other choice, can, over the years, ossify and lock you into a sort of self-defeating tunnel vision."

"That's funny," I said, "this idea of the ethical status of behavior as depending profoundly on point of view just caused another dream to pop into my head, one I had a few nights ago."

"Excellent—using one dream to cast light on another. Let's hear it. We've got enough time at least to tell it."

Let's see … I'm lying flat on my back on some gritty industrial loading dock somewhere, looking up at a sinister black man who's bending over me with a joint hanging out of his mouth. He's tall and slender and wearing a white suit, like a pimp. He looks sort of like …who's that fashisel rapper guy … oh yeah: Snoop Dogg. So Snoop seems to be getting me, his 'cargo,' ready to ship somewhere. And in the next moment, sure enough, I find myself laid out in this black limo—a hearse?—being delivered …

"All right, *digame, digame*."

"Yeah, sure, except I haven't a clue …"

"Well, you said the idea of ethical ambiguity or relativity in the Nicky dream reminded you of this recent dream."

"Did I? … I don't remember … Oh yeah, that's right."

"That might mean that there's something ethically ambiguous about Snoop Dogg, that he's not 'all black,' so to speak."

"Well, sure, he *is* wearing this spotless white suit," I chuckled.

"Come on now, get with the program here. With what do you associate a loading dock?"

"I don't know … Hard work?"

"Maybe I should say 'with whom'", the Doctor said, fine tuning the question.

And again, this bit of fine-tuning caused my synapses to jell. "My father! … Of course, Snoop Dogg is my father, who spent his whole working life only fifty feet from a loading dock! Snoop Dogg is Snoop Dad! But what is he doing, and what does it mean?"

"I'd stay right with your intuition about moral ambiguity, which caused the dream to pop in the first place, remember?"

"Yes, let's see … if Snoop is morally ambiguous—after all, despite his sinister appearance, he is awfully engaging and funny on TV talkshows—that would mean my Dad is too …"

"That's right. Take it slow. Now you're taking a fresh look at father," Dr. P. observed.

"Well, at least since the end of my relationship with Nicole I've pretty much viewed my Dad as the ideal embodiment of paternal responsibility, and that ideal has become a whip I've used to lash myself. Maybe the dream is saying there's more Snoop Dogg in my Dad than my idealizing conscience is allowing. Again, it's a matter of balancing one's perspective."

"Sounds good. What about the hearse and your prone position in it?"

"Obviously Snoop Dad is shipping me off to the cemetery. But I've read enough Jung to avoid the mistake of reading 'death' in dreams literally. It usually refers to some kind of change: ending-and-beginning, death-and-resurrection, and so forth. Wait … Dad is revealing his dark or shadow side to me, his inner Snoop Dad, and then shipping his immature, idealizing son off to the cemetery, so that his place can be taken by a son with a more realistic view of his father, right?"

"Bingo! And we didn't even run overtime," the doctor enthused. "And you know what? For being so astute today, I'm going to bend one of my own rules and let you in on a pun the dream suggested to me, one you overlooked."

"Oh? And pray tell, what would that be?" I said, rubbing my hands in anticipatory delight.

"The image of you as Snoop Dogg's load or cargo on that dock, waiting to be picked up, might cause someone to associate you with the sort of cargo the pot-smoking Snoop Dogg would be likely to transport," Dr. P. explained, unable to suppress a fiendish grin."

"You mean ... *dope*?" I asked.

"... Listen, I want you to practice a little 'active imagination' with the image of Nicky on the stoop, okay? Just sit in a comfortable chair, relax, and slowly, gently conjure her image and let it speak to you; let it continue to teach, to amplify and deepen this nascent insight you came to today. And if at some point you feel moved to converse with it, go right ahead. Don't force anything; just see what happens. Do this every now and then just for a few minutes."

So now I was getting homework, as if the analysis itself weren't enough. But it had turned out to be a grand day and I really didn't mind at all—nothing could disturb my sense of satisfaction, of just maybe, finally, beginning to "get somewhere"—other than to the local cemetery.

(5) April 2002: Chased by the Keystone Kops

As in other recent dreams, here again I'm just a bodiless point of view, this time positioned just behind the toll booths at the Weehawken, New Jersey, entrance to the Lincoln Tunnel. I'm looking right at the great yawning maws of the several tunnels before me that all swerve quickly to the right (or East) as they make their way under the Hudson towards midtown Manhattan. But I'm particularly focused on the middle tunnel, as it looms there large, cavernous and mysterious, and the reason for this is that there's a bunch of police cars, maybe five or six, speeding into that tunnel one after another, apparently in pursuit of ... me! *So again there are two of me, the point of view watching it all from behind and the "me" already in the tunnel (and hence not viewable) just barely ahead of the cops in hot pursuit.*

That's about it, except for one fascinating wrinkle: everything about the cops is cartoonish: their cars, the clubs they're waving out the windows, even their uniforms and their very bodies, look as if drawn on a Sunday newspaper funnies sheet in, say, "Popeye" or "Felix the Cat." I woke up thinking of them as the Keystone Kops.

"I assume you're not too young to recall the Keystone Kops."

"Are you kidding?" the good doctor enthused, "I had a steady diet of Keystone Kops silent flicks and Farmer Gray cartoons every weekday after school—grammar school, that is. And I still regard it as time well spent."

"God, that's funny," I said, "just as you mention those

two in the same breath—the cops and the cartoons—I'm thrown back into the dream where the cops appear *literally* as cartoon characters; and another connection strikes me as well: just as the Keystone Kops were forever chasing and never catching their 'perp,' so too Farmer Gray was forever chasing and never catching those pesky mice."

"Take it further."

"In both cases there's pursuit with intent to punish, but the pursuers are so inept, so pathetic, they're laughable. They never catch anybody; it just goes on and on."

"Yes, it does, doesn't it? … There's just no end, no closure, no resolution to some pursuits, is there?"

"Ah, I see … A brick shithouse doesn't have to fall on me, does it? Well, I guess we can end the session right here—"

"Hold on now, not just yet. The obvious hides the subtle, which in turn hides the mysterious and the hard to understand. We never settle for just the obvious here."

"Right, the term 'face value' is an oxymoron around here. We couldn't possibly read the dream as simply an unconscious expression of the comic absurdity of allowing guilt over sexual behavior (i.e., my Keystone Konscience chasing me right into Nicole's vaginal tunnel) to go on indefinitely—and be done with it, could we?" I asked in an almost farcical snide-ironic tone. "That just wouldn't do, would it?"

"So what's with the attitude? What's on your mind?" Dr. P. asked, seeming genuinely surprised by my outburst. The thing is, I was surprised too. It wasn't his catching me being thickheaded about the dream, nor was it my depression or my interstate driving anxiety, both of which had finally lifted, thank God, with a little help from my friend Paxil, and I was certainly feeling nothing but relieved over that. What I think was bothering me was that the very effectiveness of the chemical relief had only reinforced my doubts over the usefulness of analysis, or 'talk therapy,' in and of itself. My old anger over the futility of previous efforts to analyze my way to mental health was still there, simmering away on the back burner and still liable to boil over at the slightest provocation given by this latest analyst in the "parade of charlatans." So I mentally bracketed the dream and decided to go after him, this time no holds barred: "You point out my inability to bring closure on the 'sexual crime and punishment issue,' but what about your own *ad nauseam* pursuit of so-called psychological truth. You act as if there's no truth a person can ever rest in, no truth that can't be replaced by a deeper, and therefore better, shinier, one, if you just keep digging away. How is that any less slavishly compulsive than what I do? Once you accept the unconscious as a kind of psychospiritual abyss, a bottomless goldmine of revelation a la Jung, well then there's no reason ever to stop digging, is there? What did Freud call it—'analysis interminable,' wasn't it?—Well, forgive my cynicism, but it's all just a little too convenient; could this therapist's compulsion to dig deeper, ever deeper, be driven, at least in part, by considerations of income?"

Even before the words were out of my mouth, I tried, in vain, to pull them back in. "I don't believe for a moment that, after all the time we've spent together, you think that about me," Dr. P. announced with a look of grave solemnity. I was grateful for that sentiment, for it gave me a chance to do a quick and not totally graceless about-face: "No, of course I don't. But that doesn't mean I don't continue to nurse profound misgivings about—and resentment towards—psychoanalysis—because the fact is I do."

"Two things to keep in mind here," he urged. "One, you've been poorly served, professionally speaking, by at least two of your previous therapists, from what I can glean from your references to them, and you have a right to be angry about it. It's done you some damage. Two, you must try to keep in mind that intellectual skepticism is the linchpin of your defense system; it's intended to keep me—and especially *you*—from getting too close to your issues. Both of us need to be aware, as best we can in each instance, whether your anger towards therapy is coming 'legitimately,' as it were, from past maltreatment or from an instinctive self-protective anxiety."

"My dear doctor," I harrumphed in withering snideness, "again I must ask you to forgive me, but this too strikes me as just a bit too convenient—for *you*. From where I'm sitting, you seem to be mounting the analyst's classic defense against all serious challenges to his authority: 'It's your defense system talking.' Certainly you can see the heads-I-win-tails-you-lose beauty of it. Whenever I challenge you, all you have to do is play the 'resistance card,' which has the instant effect of transforming me from a speaker-of-truth-to-power into an abject patient. A moment ago I was a peer observer; now I'm just an object of study. Edward Said himself must have taken solace in his knowledge of the ingenious ways we Westerners have of practicing orientalism on ourselves."[12]

"I can understand that it must seem that way to you at times, and I won't say it never happens, what with problems of countertransference—analysts are only human, you know; we must be in a constant mode of self-critique. But over and above all that is the issue of trust, mutual trust, a *sine qua non* in any therapeutic relationship—only such trust, built up over time spent together, can slowly but surely vaporize the mutual suspicion that evolution has programmed into us—in this case, primarily your skepticism towards my authority and analytic practice."

"That all sounds nice—first-class touchy-feely rhetoric—but how can I be sure my resentment towards psychoanalysis itself isn't well-founded, that the cherished 'trust' you speak of isn't just a kind of benign accommodation on the patient's part, a predictable conditioning that deepens over time and lulls him into an uneasy truce with his own symptoms? Of course, even that (shall we call it a gradual placebo effect?) is better than nothing, I grant you, but let's not pretend there's anything authentically transformative going on here. Besides, as far as psychoanalysis itself goes, no one has ever presented convincing proof that the so-called unconscious even exists. On the contrary, persuasive arguments have been made *against* its existence, and by some of our profoundest thinkers. No less a mind than Sartre himself denied there was an unconscious, arguing that all the phenomena Freud described as unconscious (repression, resistance, sublimation, etc.) could be adequately explained as mechanisms of what he—Sartre—termed 'bad faith,'[13] which, as I understand it, is basically the 'human, all too human' tendency to deceive oneself. Where Freud would say, 'You're repressing,' Sartre would say, 'You're kidding yourself.' Supposedly it's a way of avoiding Freedom, the 'God' of existentialism, and the responsibility that goes with it.

"But Sartre is hardly alone as a serious thinker who rejects psychoanalysis—in fact, you could say the whole thrust of existential phenomenology, as the 'philosophy of consciousness' par excellence, is against the dualism of conscious/unconscious. Merleau-Ponty is close to Sartre's concept of bad faith in his view of a 'fragmented' but essentially unified consciousness with potentially conflicting intentions. For him the duality isn't between conscious and unconscious minds but between consciousness, which is free, and what he calls 'facticity' or the 'in-itself' existence of things, from which we're constantly striving to move away …"

"Do we really want to trot out a whole laundry list of theories from the anti-Freudian camp? Where would that get us?" the good doctor queried with mild annoyance.

"The *Gegensatz* or counter position is not merely 'anti-Freudian,' as you put it in another reductionist move," I countered, "it's *pro* consciousness, *pro* man-as-an-autonomous-being. Besides, I thought we were on a truth quest here; I didn't realize there were areas of inquiry that are off-limits to the quest. If there are, let me turn your own question back on you: where is all this so-called analysis getting us?"

As I said this, I saw his expression harden and thought I'd better back off a bit, this being perhaps a bit too personal a tack, and go back to more "theoretical considerations": "There's a professor of English, in California I think, named Frederick Crews who began his career as a fervent Freudian in his analysis of literature. A few years ago he did a complete about-face, totally rejecting psychoanalysis as a valid approach to either a novel or a mind. In a series of long articles appearing in *The New York Review of Books,* Crews excoriated psychoanalysis for producing such ghastly and tragic social phenomena as the so-called repressed-memory syndrome of daughters who are victimized by their (mostly female) analysts' suggestions of paternal seduction. How many phantasies of molestation were these girls subtly coached into embracing and how many innocent men had their lives destroyed by the Freudian curse?

"The irony here, of course, is that Freud himself backed off his own original 'real-seduction' hypothesis, that is, if Canadian analyst Jeffrey Masson is to be believed. According to Masson, who somehow gained access to Freud's unpublished letters in the archives about twenty years ago, Freud caved in to the prospect of social opprobrium that the 'real-seduction' theory would've certainly heaped on him. Half the fathers and uncles of the Viennese bourgeoisie would've been on his case if he had taken as true and acted on some of the things his female analysands were telling him. So he obviated the whole business by transferring all the young women's seduction memories to the realm of infantile phantasy. Problem solved—Freud's problem, that is, not his patients'.

"You see, there's enough scandal and fraud swirling around psychoanalysis to keep our tabloid press busy for … who knows?" I crowed, throwing up my hands in mock-ignorance. Dr. P, at this point resigned to my tirade, simply smiled wanly. Clearly he was not amused. Noticing this, it suddenly occurred to me that he must have regarded my entire rant as 'your defenses talking,' and not the sincere appeal of an aggrieved spirit he insisted he would have responded to. But I was too far into it now to ponder such distinctions; no matter what, I was going to recite to him every charge against his business, personal or cultural, I had accumulated over the years so as to clear the air between us at least to that degree.

"... And the existentialists are far from being the only group of high-profile thinkers who toss psychoanalysis; let us not forget those crazy poststructuralists—like Derrida, for instance, who so cunningly damns Freud by praising him. (Not surprisingly, by the way, both groups are headed up by heterodox French philosophers.) Derrida can't say enough about Freud's 'artistic' genius as an interpreter of dreams[14]: he insists that Freud talks science but practices art, that his dream analyses, in failing to distinguish clearly between the patient's memories of early events and his phantasies thereof (and even trying to justify such failure on the basis of an absolute psychic determinism), deprive us of any means of proving them false—and, as Karl Popper has shown us, a theory that can't be falsified is not scientific. But for Derrida and the poststructuralists, who are very down on science, this is cause for rejoicing since it makes Freud a sort of forerunner of their own valuation of interpretation for its own sake, for its intrinsic artistic quality of playfulness, totally apart from any considerations of 'truth.'

"But you know what? Although I resonate with all that wonderful Gallic insolence, it's only an intellectual resonance and, as such, doesn't go very deep. What does go deep is my awe for Zen and for the Czech-German writer, Franz Kafka—they share a vision of truth, or reality, or being, that eclipses totally that of psychoanalysis, or any other brand of Western psychology for that matter. As a student of Zen yourself, you know that Zen, like any form of Buddhism, rejects the belief in an individual *un*conscious as no less delusive than the belief in an individual *con*scious mind or ego—the operative word here being 'individual.' For Zen there are no individuals, just the belief in them—what *is* true is that each one of us is the entire world, only seen in each case from a different point of view. This means that what appears to us as our own individual mind with its endless round of private sensations, thoughts and feelings is, in truth, seamlessly embedded in the world at large. There simply *is* no boundary between private and public, individual and universal, inner and outer, the one and the many. Individuality is just a belief that exists in—not *my* or *your* mind—but … Mind. Consequently, science, which operates within the Cartesian subject-object or ego-object paradigm, can only be said to establish truth in the most tentative, provisional way, that is, only to the extent we take the ego as substantially real. In other words, any truth science posits—and this would certainly include the 'science' of psychoanalysis—could in principle be superseded, transcended, by a higher, deeper truth.

"That's probably why my old Zen teacher, Eido Roshi, refused the consolations of psychotherapy when his own monks subjected him to an intervention over the sex scandal he caused at Dai Bosatsu. It's probably also the reason he liked my interpretation of Kafka's parable, 'The Cell,' which I once offered in a dharma talk to the students at DBZ."[15]

"Oh, you gave a sermon during a retreat at DBZ?" Dr. P. asked, seeming genuinely impressed. "But I thought you didn't like public speaking …"

"I don't!" I shot back. "I didn't then and I don't now. But one doesn't refuse such an invitation from the Master, so I screwed up my courage and did it. It was nerve-racking, looking out at all those faces—there must've been sixty or seventy of them—all sitting absolutely still in the dharma hall and facing me in lotus position. Anyway, by the time I got to 'The Cell' in my talk, some of my nervousness had warn off and I was able to warm to one of my favorite Kafka pieces. Would you like to hear about it?"

"Yes, of course, please do tell. I have read that famous—or rather infamous—Kafka story—what's it called, oh yes, *The Metamorphosis,* the one about the poor fellow who wakes up one morning in the body of a cockroach," the good doctor chuckled.

"Actually, we don't really know if it's a cockroach," I corrected him with my compulsive scholarly precision. "Kafka doesn't give us enough description of the insect's body to assign it to a particular species—deliberately so, it seems. But that's another story. Getting back to 'The Cell,' it's only about half a page long and concerns a man who finds himself in the middle of a strange room lit by 'soft electric light.' The room has doors, but they all open onto a sheer rock face just a few inches away. So there's no escape there. Only one door leads to a second room into which the man can see from his vantage point in the first. Though strange-looking itself, things look more promising there: the princely red-and-gold-colored walls are covered by wall-length mirrors and an elaborate chandelier hangs from the ceiling. After setting us up with this less than encouraging description, the first-person narrator concludes with a sudden outburst of joy: 'I do not have to go back again, the cell is burst open, I move, I feel my body.'

"So the question is, what happened? How did the man get out of the cell? And just what *is* the cell anyway? What does it all mean? This is the way I laid it out, more or less, to the Zen students listening to me that day. I tried to shape it into a kind of koan or riddle, you know, like 'What is the sound of one hand clapping?', one of those impossible questions Zen students meditate on. So many of Kafka's short parables, head-scratchers that they are, lend themselves to koan-like treatment. Besides, who could resist a double-'K' title?"

"Excuse me, 'double-"K"' title?"

"Sure … '*K*afka *K*oans.' What other title could I possibly give my talk, or the journal article that came out of it?[16]—Anyway, since I was giving a talk and not conducting *dokhusan,* the ritualized private interview in which the roshi sternly exacts an answer to the koan from the student, *I* had to give *them* some kind of answer, and this, in essence, is the one I gave: the parable is an allegory of the human mind, or at least the psychoanalytic view of the human mind with its split between conscious and unconscious levels. These are symbolized by the two rooms. Did Kafka know about Freud and Company? He certainly did: he had a few psychoanalytic studies in his personal library and did make a few references to the early Vienna circle in his letters. Those were mixed at best, basically describing psychoanalysis as both repugnant and fascinating. So I take 'The Cell' as Kafka's considered judgment on Freud. The room with the bland light in which the man stands is the conscious mind. Kafka is saying that the bland, one-dimensional 'light' of conscious reason alone will never get us out of the trap of our own minds, which is the same as saying the trap of 'life itself.' Any presumed door/escape offered by unaided reason is a dead-end. Well then, how about the second room, which looks to the man much richer and more hopeful? That would be the unconscious mind, the colorful realm of dreams, with mirrors reflecting deep self-knowledge, and even a Jungian chandelier symbolizing the unifying Self-archetype? Surely here is the way out of the trap of neurotic modern life: the liberating exploration of the unconscious offered by the new 'science' of psychoanalysis. But Kafka passes over the unconscious too, and no less its analysis, in silence, saying nary a word about the efficacy of either. Then suddenly, without warning or explanation, the man trumpets liberation: 'I'm out of the cell, I feel my body!'

"What's happened? Kafka doesn't say because *it literally can't be said.* This is the mystery of spiritual illumination or enlightenment, satori, mokhsha—whatever name you like—Kafka-style: it eludes all telling, all narration. It happens suddenly and without warning, usually after all efforts to attain it have proven futile and been given up. In other words, having thoroughly examined his own mind, both conscious and unconscious, in vain, the man simply lets go, and in that moment of complete surrender to the trap, the trap goes 'poof'—it was a delusion, held in place by the man's own desire to escape it; the two rooms of conscious and unconscious never really existed, only the man's belief in them. So, paradoxically, psychoanalysis *can* be helpful in the quest for psychospiritual freedom, but only by revealing its own bankruptcy. In failing us, in leaving us mired in the delusive dualism of the split-level mind, it plunges us into despair, and right in the pit of that despair, lo and behold, the light of freedom flashes out. When the man ends by saying, 'I feel my body,' he means not just his own individual body but the body of the world, as it were, with which he now feels an intrinsic oneness. This is Enlightenment, capital 'E.'

"Anyway, Kafka was a master of that sort of koan-esque paradox, which is rooted in the mystical principle of the *coincidentia oppositorum*: conscious and unconscious, freedom and bondage, despair and triumph, and so on. Anything, looked at deeply enough, turns into its own opposite. And I know by now that the coincidence of opposites—the 'C.O.' as I like to call it by shorthand—is an idea that you are as strongly attracted to as I am …"

"Yes, I'm sure that's true," Dr. P. responded thoughtfully. "The mystical-alchemical idea of *conjunctio* or *coincidentia,* the subtle power of transformation of base metals into gold, is, metaphorically speaking, at the heart of Jung's vision of self-realization. What I would take issue with, however, in your elegant, anti-analytical cultural arsenal is the argument that reduces my poor man's science to a mere agent of 'despair hopefully leading to emancipation.' I'm not saying the leap from despair to freedom cannot happen—in Zen practice, which can be extreme, especially in its Rinzai form, it may well happen fairly often—just that there's no necessity for it to happen that way, and thank God for that, since deliberately courting despair can be very dangerous. From the point of view of spiritual enlightenment, analysis may well be as benighted as any other human pursuit, but the point is that it takes a benighted treatment to match and resolve similarly benighted problems. (The classic example is the South Sea Islander whose psychosis is cured by the dancing rituals of the tribal shaman. Belief and confidence in the shaman are active agents in the cure.) Unless we use one delusion to cure another, say, analysis to cure or at least alleviate neurosis, how can we prepare ourselves inwardly for that leap out of the realm of delusion altogether? In a world steeped in delusion, some delusions are helpful and some are not. I think you're undervaluing one of the most helpful."

"Am I really?" I asked in all seriousness, the time for theatrics having long passed by now. "You talk as if psychoanalysis and despair had nothing to do with one another. I tell you I have felt despair, and more than once, since I began coming here. Analysis may well shift you from a cramped cell of delusion to a roomier one, as you say, but the toll that shift takes—"

"Excuse me, what was that?"

"I said, 'the toll that shift takes …'"

"Yes, the toll … the toll," he repeated, seeming to search his mind as he did so. "There's always a toll to pay, isn't there? By the way, did you pay your toll?"

"Pay my toll? What do you mean? What toll?" I asked, puzzled.

"What toll do you think I mean?"

"Now wait a minute," I said, "that sort of 'right-back-atcha' question tells me you've gone behind my back and suddenly slipped back into your analyst's persona, which would mean you must be referring to something in the dream. Hmm … Aha, of course! My tunnel toll," I shouted, as if I'd suddenly solved the riddle of the sphinx. "But, technically speaking, the toll booths aren't even in the dream. They're only there by implication … slightly behind 'point-of-view' me."

"It doesn't matter," Dr. P. retorted, "you did mention them in a by-the-way fashion in your recounting of the dream earlier, when you were locating your vantage point. Anything you associate with your dream, particularly anything contiguous to it like these toll booths, is implicitly part of it, whether it appears explicitly in the dream or not. That's part of what you referred to in your polemic as Freud's air-tight psychic determinism, which holds that anything you say about your dream is itself symptomatic."

"You know, if I weren't so involved with these toll booths right now, I would push right back at you on that point and ask you if you don't see how close this determinism of Freud's comes to violating Popper's principle of falsifiability. There's just no way to prove a psychoanalytic interpretation wrong, is there?—But never mind that for now … Let's see, you asked me if I paid my toll, my tunnel toll—which would mean my *vaginal* tunnel toll. Apparently I haven't; I must've snuck through the tollbooth without paying since the cops are after me. But what is it I've failed to pay, what 'toll' or price is exacted for sex? It can only be the accepting of responsibility for all its consequences, in this case, Nicole's child. So my Keystone Konscience, which my unconscious views as ridiculously obsessive, is after me for bailing on Nicole and the baby, not paying the toll of fatherhood—that's exactly the way I read the dream at the top of the hour, isn't it?"

"No, not quite—earlier you read it as guilt over sex; here you're reading it as *shame* over sex, which means the social consequences of sex. The dream is showing how inseparable the two feelings are in this instance, in effect, answering the puzzlement you've often expressed to me over the apparent disconnect between your conscious feelings of shame and your dream images of guilt. Now you can see from the dream it's a conscious-to-unconscious continuum …

"… But what I'm trying to get at here is the overarching importance of point of view in some dreams, which you implicitly noted yourself in this one when you first told it. Now, bear in mind that one dream can cast light on another. Remember the 'double you' in the earlier Nicky dream—Nicky on the stoop?"

"Of course."

"Well, you have a 'double you' here too, don't you?"

"Yeesss, I do," I answered in a steady, deliberate tone as the inner light came up. "And just as the wiser disembodied or 'spiritual' me in that dream shows me a more mature 'Nicky-like' attitude to take towards myself and my problem, maybe this superior 'me' watching the cops chase 'poor guilty me' into the tunnel is doing the same.—Yes, it's only the wiser 'me' who is able to see the Keystone quality of the cops, the preposterous farce of it all. The embodied 'me' being chased obviously can't see that ... Yes, yes, that's very nice, but it's really just an elaboration—a fine one, I grant—of my earlier insight, isn't it?" I asked.

"Well, yes, but it's also more—I think it points us to another piece still missing from this dream-puzzle; perhaps I should say 'another dimension.'"

"Another dimension? I don't follow."

"Look, as you think of this dream right here and now, imagining the whole scene of it, do you see the toll booths?"

"Well, yes, of course, since we've been talking about them ..."

"Exactly. That means your present point of view is superior even to that of your spiritual 'me' in the dream. It takes in more than even that 'me' can. That gives you three 'me's.' And you can see where this is going, right? To an infinite regression of 'me's.' There's always a higher or deeper 'me' than the one manifesting in a given moment. And do you know why—because ultimately there is no 'me' in any fixed sense—true wisdom refuses to be bound.

"And do you know what I think that means for this dream?—Two things," he said, answering himself. "On a higher level, it means there's never any fixed 'me' or ego to take responsibility for anything that ever happens, good or bad. And on a lower, it means that your present, relatively mature level of 'me,' positioned as it is squarely in front of those toll booths, knows that you have indeed paid the toll, may times over in fact, in the way you've pilloried yourself relentlessly over the decades since that event. It fully appreciates the cosmic comedy—dare I say 'Kosmic Keystone Komedy'—of crime and punishment, which the gods have entitled, *What Fools These Mortals Be*. It's saying, in effect, 'Time to bring down the curtain on this komedy.'

"—And, it seems, on our own little komedy here as well. See you next time."

(6) September 2002: "Was He an Animal, That Music Could Move Him So?"

I'm standing in front of the revolving-door entrance to a tall city building, facing the street. Suddenly I become aware of something on the ground just behind me and slightly to the side. I turn to see a strange-looking creature down there on the concrete, just out of the way of the revolving door. It's too tiny to identify, no more than an inch in diameter, but as I watch it, it literally grows before my eyes, to the size of a dinner plate, the round, flat shape of which it resembles. I still can't tell what it is, whether insect or animal, but I somehow sense that, despite appearances, it's kindly, benign, even emotionally close to me. Its eyes—its only differentiated facial feature—are large and soulful, like those of a Disney cartoon animal, giving it a cuddly quality. As it breathes in and out, it contracts and expands visibly.

"So what occurs to you?"

"This one's pretty transparent, I think. There doesn't seem to be much more than the filmiest veneer between the manifest and latent levels."

"Always thinking, Herr Professor, always thinking. Don't concern yourself so much with levels. Let me worry about them," the good doctor said with avuncular reassurance.

The fact is, I was glad to hear that, glad to hear anyone volunteer to relieve me of even a modest item in my current mental baggage. After two years, the analysis, as far as I could tell, was going nowhere. I continued to be irked by a suspicion that I was wasting my time (and money). On the other hand,

I had no strong conviction of this, and so no compelling reason to end it either. Also, I was back in harness for the Fall semester at the university and worried about a female undergraduate student in my literature course who had stopped coming to class and written me a note explaining that she was extremely depressed and ashamed to tell her parents about it. I was in the middle of a ternary network of student, parents, and counseling office, with no one quite sure how to handle the situation. At home, we'd just taken in our fourth foreign exchange student, Julian, a tall, blond French kid who had utterly charmed my wife but had made a quite different impression on me ("American students are stupeed!"), this just as my nineteen-year-old son, Danny, was about to take off for a long skiing hiatus in Park City, Utah, with all his belongings stuffed into a fourteen-year-old Honda Civic the body of which showed more rust than paint.

Had I been worse off? Absolutely. I was far from forgetting my recent depression, the mere memory of which still caused me to shudder. But I couldn't say I was well off either; the ghost of the "abandoned child" continued to haunt me; so far as I could tell, the analysis had done nothing to bring me to terms with it—on the contrary, it had been the subject of many a vexing analytic session, in which we'd look at it from all conceivable angles, psychological, moral, religious, historical, even mythical. I could tell the good doctor was using everything in his therapeutic "black bag" to help me "work through the problem," including ordinary common sense, and, quite apart from the question of effectiveness, I felt a deep gratitude towards him just for that, as well as for his infinite patience with what must have seemed to him my granite-hard refractoriness:

never once did he throw up his hands in frustration with me or chide me for constantly harping on my symptoms—this in striking contrast to my previous therapists.

Sometimes I'd awaken in the morning with the matter on my mind and realize I'd been dreaming about it. Then it would linger in awareness all day long, even spilling over into the next day or two, casting a subtle pall over my entire life without and within. At other times, it would seem to slip away beneath the threshold of consciousness, yet I'd still sense a vague disquiet deep within which would often crystallize in a dream, much like the one I'd just recounted to Dr. P.

"What else could the creature on the ground be but the child?" I cried in exasperation. "It's always the child! He/She/It oozes from every pore of my being. My dreams don't even bother to disguise it anymore with symbol or metaphor. I feel nailed to a cross, the cross of a child I've never met … Just like Gregor—"

"Gregor?" Dr. P. inquired.

"Yes, Gregor Samsa, the antihero of Kafka's *Metamorphosis.*[17] At the end of part 2, the father starts bombarding him with apples from the dining room fruit bowl in an effort to drive him back into his room after he's 'broken out'—of course it had only been to help his mother who had fainted at the sight of his hideous brown bug body. But Dad's not interested in excuses; his only concern—"

"—Excuse me, you just said 'Dad.'"

"Yes, Gregor's father," I clarified.

"But why would you refer to him as 'Dad'; that's awfully personal, isn't it? That is, unless you were being ironic, and even then …"

"No, I wasn't being ironic," I admitted, considering the implication. "I can't deny I've always identified very closely with Gregor. That's partly Kafka's doing: although he tells the story in the third person, he never allows the narrator to see or experience more than Gregor does. He ties the reader right to Gregor's hard shell of a back. It's an extremely powerful technique. But my identification, I'm sure, is more deeply rooted in my sympathy for Gregor's doomed plight, his growing awareness that he's imprisoned in the insect body for the duration, that it's his destiny. And as a reader, you come to realize that the father has played a key role in the creation of that insect body, which is the physical manifestation of Gregor's low self-regard.

"Anyway, when father finally hurls the equivalent of a major-league fastball into the middle of Gregor's back, and it lodges there, the narrator says, '... but he felt as if nailed fast and just stretched out in the total bewilderment of all his senses.'"

"And so you feel an empathy with the Christlike Gregor since you too are 'nailed to a cross'—your cross being the guilt and shame you feel over the so-called abandoned child?"

"Yes ... Sometimes, like lately, those feelings become so intense that I feel every bit as vile and hideous as I imagine Gregor looks. And I feel intensely Gregor's anguish as he's forced to suffer a kind of crucifixion at the hands of his own father."

"Hence your half-conscious use of the intimate 'Dad' in telling of the father's aggressive behavior."

"I guess so. But there's more to it ... There's something about the *way* the father crucifies Gregor, the 'style' of the violence, I guess you'd call it, that pulls me in. It's that the father does it all playfully, … can you believe? He seems to take some sadistic pleasure in flinging those apples and nailing his son to the cross of self-loathing. It brings up unhappy memories for me of childhood years at the lunch table in my home. We'd all be there, my Mom, my Dad, my sister and I. School was only two blocks away so we could run home for lunch, from noon sharp to 12:30. Since my father worked evenings, this would be our main meal of the day. And having to face, day after day, year after year, a shift he loathed, doing a job he hated—I guess this built up in him a resentment, an anger, he knew no other way to discharge than to hurl what—ever since I read *The Metamorphosis*—I think of as verbal apples at me. But the 'apples' were 'playfully' thrown, just as in Gregor's case (except for the last one), in the sense that they were amusing, teasing little barbs he would smile or chuckle over as he tossed them off, one after another, lunch after lunch after lunch: 'Dennis would never do that … never say that … Dennis isn't the type to … Do you think Dennis would like …' and so forth. And he'd just keep spitting those harmless little quips out at my expense, all directed at his captive audience, my Mom and sister, who never once told him to knock it off, never told him to spit out what was really on his mind, that he couldn't face another day looking up shipping rates in that God-forsaken traffic department, and that he wouldn't have had to if he didn't have us two brats to support."

"Your father was, as they say, between a rock and a hard place," Dr. P. mused, "stuck between conscience and personal need. Needling you was the only way he knew of defusing his own stress, his anger and anxiety, even grief, over a life he felt was slipping away. You need to know that this was largely unconscious behavior on his part. Not that that made its consequences any less harmful to your psychological growth—it's clear that your extremely harsh, punitive conscience is related to the father who teased and tortured, who took perverse delight in nailing—needling—you over and over again, never letting you off the hook, so to speak. There came a point, no doubt by early adolescence, when you unconsciously incorporated (the technical term is 'introjected') that needling authority into your psyche. After that you no longer needed father, you had your own inner needle, which I think remained more or less inactive, that is, latent, until you learned of Nicole's pregnancy—"

"No, actually now that I think about it, there was one earlier prick of the needle," I corrected.

"Oh?"

"Yes. When I was a junior in college, I dated a student nurse—Jennifer—who was, as the boys used to say, very fast, light years ahead of poor virginal me. (My friends actually called us "Vaginal" and "Virginal," "Vaj" and "Virge.") The pressure she put on me to 'seduce' her was enormous, but I guess I just wasn't quite ready to take that leap. In fact, I'm sure I wasn't because I developed this painful obsession with my nose that lasted about as long as the relationship. All summer long, while I was seeing Jenn, I was plagued by feelings of anxiety and depression over my nose, of all things. And of course I had no idea why—it just seemed to be always in my way, always there, right in front of me, a strange object between my eyes that followed me whichever way I looked. For months it drove me crazy. Now, at that time, around 1962, I'd had no education in depth psychology. I'd never thought in psychological terms and so had no clue that my nose might be a matter of phallic sublimation—moving the penis up to the nose—in order to disguise the real issue, which was my desire for Jenn."

"Actually, what you're telling me sounds more like guilt from mother over sex than sadistic, shame-inducing needling from father. Or should I say rather that the two emotions are inseparable here, just as you yourself have always thought of them as curiously intertwined in your problem. For mother sex was always, as you've put it, 'the gorilla in the room'; so too the penis hiding in plain sight as your nose. And father's needling has a phallic 'goosing' aspect to it (you just described this painful nose episode as 'a prick of the needle'). Your inner needle might've been unconsciously challenging you to put the make on Jennifer, even as it ridiculed you as inferior and worthy only of cutting criticism.

"And by the way, let's not overlook the obvious connection between Dad the needler and the sinister Snoop Dad figure in your dream of the loading dock. Here you can see clearly how your own shame caused you to idealize to an extreme degree your father's sense of familial responsibility, something which, when viewed more objectively, takes on a much darker aspect."

The doctor paused for a moment, then continued in a reflective vein. "All the strains of emotional pain blend together to cripple us to one degree or another. Our parents can't help it, and we can't either when we inflict the same or similar burdens on the children we love. And on and on it goes down through the generations. Only one thing I know can break the chain of ignorance, and that thing is what we are doing right here and now. If you ever come up with anything better, let me know."

I felt deeply moved, both by the suffering I had just succeeded in articulating to him (and even more to myself) and the simple empathy of the doctor's response. Needing a moment to let it all settle, I looked around the small consulting room and noticed, without being in the least bothered by the fact, that the room was particularly close that day, probably because the heat had just been turned on for a rare September cold snap, releasing a faint stale odor of dust particles into the air. Dr. P. didn't seem to mind it. On the contrary, he impressed me as someone who paid little attention to his physical surroundings in general, lost as he usually was in the realm of ideas. Even the small, straight-backed chair he sat on, hardly adequate for his large frame, seemed designed to deny him comfort and keep his attention steadily focused on the important business at hand. I found his dedication admirable.

"But let's get back to that small, soulful creature just behind you in the dream. It's a rich, overdetermined image. Say more about it."

"I said before that I felt nailed to it, or to the burden of it, like Gregor who is 'nailed fast' … Oh, I don't know, I'm sure you're right about its being highly condensed. I mean, it's the child all right, what with the 'gestation' that takes place in the dream right before my eyes, from zygote to full term and so forth; but in the sense that it's Gregor (it does look a little like him and it did remind me of him), and I have always strongly identified with Gregor, well … it's also *me.* Derrida would call it a signifier, I'm sure, an image that can't be pinned down to a precise, unequivocal meaning—like the cobra under the boardwalk.

The most I can say is, whatever way you look at it, it evokes both pain and compassion—"

"Ah, but that's good," Dr. P. hastened to add. "Unlike the cobra, it's not evoking just pain anymore. Pain's partner or complement, compassion, has finally been aroused, whether you feel it yet in conscious awareness or not."

"These so-called 'dream signifiers,' these dynamic images, remind me of musical chairs," I snickered. "The instant you grasp at one, trying to take possession of it as 'my official meaning,' it's gone … Wait a minute, wait just a minute … thinking of music, a dream just popped into my head, one I had last night. It's about music, in fact, about one of my favorite pieces, the *'Rach 3'* or Rachmaninoff's *Third Piano Concerto. A young pianist, very friendly, very well dressed, is sitting at a grand piano nearby, a Bösendorfer, playing the* Rach 3. *The room is dark, possibly a lounge, and there are some people, three or four, lying asleep on the rug around the piano. For some reason these people make it hard for me to get to the piano to practice. I need to practice the* Rach 3 … *That's about it, I guess."*

"You know the drill," Dr. P. nodded.

"Well, I just love the *Rach 3,* a marvelous, gigantic, epic-scale concerto. It's got everything: drama, conflict, adventure, tenderness, gorgeous melodies, a structural arc with a heart-pounding coda—everything you look for in a great and serious work. The only piano concerto I know that tops it for vastness of scale is the Busoni … It's funny because, although I've known Rachmaninoff's *Second Concerto* my entire adult life—that's the popular one with the melody that became a hit song in the 1940's, what is it … oh yes, 'Full Moon and Empty Arms'—

I only discovered the *Third* when I saw the movie, *Shine,* a few years ago, in which the concerto was featured."

"Yes, I saw that film: a young student pianist at the London Conservatory plays the piece at his performance exam, and almost kills himself in the process. Isn't that right?"

"Yes. It becomes too much for him. But, ironically, he recovers from his breakdown a completely changed man, a kind of lovable loon who now plays music for the sheer joy of it rather than as 'serious business.' What's more, it's a true story, or at least based on one: the life of an Australian pianist."

"So, why do you think you're dreaming about the *Rach 3*?"

"Apart from the fact that I love the concerto and loved the movie, I haven't a clue," I shrugged.

"Oh, come now, you're either being dull today or you're repressing."

"Thanks a lot," I sneered, "Why don't you try sitting at this end of the conversation for a change? If *you* draw a blank, you can keep it to yourself. If *I* do, I'm immediately exposed as a dullard."

"Come now, 'Gregor,' stop whining. Step back a ways in your mind and take a look at the whole dream. Isn't there anything it reminds you of?"

"Let's see, … maybe I'm not so dull after all, because, when you put that sort of question to me, it usually means … yes … it usually means you want me to see a dream as reflecting the analytic process itself … and, well I'll be damned, it does indeed, doesn't it?" I asked the good doctor with a big smile. He smiled back good-naturedly, not saying a word. "The concerto is the analysis," I went on, "the epic adventure, the risk, the danger of it. The kid in *Shine* breaks down, completely falls apart, but he keeps going till he comes out the bottom of it transformed, enlightened, you might say, because other people don't have a clue about his crazy wisdom. As the one undergoing the process, that would be me. But I'm getting ahead of myself because in the dream I'm at a much earlier stage, probably where I actually am now, and I'm not even at the piano, someone else is ... wait, who else could it be, of course, but you? You're playing the music, guiding the process, as it were, and I'm your student, your protégé, who needs to practice if he expects to become as accomplished as the master."

"Well, if you insist," the good doctor oozed in all mock-unctuousness. "But never mind, go on."

"It's all about self-realization, isn't it?" I asked rhetorically. "It's kind of a summary dream, a stock-taking dream, and an encouragement to 'soldier on.' It's telling me I'm on the path, following the Way, as they say in Zen."

"Yes, and there are other elements, both in the dream and directly associated with it, that support this view. Can you spot them?"

Feeling buoyed by the dream's welcome revelation that I wasn't wasting my time, that with this analysis I was doing something intrinsically noble and good, I could re-address the dream in a mood of relaxed playfulness, which always yielded fruit when I interpreted literary works and stood me in good stead in this moment as well. "Let's see, there are those sleeping bodies on the floor surrounding the piano, keeping me from getting to the piano to practice ... to practice music, make music. Living the creative life is self-realization, being free to play your tune, sing your song. The sleeping bodies are hindrances, obstacles that must be overcome in the course of the analysis … the fact that they're sleeping means they're unconscious, still unconscious. The room is dark like a lounge, a *night*club lounge. They're asleep in the night of the unconscious, and as they wake up in the course of analysis one by one and move away, I'll have easier access to the piano … Will that about do it?" I asked, just a bit too smugly.

"Not quite. I'm the pianist in the dream, am I not?"

"Yes, I already said that."

"Take it easy. Work with me here. If I'm the pianist, and I remind you of the young pianist in the movie, *Shine,* then there should be some link between us, should there not?"

"I suppose so, but other than the fact that he's young and you're considerably younger than I am, I don't see … Oh, hang on, … he's been through his ordeal and emerged from it a wise child; now his response to every moment is one of utter delight; and you've been through this process yourself and so are in a position to help poor benighted yokels like *moi.* Right?"

"Yes—and do you remember the pianist's name?"

"Why yes, it's … ah, David … David … Helfgott. My God, how supremely right! Helfgott: 'help' from 'God,' divine help, which, God knows, I certainly need."

"And which you're getting, not so much from me, of course, I'm just a facilitator, a guide, trying to help you find your own inner guide, your deepest Self or 'helping God,' which is symbolically projected onto me as the dream music-maker."

I just sat there, slouched on the chair, totally done in. "From Gregor Samsa to the music of the spheres … We've come a long way today," I mused, half to myself. "Today was almost a concerto in itself … You know, they say Kafka didn't care much for music. I find that very hard to believe, someone with his ear for language. But interestingly, his narrator makes a point of saying that Gregor loved it. It's one of the deeply *adagio* moments in the story, achingly poignant. It's in part 3 after dinner when the sister plays the violin in the living room for the amusement of the three male lodgers. Gregor can hear the strains from his room, all the better since the family has recently taken to leaving the door open an inch or two in the evening. The music lures him out into the living room, out of his now-filthy insect's cave into the circle of human society. As he slowly creeps along the floor ever closer to his sister who is lost in the playing, his body caked from neglect in rubbish and dust balls, the narrator asks, 'Was he an animal, that music could move him so?' Strictly speaking, the narrator is asking the question, but he's really just paraphrasing Gregor's own question to himself: 'Am I an animal, that music can move me so?' The technique is called 'inner monologue' and is part of Kafka's strategy of binding the reader to his character's destiny. And you know something, that's exactly what it does—certainly for me. Sometimes in the wake of a piece of music in which I've been totally absorbed, I'll find myself asking, 'Can I be so base when I'm capable of such a response, when I can lose myself like this in the music of the spheres?' Gregor is asking from the depths what sort of being he is; his whole season in hell, which is what the story tells, has been a struggle between two self-images, the insect he loathes but cannot escape and the spiritual identity he craves but cannot attain. Gregor is literary proof of the Buddha's First Noble Truth that life is suffering. The care and concern over what sort of being I am is misery."

Dr. P. looked at me long and thoughtfully, then turned aside and reflected, "The struggle between self-images you mention reminds me of Nietzsche's metaphor for man as a bridge, a transition between animal and superman. Maybe he means, slyly, a bridge between opposed images neither of which man is at all. Maybe he's saying that man should learn to be content to be just this—a bridge, a connection. How much more fun to be the connection between things than to be any particular thing itself—especially if there *are* no things in themselves, just images of them."

"How did Goethe put it, 'Everything transitory is but an image.'"[18]

"Yes, but don't forget Nietzsche's own complement to that insight," the good doctor cautioned, "'Everything *eternal* is but an image.'"[19]

"Sounds good to me," I smiled. "But at this point that's all I've got—the sound of it."

"That's all you need."

(7) March 2003: Pinocchio

I'm standing in a dark, seemingly limitless space that's being lit up by a vast conflagration. Masses of flame billow up high above me into black nothingness. If they weren't so lethal, you could almost regard them as beautiful, with their sweeping undulations and permutations of red-gold-yellow hues. But this fire is anything but an object of contemplation. It's mean, ravenous and heading straight for me, its advanced tongues already licking my feet. Although I feel no sense of physical pain, the dread that would normally anticipate such pain is there in abundance. As the flames come over me, I suddenly realize that their point of concentrated attack is my nose, which has just grown into some sort of physical monstrosity, as out of proportion to my face as a macaw parrot's beak is to its. In quick, consumptive fury, the fire burns though my Cyranoid nose, causing the outsized organ to come loose and tumble down onto some indistinct smoke-covered surface below my feet, even as it continues to burn like beef on a grill.

"Charming."

"Isn't it though? I had this dream—uh nightmare—a few nights ago but it's a close replica of a dream I've had on and off ever since my breakup with Nicole."

As I sat there and watched him watch me, waiting for me to hold forth in a blaze of inspired free associations, I felt myself just slump, both inside and out. I knew well what the dream meant, or thought I knew, with its obvious infernal-purgatorial-phallic imagery, but I couldn't summon the energy required to attend to it properly. We'd been over this ground so many times already by now, the arena of sexual crime and punishment, with its two arch villains of parents and HMC (Holy Mother the Church), and the prospect of covering it yet again almost made me want to gag in an emotional sense. I felt as spent as the gray, gloomy weather that filled the frame of the office window, with its listless smattering of flurries marking the end of yet another endless Syracuse winter. It was then I realized that a fair part of the usual resistance to self-inquiry in analysis was not so much to the painful emotions of fear, anger, guilt and so on, as to the sheer tedium of repetition. It was perseverance as much as courage that analysis demanded. Again with ignorant old Mom and Dad, again with benighted, if indeed not ax-grinding, Father so-and-so, S.J., naïve yet lethal Sister so-and-so, again with sin, fear of damnation, eternal abandonment, isolation, loneliness … Yet Dr. P.'s unfailingly astute, attentive demeanor, hour after tedious hour, was a living demonstration to me of how necessary it all was, even the tedium.

Quickly reading my body language, he urged, "Come on now, you know that attention must be paid to whatever you're dreaming about. No matter how often we sift through these themes, if you continue to dream about them, we need to keep sifting."

"I suppose that goes for all the 'frustration' dreams I've told of here too," I snorted, "like the never-ending series of mad rushes around campus trying to find my classroom, or the infinite variations on the theme of being stranded in some European city—London, Prague, Stuttgart—unable to find my way back to the hotel or the airport. Or having a map but also having something wrong with my eyes so that I can't read it. These dreams recur so often they bore me. Or rather they anger me, since I can't for the life of me figure out what the cause of all this frustration is. Anytime we examine one of these dreams and I begin to feel I'm getting a handle on them, I'll dream another two or three of them and realize I've gotten nowhere. Their very frequency seems to mock my ineptness and that pisses me off."

"I have my suspicions about these dreams but I'm not prepared to reveal them just yet. Anyway it'll all come out in the wash."

"Interesting metaphor, because that's just how I'm feeling these days: all washed out. Right now it all seems so pointless. How do I know anything's really happening here? I mean, we analyze dream after dream—I'll admit you have great skill in this area; you could've been a first-rate literary critic, or 'critter,' as my wife often calls me—and you always, or almost always, manage to ferret out some subtle yet dazzlingly apt connection between a dream image and something I've told you about my life, … like my friend Eric's head wound in last week's dream and my wife's compassion for those with mental problems or 'head wounds,' and how I might unconsciously perceive that as one strand of her attachment to me, and so on … But the proof, as they say, is in the pudding, and I'm not getting enough to eat here. On the contrary, I work and work and get hungrier and hungrier. I'm sorry, but I just don't see any long-term pay-off. What are the benchmarks and how can I tell where I stand in relation to them?"

"How are you doing with driving on the interstate?"

"Fine … I'll give you that …"

“And the tunnels and bridges and airplanes?”

“They’re all right, although I’ve only flown once since …”

“Let’s not quibble … How easily the progress we *do* make gets taken for granted. Anxiety issues often go first, whereas those related to depression, obsession and guilt often lie deeper and take longer. I would say you’re pretty much on schedule.”

“But I feel *more*, not less, entangled in all the guilt and remorse of the past, *more* obsessed with all the moral questions surrounding Nicole and the child—even *more* self-absorbed than I was before I began coming here. How can that be therapeutic?”

“It’s all part of the struggle to work through these heavy issues. As you de-repress, you confront the painful thoughts and feelings you’ve been avoiding. This can be difficult and slow going. (You know this.) It’s the reason so many people who could benefit from analysis avoid it like death and even many who do undergo it fail to get very far and drop out. It takes real courage and perseverance—true grit. Let yourself be encouraged by the fact that you’ve demonstrated these qualities. If you stick with it and continue to give yourself to the process, you will eventually be glad you did.”

Tempted though I was to content myself with these consoling words and this rare praise, my torturous skepticism and the bilious exasperation it generated would not allow me to back off. As so often before, I again felt driven to give the good doctor a bitter taste of my own profound sense of doubt: “I read an article in a recent issue of *Der Spiegel*, the German news magazine, that said that about half of all German psychotherapists not only no longer believe in the efficacy of psychodynamic psychotherapy but even fear it may cause harm. I just can't help sharing their suspicion that this ceaseless self-absorption, this quagmire of analytic self-review, is *itself* pathological—what do they call it when the treatment is the problem ... oh yes, iatrogenic illness ... physician- or treatment-induced illness. How can you overcome anything with which you just keep banging yourself over the head? Simple logic says the headache can only get worse. In this case the headache is oneself, one's own ego or sense of individuality. This is 'the world' that Jesus says is too much with us ...

"Zen offered me the prospect of escaping the suffocating confines of my own ego—that's what pulled me into it. Of course, I didn't really appreciate the fiendishly subtle nature of the trap of 'spiritual materialism' at the time—that's Trungpa's[20] expression—and the various ways one's own metaphysical cravings could actually strengthen the ego and undermine the spiritual quest. But that's a story for another session. It wasn't until the mid-eighties, when I started nosing around the Eastern wisdom traditions—Hinduism, Tibetan Buddhism, Taoism, Zen—that it dawned on me it might be possible to live entirely free of bondage to one's own self-image. That's something almost impossible for us moderns to imagine—and especially us modern Americans living here in the storied land of the rugged individual. And yet cultural historians tell us that the image of self as we understand it today is a relatively recent invention. Some say the awareness of one's separate selfhood was a fairly rare psychological condition in the West until the Renaissance when mirrors began to be mass-produced and widely owned. Imagine that. Such a sea change in human consciousness brought about by a piece of glass!

Many also believe that European romanticism, with its glorification of the creative ego, consolidated the change the Renaissance set off. Of course, one can quibble about chronology and relative influence, but what seems clear is that the human ego has by now grown into some rapacious behemoth, threatening the well being of both the individual and society with its implacable needs and cravings.

"And do you know what the kicker is in all this? There ain't none! This realization never fails to blow my mind: the self-image, which we never leave home without, is a picture of something that doesn't exist. I love the way that Canadian housewife puts it in Kapleau's *Three Pillars of Zen.* Her awe-struck words at her moment of insight are seared into my brain: 'Slowly my focus changed: "*I*'m dead! There's nothing to call *me!* There never was a *me!* It's an allegory, a mental image, a pattern upon which nothing was ever modeled:" I grew dizzy with delight.'[21] From what I can tell, it took that woman many years of meditation to come to that awakening, to pull up, root by tenacious root, the profoundly conditioned sense of herself as a discrete being, separate and apart from the rest of the world. And here you and I sit, apparently doing the very opposite, putting relentless focus on *this mind of mine* as housed in *this body of mine.* I fear that analysis and Buddhism may be working at cross-purposes. It can only come to a bad end."

Dr. P., as always, listened attentively, then shifted in his chair as he weighed his words, and spoke: "You know that I'm in sympathy with much of what you've said. You'll recall our discussion of Kafka's Gregor some time ago and your view of him as struggling with good and bad self-images."

"Of course."

"Do you also happen to recall my reference in that conversation to Nietzsche and his image of man as a transition-stage between ape and superman? And my own speculation that maybe man is just that: a transition, a bridge, a connection, but not along any evolutionary timeline—evolution's not the issue here—rather a point or seat of awareness connecting the vast array of phenomena that come and go. Do you remember?"

"Yes, I think so."

"Well, if you do, then you can see the extent to which I share your view of the delusion of ego—and again I must emphasize that I'm speaking here of ego in the Buddhist and not the Freudian sense—as a discrete consciousness. Fundamentally, there *are* no human beings that exist as separate centers of awareness—you're quite right on that. But as I've said before, the question then becomes very practical: how does a 'non-existent' human being most efficiently get to that vantage point from which he can realize and appreciate such a liberating truth? (And by the way, I call this truth, the truth of enlightenment, 'liberating' because once you realize your own fundamental emptiness, you're free and the whole burden of individual responsibility for events slides off your shoulders.) If we *can* get there from here, what's the best route? My answer to that, as you know only too well, is *this*. What you call 'obsessing over problems' I call 'working through them.' What you and *Der Spiegel* call 'the inadequacy of analysis' I call 'the inadequacy of professional training of therapists.' I must admit it's a crapshoot when a person decides to commit to a therapist. It's beyond difficult to know what you're getting into … to know whether the person to whom you're entrusting your well-being really understands what he's doing, regardless of how intelligent he may seem, or whether the academic department or institute that spawned him really knows either, for that matter. For example, an astute, competent analyst is always carefully aware of his own words, of the particular way he puts things to a patient, especially painful truths the patient needs to face; he knows enough to avoid phrasing things in a way that will exacerbate the negativity already built into the patient's overly self-critical point of view, while at the same time nudging the patient to confront what needs to be confronted. An analyst-in-training I was supervising some years ago was conducting a session with a particularly self-critical patient. I was listening in from behind a one-way mirror. When the patient brought up for the umpteenth time a complaint of remorse over an old slight to his younger brother from when they were kids, the analyst huffed and said, 'What, *that* again!? Are you obsessed with it?' Now, you can imagine what the patient learned from this exchange: 1) 'It's true; even my analyst knows I'm a shit'; and 2) 'There are certain things, like symptoms, I must not talk about here.' I never, ever upbraid a patient for talking about symptoms. Never. After all, that's where the pain is, and not without good reason. Symptoms are organically constituted. They are, to paraphrase Freud, a *via regia* or royal road to the underlying pathology causing them. What conceivable reason could there be to avoid discussing them? … Oh yes, I forgot, we don't want to bore the analyst with repetitious whining, do we?"

This last remark, uttered by the good doctor with exaggerated snootiness, caused me to guffaw involuntarily. It was definitely therapeutic. But then he immediately turned serious again, picking up the thread of his argument: “So what I’m saying is, the problem lies largely in the difficulty of establishing a ‘quality control’ of professionals, as well as in the intrinsic difficulty of the analytic process itself even when conducted under ideal conditions. Without it or something like it, the Way to Illumination is indeed fraught with danger. You’ve been to Zen monasteries for extended retreats and become acquainted with experienced students and even monks and high-ranking officers in residence there, haven’t you?”

“Well, yes, I have, at least at one particular monastery.”

“Well, what’s your summary judgment of the caliber of character of the people you’ve encountered there?”

“Why do I get the funny feeling you’re leading the witness here—I’d have to say they come in all shapes and sizes, just like people ‘on the outside.’ I have not, I must admit, come across any shining paragons of virtue, if that’s what you’re getting at.”

“No, no, not quite that—I understand very well that spiritual insight and virtue do not have the conventional clichéd one-to-one correspondence; take Trungpa for instance. What I mean is, would you say Zen monks and students are paragons of mental health? Has their practice made them happy, healthy and wholesome, so to speak? Would they qualify for the ‘after’ picture in a therapist’s ‘before’ and ‘after’ ad for his services?”

“My honest impression is, they would not. Even the monks I came to know somewhat, though decent men for the most part, struck me as just as insecure and grasping as I am, or Joe the plumber is. And some were definitely in need of counseling. One, I was told, had a fondness for masturbating into the kitchen sink, and not particularly caring who was around to witness it either. (Not that that scandalizes me personally, but, c'mon man, that sink is where the dinner veggies are cut and rinsed!) Another monk was a misogynist, and proud of it. He said he would've been happy to see women banned from the monastery grounds entirely, not excepting the nuns. A third monk said he was only at peace during retreats [*sesshin*] when silence was enjoined on everybody for a week. And this is not to mention the scores of lay students who came and went, the ex (?) druggies and alcoholics and just generally inept, incompetent social misfits, all looking and longing for that Highway to Heaven. (During my first retreat, one student who had recently committed suicide was memorialized in a group chant.) —But you know it's no secret that misfits and malcontents are drawn to religious movements, just as they are to *your* profession, in the hope of finding some idealized solution to their personal problems."

"Yes, and that's precisely my point. We must all be disabused of such idealism, of all hope of finding a panacea, a magic wand, a silver bullet, whatever the movement or ideology may be. Idealizing fantasy, even—no, especially!—of the religious sort, is just another defense, an impediment, to true transformation. You in particular, Herr Professor, need to learn that meditation, by itself, is almost never enough to attain mastery of the transpersonal levels of mind, not to speak of lasting enlightenment. In fact, Vedanta Hinduism itself teaches that unresolved psychological conflicts on the egoic level return on the transpersonal levels—what Ken Wilber calls the 'causal bands' on the spectrum of consciousness in

Vedanta psychology[22]—in even more severe form, and have to be dealt with again. Meditation alone cannot dissolve our deepest emotional problems. In my ideal world, analysis would partly precede meditation on the spiritual path, but at the very least it should parallel it. And while I can't wave my therapist's wand and so dispel your painful doubts about what we're doing here, I can at least offer you a few references to recent research on the unconscious. If you find it persuasive, it might help to buttress your faith in the validity of depth psychology and dynamic psychotherapy."

With that, Dr. P. handed me a piece of notepaper on which he'd jotted down the names of authors and titles of a handful of current research studies in psychoanalysis. As he did so, he said, "I wouldn't do this with most patients; the process usually works better if the wheels and gear shifts of it are hidden away in the analyst's head; but in your case I make an exception, since you're afflicted with a little bit of knowledge, just enough to cause trouble. So, in hopes of clearing up the affliction, I'm giving you a bit of the 'hair of the dog,' so to speak."

I was touched by the doctor's thoughtfulness, as evidenced by the trouble he took to assemble this little bibliography. It meant he didn't regard my doubts about the validity of the process as trivial, nor as entirely reducible to an intellectual defense mechanism. I quickly scanned the names on the paper, recognizing only two: Robert Langs and Mark Epstein. Almost as if registering this fact telepathically, he proceeded to comment on just these two references: "Langs is perhaps the reigning monarch these days in the field of research in psychoanalytic theory and technique. And I included Mark Epstein's

Thoughts without a Thinker as a powerful argument for combining dynamic therapy with meditation on the psychospiritual path, as opposed to doing either one by itself."[23]

"Thank you," I sighed, not knowing quite how to feel about the list. "I find myself in the awkward position of having to do some homework reading, for the sake of my therapy, to convince myself of a view of human nature which, to speak with Kafka, 'I do not love but by which I am possessed': that we're all essentially puppets being jerked around by a puppet-master we've come to know as the unconscious."

"Yes, in a way, but puppets struggling to become autonomous beings."

"Yeah, … Pinocchio longing to be a real boy," I said barely audibly, more to myself than the doctor.

"Pinocchio?"

"Yeah, you know, Gipetto's puppet, his substitute son."

"Fascinating," Dr. P. suddenly beamed, "how the mind, when allowed to go its own way, always brings us back to the business at hand, in this instance, first to puppets as a metaphor for man dancing to the tune of the unconscious, and from there to the particular example of Pinocchio."

"I'm sorry, I must be running out of gas. What's fascinating about it? And just how is Pinocchio the 'business at hand'?"

"Think about poor little Pinocchio. Do you happen to recall another liability he had, besides being made of wood (though not unconnected with this fact either)?"

"Another liability?" I asked scratching my head. "I remember he got swallowed up by a whale and sort of ran into his father—Gipetto—deep inside the whale's belly. The old man was actually seated at a little table eating."

"A misfortune, or perhaps good fortune, depending on how you look at it, but not a liability, not something fearful to which Pinocchio was subject ..."

"Hmm ... Let me think: a liability 'not unconnected with wood,' you said. I suppose you could say he was subject to catching fire and burning to ashes, but then again, who isn't?" I snorted. "You don't need to be made of wood to ... wai wai wait!" I said raising my hands slightly, palms out. "*I'm* on fire, *I'm* burning up in the dream!" I said, as much questioning as declaring the fact.

"Good, good, stay with it—there's more still," the doctor urged.

"More?" I asked incredulously. "What more could there be? ..." And just as I put this half-serious question, there popped into my mind a very old memory, possibly even the oldest left to me. "You know," I said to the good man wistfully, for I believe I was almost in a state of reverie at this point, "*Pinocchio* happens to be the first story I ever heard. I couldn't have been more than two or three. The reason I know this is that I have this visual memory of the living room in our Hoboken flat prior to our move to the farm in upstate New York. Also, I remember sitting in my father's lap in an armchair so I had to be a toddler. I can still feel myself nestled in his right arm as he held the book open in front of us. I'll never forget the awe that quickened me as he related all these strange facts and events—a little boy made of wood ... out in the world on his own ... reuniting with his father in the whale's belly ..."

"Any other strange facts or events come to mind?"

"Oh, that's right, your question about a liability ... to do with wood ... Aaah, oh ... my ... God, of course, how could

I forget *that?*—Whenever Pinocchio would tell a lie, his nose would grow longer! I remember being astonished to learn this as my Dad read it to me. And then, a few pages later, the first test case: Pinocchio tells some little fib and, sure enough, his nose grows. I can still see the story text on the right-hand page, and on the left an illustration. It was an illustrated edition, with simple pencil drawings, little more than stick figures, but to my three-year-old imagination, they were as powerful as Dali's melting watches. Pinocchio's nose is about three feet long and his eyes are bugging out in panic at the fact. Most alarming of all, a bird is perched on the nose close to midpoint pecking away at it, already about halfway through it. I don't know what horrified me more as I tried to grasp all this: the fact that, under certain conditions, i.e., if you did something bad, your nose could visibly grow or that, having thus grown, it could be chewed off by a bird …"

Dr. Purper sat there patiently and attentively, refraining from interjecting anything until he was sure my memory had spent itself. When it had, he sat up straight, brought his hands together and said in the softest of tones, as if still wary of being intrusive, "So, we see from the story of Pinocchio just how early your alienation from your nose began; and all the psychological mischief to which this alienation has led in the course of your life, right up to and including the dream you reported today. Do you still feel, as you clearly did at the top of the hour, that this ground couldn't possibly be worth going over again?"

"Certainly not … I feel like a fool."

"No need for that," the doctor assured me. "These lessons about the way an analysis unfolds need to be learned again and again—by all of us. But just look at what we can now see. A Freudian might call this a textbook case of the Oedipal drama: father reads baby son a tale in which boy is threatened with loss of nose, i.e., displaced phallic member, if he behaves 'badly.' The nose is a classic sublimation or upward displacement of the penis, right on the same vertical bodily axis—"

"But how could a baby possibly understand—"

"Understanding has nothing to do with it. A baby doesn't 'understand,' he *lives* these truths, 'understand'? He *lives* them. A baby knows need, desire, intimacy. And, of course, fear—fear of annihilation, which we can read as loss of intimacy (which includes feeding) or abandonment. You could say for a baby life and death are almost always on the line. Bruno Bettelheim[24] notwithstanding, I've never been a fan of parents' reading Grimm's fairy tales to their pre-schoolers: they're far too violent—all those maimings and dismemberments. Maybe in some cases those tales can be a catharsis for a toddler's anxieties, as Bettelheim claims, but who says it can't also go the other way, as it apparently did in yours? I mean, Daddy reads a text to you containing an appalling image—little Pinocchio getting his nose pecked off—and it sticks deep inside the recesses of a three-year-old's memory. Remember, a baby is what Freud called 'polymorphous perverse,' meaning the genitals have not yet been so clearly marked off as '*the* erogenous zone.' Rather, it is still to some extent an erogenous organism in toto, so that one bodily protrusion, say a nose, has about as much erotic valence as another, say a penis. Obviously, the particular symbolism of nose for penis, or any other symbol for that matter, can only become meaningful—and functional—once the differentiation between conscious and unconscious levels has become consolidated, say, around six or seven, with the onset of the so-called latency period. This primordial split in the human mind is precisely what symbols, particularly dream symbols, are meant to help heal. They're bridges, as Jung called them."

"Yes, and I can see how many of mine I burned once the enormous complications of puberty hit me," I said shaking my head in wonder. "The prolonged grief over masturbation (care of Holy Mother the Church) and the extreme escalation of all that guilt into my nose obsession when I moved into the fast lane with Jennifer in junior year college. Then, of course, the nasal-phallic inferno that has haunted me for over thirty years right up to and including my nightmare this week."

"And don't forget your sniffing compulsion around mother when you were four or five."

"Yes, yes, being unable to get the nasal passage clean and clear enough, no matter how hard, no matter how obnoxiously, I sniffed. It's as if I couldn't do enough to make myself 'presentable' to her … Man, talk about charting a particular line of pathological development! … But listen, Dr. P., how seriously, how literally, do you take all this Oedipal stuff?"

"The question, Herr Professor, is how seriously, how literally, do *you* take it?"

(8) August 2003: Goosed in the Parking Lot

I'm in my car in the A&P parking lot on 14th St. and Willow Ave. in Hoboken, about to pull out onto Willow heading south. There's traffic passing by so I have to wait for an opening. Checking my outside mirror, I see in it a car pulling up behind me containing several passengers. Looking into my rearview mirror to see what I can see, I'm startled to discover my father behind the wheel and the car filled with my family and relatives, maybe six people total. Apparently short on patience (here as in waking life), Dad slowly creeps up behind me to the point of touching bumpers. Then he starts giving his car gas, trying to nudge me forward and, I assume, out into the street, apparently unconcerned with the traffic. But, of course, I am concerned with it, very much concerned. So there's this forward lurching going on, Dad giving it gas and me pressing the brakes.

"This is a dream I had in the early seventies the memory of which stays with me, so I thought it'd be a good idea to take it up here."

"Very good," the doctor nodded. "Old dreams, new dreams or anything in between. If they're on your mind, they're percolating in the unconscious, which knows no statute of limitations, and therefore grist for the mill here—pardon the very mixed metaphor."

It was high summer, the dog days, and Dr. P. had two large fans going, which almost made enough white noise to cause a hearing problem between us. Corpulent as he was, I don't think a room could ever be too cool for him. It was our first session upon my return from the annual two-week family vacation on Cape Cod where we'd been renting a summerhouse almost every season since the mid-eighties. Over the years we would spend most of our days there with my sister, Iris, and her fiancée, Ron, who would drive up from New Jersey to join us. It was two weeks of pure fun and relaxation—afternoons lolling on the various beaches dotting the Lower Cape, screwing up our courage to jump into the cold surf and then being proud of the accomplishment, lazily checking out the bookstores in Chatham or Hyannis or P' town, evening barbeques with a steady flow of wine and beer.

In the summer of 1985, our very first time there, my Dad was part of the gang, but it was to be his only Cape vacation. He would be gone by the next one. Maybe that poignant fact had been on my mind these past few days back in Syracuse, causing me to recall the dream which I then told Dr. P. in this first return session. To be sure, it was a dream of conflict, but then that last vacation spent with my Dad on the Cape had not been without its little skirmishes either. The one that stands out in my mind is the argument we had over Zen. It was the very first evening, shortly after our arrival, and we were all unwinding with a glass of wine following the long drive. I was "holding forth" to the family on the exotic wonder of this new a-religious religion I had recently discovered, having steeped myself in its bizarre yet seductive comic lore and even taken up its practice in the form of a meditation called "counting the breath." Of course, I was already in a position to offer those punchy Zen answers to everyone's deepest spiritual questions and doubts, and did so with relish, which apparently quickly began to irk my Dad (the others were too polite to call me on anything), who suddenly asked, "What would Zen say Iris is?" With outrageous flippancy I replied, "Why, nothing, Dad, nothing at all, just like anybody or anything else." In scoffing dismissal he shot back, "That's absurd! I could never take seriously a view of the world that had as its basis … nothing! Ridiculous!" I knew as I launched into a wordy explication of the doctrine of *sunyata,* emphasizing the concept's remoteness from Western privative and nihilistic senses of "nothingness," that I had no chance of converting Dad to the cause. The problem, however, was not that he had no mystical side to his temperament, no sense of paradox or mystery. On the contrary, he was very much open to the mystical sensibility, having discovered that side of himself late in life, no doubt in consequence of the loss, nine years earlier, of his life's partner and true soul mate, my mother. In his last years he'd read Blake no less, actually slogging through those crushing self-invented epic mythologies that I could never quite bring myself to approach. (The *Songs of Innocence and Experience* were quite enough for me, thank you.) His pocketbook copies were dog-eared and full of marginal notes. But my Dad, it seems, had a particularly vexing impediment to entering the mystical path that caused him some considerable anguish, one I'd heard him mention before and that he now brought up again in a calmer phase of the same conversation. He said simply, "I have no way of knowing whether anything I experience in a mystical revelation is true. How can I tell whether it's true?" I was struck by this "confession," in particular by the sense of sincere disappointment and exclusion with which it was made. Again, I tried to "negotiate" the issue with him (this time intending to help rather than impress), pointing out the paradox that the deepest spiritual "truths" were beyond even categories as basic as truth and falsehood, but, like most of us, he was far from being ready to let go of this ingrained moral value, conditioned over a lifetime. I remember feeling sympathy for the painful spiritual frustration this problem had to be causing him, imposed on him as it was by his own mind, and at the same time an utter impotence to help him get past it.

As I related this bit of personal history to Dr. P. in my stream of associations to the dream, I thought I could discern in his expression just the barest trace of a softening, a compassion perhaps, for my Dad and probably also for me in my helplessness. "You should be grateful to your parents," he said, "who, with all their faults, nevertheless managed to bring you up as a person capable of empathy for others, even for the father who seemed to have too little for you as you were growing up ..."

"Please don't misunderstand, Dr. Purper," I interrupted emphatically, "I certainly don't mean to tar them black. Although I still feel anger towards him or her on occasion, I'm well past the parent-bashing phase of young adulthood. It's just that the very nature of what we do here steers us towards the unhealthy, the problematic, aspects of the relationships, at the expense, I'm afraid, of the many things I can recall with warmth—such as, in my father's case, the Sunday afternoons of my boyhood when he'd take me to the ball field and hit fungoes to me so I could practice my outfielding skills, or the time I precipitously resigned my scholarship and withdrew from graduate school in an emotional crisis over career choice. That sent my mother into a fit of semi-hysteria, while he simply counseled calmness and patience, which gave me the few days of breathing room I needed to work things out for myself. (I returned to school.) Even the Pinocchio episode early on, whatever nefarious part it may have played in my nascent psychopathology, I still, and will always, recall with deep affection for my Dad. I can't tell you how much it means to me that he took the time and trouble, after a long day at the office, to read to me and instill in me a love of stories that would lead me to my life's work."

"Yes," the doctor said supportively, "you paint an endearing portrait of the wise father who carefully attends to the well being and sound growth of his son. As you well recognize, it's important, for the sake of a balanced perspective, to keep that in mind while we examine—as we must—the less savory aspects of the relationship. Which brings us back to your dream. But then, I don't wish to be accused of 'leading the witness,' so I'll just say there's definitely some fathering going on in it. How would you characterize it?"

"Not to worry, you're not leading me anywhere I haven't already gone many times on my own. It is, after all, a dream that's haunted me for a long time. To me, the most striking thing about it is his gas pedal versus my brakes, such an apt image of the clash of wills. He's trying to push me out while I'm trying to hold back. That much is obvious. What's less obvious is the issue ..."

"Just let your mind play with it."

"Well, the parking lot is safe; the cars in it are all stationary and positioned in order, while the street traffic outside the lot is moving and obviously less safe. You have to be especially careful on entering it, pick the right opening and so forth—"

"Yes, you have to pick the right opening, don't you, or you could get seriously hurt," Dr. P. seconded, as he cast a certain shrewd and knowing look my way that gave me pause.

"Oh yes, yes! . . .That just confirms my own view of the dream. It complements it. You're uncovering a sexual component that had escaped me but that fits so well with my more familial-social interpretation. I've always seen my father here as trying to nudge me out of the safe, self-centered harbor of bachelorhood into the dangerous flowing stream of marriage and family—even though he never behaved that way in waking life. I married late, at thirty-one, but he never bugged me about it."

"There are such things as unconscious attitudinal influences."

"Who am I to deny it? The thing is, I originally had the dream after the affair with Nicole, I guess around 1971, so I've always read it as a sort of primitive paternal prohibition or sanction against the single life, an enforcement of the command to add my link to the chain of generations—a command I had, of course, just violated ... But you've just hinted at a rather obvious sexual symbolism ('obvious' once you see it, of course) in the dream that fits seamlessly: the vaginal opening in traffic, the phallic car that enters it, the father's goosing of the son with his own phallic car in a sadistic effort to make him take the plunge, the dangerous social entanglements lurking behind, and in front of, the presumably private act of intercourse, which is anything *but* in a psychological sense ... I'm pushing thirty and I'm feeling strong familial pressure, unconscious though it be, to commit to a woman, a wife, a family—to get out there into the heady stream of mature-adult family life. But I'm hitting the brakes hard, resisting my father's command … You know, I'll admit I had all sorts of anxieties even at thirty about taking on the 'onus' of wife and children, doubts about my ability to handle it all, even though I was gainfully employed and financially able to support a family, however modestly. The doubts were, of course, psychological, not financial—I just knew there was something askew in myself, something bent, that I needed to straighten out before being ready for what Zorba calls 'the foool catastrophe.' But even all that was trumped by the chief motive for my resistance: I simply did not love Nicole, nor she me. Forcing ourselves into a loveless marriage, or, in terms of the dream, allowing myself to be pushed into the commitment that filling the vaginal opening only too often entails, even for the child's sake, would've been suicidal, certainly for me."

"Yes, it would have, and I think the dream supports that view. Your resistance to the authoritarian command of the Father Almighty is actually a sign of inner strength, not weakness. There's a paradox for you. You've never had any trouble feeling the 'shame' of your so-called avoidance of responsibility in the matter, but the dream, as so often, is compensatory, showing you the other side, the deep courage, integrity and plain common sense of acting, in this instance, against the power of convention, however profound, however seemingly righteous. It takes guts to allow yourself to be seen, even in your own eyes, as a shirker, for the sake of a deeper principle of self-integrity.

"But listen," Dr. P. said, energetically shifting gears. "I want to go back for a moment to the image of the street traffic in the dream. Now my German is certainly not up to snuff, but if I accurately recall my few paltry attempts years ago to read Freud in the original language—I believe it was the *New Introductory Lectures on Psychoanalysis*—the word for traffic and the word for intercourse, while merely synonymous in English, are in fact *identical* in German, are they not?"

My jaw dropped. I was still not over my admiration for his easy spotting of the dream's sexual theme that I, even over the course of years, had failed to notice, and here he was, deepening and enriching that theme with the sort of linguistic interpretation that was right out of my own supposed area of expertise. "Why, yes, they are," I answered sheepishly. "The word is *Verkehr.* There's *Autoverkehr* and *Geschlechtsverkehr,* meaning 'auto traffic' and 'sexual intercourse,' respectively. Intercourse is traffic and traffic is intercourse. That would be, for a dreamer like me with German as a second language, a spot-on pun underlining the sexual symbolism: trafficking in the wrong opening can have dire consequences. Reading *Verkehr* this way also supports your alternative view of the dream as a gutsy refusal on my part to bow to convention—which of course I like very much. It's not that entering *any* opening in the traffic will, inevitably, have dire consequences—that would read the dream as representing *any* sex act as guilty, that is, sex *per se* as guilty—but that entering the *wrong* opening, marrying the wrong girl, could be catastrophic. This latter is an encouraging Jungian point of view, it seems to me, contrasting sharply with the other more Freudian, and decidedly pessimistic, view."

"By all means, accept the Jungian viewpoint here," Dr. P. advised.

As I took in his words, I heard a muffled yet hearty gust

of laughter coming up through the floor from Dr. Farinelli's consulting room below us. Then the cracking noise of the door shutting as yet another 'well adjusted' patient was sent back out into the world. There was something about the notion of "traffic," the sexual traffic in the dream, traffic in and out of the chairopractor's office below, the rush-hour traffic building up audibly outside on Genesee St. even as we talked, that continued to preoccupy me. The effort required to alight on the connection in my mind while attending to the session was, I decided, too much, so, naturally, the instant I dropped the matter, it popped into consciousness all on its own in the form of a bit of German literary text I knew only too well: "In diesem Augenblick ging über die Brücke ein geradezu unendlicher *Verkehr*." I actually declaimed the words right there, spontaneously reading them from a mental screen and cutting the good doctor off in mid-sentence.

"Excuse me?" he said, regarding me quizzically.

"Verkehr! Verkehr!" I answered with elation, which apparently only added to his perplexity. "It's the final sentence of Kafka's short story, 'Das Urteil' ("The Judgment"): 'At this moment an unending stream of *traffic* was just going over the bridge.'[25] Certain critics have read the word 'traffic,' that is, 'Verkehr' in that climactic sentence as … well, 'climactic.' What I mean is, while the sentence is certainly describing the actual vehicular traffic going by in the street at that moment, they argue it's also conveying an oblique reference to orgasm. What orgasm or whose orgasm is hard to say. The story, which like so many others by Kafka concerns a lethal confrontation between father and son, is only about fifteen pages long and is one of Kafka's least accessible, written in the style of a dream, by which I do *not* mean nebulous—on the contrary, it has the super-clarity of detail and a-linear narrative sequence actually experienced in dreams. Kafka wrote the whole thing down in one feverish night and considered the experience a rare occurrence of what he called 'pure writing,' that is, a creative act untainted by the ego the textual product of which was to be preserved from all editorial tampering by the ego. So the story retains the rough quality of a first draft. At least one critic claims Kafka himself experienced orgasm during the writing, so ecstatic was the creative flow, so that the 'traffic/intercourse' reference at the end may refer to the author himself. Of course, nobody really knows.

"Does all this figure into my own dream of the risk involved in moving into the flow of 'traffic'?—I wouldn't be at all surprised," I answered, anticipating Dr. P.'s question, "especially when you consider how long I've been aware of these facts—or rather speculations—about Kafka and how striking the parallels are between the story's protagonist, Georg Bendemann, and yours truly … beginning with the end: the traffic flowing by is bridge traffic, which is the last thing Georg sees before he lets go of the iron bars of the bridge railing, falling into the river below in an act of self-execution. You can't easily call it suicide because he dies carrying out the sentence his own father has pronounced on him of execution by drowning. Now, my Dad in my dream is less harsh: he's just teasingly trying to 'goose' me out into the traffic. He's subjecting me to potential danger, not certain death. But the question for both father-son scenarios is: how has it come to this, to such brutal, tyrannical mockeries of patriarchal justice? Nor is the element of mockery gratuitous or melodramatic here;

both fathers show streaks of gallows humor, my Dad with his phallic goosing, as if he would threaten me with serious injury (castration?) or death for my failure to commit-by-marriage to the opening I'd dared to 'traffic' in; Georg's father with his farcical kangeroo court, set up for the sole purpose of handing his own son a death sentence, a *Todesurteil*. But the thing is, in both dream scenarios the actual motives behind these harsh patriarchal judgments are shrouded in obscurity, even triviality. Sure, Georg's father levels all sorts of vague charges against him: never a son to be proud of … took so long to grow up … practicing deceit against all of us, and so on. And my father obviously thinks I'm stalling (no pun!) on my filial duty to assume the role of *paterfamilias,* that I too am taking 'too long to grow up.' And Kafka himself was convinced his father felt this way about him, as the famous long letter he wrote to the old man, which his mother wisely intercepted, makes perfectly clear. But this damned vagueness of the lethal motives of authority—which by the way runs through Kafka's works—just gives me the sense that the son's guilt is somehow existential, I mean in the strict sense that it's built into the very fabric of his existence from birth and therefore cannot be articulated in any bill of particulars. (The elemental nature of this filial guilt might explain why it should manifest in dreams, those denizens of the unconscious, while remaining apparently absent from waking life, as in my own case.) Such charges as are given always seem made up on the spot. The fact is, sons are simply *schuldig,* that is, again, in the German word's double sense of 'guilty before' and 'in debt to' their fathers. Every son, I guess, must find his own way of expiating that guilt or paying that 'debt.' Kafka's way, of course, was writing; also, he did finally get engaged (for the second time, actually) at the end of his life, but died of tuberculosis before he could marry. As for me … well, I'm here."

"But, as it turns out, you *did* marry, and you *did* have children. Didn't that pay the debt?" Dr. P. asked.

"All I can say is, as long as I continue to be plagued by these feelings of deep shame, irrational though they be, I can only consider it a case of too little too late—at least in the eyes of my own kangeroo court," I said, unable to suppress a resigned smirk. "And no other court really counts, does it?"

"You know, you have an extremely harsh conscience," he said in a tone that seemed almost like perverse admiration.

"Is that a criticism or a compliment," I asked.

"Neither," he answered, "—it's a wonder."

"So's Godzilla."

(9) December 2003: A Crawling Baby, Unattended

This dream has two scenes. In the first, I've adopted a ten-year-old boy and am walking down the street with him, my arm over his shoulder. As we stroll, I tell him a story: "A boy lost his father. He didn't know what to do. His friend's older brother comes home from the war and adopts him. The end."

In the second scene, I find myself in an apartment with several small children, unattended. One of them is just a baby crawling around the floor. I leave the apartment and, as I walk down the corridor towards the exit, I pass a woman and tell her, "There's a baby crawling around in there [pointing towards the apartment door] unattended by an adult." Just then I realize the building's on fire. Hurrying out, I run about a block and duck into a 7-Eleven (it seems I'm in Hoboken) to tell the proprietor, a woman, about the fire. Coming out of the store, I head back towards the apartment building, but slowly and stealthily, so as to sneak past what looks like a dark marauding band of terrorists also heading for the building. As I cautiously make my way, I keep asking myself, "Where's my son?"

"Here we go again, huh?" I said with an embarrassed smile.

"I'm sorry, what do you mean?"

"You know exactly what I mean. Here we go again playing the same old broken record. It must be all you can do not to scream. Tell me, just how do you stand it?" I asked, partly in earnest and partly to deflect my embarrassment.

"Herr Professor, how little credit you give me. Even after all this time, you still feel the need to apologize for your problems, as if out of fear I might get bored with you and show you the door."

"I think what I'm apologizing for is my seeming inability to get over them, or at least to make progress I can identify and take heart from. It all seems to be just so much wheel-spinning. Round and round we go ..."

"Two things," Dr. P. said sternly. "First, I want you to notice the two faces you present to the therapist: the first, predominant up to now, has been the face of protest and skepticism, the seasoned intellectual bent on crossing swords with the therapist, jabbing at his philosophical vulnerabilities, in order to prove himself an equal if not a superior. The second, emerging gradually of late and in plain view today, is the face of diffidence and low self-regard, the apology for not 'doing better,' the faintly obsequious deference to the therapist who has the power to confer or withhold esteem. To some extent, the first face has been a mask for the second, and, to the extent that you finally feel sufficiently comfortable here to begin to show the second, you are, strange as it may sound, indeed making progress. The masks must be stripped away, one by one, and as we go deeper, there will naturally be more sensitivity and pain, but also, in their wake, healing. Your professorial persona has served you well in protecting you from the slings and arrows of denigration and ridicule that began with parents, but, as you know, that fortress becomes a prison, which will, if left intact, eventually asphyxiate you. Neither of these faces, nor any of the permutations around and between them, is the real you, as you've learned from your Zen practice, but while Zen may give you glimpses of 'your True Face before your parents were born,' it takes analysis or its equivalent to prepare you to realize that Face fully, to move into It and be It comfortably.

"The other thing has to do with the discouraging sense of stagnation in the therapeutic process. Some degree of this—not stagnation but the sense of it—is to be expected as we move into the middle phases of analysis. It's analogous to the 'mystical desert' of which St. John of the Cross and many others speak in the great mystical tracts. The honeymoon phase of analysis is over and—"

"—Excuse me," I broke in. "Did you say 'honeymoon phase'? Where, may I ask, was I during this so-called *honeymoon*!" I insisted with snide incredulity.

"Oh, we had one, despite what you may think, only it was juiced with passionate squabbling rather than sex, not unlike many honeymoons. Anyway, this desert phase we're entering now is an especially dangerous time because the temptation to drop out can become very strong. I pointed out a moment ago how genuine progress can wear the mask of regress: if you feel worse, you're probably getting better. ('No pain, no gain,' as the athletes say.) It can also wear the mask of 'nothing happening,' a sometimes extended period of dull aridity that can become more painful than pain itself. In establishing contact with the unconscious as we've done, a number of subliminal processes have been set in motion that need time to come to fruition. So you must constantly renew your faith in an inner movement you can barely sense, if you can sense it at all, but which will continue to be reflected in the dreams we analyze.

“But whatever the dangers and risks and pitfalls of analysis—and of course they are real, since what we’re doing, this deep self-inquiry, is profound—there’s one thing you can be sure of: I will never show you the door. I will never, ever, abandon you—no matter what.”

As the good doctor said this last, he modulated his voice from a hortatory to an unmistakably paternal tone, this man who was some dozen years my junior, and the obvious sincerity with which he spoke, grounded in his deep familiarity with my fears of abandonment stretching back to the earliest years of life, banished any trace of irony or cynicism from my skeptical mind. “It almost seems as if you’re trying to act the part of some sort of ideal parent, filling in some of the emotional gaps left by my ‘all too human’ ones,” I said with a chuckle.

“Very astute of you. That’s the *in loco parentis* function a decent therapist never loses sight of. You get ‘re-parented’ here, care of yours truly. (No extra charge, by the way.) As we examine the early experiences and release painful feelings, we also try to respond with the nurturing concern the original caregiver, for whatever reasons, didn’t or couldn’t provide. In a sense, you get to do childhood all over again. Of course, it would’ve been better had it gone right the first time, but that’s life …

“So, how about we get to the dream?”

“Yes, of course, the dream,” I echoed. “Actually, now I think of it, it’s not really much of a leap to the dream from the reassurances you’ve just given me—for which by the way I’m deeply grateful. I’m dreaming about one, or several, potentially abandoned kids and trying in the dream to find some way to address the situation. Maybe I’m trying to help them the way you’re trying to help me.”

"Do you think it's also possible you identify with those kids, and that in trying to help them, you're trying to help yourself?" he probed.

"Why not?" I asked rhetorically, only half in jest. "As I understand it, identities in dreams are not so fixed as they are in waking life. I can be more than one character in a dream, as it were, not just the protagonist in the drama—"

"—Yes, that's right out of the psychoanalyst's handbook," Dr. P. chimed in. "In fact, that celebrated analyst of the counterculture era, Fritz Perls, claimed that the dreamer is, in fact, *all* the characters in the dream, and everything else in it besides—house, furniture, weather, umbrella stand. That's why he'd have his analysand groupies improvise mini-psychodramas by having them literally act out all the various significant elements in their dreams: 'Okay, now be the wall, … now be the gun … now the sunset.'"

"I love that idea. It appeals strongly to my sense of literary creativity. It shows the dreamer's ultimate identity is always that of 'author of the story,' not any particular character or thing *within* the story. It's a matter of levels of awareness: the dream is the dreamer's creation; and even though he may *seem* to identify with the protagonist, usually a replica of his conventional ego-identity, in the sense that he looks out at the world of the dream through that self-replica's eyes, on a deeper level he's the author, a quasi God from whom everything that constitutes the world of the dream issues, including those forces in it that appear to threaten him. It's a split-identity, double-focus sort of thing, something my friend Kafka was well aware of and loved to play with.[26]

"Not to stray too far from the business at hand, but this

little 'narrative theory' of mine is also a trope I've found very useful for expressing my spiritual point of view."

"How do you mean?"

"It's simple really. Think of all human beings as characters in stories (read: lives) they themselves are writing, only without knowing it. Once you accept the conventional Eastern view of enlightenment as the realization of your Oneness with everything, then this 'narrative view' of human life becomes perfectly logical. Those few who succeed in realizing that Oneness advance in status from unconscious protagonist in their own story to conscious narrator/author/creator of that story. In fact, the whole distinction between story and storyteller evaporates. The dancer is seen to *be* the dance; the one signifying *is* the thing signified; we *are* our stories. This is to become God, to realize one's own divinity. Oh yes, an added bonus is that, to such an enlightened one, no story has any meaning outside itself. There are no hidden meanings in or behind any story. Why? Because there *is* no 'behind,' no 'outside of'; even the sense of hiddenness is just another aspect *within* the story. (From this 'authorial' point of view, even your vaunted unconscious, Dr. P., doesn't exist.) This should appeal to students of literature in academe, fed up with their symbol-hunting, post-al, know-it-all professors, who incessantly deign to tell them what the tale or poem '*really* means'—"

"Excuse me, Herr Professor," the doctor interrupted, "a question if you will, which I ask both out of genuine curiosity about the answer as well as to lead us back closer to your dream: Does this view of yours, that each of us *is* his own story or drama or, to put it baldly, life—does this view mitigate the feelings of shame and guilt that are manifest in so many of your dreams and that have, as you've revealed here, plagued you for most of your adult life?"

"To be honest, I would have to say, to some extent, yes, but not nearly profoundly enough, not to the point where I can regard them with the same benign indifference I regard other things.—And please, don't misunderstand my use of the word 'indifference' here—it's really the idea of equanimity I'm getting at."

"Yes, yes, of course. So what you're saying is that, even by your own 'lights,' you're not yet fully enlightened."

"Nice one—and yes, that's exactly what I'm saying—which is why I'm here, I suppose, to try to clear away enough of the debris of character so as to move out into the limitless authorial space of my story. Kafka said everyone has access to God, only each a different access. Well, what's more different about each of us than our stories, our very lives. Each life is a different door to the Law, one of Kafka's code words for God."

"So, which feelings in particular do you experience in this dream of the unattended children?" asked Dr. P, putting my mind's nose to the grindstone lest the entire hour be lost to lofty metaphysical speculation.

"Well, obviously the discussion we've just had makes that question quite problematic because the answer would depend on the identity or point of view from which I'm experiencing," I said with not a little self-satisfaction. The grimace contorting the good doctor's face told me I'd better get off the relativism schneid but fast: "But I'll assume you mean my feelings as protagonist," I added quickly. He allowed a wan smile. "Even there, though, the answer's not so simple," I continued.

"I mean, yeah, at first blush, it sure looks like I'm running out on those children in the apartment, which matches up only too well with my feelings of shame over 'abandoning' the child—er, *my* child [the doctor nodded]—with Nicole. Alerting two women to the situation, the one in the hallway and then the store manager, strikes me as trying to rationalize leaving the whole 'catastrophe'—the fire certainly makes it a potential catastrophe—in 'the woman's' capable hands. But clearly this rationalization is not successful. I literally don't 'get away with it,' since, on leaving the store, I turn back towards the apartment building."

"I'm not sure I follow ..."

I knew very well he 'followed' me, that he was just feigning uncertainty as a way of prodding me to articulate the rest of the dream as clearly and emphatically as possible because he knew what I was about to say should be burned into my psyche forever: "My return means I'm dropping all rationalization, all pretense, all effort to overcome this issue by running away from it. I'm heading right back into that fire to rescue those kids."

"I see. Does that mean Nicole can expect a phone call from you this evening?"

"No, no, of course not," I said. "That's reading the return segment of the dream entirely too literally; the dream is much more subtle, more artful, than that, I think."

"Ah, I see, go on," he encouraged, a step ahead of me as usual.

"Going back, I think, means the kind of 'going back' or 'return' we're doing here—you know, going back into that emotional fire, sitting on the 'hot seat' of therapy until the issue burns itself out—I would even go so far as to say rescuing the kid, or kids, or crawling baby, means using therapy to rescue myself, since, if Perls is right, I'm the kid too and God knows I need rescuing."

"Yes, and isn't that just what you're doing for yourself in that first scene as you walk down the street with your arm over the shoulder of your newly adopted ten-year-old son? Coming here means taking care of yourself, helping yourself to grow up. That therapy is implied in this scene is also revealed by the little story you—in the identity of a more mature, wiser self—tell your boyish self about another young boy who is himself rescued by a father. Therapy is often represented in dreams by tropes or images of self-reflection since self-reflection is precisely what we do here …

" … And, getting back to the dream's second scene, it's not only the fire of difficult de-repressed emotions you're entering by coming here, you're also encountering something else most people would rather avoid … hmm?"

"Let's see, what could that be? The only puzzle piece left would be the … yes, the dark marauding gang of terrorists who are also heading for the apartment building. Well, if I'm to be honest here, and remain consistent with the interpretation of the dream I've worked out so far, I'd have to view those terrorists as an expression of my own darkest, most dangerous impulses—Jung would call it my shadow, right?" Again, Dr. P. nodded at least tentative agreement. "And I guess the joke's on me here," I said, suddenly feeling disappointed, "since it's pretty clear I'm avoiding those terrorists, literally trying to sneak by them, stay out of their way, as they head for those kids in the building, for who knows what murderous purposes. It amounts to consigning the whole issue to my shadow, who always has the simplest solution: fuck ’em, kill ’em—doesn’t it?” I asked, lowering my head.

“Now, just a minute, slow down …” Dr. P. cautioned me with great deliberateness, including the deftest use of his hands as brakes to my cascading thoughts. “It’s very important you notice here your habit, almost a reflex, of interpreting in a way that casts you in the worst possible light. So, just to be clear, we’re learning *two* things here: what the dream most likely means and how you tend to read your dreams through the harshly critical filter of conscience. In the first place, there are two ways of avoiding the shadow, one good and one not so good. The not-so-good way is to avoid acknowledging you even have one, which is what most people do who project their own baser tendencies onto others and then read those others as threatening to them in some way. That’s explains how irrational prejudices arise and flourish as they do. That’s obviously not the case here. Your avoidance of your shadow in the dream is perfectly sane and rational, wise even. That avoidance is based on an acknowledgment of its dangerous nature, which can only come from a careful consideration of that nature, which is one of the things we’ve been doing here. It’s not your business to fight the shadow, nor, for that matter, to become bosom buddies with it—both sentimental illusions—but rather to become aware of it, familiar with its ways, so as to react always in a manner you yourself judge to be optimal—which is exactly what you do in the dream. Notice that you slip ahead of the terrorists, presumably to get to the children in the apartment building before they do, thereby saving them from the terrorists’ nefarious designs, whatever they may be. That’s you behaving in a way that shows you’re in charge here, not 'they,' or not 'It.' You've headed the shadow off at the pass, so to speak, foiling its perfidy, because you decided that, all things considered, that was in everyone's best interest. And that's something you can only do by understanding how the shadow works."

Dr. P. fell silent for a few moments, letting this corrective take on the shadow and my relationship to it just simmer between us. Then he went on: "I said a few moments ago that, with respect to this dream, we were observing two things: the dream itself and how you tend to read it … Enough said?" I nodded, sobered. "You can also see here one of the reasons why it's hard, if not impossible, to do analysis on your own; you need a more or less neutral perspective to protect you from your own blind spots."

Then, slowly shifting positions in his uncomfortable chair, apparently to indicate a change of subject, he looked at me and said, "By the way, I had a notion the other day that I wanted to run by you: What would you think of the idea of making a confession?"

"Excuse me?" I said with obvious consternation, leaning my head forward toward his. I couldn't believe I was hearing what I was afraid I was hearing.

"A confession … to a priest. I have a friend, a Father Tom Considine, at St. Joseph's Abbey in Spencer, Massachusetts, who happens to be a wonderful spiritual mentor. You could maybe join a closed weekend retreat at the abbey and have a chat with him—"

"—Wait, please wait, Dr. Purper," I interrupted, still trying to get my bearings. "Surely you're not serious … You're proposing with a straight face that I confess my sins to a priest, that I resume my subservient allegiance to a draconian institution that happens to be one of the major reasons I sit here before you today?"

"I'm not suggesting you 'join up,' just that you talk to a man who knows how to listen. Catholic confession these days has come a long way from the medieval ordeal it was in our childhoods. It's much more like pastoral counseling now, without all the categories and numbers of sins; it's more like coming *here*, the attitude being one of seeking to heal rather than judge. It's much more in the spirit of *tout comprendre c'est tout pardonner,* 'to understand all is to forgive all' ... Anyway, the strategy I have in mind is, once again, of the 'hair-of-the-dog' variety: what has been induced by the moral suasion of Holy Mother Church—this persistent sense of shame and sin—might also be exorcized thereby. Something in the unconscious might just respond to the powerful cleansing ritual of confession, scoff as you may. Obviously that sacrament was once a dominant force in your life and, doubtless, still is unconsciously ... I just thought it might be worth a try. You have nothing to lose by it."

"Oh, you really think so?" I retorted with mock sincerity. "Nothing to lose, you say. That's nice, that's very nice ... Have I mentioned here the last closed Catholic retreat I ever made?"

"I don't think so."

"Well, let me tell you all about it. It was the Spring of my senior year at St. Peter's Prep, an all-boys school. They bussed the forty or so of us in my class off to—what was it called—ah yes, the Gonzaga Retreat House, somewhere out in the western boonies of New Jersey, for a weekend of spiritual fun and games. We were all about seventeen, therefore all adept onanists on the cusp of graduation, which meant this was the Jebbies' last chance to cripple our healthy sexual instincts for life. And boy did they pull out all the stops—everything short of water-boarding. There were the sagacious counseling sessions in which we'd break up into small groups and huddle around one of the priests who would dispense a plethora of strategies for outwitting Satan whenever the Prince of Darkness took it upon himself to invade our penises: wear loose clothing, don't sleep on your stomach, bury, or better yet, burn the porn (better the porn than you!), and other such matchless tactical gems calculated to steer the adolescent male psyche into the safe harbor of mature repression. Even better were the twice-daily sermons in the darkened chapel delivered by the retreat master—Father … Callahan, Hanrahan, Hooligan, Hannigan? … Who can remember? If you've heard one boozy Irish Jebby preach the evils of eros, you've heard them all. I remember particularly the last talk, the climactic rhetorical surge intended to strike deepest, to sear itself into youthful memory. And the climax of the climax, the cautionary tale of moral tragedy featuring that ill-starred teenage couple, Johnny and Betty Lou, who just couldn't keep their horny little hands off each other, such that their bestial desires impelled them to pull over to the shoulder of the interstate … and do the dirty deed (the back seat was just roomy enough). Oh, the Shakespearean pathos of the good father's declamation as he pointed East to describe the fateful sixteen-wheeler that came barreling down the right lane of the interstate doing a crisp 70, the sleep-deprived driver taking just a second, a nanosecond really, no more than that, to nod off, but alas, long enough to veer three feet to the right, just enough off course to send poor

Johnny and Betty Lou plunging downward to join the Marquis de Sade, Hugh Hefner and the entire Western-historical population of loathsome voluptuaries in the ravenous flames of eternal damnation."

I paused for a breath and to savor the droll smile, Mona-Lisa-like, on Dr. P.'s face. I was having fun and he was not of a mind to spoil it. "But if the hell sermon was the *pièce de résistance*," I said, holding up a finger to signal the resumption of my tale, "the coup de grace, delivered on Saturday night, was the peroration on the Shroud of Turin. What the hell sermon packed in fear, the shroud sermon packed in shame, or more precisely, unworthiness, two emotions which, when combined, could be counted on to act as a more potent depressant of the libido than even saltpeter itself... which substance, by the way, I still suspect they were adding to the food for good measure ...When I think back on that lugubrious homily, I can almost agree with that French wit—was it Sartre?—who pronounced Christianity and psychoanalysis the West's two greatest monuments to suffering. (Would you agree with at least half of that, Dr. P?) As Father Callahan intoned the familiar Good Friday tropes—the crucified Christ, the nails through emaciated limbs, the almost wraith-like corpse—he passed around to us these little wallet-sized cards showing the bust imprint of the God-man's image left on the shroud for future Catholics to beat their breasts over. And as he did so, he used all his powers of persuasion to make damn well sure we understood that *we*—not the Romans, not Pontius Pilate, not even the Jews (well, maybe the Jews a little)—but *we* seventeen-year-old boys sitting there hushed had caused this ... this theocide by our sinful (read: sexual) natures. Never mind the question what sort of heavenly Father could only be propitiated by the death of his own son. Never mind behavior behavior schmehavior!—it was our fallen *natures* that did it; and since no one has ever seen a 'nature'—let alone a theocidal one—that makes it a mystical issue, and since mystical reality transcends time, it turns out we *are* responsible for what happened two thousand years ago …

"Remember Father York, my old high-school Greek teacher I told you about early on? Well, this retreat master, Father Callahan, was the anti-York. He rode home with us on the bus Sunday afternoon. He sat about two seats in front of me across the aisle, which gave me a chance to observe him a little. What stood out is that he sat ramrod still the entire trip, never turning his head, never engaging anyone in conversation—as if kicking back and showing a little humanity might tarnish the brilliance of the infernal masterpiece he'd just created … Oh yeah, he did have one thing in common with his opposite number: he suffered a nervous breakdown. According to the grapevine, it happened about two years after our retreat. I guess it just goes to show that psychosis is no respecter of character; it happens to both good and bad. (Hmm, just like Enlightenment.) Still, it pains me to say that one Callahan can probably snuff out the youthful inspiration sparked by twenty Yorks."

I let my gaze linger on Dr. P, who had been listening with his head resting on his palm. After a moment he shifted, inhaled deeply and said, "So, can I take that as a definite maybe?"

"You can take it any way you like," I laughed. "I'm not going. I've had quite enough of spiritual retreats for this lifetime, thank you, be they of the Buddhist or the Christian variety."

"Oh, that's right," he recalled. "You've done *sesshin* at the zendo in the Catskills, haven't you? I'd like to hear more about that sometime—not now, of course, we're quite out of time … So, I'll see you in the first week of the new year, right?"

"I'll be here."

"Well, Merry Christmas."

"Happy holidays."

PART TWO: EDUCATION

(10) April 2004: Entering the Enclave of Avatar

I'm admitted to a moderately large, well-lit room that seems to be part gymnasium and part assembly hall. I recognize it as the headquarters of Avatar, an actual organization for psychospiritual growth prominent in the 90's. The room is occupied by several young to middle-aged adults, both men and women, who are working out vigorously on high-tech gym equipment, such as Nordic Tracks and similar contraptions. They all look like demigods: strong, beautiful beings at the peak of physical and, I sense, mental fitness: mens sana in corpore sano, you know? And they're all wearing these tight-fitting leotard-type outfits that display their corporeal perfection. I'm in awe of them as I stand there watching them move. Still, I have my doubts. For one thing, somebody braced the door shut after I was let in, making me uneasy; for another, I'd been through many such programs before and they had all failed, however promising they'd looked at first. I express my skepticism to the Avatar masters who merely smile benignly. But my doubts continue to plague me until finally I decide to leave. I remove the door brace and step out, proving to myself they can't keep me there by force. Now outside, I look around at a seedy neighborhood and start hunting for my car, which I have trouble finding.

"So?"

"No mystery here—"

"—Don't say that, and don't think it either! When you do, you foreclose on the possibility of discovery, serendipity—precisely the place where the deepest insights lie. There is *always* mystery."

"Okay, okay, I was merely suggesting that I think I have a pretty good handle on the main theme of this dream …" Actually, I was surprised by my own enthusiasm for interpreting the dream, as I had reached at this point a kind of nadir of indifference to the analysis, no longer much caring whether I was making progress, nor even what progress meant in analytic terms. Therapy had become just something I did on Thursday afternoons from 4 to 5 p.m. It was like doing the laundry or shopping for the week's groceries, a chore one neither minded nor particularly enjoyed. Without realizing it I would forget, again and again, Dr. P.'s warning that I had entered analysis' version of the mystic's Dark Night of the Soul, the acutely trying middle phase on the path compounded of doubt (which had always been there), misery (nothing ever changes) and boredom (so what?). Well, if I was crossing an inner dessert, this must surely be the middle of that dessert at high noon, the Sun's Anvil that daunted even the persevering Lawrence of Arabia. This was the very phase of my old Zen practice Dr. P. had implied I copped out on in our first session (an implication I protested then and still do). Here I was facing it again. St. John of the Cross, in *The Ascent of Mount Carmel,* even describes it with the metaphor of the 'mystical dessert,' a parched and parching place with scant affect for the heart nor stimulus for the imagination, just the same old same old same old …

Nor had the good doctor and I ceased with our theoretical skirmishes, just that they became more amicable, personalized and psychologized, with yours truly the object of the psychologizing more often than not. Such as in the hour preceding this one when he suddenly asked me, in the midst of one of my rants against the theory of the unconscious, "So tell me, how come you're a specialist in the field of German romanticism, a movement infatuated with its discovery of an unconscious mind, a 'passive consciousness' as those thinkers put it, when week after week you come here to me and fight tooth-and-nail against that very notion? One would think you would've preferred studying their enlightened predecessors, Lessing and Rousseau and Kant, those champions of a much more sanguine conception of the mind as a free and autonomous entity, a power monolithically guided by reason. That seems so much better suited to your taste and temperament. How is it the disconnect doesn't drive you crazy."

"Sometimes it *does,*" I admitted, "but with me it's the same as with Kafka: the two of us are both obsessed and repelled by the idea of an unconscious mind; it's something you just can't ignore, the sense of an abyss *inside* you to which you're drawn as if to the edge of a ledge of a skyscraper. Sometimes it strikes me as the only thing truly worth studying, the only thing in creation mysterious and deep enough to hold out promise of a remedy for human suffering, a remedy that works. But of course, anything that powerful is bound to be double-edged; it has to be as dangerous as it is promising, which, I suppose, is why so many hero myths have a dragon or some such monster guarding the treasure-trove. But I want that treasure, and studying the European Enlightenment is, as far as I can see, not the shortest route to it, however strong my ideological sympathies for that movement may be. For me ideology—even one touting reason—is one thing, the heart another; and my heart lies with the romantics: they courted mystery."

And so it would go at times, he baiting me with probing questions of an ostensibly intellectual nature that were designed to make me aware of certain contradictions in my psychological make-up, and I either responding in a way that satisfied me, as here, or, as more often happened, not, which meant the matter was something I needed to look at. Such as in a session not long heretofore in which he casually mentioned how curious he found it that I, as someone generally enamored of postmodernism, had not embraced the playful postmodern idea of the poly-authorship, or even non-authorship, of a novel; that is, a novel having, via a form of hypertext software, so many contributors to its writing that the very concept of authorship was rendered irrelevant. I didn't know what to say; I had no good reason or explanation, but yes, it was true, I found the idea repugnant. To which his response was to wonder, rhetorically, whether my repugnance didn't come out of a fierce desire to retain the traditional category of individual authorship, to keep full control over and credit for anything I wrote, since this was my most important way of affirming my self-worth. This, he concluded, from someone who had spent almost a decade practicing Zen for the sole purpose of breaking his connection to the personal ego. This was a humbling insight, to say the least. Nor, having by now become a bit more honest with myself, was I tempted to argue psychological reductionism on his part ("Your rant over 'the death of the author' is nothing but …"). He'd nailed me and I knew it.

So my analysis had become an open-ended exercise in tedium, punctuated by occasional painful encounters with my own hypocrisy and rare moments of élan when I felt I had something illuminating to say about a dream, such as the one I'd just presented. "By all means," the doctor enthused, inviting me to hold forth.

"Well, I think there's no question but that the dream is about the analysis and my persistent ambivalence about its validity and value. All the dreams I've had in the last few years featuring so-called Human Potential groups—TM, Lifespring, Scientology and so forth—have really been about my experience here with you. Like this Avatar dream, they're all riddled with doubt on my part, doubt despite the shining promise, and usually it's not long before I'm looking for the nearest exit. Actually, I did do some Avatar training, three or four days anyway, about two years before I started coming here. It was with a woman in Ithaca, her name was Elena ... Elena Iglesias, and on the final day of training I did have some kind of satori efflorescence. Each one is different, unique, yet they all include the basic experience of a falling-away of the sense of separation from anything you're aware of, as if everything your consciousness touches is some aspect of yourself dissolving into bliss as you touch it. The joy is indescribable and you feel utterly nourished—the ultimate chicken soup for the soul. The trouble was, I found the consciousness-raising exercises tedious beyond endurance, the more so with my obsessive-compulsive tendencies, which drove me to repeat them until they were 'perfect.' Not surprisingly, I abandoned the whole regimen two days after getting home and haven't done it since ... umm, with one exception: I still practice looking at objects, people or even thoughts—anything really—as if they were complete phenomena in and of themselves, without any reference to anything else. It's amazing how things open up to you when you strip them entirely of their connection, their reference, to other things. I think it's these references, which are entirely made up by the mind, that the Zen masters refer to as 'delusion.' Ultimately, nothing refers to, or finds its meaning in, anything else—a form of dualism; things mean always and only themselves, and when that is seen to be the case, as in satori, then these self-referential things are all that exists, and right there is the great Oneness. So, despite its failure for me as a program, I *am* indebted to Avatar for helping me learn—or rather, *re*-learn—how to look at things through innocent eyes."

"Thanks for the lecture on the epistemology of mysticism, Herr Professor, but could we please get back to the dream and your reading of it as a reflection of the analytical situation here?"

"Of course. As I said, it's no great mys—uh, enigma. On the manifest level, you appear, not as yourself, not even as an individual, but as an oligarchy, a small cadre of 'Masters,' supremely wise and enlightened, who welcome me to the inner sanctum where the magic of transformation happens—"

"Well, that part of your interpretation is certainly beyond dispute," Dr. P. quipped with mock-smugness.

"Not so fast, Paracelsus," I shot right back at him, "don't overlook the door that gets immediately barred shut behind me once I'm in. That certainly gives me pause and plants the seed of doubt in me eventually leading to my bolting."

"Of course it does. The barred door symbolizes, among other things, the claustrum that the analytic situation is for you, as it is for most. It's terrifying to submit to sober, honest self-inquiry, to let go of all escape routes and stay put long enough to confront (and hopefully subdue) whatever chimaeras may rise up out of the Pandora's box of the unconscious. I would say the dream is showing you the deep anxieties you have about this, especially as we go deeper. Typically in the middle phase of analysis, these anxieties get paved over by a surface mood of tedium, boredom, ennui, such as you've been complaining of for some time now. And intellectually in your case, that mood gets rationalized, justified, if you will, by all your 'sound arguments' against the theory of the unconscious. But notice that the door is barred from the inside, not the outside, indicating that its purpose is more to keep others out than you in, in other words, to guarantee confidentiality; you could leave any time you choose to, and you do. But what happens when you unbar the door and escape the Avatar claustrum out into the street: you see around you a seedy neighborhood with your car nowhere in sight. What is that telling you?"

"I don't know … maybe that Avatar should move to a more upscale neighborhood," I chortled.

"Come on, come on, you can do better than that."

"Well, I suppose it's telling me that, as scary as the claustrum of analysis may be, it's preferable to the 'seediness' of the unexamined life out in the world, and maybe I should turn right around and go back in."

"Yes, precisely. After all, you'll never find your 'car,' that is, your direction in life, out there, since it's really *in here*, isn't it? The paradox so beautifully captured in the dream is that your direction is right here in this locked room: in order to really get somewhere, you must agree to stay put! You must put aside your fears and commit!"

Again, as with the question of authorship and so many others, I was stunned by the aptness of the man's interpretation and his succinct way of putting it. It had a compacted, Zen-like power that totally defused whatever counter-arguments I might ordinarily have been moved to raise. It carried its own unassailable truth, like the solution to a koan, and I actually felt a twinge of gratitude as I bowed inwardly to it. It was bracing to be told a truth beyond doubt.

Nevertheless, I had my questions. (There were always questions.) "But how do you *do* that? How do you 'put aside your fears,' as you say? How do you 'commit?'"

"Don't fret over it," he reassured. "It's not entirely voluntary. Your job is just to keep doing your best. Then, at some indeterminate point ex post facto, you'll realize that a deep commitment has in fact taken place, that your spiritual weight has somehow shifted from the rim to the hub of the wheel. The matter is ultimately out of your hands and in those of your unconscious."

"But it sure sounded a moment ago as if you were telling *me,* and not my unconscious, to cast aside fear, etc."

"I *was* telling *you—all* of you."

"Ah, I see. You talk to me as if there were no schism, no 'wound of consciousness,' as one thinker put it, as if healing had already taken place."

"Sure, sometimes. There are moments when the famous AA nostrum, 'Fake it until you make it,' is definitely called for. If I keep treating you as a healed being, eventually you'll become one."

"Speaking of noble humanitarian groups like AA," I said, as a segue back to the dream, "there is, as we've seen, one of them in the dream: Avatar. I read Avatar earlier as a thinly veiled, pluralized image of you, the Master-Healer-Teacher, and so forth. But other associations to Avatar come to mind as well. For one thing, it's a word American Zen tosses around all the time to indicate anyone or anything, even a situation, that helps raise consciousness towards Enlightenment. It's a term often applied to those who make us suffer in life, helping us to avoid feeling hatred towards such noxious people by viewing them as spurs, painful though they be, to awakening, spurs sent by the compassionate Buddha himself."

"Are you hinting that I might be such an avatar for you?" asked Dr. P., again in that tone of mock-smugness.

"Well, I don't know whether you're an emissary of the compassionate Buddha, so don't flatter yourself. On the other hand, the part about making me suffer does ring true."

He laughed a hearty belly laugh, as did I.

"But that's not really what I'm aiming at here. Avatar, as a closed group, a secret society, into which you must be initiated via a prescribed course of instruction, with a hierarchy of masters, and levels of accomplishment, rituals, ceremonies, symbolic garb and always a group of novices coming in—it reminds me of the underground stream of secret organizations, most of them humanitarian, in this country and in Europe going back centuries at least as far as the Renaissance. You know, the Rosicrucians, Freemasons, and so on. Germany has an especially rich history of such heterodox groups, like the *Rosenkreutzer*, who still flourish today, possibly because the forced conversion to Christianity in the early Middle Ages never sat well with the Germanic peoples. The old paganism had to find underground ways to leak out, at least until Wagner came along and made it mainstream again.

"Anyway, there's a kind of traditional German novel called the *Bildungsroman,* or 'novel of inner education,' that has always been dear to my heart. This sort of book begins with the hero's early childhood and traces his growth and development up to nascent adulthood in which he finds his rightful place in society, and there it brakes off. The most famous examples, I suppose, would be Goethe's *Wilhelm Meister's Apprenticeship* (1795), which sort of set the modern standard; Thomas Mann's *The Magic Mountain* (1924), a daunting read even for the dedicated; and—my particular favorites—most of Hermann Hesse's mature novels, such as *Demian, Siddhartha,* and *The Glass Bead Game,* all post World War I. The thing about all these 'formula-novels' is that there's always some kind of secret group or enclave of wise masters in the background keeping a protective eye on the hero as he grows up. Why? Because he's been spotted as a gifted individual with high potential, someone who will one day be worthy of induction into the elite group and who will help to build a utopian society of brilliant artists, profound intellectuals and wise statesmen, a small society to begin with that will eventually come out of hiding and replace the present insane mainstream civilization that is bound to destroy itself through wars and various forms of oppression almost any day now. (This sort of novel usually pictures an exhausted, desiccated society bent on self-destruction 'almost any day now'—Armageddon looms on the horizon.)

"I guess the reason I'm belaboring this is that I can't help sometimes thinking of *you* as an envoy or representative of such a secret society, and that, through this analysis, you're preparing me to enter it, helping me to become worthy.

You're my certificate of entrance into the enclave of Avatar, as it were. I know it's just a silly fantasy, but it's one that's strong enough to have gotten into a dream, isn't it?"

"I definitely do *not* think it's a silly fantasy," Dr. P. hastened to contradict. "On the contrary, the dream can certainly be read as an allegory of your struggle to accept admission into the fraternity of brothers and sisters who have achieved what Jung and others would call self-realization. And that is a small and exclusive society for sure—you might even call it 'secret' in the sense that most people have no real awareness of the supreme value of psychospiritual maturity. The Philosopher's Stone is certainly well hidden from the vast huddled masses, partially by reason of their preoccupation with the struggle for survival but also, to some extent, through their own blindness. And such blindness is at least partly willful for the simple reason that self-realization is damned hard. In any society only a few will be attracted to it. This gives it a certain de facto elitism that accounts for the air of charisma surrounding the secret fellowships dedicated to preserving access to it in myths and novels like your *Bildungsroman*.

"Now obviously what first brought you here was a strong need to free yourself from the pain of your so-called neurotic symptoms, the fears and depressions and obsessions and so forth. This is what happens in Freudian psychoanalysis. You get liberated from your personal unhappiness, but, alas, only in order to expose yourself to the general unhappiness of the world, as Freud himself so cheerfully put it. Not a very alluring prospect, I think you'll grant. But here we go further than that; we view relative freedom from neurosis, not as an end in itself (although one certainly *could* do that), but as a springboard for the pursuit of total self-transformation, the ultimate blossoming of human potential, which of course implies the enjoyment of such supreme quasi-divine qualities as spiritual freedom and bliss. Call it self-realization, call it individuation, or enlightenment, satori, mokhsha, the Kingdom of Heaven, the perennial philosophy, Being, Reality or any other of the countless names the world's cultures have given it. It's every human being's birthright. It's what distinguishes Jung from Freud and separates the spiritually serious from the frivolous and indifferent. It's the positive complement to Freud's negative side of the coin: we attend not only to freedom *from* but freedom *for.* Of course, Freud dismissed all of Jung's preoccupation with transpersonal states of consciousness as mystical rubbish. Eventually it led to the profound break between them around 1913."

"Now who's giving lectures?" I teased. "... But you know, of all the expressions you listed for ... *It,* the *summum bonum*—now *there's* another name!—the one that really lit up for me was 'satori,' the Japanese Zen term. Of course, it, and the roughly synonymous *kensho,* were spiritual concepts bandied about endlessly in the various Zen communities I frequented in the 80's and 90's, to the extent that they were drained dry of all their inspirational quality and moved to the cemetery of dead mantras, like all those 'Hail Mary's' that make up the Catholic rosary. But all that is in sharp contrast to the very first time I heard the word spoken, which was during a group primal therapy session in L.A. in 1974—"

"—Yes, you've alluded to your youthful left-coast adventure in the jungles of the Human Potential Movement several times now. I think it's time for you to tell me a little more about counter-culture therapy, California style, don't you think?"

"My pleasure. That too, it turns out, involved a kind of hermetic society. As I said, my first 'encounter with "satori"' took place during a group session held at a Primal Therapy spin-off institute or center, one based largely on the principles articulated by Arthur Janov in his book, *The Primal Scream,* which caused quite a sensation in the early 70's. But this center, called the Feeling Awareness Center and located in Venice, had disowned Janov and his Primal Institute in Beverly Hills because it felt the sickest patients there were being neglected, written off as failures basically, which led to several suicides. Anyway, one evening as group was breaking up, Mike—that's Mike Majors, the head honcho—dismissed us with words much like the following: 'We've done some good work here tonight, people ... Remember, on any given night you can leave here on a satori high, if you just give yourself to the process.' I didn't know what he meant, just that it sounded like something desirable, the more so with that exotic Japanese tone. So, of course, I ran right home and looked it up and found a definition pretty close to my intuited sense of it. But for the first time, I think, just that casual dropping of the term by Mike opened my eyes to the possibility of a therapy or a practice that might be for the sake of something more, something finer and higher, than the mere excision of symptoms. It was my first, small, groping step back to some kind of spirituality after wandering for more than a decade in a dessert of angry agnosticism.

"But to begin at the beginning, Dottie and I had packed all our belongings into an aging Buick Skylark in May of 1974 and driven cross-country on I-80 to L.A. That was just after I'd been awarded tenure at Syracuse and been given a year-long research leave at half-pay. I figured, what with children and the harness of a career on the horizon, this might be the last opportunity I'd ever have to straighten out my inner life (the situation with Nicole and the child was still freshly painful then), so I'd better grab it. The Feeling Awareness Center, located just off Venice Boulevard, was my virtual home for about ten months in 1974-75. Though Dottie and I had an apartment on Sepulveda and she was little more than a bride at that time, I spent most of my time at the center working hard to shed my neurosis. Looking back, I can see how frightfully I neglected her at the start of our marriage and to this day I'm grateful to her for sticking by me, even braving the anxiety of knowing that such therapies were notorious for braking up marriages presumably based on neurotic dependency.

"Initially, on arriving in L.A. in early June, I tried, and failed, to get into Janov's place. They rejected me—*by postcard*—about a week after my interview, giving me no reasons. At first, I was crushed since for over a year I'd been embellishing this scenario in my imagination of finding the elixir, the panacea, at the shrine-like Primal Institute, this monument to Janov's pioneering genius. But as it turned out, I didn't even get to see the man himself at my interview. It was his wife and associate, Vivian, who handled 'my case.' I'll never forget how she entered the interview room, dabbing at her eyes and nose with a tissue, overcome, I had no doubt, by a patient's emotionally wrenching, though profoundly healing, therapeutic breakthrough. She sat down behind the desk, picked up my application from the top of a pile about four inches thick and perused it.

Still sniffling a bit, she mumbled something like, 'Hmm … phobias. Unusual. They seem to be passé these days.' Inwardly I cringed at this judgment of being neurotically out of date. Could having an old-fashioned phobia bar one from admission to the therapeutic sancta sanctorum? Oh God!

"So Dottie and I hung around L.A. for a few weeks. I just couldn't bring myself to pack it in and head back East. Eventually, word came to me through the grapevine of this alternative group in Venice. I went there to have a look and was surprisingly impressed. I met Mike straight off, who was there with two or three of his best therapists. They pitched themselves and their enterprise well. Mike was an ex-lawyer who early in his career hit a wall, chucked it all and went in an entirely different direction, eventually leading to his founding of the center. Then in his mid-thirties, he was exceedingly handsome, with wavy black hair and a set of steel-blue eyes that looked straight into your soul. He spoke with a quiet charisma that I found slightly mesmerizing. He explained their program and their differences with Janov (without rancor), and gently asserted that I'd be much better off with them. Within a week I began my Feeling Awareness Training.

"Though following the core of Janov's basic therapeutic regimen, which revolved around 'primaling,' Mike Majors was too broadly educated to simply ignore older currents of psychodynamic therapy. So what he taught his therapists included a generous philosophical overlay of Carl Jung and a pragmatic dose of Wilhelm Reich: self-realization, traumatic birth memories, the collective unconscious, body armoring and the importance of opening the body up to 'the Reichean orgasm,' which meant basically blissing out the entire body and not just the puny, circumscribed genital area. (I never ran into anyone there who was against this.) To this end his therapists were trained not only in the 'house therapy' but in a smorgasbord of counterculture body therapies as well: bioenergetics, Rolfing, chiropractic, Alexander technique and others. I actually tried the Alexander thing myself, for about a month, to loosen up and strengthen my lower-back muscles, which had often betrayed me. I remember it as a rather gentle manipulation of muscles and joints by the therapist, in my case a very voluptuous young woman in tight leotards—Judith something or other. I lay on a massage table on my back while she variously raised, lowered and bent each leg in turn, telling me as she did so how similar my build was to that of Muhammed Ali. To avoid embarrassment, I did my best to concentrate on my last tax return."

"I hope this sordid tale at least has a happy ending," the man indulged himself.

"Never mind," I reproved him. "… But the Holy Grail at the FAC (Feeling Awareness Center) was the primal, Janov's signal invention, or rather discovery, since he is said to have stumbled on this uniquely healing release of feeling-memory while observing the deep abreaction of a young boy patient. Everything at the FAC was aimed at getting some thirty or so of us patients, all lying on mattresses and screaming our bloody heads off, to experience a primal. It was always a scene of 'controlled chaos,' as Mike called it. The building was this huge ex-photography studio with an enormous central space comparable to a gymnasium. The room was dimly lit and thickly carpeted but otherwise virtually bare except for the many single-bed mattresses spread all around the floor in no particular order. You'd report in at 7 p.m., strip down to your skivvies (both sexes), lie down on your back on a mattress, bend your legs and do a few minutes of deep abdominal breathing (to aid in bringing up feelings). Then you'd simply 'go with' whatever came up: anger at Mommy, Daddy, boss, husband; fear of co-worker or neighbor; sadness over death of dog—whatever. A crew of therapists would work the room, flitting from mattress to mattress as needed, helping one, then another, then the next, to 'get to their feelings.' Once a patient struck emotional gold, they'd usually move on to another mattress. The main thing was to get as deeply as possible into the expression of that feeling, to become one with it, in the hope that it might lead to that *summum bonum*, the Primal, that precious release of ur-feeling, invariably tied to some painful experience of early childhood. So you just 'primaled' your way to mental health."

" Of course, we now know that sheer emotional ventilation in and of itself is not profoundly healing or transformative. In fact, it can even be dangerous for some ..."

"Yes, yes, I know, and, with all its sincere efforts to uphold standards of honesty and integrity, there were certainly a number of oddballs always skulking around the FAC. (There was one woman there in her fifties who spoke in a basso profundo whiskey voice and wore absurdly cut-off jeans shorts, and who constantly professed a ravenous passion for Jewish men. She thought I was one, a notion of which I hastened to disabuse her.) But I must take issue with your characterization of the therapy as sheer emotionalizing. There was always an attempt to link feelings with early experience, to realize a total noetic-affective gestalt, so to speak; it was ultimately a deep, organic understanding that was seen to be healing. If you're going to critique the therapy, I think you have to do it on its own terms. And believe me, I hold no particular brief in its favor. While I don't regret having done it—it *was* an adventure—I'm at a loss to say whether it did me any real good. I think I left even more depressed than when I arrived …

"… Oh yeah, don't let me forget the epilog chapter to my little picaresque tale, California style. The last in the amalgam of mind and body therapies I sampled at the FAC was Scientology. For about the final six weeks of my program, I went 'on the cans,' as they say in the patois of L. Ron Hubbard's 'science of the mind.' The cans are two little metal cylinders that look like Del Monte tomato sauce cans, minus the labels, and are held by the client, one in each hand, and connected by wires to a galvanometer that's read by an 'auditor.' The auditor runs you through endless lists of prepared questions on various traumas from early life with the aim of 'clearing' the repressed emotional charges, called 'engrams,' from the mind. Apparently the meter, in monitoring fluctuations in the electric current in the client's hands as the questions are put to him, tells the auditor something about the emotional charge a given trauma still has for the client.

"Anyway, it was an optional, tying-up-loose-ends sort of thing my personal therapist, Bobby, recommended to me. Bobby also audited me himself. At the end he paraded me around the place as a sort of model client, crowing to his therapist cronies that I had actually achieved something called 'a grade 4 release.' I had no idea what that meant. I only know I found the whole business unimaginably tedious and felt no different as a result of it.

"The only thing I found even vaguely interesting about Scientology was its dark, if brief, history at the FAC. It seems Tina Eberhard, Mike's associate at the center and longtime girlfriend, was in fact a refugee from the L.A. Scientology establishment, after having climbed her way high into its upper echelons, then becoming disenchanted with it and finally bolting—apparently not an easy thing to do. The thing was, she smuggled out with her many of the organization's top-secret 'run-downs' (lists of questions) and techniques and incorporated them into the FAC curriculum. According to her and Mike, no one in the L.A. Scientology organization was aware of this, and they urged on all of us at the Center the need to keep our mouths shut about it. One secret society pilfering the secrets of another. How cloak-and-dagger can you get? To bring home his point, Mike took pains to inform us in lurid detail that L. Ron, the founder of Scientology, was a madman sitting on his yacht somewhere in the Mediterranean, ready to dispatch his goons to any venue on the planet where the interests of his 'church' were threatened. So mum was the word."

Dr. P. sat there, wearing the satisfied expression of someone who had just been told a good story. However, being the highly intelligent, sensitive man he was, he had also been listening with the discriminating ear of the therapist: "Fascinating. And you lived to tell the tale … I wonder if I could just roll the tape back a ways for a moment; I was struck by something you said near the beginning of your story. You wondered, during the interview with Vivian Janov, whether your out-of-date phobia might possibly—how did you put it—'*bar*' you from admission to the therapeutic sancta sanctorum. There again, you see, we have the barred door, only in this instance you're on the *outside* of it wanting *in*, in precise counterpoint to the situation in your dream. Perhaps you're as afraid of missing out on the analysis (if you quit and return to the 'seedy outside world') as you are of committing to it. A profound conflict that, but it does seem to be where you stand at this juncture. It's reflected, as we observed earlier, in your mood of tedium and virtual paralysis—the sense that nothing's moving, here or in your life.

"We simply have to hang in there and keep at it until, one day, we find you've moved the leg that's clinging to the wheel's rim to its hub."

"Well, I'm not going anywhere," I said.

"Yes, that's just the point, isn't it?"

(11) October 2004: The Rules of the Game

It seems my building on campus is being gutted and all faculty are being moved to another location. I can't find my book bag and other incidentals and wind up getting left behind. Once outside on the quad, I run into my old German professor from college, Dr. Condoyannis, and we fall into a discussion of C.F. Meyer, the Swiss realist writer who is one of my research interests. Dr. C. seems to know so much more than I do and, in fact, shows frustration with my deficient knowledge, for example, of the complex relationship between Meyer and baseball (yes, baseball!). Just then I notice about a dozen girl scouts standing nearby and listening to our conversation, or, more precisely, to Dr. C. as he exposes my ignorance. Growing angry, I tell him to move away from them so as to continue the conversation in private. Once off by ourselves, I upbraid him for not being sensitive to matters of confidentiality.

I ask him how it is he knows so much about Meyer. Has he researched the subject? (I'd feel so much better if he has.) He says yes. I ask why. He answers, "I thought I could learn about myself through him. Also, I was hoping I could use his works to study social issues like civil rights." This bothers me a little because such matters don't particularly interest me intellectually. Just then, Dr. C's whole appearance—looks, manner and speech—morphs into a kind of avuncular informality. He now looks like a balding, qvetching, though still highly intelligent, Jewish professor. He prattles on about C.F. Meyer and baseball, but now the chat is much more casual and my sense is that we are much closer to being equals, although he's still superior in knowledge.

"Looks like today's going to be an interesting session," Dr. P. smiled, rubbing his hands in anticipation.

"How so?" I asked, intrigued by this response.

"All in good time," he answered with irritating opacity. It was, in any case, already an interesting session for me the moment I entered the premises—and this on two counts. One was that Dr. P. had just moved quarters from the rented suite we'd been meeting in up to then to the basement of his home in Eastwood, on the north side of Syracuse, and this was our first session in the new venue. October, with its mild weather, was the ideal time for such a move. The change—probably intended to economize: he kept a second office in Oswego—was certainly salutary for me, as the basement, in contrast to the drab office building, was enchanting. It had all the charm, all the intellectual and aesthetic stimulation, the office lacked: there were books everywhere, not only decorating every wall ceiling to floor, but also in piles on desks and tables and even the floor. And not only his professional library, but sections on literature, history, art, religion, philosophy and language. Here the evidence abounded for my long-held suspicion that the good doctor was, in fact, a genuine polymath. He knew a lot about almost everything. Next to many of the books, in and around and under them, were sheaves of paper covered with word-processed text—some sheaves thinner and some thicker, some even of book-thickness. These were unpublished articles and monographs authored by the man himself. When I asked him what he intended to do with them, he said, "Nothing special. Maybe somebody will organize and publish them as my collected papers after I'm gone. It doesn't really concern me." Paintings, mostly copies, filled the limited available wall space:

a Jackson Pollock here, an Edward Hopper there, a few portraits of intellectual heroes (William James, Freud, Nietzsche) interspersed among them. Also busts and statuettes, brass Buddhas, Russian orthodox iconography, and other religious arcana I didn't recognize, not to mention replicas of alchemical vessels and glyphs on parchment scrolls. As a kind of underground sanctuary, it all combined to give me a thrilling sense of having passed through the gates of the collective unconscious itself, as if from then on he and I would be operating from *within* it, not just talking *about* it.

The other note of interest concerned a change in the man himself, or at least in his physical appearance. After a moment of puzzlement over 'something new and different' about him, it suddenly struck me that he had tinted his beard, now fully grown, jet black. This gave his already penetrating visage an aspect bordering on ferocity, not unlike those photos of a middle-aged Karl Marx at the end of a long day toiling in the dusty archives of the British Museum. In Dr. P.'s case the 'ferocity' was, thank God, leavened by his unfailing readiness to laugh or smile. Needless to say, I couldn't let this rare opportunity to tease him slip by, so I affected a quizzical expression as I carefully eyed him, mumbling things like, "There's something … What the … Is it possible? …" and so on until he caught on to my ruse and averred jauntily, "Just freshening things up a bit. Nothing wrong with that. New digs, new beard. The one celebrates the other."

"My congratulations!" I said, now feigning sincerity. "Who says a spiritual man has to be oblivious to his own appearance? These days, hair-shirt austerity as a sign of spirituality is as phony as a three-dollar bill. I'm partial to the Buddhist concept of the Middle Path myself—you know, indulge in any pleasure or creature comfort you like, as long as you don't get attached. The young Krishnamurti himself was said to be especially fond of London tailors and owned several suits made of their finest fabrics."

Dr. P. merely smiled wryly at my joking pretense, and then rolled his eyes as if to indicate it was time to move on. I prepared to do so, reluctantly, as I would have been more than happy to spend the whole hour kibitzing with him. As far as the analysis was concerned, I continued to feel mired in a swamp of ennui. I'd given up hope of things ever being any different. Hope was a burden I was tired of carrying. No matter how many dreams we examined, whatever twisted structure underlay my persistent moods of guilt and self-loathing seemed to remain intact, all unaffected by the diligent effort we were making. Again and again I complained to the man of this sense of stagnation, and each time he would reassure me that unconscious processes had been set in motion that, in the fullness of time, would bear fruit. It became like a ritualized call and response: "Dominus vobiscum … Et cum spiritu tuo … I'm sinking into the swamp … Just hang in there …"

And so I welcomed even minor alterations in our routine: the new basement consulting room with all its intellectual distractions, even the new and shiny black beard. But of course I knew these changes were merely cosmetic and that their stimulation would quickly wear off, revealing me to be still stuck in the same old same old. That's why I perked up when Dr. P. responded to my dream narrative by enthusing, however tongue-in-cheek, over "an interesting session" to follow. I hadn't a clue as to what made him say that, but I knew

I was ready for something—anything—interesting, even if it meant, as I suspected it did, rough sailing for me. (It seems boredom can become a powerful motivation to "get on with it" in analysis.)

"I don't see anything particularly compelling about this dream, certainly nothing that would move you to predict 'an interesting session,'" I said airily. (I was, of course, baiting him. Would he bite?)

"Is that so?" he responded, drawing out the "sooo" hyperbolically. (He didn't.)

"Yeah, that's sooo. I'm switching offices on campus and I run into my old professor from undergraduate days. We talk about C.F. Meyer. He turns into an old *jiddischer Vater* and we finish our pleasant chat. Where's the momentous significance?"

"How profoundly subtle repression can be," he said in wonder. "Do you realize that your perfunctory summary of the dream entirely omitted mention of the crucial conflict it expressed, a conflict you fully elaborated in your narrative at the top of the hour?"

"Conflict? What conflict?" I asked, annoyed. "... Oh, you mean when Dr. Condoyannis criticizes me for deficiencies in my knowledge of Meyer?"

"You're close, but your focus is too narrow. Take a wide shot, as they say on a movie set, a context shot. You and your old professor are not chatting in a vacuum, are you?"

"No, no, we're not; some girl scouts are nearby listening in. In fact, that's what causes the problem, I guess, more than the criticism itself; it's that he's sort of letting a third party in on a professional exchange between us that should really be confidential. Is that it?"

"That's the *beginning* of it," Dr. P. emphasized. "But we still have a ways to go; after all, what does all that have to do with anything? What's it mean?"

"I don't know … Dr. Condoyannis was my first German professor in college. In fact, I had him for Russian too. I must've taken close to ten courses with the man. And what a strange bird he was. A man almost totally without humor, in or out of class, with this impregnable façade of formality. He strode into class at the top of the hour, gave us our lesson and strode out at the end. No more, no less. He was a small, impeccably dressed man and spoke in a rich, sensuous baritone, but always only in a low drone, entirely without inflection. I often thought, what a waste of a great voice. But his command of languages was unimpeachable. His research was mostly in textbooks and dictionaries, the practical, applied side of linguistic scholarship. Would you believe, he actually composed a Russian-English science dictionary! Lists, taxonomies, definitions—that sort of thing was his forte. I always felt imaginative literature was an utterly foreign body to him; he hadn't the slightest idea what to do with all those messy German stories, plays and poems, not to mention us messy students. So he'd hide, figuratively, behind a note-covered bluebook whose contents he would drone to us—almost like a bored priest chanting High Mass—or, more often, simply read the German text and translate.

"I often wondered about his personal life, probably for the very reason that he kept it so hermetically sealed off from us. Was he married? Did he have kids? (Unimaginable.) What did he do in his spare time, work on revising his dictionaries? Did he wear the ever-present suit and tie in the privacy of his own home? …"

"Interesting, to a psychologist at least," Dr. P. said. "A man who becomes very interesting by virtue of being strikingly *un*interesting. It's a neat paradox, sort of parallel to the situation of the writer J.D. Salinger, who has become famous (some would say 'infamous') for insisting on total anonymity. The attempt to erase oneself always draws attention ... But back to the dream. Let me ask you: is there anything about this particular uneasy—indeed, upsetting—situation in the dream, you and Dr. C., with the girl scouts getting an earful, that reminds you of anything that's come up in recent weeks?"

"'Come up?'—you mean *here*?"

"Yes."

"Well, I certainly haven't run into any girl scouts around here—or any other third parties," I said. It was the best quip I could come up with. I always felt uneasy when Dr. P. asked me that type of question, a question of the recall of recent events, especially those comprising interactions between us. I always felt put on the spot, like a student in class who hadn't done the reading assignment, and my almost instinctual response was to crack wise. At the same time, I was, at this point in the analytic process, getting better at catching myself using wit and humor to deflect difficult issues, so, eager as I was to make anything resembling progress, I stopped and considered his question carefully: "Well, if it's come up here, it must involve ... *you*, which, I suppose, would make Dr. C. in the dream an imago of *you*. Am I way off here?"

"No, quite the contrary—in fact, I wonder at your seeming reluctance to consider the possibility," he responded, again making me uneasy and somewhat defensive.

"*Am* I being reluctant? Or is it just that I honestly see

almost no resemblance between you and Dr. C. Come on, you're entirely different types! In fact, I would almost call him the 'anti-Dr. P.'"

"Hmm, interesting: Dr. C. … Dr. P. … Dr. C.P., and that would be me: Charles Purper."

"Oh, that's clever all right, but really now, it's no more than a textbook example of what my Jesuit philosophy professors back in college used to call 'casuistry' (they were experts at it themselves): the subtle manipulation of facts to produce a specious argument." I only half believed what I was saying. It was more a hope or a wish. But why was I so reluctant to go with him on this? Why did it bother me if the conversation in the dream was really between him and me. Sure, it did contain disagreement and acrimony but so had any number of actual exchanges between us right from the start, including this one. We'd had more than our fair share of verbal confrontations, including several in which I had even questioned the validity of what we were doing. In fact, he knew very well I *still* wasn't entirely convinced. So what unpalatable truth could lie hidden in this dream conversation that I didn't want to look at?

"Casuistry, is it now? … Is it really such a stretch to see Dr. C. as a cover for me? An imago in dreams is quite often a phantastic distortion of the real person, so the element of contrast certainly doesn't rule it out—on the contrary, the contrast, as a sort of differential symmetry, can actually point to it. And if you look closely, there *are* similarities between us: the title 'doctor,' with you as student/client; the teacher's corrective criticism: what patient doesn't at times feel criticized by his therapist? And the not-at-all trivial fact of a shift in venue: you run into Dr. C., literally, as you're moving to another office;

and, of course, you and I are meeting here today in this basement office for the first time."

"But what possible significance could a change of location have? Doesn't my unconscious have better things to worry about?" The quipster was back again in full force.

"That question brings me back to my own question of a moment ago: can you think of anything that's come up in a session recently that might throw light on the dream triangle of you, Dr. C. and the girl scouts?"

"For the life of me, I can't think of anything ..."

"Do you remember what we talked about last week?"

"Last week ... I'm embarrassed to say ... well, I don't think we did any dream analysis, since, if memory serves, I didn't bring a dream."

"That's right, you didn't."

"I think we talked about ... the analysis itself ... I was voicing my usual complaints and that, as I remember, led to a discussion of the parameters, er ... the framework in which analysis occurs. What are the optimal conditions for conducting an analysis—that sort of thing ... Oh yeah, you mentioned someone, a colleague I think, who's come up with a list of conditions that should always be firmly in place throughout the course of an analysis—yes, that's right, 'the rules of the game,' so to speak. Was it Long, Langley—something like that? ..."

"Langs, Robert Langs. Yes, as I mentioned last week, he's developed these eight or nine ground rules or frame conditions for analysis[27] based on extensive research in the area of unconscious motivation, particularly the aspect of discrepancy, and sometimes even conflict, between the conscious and unconscious points of view on the optimal conditions for therapy—"

"—Yes, you said he believes the unconscious viewpoint is deeper and wiser than the conscious and is generally to be adhered to in establishing boundaries for therapy. He thinks conscious judgments are superficial and mainly concerned with short-term gains, often to the detriment or even total sabotaging of the therapeutic process … So, what about it? …"

And, of course, just as I put this question, the answer popped onto my mental screen like the opening of a surprise e-mail, and I understood immediately and fully the reason for all of Dr. P.'s leading questions as well as the reason for all my uneasiness about the direction of our discussion. "Oh … ," I half moaned, "so you think the dream is telling me I ought to complain about the way you're running therapy, based on the way I rebuke your imago, Dr. C., in the dream for his indiscretion?"

"Well," Dr. P. answered evenly, "I think it's worth considering, don't you?"

"I don't know. This is awkward, to say the least. How could I possibly know whether you're sailing a tight ship here? I mean, certainly nothing screams out at me; there's no obvious incompetence or abuse; and besides, I'm not trained to judge such …"

"No, of course you're not, and I'm not asking you to. What I *am* asking is that you consider carefully whether your unconscious may not be telling you, through the dream, that I'm breaching certain ground rules here that *it* sees as in your best interest for the analysis. Am I screwing up from *its* standpoint? … Let's put it this way, I'm asking you straight out, are you getting any sense that I'm failing you in any way?"

What a question! I was utterly stunned by it, despite the

fact that something in me knew from the beginning that this was where the discussion was heading. Its honesty and courage were disarming, its sincere concern moving, and, not being used to such brutal candor in my dealings with even those closest to me, I didn't know what to say. How often in life does an authority figure turn the reins over to you and ask you, genuinely, to judge him? My first impulse was to reassure the good doctor that all was well, even though, in view of my by now chronic sense of stagnation, I had no idea whether this was so, just out of gratitude for his openness. This response I immediately rejected, on the grounds that his honesty demanded the like in equal measure from me, if I was up to it. So, screwing up my courage, I simply said, "Look, Dr. P., I really don't know whether you're failing me. All I know is that things seem to me to be pretty much at a standstill. Whether that indicates a problem in and of itself, or just business as usual, I don't feel able to judge. But I certainly am willing to examine the dream as a possible indication that something is wrong with the set-up, especially since I see now that that's what your leading questions were nudging me to do."

"Now you see what I meant at the start when I said today was going to be an interesting session," he chuckled.

"Seriously? You read the dream that quickly?"

"What was there to read? Teacher gets scolded by student for indiscretion. Last week I told you all about Langs and how his list of 'game rules' attempts to obviate just such liabilities of analysis. You, of course, repressed the memory of last week's discussion, which would've lit up the dream for you, until I managed to tease it out of you. It's completely understandable that you'd resist awareness of such a sensitive matter since it puts both of us on the hot seat, me for integrity and you with the burden of questioning same. But, there it is …"

"Well, since there's nothing left but to face it …" I said wearily. I had the lonely feeling I was navigating without a compass, or, more precisely, since Dr. P. *was* my compass, with an instrument the accuracy of which—for the moment at least—was not to be trusted. "Let's see, … I guess the indiscretion theme in the dream is the clearest link to Langs. I tell Dr. C. in anger he shouldn't be criticizing me within earshot of the girl scouts. Langs puts that right up front, rule number 2 or 3, as I recall from your summary. As might be expected, his insistence on privacy and confidentiality is absolute. But then, that doesn't make any sense to me: you certainly haven't exposed my 'confessions' here to any third party or parties, at least not to any I'd know about, so …"

"Easy, let's not be too hastily dismissive here," Dr. P. cautioned. "Obviously there've been no third parties here in the 'claustrum,' within earshot so to speak, but there are other ways to compromise confidentiality …"

"Well, if not here, then where? How? We have no outside contact with each other, and even if you were to speak about me indiscreetly to a third party on the outside, I'd have no way of knowing it and so no reason to be accusatory, consciously or unconsciously, right?"

"Yes, I agree, consciously anyway, but are you sure we've had no contact on the outside?"

"Well, if you're thinking about that time we ran into each other at the bookstore about a year ago, I dismiss that out of hand. Nothing even close to being 'tainted' happened."

"Agreed. That, however, is not what I'm thinking of.

This was more recent—only weeks ago, in fact."

"What?" I asked open-mouthed.

"Actually, you could almost say this outside contact was pre-arranged," he said smiling, as if ironically implying something quasi sinister.

"Come on now," I said, "you're being ridic—" and for the second time in the hour the veil of repression lifted to reveal my clear memory of a brief meeting between us during intermission at a Syracuse Symphony concert about a month earlier. Mischa Dichter had just given a rapturous performance of the Brahms *Second Piano Concerto*, and, during the break, I was strolling among the gratified listeners sipping champagne in the lobby when I spotted the good doctor leaning against a marble pillar chatting with two attractive women. One was in his age range and the other considerably younger, so I naturally took them to be his wife and daughter. Interestingly, he was correct to say the meeting was not entirely by chance, since in parting at the end of our previous session it came up that we both had tickets to the weekend concert and that, who could tell but that we just might run into each other there. Did I have a semi-conscious eye out for the man during intermission, curious to observe him in ordinary social circumstances? Perhaps, but it was certainly not a priority. In any case, I went up to him with a friendly greeting, which he returned and then introduced me to his two companions. We exchanged a few brief pleasantries and wished each other further musical enjoyment, upon which I returned to my seat.

"Oh, of course, the SSO concert last month," I gushed, slapping my forehead. "How could I forget that?" I said laughing, upon which Dr. P. raised an index finger in gentle reproof and grimaced. "But there again," I retorted, "where's the harm? It was nothing more than the briefest social exchange. Nothing even the least untoward happened."

"Again, I would ask you to slow down a bit and examine the encounter, brief as it was, a little more carefully. Are you quite sure there was nothing unseemly about it?" the doctor asked, in a way that suggested he thought there might be. And the amazing thing was that I believed I knew, albeit to my dismay, what he was getting at. Again and again, as he had by now done so often, he pulled me back ever so gently from my posture of avoidance, of a studied careless inattention, nudging me towards awareness of an unpleasant truth concealed in an otherwise banal social encounter. A truth unpleasant for both of us.

"Well, you know ..." I said, hedging, "I did come away from that moment with a kind of funny feeling."

"Funny?"

"Yes, unpleasantly so, I must admit."

"Yes ... go on."

"I just felt odd, or awkward, I think, about the way you introduced me to your companions—so much so, in fact, that I blocked out awareness of your identification of them. I still don't know who they were—or are. I assume they were your family but I don't know."

"Say more about the funny feeling, ... the awkwardness," he said, without a trace of self-consciousness, so far as I could tell.

"God—talk about awkward—*this* is awkward ... "

"I know. Just do the best you can."

"... I just had the sense—how can I put this—the sense

that the cool, formal way you introduced me put a chill on the encounter. I mean, you introduced me by name alone; you didn't offer any further information about me. I felt I was an abstraction in the eyes of the ladies and that I stood at some remove in yours. I had the feeling that this … laconic coolness on your part actually had the paradoxical effect of giving me away, so to speak, as a patient, though your conscious intention was probably the very opposite, to protect that identity … Am I going too far with this?"

"Not necessarily."

"Was this an indiscretion on your part, a 'Langsian' violation of confidentiality? I don't know. If we read the dream this way, I guess it was. But my feeling is that, even if it was, it happened ninety to ninety-five percent unconsciously in both of us. An unconscious psychodrama. So there's certainly no blame to be cast."

"No, that's right. We're not here to blame, just to understand."

"If we accept this, that makes the girl scouts in the dream stand-ins for your lady companions, I suppose. Why are they cast as girl scouts, I wonder—could it be the idea of innocent ears, tainted by—forgive me—your … 'laconic indiscretion?'"

"That sounds about right … I did have some sense of all this when it happened, but it was, well, … inarticulate, and I dropped the matter. But the unconscious, which as we know is itself interpersonal or transpersonal in its deeper ranges, obviously didn't. So when you told the dream at the top of the hour, I recognized it as an opportunity to get at that moment from your end. Actually, the whole interpretation you've laid out rings true to me, which means you've given me some homework to do, some important self-examination. But that's what we do here: we engage in dialogue and the learning is interpersonal. It's not just you under the lens, it's *us.* That's certainly the way Jung envisioned the therapeutic hour, patient and analyst engaged in a dialectic of growth, and that's another way in which he broke from Freud and the classical couch behind which the analyst sits in Olympian silence—forever a tabula rasa to the patient."

"Ah yes, the classical ideal: the analyst as blank slate, supposedly making him an ideal screen on which the patient can project and transfer all sorts of interesting things." I was expanding the doctor's point because I needed a buffer for my own next point, also unpleasantly confrontational, yet invited, as though via some synchronic magic of the unconscious, by his words. "You know," I continued, "Langs also makes a big deal of this idea of the therapist's impersonality, much like Freud himself ... and there is that sequence in the dream in which Dr. C. gives rather ample answers to my questions concerning his interest in C.F. Meyer. Dr. C. is telling me quite personal things about himself here—way out of character for someone who worked awfully hard to remain a social cipher. As I see it, he basically reveals two things: 1) that he's hoping Meyer will teach him about himself, that Meyer's writings will become a sort of framework for self-analysis (which, by the way, might make Meyer an imago of Jung [a "teacher" of yours], both men having been favorite sons of Zurich); and 2) that Meyer's works will serve as something of a primer of civil rights issues ... I must say, both revelations are sparking intense associative flashes in my mind, things that hadn't occurred to me before the session."

"By all means, let's hear about them," Dr. P. responded, with what seemed like genuine curiosity.

"Yes … Well, assuming Dr. C. *is* your imago, the first item, about self-inquiry, is really about *your* personal motives for choosing psychology as a career, the strongest of these being a desire for self-knowledge. The reason I say this is that I know Meyer, as a writer of historical fiction, to have been an astute 'depth-psychologist,' before there even was a depth psychology, at least as we know it today. This certainly strengthens the connection to Jung I just mentioned. Meyer's characters are riddled with 'neurotic' and even 'psychotic' problems: one character—female—is a transvestite with a father complex; another unconsciously projects his own religious prejudices onto others, in effect demonizing them; and a third does a 17th-century version of a psychoanalysis on still another character, a kind of proto-analysis, replete with such themes as repression, deferred action (*Nachträglichkeit*) and even the Oedipus complex. Freud himself, who often paid tribute to poets and writers—Dostoevsky and Goethe, for example—for their natural psychological insight, said in his letters to Fliess that he learned a great deal from Meyer's works. That, as I see it, makes those works something of a textbook on psychoanalysis in the dream, with you, in the guise of Dr. C., telling me something quite personal about your inner life. Now, in the context of Langs's, shall we say, … 'stodgy' rule against personal revelations by the therapist, that may seem like small potatoes, but the second revelation which follows immediately on the first turns out, I think, to be potentially more culpable: Dr. C. says he also expects Meyer's writings to teach him about issues of civil rights. Likewise a harmless, even banal, admission, you might say. But what if I tell you—and mind you, no one but I could know this—that socio-political matters such as civil rights, the oppression of minority groups, and so forth, have never particularly interested me; that whatever energy I've managed in my life to give to these problems has always been scraped together under the lash of conscience; and finally, that Dr. C.'s, i.e., *your*, expression of the nobler, selfless antithetical attitude in the dream makes me feel distinctly uneasy, in the dream, that is?—Well then, considering the fact that you've expressed your left-liberal political views here quite often, and even made a point of saying how important you believe it is to develop a sense of social justice and even become active in worthy causes, one could, it seems to me, certainly argue for a reading of the dream as an unconscious protest on my part against your attempt, intentional or not, to shape me into a little tin epigone of you. My unconscious, it seems, doesn't want me to be re-made in your image—it has its own plans, thank you very much!"

I have no idea how that syllogism managed to come out the way it did. I only know that, once I started down its labyrinthine path, I had to keep it together until it was done. I had accused the man, in a rhetorical flourish that probably concealed as much as it revealed, of telling me too much about himself, of revealing lofty values he held dear that nevertheless had the oppressive effect on me, in the therapeutic hour, of didactic impositions. I needed him to help me find my own way, not his.

His reaction was hard to read. For a man rarely at a loss for words, he seemed just that. Then again, he was probably just processing my "analysis interminable" and considering his response. I have no doubt its sense was crystal clear to him, but I'm also convinced he wasn't expecting it. From my dream narrative he had foreseen the discussion of Langs, and probably even anticipated that of the encounter at the symphony, his 'sin' against confidentiality, but this accusation of a further 'violation,' now of impersonality, had apparently blindsided him. After a long moment, he said in his patented, most endearing deadpan, "You know, Langs's rules are not graven in stone tablets. They're not the ten commandments."

"I know, I know," I hastened to agree; and I did agree. The last thing I needed was the burden of monitoring my analyst for arbitrary rules violations. My tendency towards scrupulosity was already noxious. But still, the interpretation I'd offered of Meyer had suggested itself; it was a spontaneous product of the session and therefore, by definition, worthy of serious consideration.[28] Of course, the good doctor knew this only too well. "More homework for me, I guess," he said sheepishly. "But seriously, the rule against personal revelation is not one that sits well with me, be it from the high court of Freud or Langs. It just strikes me as unnatural, especially in therapeutic relationships of long standing, as this one certainly is by now. However, that said, I would emphasize that discretion in this area is paramount, and if I have on occasion been careless in allowing my personal values to color our dialogue in even a subtly coercive way, I sincerely beg your pardon and vow to correct the tendency.

"Not to belabor the matter," he said, apparently as an afterthought, "but there may well be good reason in Langs's particular case for favoring the spirit over the letter of the law. I actually knew him years ago. In fact, I studied under him at the Lenox Hill Psychotherapy Program in New York City.

He was one tough son-of-a-gun, I can tell you, and he did not suffer fools gladly. No one thought he was an easy man to get along with. On the other hand, everything he's ever said, presented or written implies he has an essential fear of death, a fear that some say filtered into his scholarship—which by the way is prodigious. One might cite as an example this very rule insisting on the therapist's impersonality. It's easy to see how a therapist in thrall to a fear of death might come to regard any self-disclosure to a patient as a window of vulnerability. To be known by the patient is to be vulnerable; better to remain opaque. By this reasoning, for Langs each successful therapeutic outcome, resulting from strict adherence to the rules of the game, represents, unconsciously of course, another triumph over death … As Jung said, there's no purely objective research, even in science; there's always a vital strain of subjective value that leaches into the factual observations and blends with them."

"Did anyone ever have the guts to suggest this interpretation to Langs himself?" I asked.

"Thank God, there was no need," Dr. P. snorted. "It was *his* interpretation to begin with."

Shaking my head in amazement, I got up to leave. Halfway up the stairs, Dr. P. called out after me, "Ach ja, Herr Professor, remember to give your old, qvetching Jewish uncle my best regards next time you see him. Now there's a man after my own heart—born a blank slate, dies an open book. Ask him why he showed up just when you happened to be moving your office."

(12) May 2005: The Cell

It's between twilight and darkness at the end of a beautiful day. I find myself standing on a corner of the town square in the village of Oxford, New York, wondering how I got there from Hoboken, where I apparently still live with my family. (It's not clear which *family, the one of origin, my current one, or both.) Although I have many relatives, particularly cousins, in and around Oxford, none of them seem to be at home just then. My sense is they're all away on vacation. My problem is how to get back home to Hoboken, especially since I have no car. I take out my cell phone and, fumbling with it in the deepening darkness, finally manage to call my mother's number. However, my young son Danny, age about five or six here (twenty-two in reality), picks up the phone. I talk to him for a minute and ask him to "put Mom on." He puts the phone down and I wait—and wait. Mom never comes. Finally, I shout into the phone in frustration and close it up, now even more concerned about getting home. But then it occurs to me to wonder why it's so important to contact her anyway. After all, what can she really do to help? …*

"… She who?"

"Excuse me?"

"Exactly who is it that can't help?" he asked, as if he hadn't been paying attention. Of course, I knew well by then that such a question usually meant just the opposite: *I* hadn't been paying attention. "You began by saying you'd placed a call to your mother. Then you tell your son to put 'Mom' on, which sounds as if you're asking for *his* mother, i.e., your wife.

Finally, you say, 'Mom never comes,' which again sounds like *your* mother. Whom are you asking for help? Whom are you trying to reach?"

Now, it wouldn't be accurate to say Dr. P.'s question came as a complete surprise. Certainly I'd had a vague, inchoate sense of confusion, even ambiguity, surrounding the identity of "Mom" in the dream, and yet, in the two days since I'd had it, during which I'd mulled it over quite a bit, this sense had somehow never reached a threshold of awareness that would have caused me to focus on it and realize it to be the key to an insightful interpretation. Indeed, this very consideration led me to the secondary or meta-insight that it's almost impossible to psychoanalyze oneself: there are just too many blind spots, avoidances, slight, moderate and profound repressions and the like to get very far. Man's capacity for self-deception is, literally, mind-numbing. There's no doing without that neutral, yet attentive and sympathetic other party to keep one on course. In spite of my continuing, by now resigned, feeling of futility about the analysis in general, I couldn't help also feeling a deep gratitude to the good doctor for his unfailing alertness to the revealing contradictions coming from my side of the dialogue. In fact, I felt moved to tell him so just then, and I did. I told him just this astute attentiveness on his part, along with the frequent spot-on brilliance of his *aperçus*, had a salutary effect on my depressing sense of stagnation. Maybe something good was happening after all. But whether I was getting anywhere or not, he at least knew me, and my style of avoidance, better than I did. And he did seem to appreciate my expression of gratitude; after all, he was in a very real sense carrying my sack of rocks along with me, and no doubt needed occasional encouragement just as I did.

"So, you think the dream is all about the confusion over who 'Mom' is, eh?"

"I don't know. I just asked a question," he said laconically. So much for compliments, I thought. The man is not to be plied by the sweet ghee of words. "All right," I said, "let's assume it is and see where it takes us. I had an inkling anyway; you just crystallized it."

"Fine."

"I know that individual identities can be fluid in dreams, just like all other conceptual categories. Didn't Freud say something to the effect that the only word the unconscious does not recognize is 'no,' that it's the only realm where the law of non-contradiction does not apply? Things there can be both true and false, good and evil, beautiful and hideous, and so on?"

"Quite right."

"Well, that seems to be the case in my dream: 'Mom' is a shifting identity. As you so astutely noted, I refer to 'Mom' three times in fairly rapid sequence: first it's mine, then Danny's, and finally mine again."

"What do you make of that?"

"Whatever else it may mean, the dream is certainly telling me that deep down I make no sharp distinction between my wife and my mother, that I, in effect, married my mother."

"You're far from being alone on that count, Herr Professor Oedipus," he reassured me. "The men of whom that is not true are few and far between. Transference, as a psychological phenomenon, is not confined to psychotherapy. Whenever the buttons of repression are pressed, we all unconsciously make others—mates, friends, relatives, associates, bosses—into parents. And we do it over and over again, which makes it what analysis calls a 'repetition compulsion,' an attempt, without end, to work out unfinished business from early life. Of course, since it's all going on unconsciously, we never understand why certain people cause us so much misery and why we feel compelled to react to them the way we do. What's worse, we're doomed to keep enacting the same painful scenarios unless we're fortunate enough to come across analysis or some equivalent liberating process. That currently popular definition of madness—doing the same thing over and over and each time expecting a different result—would seem to apply here, except that then we'd have to classify most of humanity as mad. (Then again, if the shoe fits …) Only through analysis or a bolt of psychospiritual lightning can we clearly see what we've been up to and, as Jung says, withdraw the projection. Either way, consciously or not, the day of reckoning does come in any marriage. Those with some self-awareness certainly have a leg up on those who remain asleep in any attempt to recast the relationship on firmer ground.

"But I digress. The point here, as I think you already recognize, is that this very moment is an invaluable opportunity for you to, shall we say, up the reality quotient of your own marriage."

"*My* marriage? But I've been married for over thirty years. I've already had a dozen 'days of reckoning.' How many more could there be in the pipeline, for God's sake!"

"How many sessions does it take to cure a neurosis?" he said, answering my question with his own. "How many hours on the *zafu* to reach Enlightenment? Such things are imponderable. It's best not to ask; just keep trekking until the question becomes irrelevant. Actually, that irrelevancy is the answer."

I pondered that for a moment and then turned my thoughts to the dream. "I guess my attempt to reach my Mom on the phone is transparent enough, especially in view of the fact that I fail to do so. It's clear by now that this kind of 'Mom dream,' where I can't make contact with her and become anxious, goes back to the earliest times. How often have we talked here about my Mom's inability to breast-feed me in infancy and the terrible colic I had during the first six months, until I was finally brought to a specialist who simply changed my formula and resolved the issue? And how depressed my Mom was during that period, not only because of the post-partum thing but also the terrible feelings of guilt and failure she must've struggled with from judging herself an inadequate mother. She told me I did nothing but cry ferociously in those early months, which, as it turned out, was inevitable since I was starving ... Jesus, she must've wanted to throw me out the window, an urge for which she also must've crucified herself, God-fearing Catholic that she was.

"Anyway, that was the bleak situation into which I was *geworfen,* as Heidegger might say:[29] a mother crushed by depression and guilt, almost to the point of paralysis; and you can probably throw suppressed rage into the mix: after all, who else but little ol' screaming me-me was doing all this to her? ... The complete absence of what we'd today call 'a support system' to help her through it (her doctor prescribed long walks!); no mental-health professional at the ready with a Xanax or Valium prescription, to at least take the edge off it for her; alone together in an empty flat, my father at work, my sister not yet born, listening, the two of us, to Martin Block's *Make-Believe Ballroom* show every morning on the radio. I can still remember the lead-in theme song: 'It's *Make-Believe Ballroom* time … so come on in and …' It's possible that that song, with its cool swing rhythm, is my earliest memory.

"Anyway, I guess anxiety and frustration dreams over my inability to reach my Mom, to connect with her—as here by phone—show how profound the impact of those early months must have been. It's still very much here inside me at sixty-three."

"Yes, it is," he seconded, "and note also that the lack of contact, the disconnect, affected you on two levels, the physical and the emotional. You weren't getting much of either kind of nourishment, which breast-feeding, by its very nature, provides in full. And even though your Mom no doubt did her level best to care for you, those dark feelings that afflicted her couldn't help but transfer themselves to you in some measure, infants being the super-sensitive little creatures they are. Studies show that children, especially infants, raised by depressed parents are, as adults, far more vulnerable to it themselves than others."

"You know," I said plaintively, "I can commiserate with my Mom as I think back on her situation in my infancy: the isolation, and the depression exacerbated by it, the helplessness, the confusion … the despair, but I must confess it's more an intellectual commiseration than anything from the heart … Even as I imagine those sad circumstances here with you, the feeling in me at the center of it all is anger … rage, even. Yeah, I know, she couldn't help it, she was a victim herself, and all the other wise counsel I get from my sister, not to mention my own conscience … But none of that touches the anger I feel for having been deprived of the chance to meet the world on fair terms (Yeah, right: what's 'fair,' what's 'normal?' But none of that matters to the anger!). I feel as if I've been playing catch-up my whole life … Damn it, we ought to live in a utopia in which no one is allowed to become a parent until they've been given a seal of approval by a wise council of elders!" And as I said that, with a conviction made fierce by my own anger, I happened to catch the look of pained incredulity on Dr. P.'s face, his deeply democratic soul offended by the elitist arrogance I had imbibed from Goethe and Hesse, but which my American half, of course, took with a grain of salt. That look, making me aware as it did of the absurdity of my rant, caused me to burst into laughter that was probably even more frightening than the anger preceding it.

Realizing, finally, that I'd come to my senses, the good doctor gave a faint smile and explained, "I know how confusing, how disorienting, such feelings can be because it's a case of your ego-ideal being in conflict with your instincts: you know up here," he said, pointing to his brow, "how horrendous your mother's circumstances were and that the only rational response to them is compassion for her; but, having been at the other end of that short stick, your anger is blocking that response. You must understand that particular emotional inhibition clearly and not beat yourself up over it. On the contrary, have the courage to feel the rage in its full force, right this moment as you're experiencing it; let it fill your body and have its inning in the game, so to speak, without your worrying about the right or the wrong of it, anymore than an infant would that knows only what it needs. (You don't need to actually *do* anything; just let the tendrils of your mind caress the feeling.) Once it's run its course, you'll find yourself feeling the compassion with no effort at all. There's really no other way …

"… But back to the theme of 'Mom's' ambiguous identity in the dream. You've already detected a mingling of Mom and Dottie. Let's look at that—"

"—No sir, *you* detected that. I 'inkled' it but no more than that. All I did was draw the rather obvious conclusion that I married my mother, which, by the logic of psychoanalysis, means that at least part of my attachment to Dottie, even after thirty years, is an effort to make a kind of contact with her that is doomed to failure, no?"

"How do you mean?"

"Well, the mere fact that my asking to speak with *Danny's* Mom in the dream is sandwiched by two mentions of *my* Mom strongly suggests it's my own Mom I'm really trying to get in touch with, and that my 'mistaken' request to speak with Danny's Mom—my wife—is my unconscious' way of lowering the veil on the transference. An ostensible slip of the tongue reveals the truth … And you know, I do feel a strong leaning towards such a view, not only on account of the dream but also on the basis of certain subtle behavioral patterns I've observed in myself over the course of my marriage, tiny reactions to things Dottie would say, things that would press my buttons. These reactions would be almost wholly internal, with just the barest flinching or facial twitch as evidence of them. Maybe she'd tell me I wasn't doing enough around the house—this would be when the kids were little and she was terribly overworked—and I'd find myself instinctively grasping for arguments in my own defense. It was almost as if I were watching myself acting out this robotic behavior, and I'd be reminded of the same lame attempts at self-justification I'd tried, in vain, on my mother oh so long ago, and I'd feel the raw manipulative power of both women over me. In those moments I'd feel directly the dead weight of my own conditioning."

"And were you able to take the next step and feel the paradox of liberation from that conditioning; in the very seeing of it did you feel free of it?" he asked.

"Sorry, I can't give you a ringing endorsement of the truth of that paradox, much as I'd like to. What I *can* say is that, in seeing it, I was sometimes able at least to consider Dottie's complaint a bit more objectively, on its own merits, rather than as something I absolutely had to prove wrong like a lawyer arguing a case."

"No small achievement there," he said. "In fact, you should regard such incidents as momentary deepenings of consciousness. They, along with the kind of dream analysis we're doing here, will, in time, evolve into a healthy differentiation of these two most important women in your life. Taking Dottie's complaints 'on their own merits,' as you put it, amounts to taking *Dottie* on *her* own merits, and less and less as a projected imago of your mother. Less and less will you try to get from Dottie what only your mother could have given you. I would even say the dream, in lifting the veil of transference, however tentatively, is an important step for you in the process of that differentiation.

"But we're far from done with this dream, I think. What else can you 'unpack' from it, as the literary critics put it?"

"Hmm … I guess what strikes me is that the entire discussion up to now has focused on my relationship with a person—or person*s*—who are not even present in the dream: my Mom and/or Dottie. But little Danny *is* there, and obviously there for a reason. I'm sure it's no accident that he, and no one else, picks up the phone, don't you think?"

"I do, indeed," Dr. P. answered, cuing me to go on.

"I …don't … know, … nothing in particular occurs to me. My relationship with Danny has always been good, better than that even. I am crazy about the kid, but there's no denying he does sharply disappoint me in the dream. I know he's only six or so, but at six Danny certainly would've had no trouble calling someone to the phone, or going and fetching them … "

"Who is it he fails to fetch?" Dr. P. asked.

"What? … What do you mean? We've just been through all that. It's my mother, or his mother, or both."

"Is that all there is to it?"

"I don't follow you. We just discussed the transference of identities, and you agreed that … Oh, wait, … I get it," I said, slumping a little and feeling suddenly crestfallen. "If Dottie isn't Dottie, or at least not *just* Dottie, in the dream, then maybe Danny isn't just Danny either … Ohhh no, it must be the child … the child who's always been a blank slate to me, with Danny filling in the blank. And that would make his Mom Nicole, and that would explain my anger at 'Danny' in a way I don't like. No, I don't like it at all."

"I don't understand."

"Isn't it obvious? I'm angry at 'Danny'—the child—for being in the way, for aborting the connection to … to … well, hold on … it's certainly not Nicole, whom I never really loved, so it must be … my Mom! Again my Mom at the bottom of it. The child in the way of my connection to my Mom … Yes, it does make a weird kind of sense. I remember feeling so rotten just after I'd broken off with Nicole … oh yeah, on the *phone,* if you'll recall. It was that same Christmas vacation and I was staying at my parents' house, and I kept feeling this demonic urge, almost a compulsion, to confess the whole business to my Mom, so that somehow she could wash away the guilt and shame … make it all right. I knew perfectly well there was nothing in reality she could do for me, that it only would've upset her terribly, so I knew I had to keep my mouth shut."

"Yes, the 'adult you' knew that, but the infant was still trying to get fed, to be nourished and comforted—to be loved. Even as a grown man, you were feeling the very same desperation you suffered then, in the earliest years of life, utterly dependent on a mother who couldn't respond, at least not the way you needed her to. And since the root experience was deeply repressed, with probably only somatic memory 'recording' the first months, the feelings felt demonic to you, totally out of control. That's why you felt driven to seek love and forgiveness from mother for the 'bad thing' you had done, just as you no doubt felt responsible for how bad she felt in those early years."

I was caught up in a swirl of emotion—anxiety, guilt, sadness, longing; yet also, in the midst of it all, there was a sense of connection, of being in touch, not, to be sure, with any font of maternal balsam, but at least with my own pain, and this part of it was bracing. I felt some degree of integration, even within the chaos, and allowed myself to bask in it.

"I was struck," the doctor continued, "by a word you used when you were describing your anger in the dream towards the child for being in the way. You said he was 'aborting the connection' to mother …"

"Ah, … I see what you're implying. You think I'm disguising a wish I harbored to abort Nicole's child by an act of reversal, a projection of responsibility for the abortion onto its object?"

"Well?"

"I don't know. I suppose it's possible. It would certainly follow from my anger towards 'Danny': a wish to get rid of him for being evidence of the 'sin' disconnecting me from Mom … the 'evil fruit' of illicit sex; and it would also help to account for the outsized load of guilt I've been carrying for so long … Talk about a no-win situation: If I acknowledge the child, my real Mom condemns me; if I get rid of it, my inner Mom does—inner Mom being the one-two punch of mother and Holy Mother the Church. Maybe what actually did happen, my abandonment of the child, along with his mother, was a compromise between abortion and acknowledgment."

"Could be, but remember, you did offer to marry Nicole."

"Yes, I did, but my heart wasn't in it."

"We can't really help what's in our hearts, can we; we can only control our behavior, and not always even that," Dr. P. consoled.

We sat in silence for a long moment, letting what had just transpired vibrate between us. I felt, palpably, the truth of the old saw that a burden shared is a burden halved, and was grateful. "You know," I finally said, "it just strikes me that three women are wrapped up in the little word 'Mom' in this dream: Dottie, Nicole and my mother. I know that, for psychoanalysis, dreams are supposed to be highly condensed, but this is ridiculous."

"Yes," Dr. P. nodded, "condensed, and sometimes even archaeologically so."

"What do you mean?"

" In his late essay, *Civilization and its Discontents,* Freud compares the psyche to an ancient city that's still extant, like Rome. He says that, just as a skilled archaeologist can see traces of several historically successive phases of the city as he digs, all superimposed on each other, so too will an analysand inevitably come to recognize many of the significant others of adult life as mother or father imagos all superimposed over the parental prototype. Each new woman, or man, who comes along is a new layer or stratum that embeds itself in the succession of images grounded in the original. Hence Dottie is Nicole is mother. Of course, I'm vastly oversimplifying here, omitting entirely the other pole in the dialectic, differentiation. The thing is, as analysis proceeds, differentiation becomes stronger, clearer, until each significant other is significant largely in his or her own right. At least, that's the ideal outcome."

"So my call to 'Mom' is really an attempt to get in touch with three women, each for different reasons," I mused.[30]

"Maybe more, who knows?" he said jauntily. "But you see, just here is where the archaeological analogy breaks down. In the world it's the *current* topography of the city that counts; that's the one people actually live on, the ancient, buried surfaces being of merely historical interest to a few. With analysis it's the other way around: it's the original, the prototype—mother—who far outweighs all those who come after in psychic significance, they being largely projections of her. So much *élan vital* is wrapped up in the original … And by the way, such a view does not lend aid and comfort to those who regard psychoanalysis as some aberrant rumination over a remote past shrouded in the mists of personal pre-history. On the contrary, everything in the unconscious is alive and co-present—commingled, you might say—with everything in the conscious mind, the reason being that time does not exist in the unconscious, which means it makes no sense to speak of temporal distance between the two realms. Separation there is, I'm sure, but not of a temporal nature. Repression is always going on *right now*."

"It's funny," I said, letting the dream resonate, "I've never liked the telephone. I mean, I'm not what the kids would call 'hip' to the current technological revolution in general—i-pods, i-phones and blackberries are all like so many electronic Rubik's Cubes to me—but you'd think I would at least have come to terms with the ordinary telephone by now. I make as few calls as humanly possible and take even fewer. As soon as a call shifts from some pressing matter of business to 'so what else is going on,' I'm like a claustrophobic (which I also am) looking to get out. Maybe this semi-latent anxiety of mine over the telephone, or rather its high-tech devil's spawn, the cell phone, is why the dream uses it to stage a scenario of some of my deepest issues … Phones are just trouble."

"Especially when you're depending on one to contact someone who can't be reached," Dr. P. added, as if to help me consolidate what I'd just learned about myself. And as I was nodding to indicate his point was not lost on me, a curious association, also sparked by the good doctor's remark, popped into my head which I couldn't resist sharing with him: "You know, about fifteen years ago when I was doing research on the poet Rilke's influence on the Trappist monk, Thomas Merton,

I was struck by a comment Rilke wrote in a letter to his patron at that time, Princess Marie von Thurn und Taxis, to the effect that Christianity was severely hampered as a religion by the imposition on its adherents of a 'telephone to God'—in the person of Christ. 'No one comes to the Father except through me,' and so forth. Rilke was writing from Spain and had just toured the famous 'crucifixion crosses' in Andalusia memorializing the victims of the Inquisition. He went on to say in the letter … what was it … something like 'the very human founder of the "other" religion in Spain, Mohammed, managed quite nicely, thank you, to set up a direct line to God for his followers.' (I'll pass over in silence the sobering historical context this gives to the atrocity of 9/11.) But the question of whether you need a 'phone'—a mediator—to reach God strikes me as oddly parallel to the question whether I could ever—in the dream, that is—have reached my mother by phone. Now, my first impulse is to preempt the whole discussion of this terribly important issue by asserting flatly that, in both instances, the religious and the familial, a mediator is neither necessary nor, indeed, possible. The reason for this, which you'll forgive me for casting in deconstructionist terms, is that there really is no 'transcendental signified' waiting to be reached through a mediating signifier. The pursuit of the signified—be it God, the Nurturing Mother, or any other panacea—is the pursuit of a phantasm, for the simple reason that this very moment, here and now, is all there ever really is and all we ever really need. Seek and ye shall *not* find, says Zen, since you—the deep You we call Self which is totally self-sufficient—already are that which you seek. What's called for, it seems to me, is not seeking but recognition, Self-recognition, and recognition is always immediate; it does not take place in time, in the same sense that the relation between the conscious and the unconscious, as you mentioned earlier, is not temporal. Better to call it ontological, a matter of intertwined strata of being, immune to time. I think my little epiphany at the end of the dream is an instance of this sort of recognition: 'Why am I trying to reach Mom. What can she really do for me?'

"However, having said that, let me add the important qualification that a so-called mediator—be it a saint, a mantra, a koan or even a cell phone—can, if carefully chosen, be helpful on the 'non-path' of recognition, provided it lead the individual to an ultimate awareness of its own uselessness. As the Buddha said, once the raft has planted you on the other shore of the river, you don't hoist it on your back and carry it around. You leave it behind. He might have added that you never really needed the raft anyway; you always already *were* on the other shore. You see, that's the astonishing paradox of it: the instant you see, deeply, that the raft can't get you anywhere, you realize that even the raft itself was part of the destination, that there never was anywhere to go: what you regarded as a means was already an aspect of the end. In truth, there are neither means nor ends, just things as they are.

"Anyway, that's one problem with mediators: the lingering attachment to them. The other is their reification by organized religions into doctrinal icons that are then imposed on the flock in blanket fashion: Jesus as the 'one-size-fits-all' mediator, for example. Now, there's nothing wrong with the idea of Jesus (or the Buddha, or 'the sound of one hand clapping') as mediator—for certain people. The 'fit' between mediator and mind is a delicate psychospiritual matter that must be worked out carefully in each instance. The German romantic poet Novalis, a mystic of astonishing depth for someone who died so young, went so far as to say that anyone with any self-awareness at all should be entirely free to select her own mediator, that even the slightest coercion in the matter could be injurious to her spiritual life. I remember reading in Kapleau[31] about a Zen student who told the roshi in *dokusan*[32] that he'd been meditating on the koan *mu,*[33] the one assigned to most beginners, for three years but hated it and didn't feel he was getting anywhere. The roshi, in wide-eyed astonishment, said, 'And you never will get anywhere like that! Why didn't you say so in the first place!' Different strokes, as they used to say."

I suddenly realized I had lapsed into lecturing and reflexively ran my finger along an eyebrow to check whether the traditional Zen curse of elongated eyebrows for too much blather about spiritual things might have struck. Recognizing the gesture, Dr. P. laughed and said, "Don't worry, they're fine," then adding, "I would definitely say this dream is a big step in your individuation process; it shows you're coming to see the necessity of letting go of your mother as your own 'raft to the other shore' of integrity. What's even more important is that this insight occurs to you *within the dream itself,* in that final questioning of the need to connect to her after all. That shows the truth is sinking in. And I'm sure I needn't point out that, as that need withers, an authentic, healthy relationship to mother grows."

We both stood up, and as I headed up the stairs and out into the crisp, beautiful Syracuse spring, so long in coming as usual, I felt something I hadn't felt in a long time, the faint stirring of a seed of hope.

(13) November 2005: Manhattan Mandala

The sun is just setting on a beautiful late spring day in Manhattan as I find myself standing at the northernmost point on the rim of a huge traffic circle, facing southward. It looks a little like Columbus Circle, but it's so much bigger, almost the size of the massive Place de la Concorde in Paris. If you think of this circle as a clock face, I need to get from twelve o'clock to six, on my way towards lower Manhattan. Somehow I know that once I get to six o'clock, I'll have to choose to go either east (left) towards the sunlit green fields of Long Island or west (right) towards the dark, dingy confines of Hoboken. I can actually see the vague outlines of the two areas off on the southeastern and southwestern horizons from where I'm standing. Interestingly, the skyscrapers are no obstacles to my vision.

I decide to make my way down along the northwestern arc of the circle towards nine o'clock. Just as I get to nine and set myself to tackle the lower arc, I'm confronted by an elderly black man, on whose property I'm apparently trespassing. He says to me, "Man, don't you know this is one of the biggest squares in the world?" He speaks the words in a tone expressive of concern for my well-being, as if to say, "You be careful now!"

"Actually, that's the earlier of two dreams I've had this week, so I told it first; but, believe me, the second one's a pip."

"Hmm."

"Yeah, that's what I said this morning as I mulled both over coffee." That smart-ass remark was the only bit of sarcasm

I'd managed to conjure up for days and was an expression of my gathering mood of late, which had turned ominously dark. The hope that stirred in May and sustained me through the summer had come completely undone, and then some, over a period of weeks in the Fall that followed. The sequence of events leading to this nadir was as follows: near the end of a summer that had been both relaxing and productive, it occurred to me one day that, apart from my weekly meetings with Dr. P., I had allowed the spiritual dimension of my life to grow languid. I'd stopped meditating and had drifted away from my reading in Krishnamurti, Balsekar and others who had inspired and sustained me for so long. Casting about for some new inspiration (above and beyond that offered by any given moment, as the sages insist), I came across a face in the annual catalogue of the Omega Institute in Rhinebeck, New York. Omega is a unique sort of "mall" for spiritual shoppers, a rural retreat center offering the gamut of New Age services from yoga classes to *ch'i kung* breathing training to art therapy and beyond. It's located in the Hudson Valley region about an hour north of New York City. The face belonged to a forty-ish man named Adyashanti and accompanied a brief description of the weekend retreat he was slated to conduct in late September, aimed at helping people "to awaken to their true nature." It was not so much the description that caught my eye, which was Human-Potential boilerplate, but the face in the catalogue photo. It riveted me. It had nothing in common with the smiles of strained ecstasy pasted on the faces of so many teachers and gurus in the various New Age magazines and brochures, smiles that scream at you, "Look at me! See how together I am!" This face, of an American with shaved head and liquid blue eyes, was truly radiant. It said simply, "I'm here for you, if you need me."

I decided to attend the retreat but I wanted to run the idea past Dr. P. before committing. He had no problem with it and, in fact, encouraged me to go, taking a sort of synchronistic attitude towards it that I found delightful: "If you feel that strongly about it, you're probably meant to do it." So down I drove from Syracuse to Omega on a gorgeous Friday afternoon in September, checking in around six o'clock. The retreat ran from Friday evening till lunch on Sunday and consisted of rotating talks, Q and A sessions and meditation periods. It all took place in a large auditorium full to capacity with veteran followers, including many from foreign countries, along with first-timers like myself, curious to see what all the fuss was about. The packed house attested to the considerable reputation this still-young man had acquired on the "guru circuit" over the course of a dozen years or so.

At around eight p.m., "Adya" appeared and took his seat at center stage, facing his rapt audience. Surrounded by a few tall vases and garlands of flowers, he was dressed informally in chinos and an open-collared shirt displaying some sort of pink neo-Vedanta brocade pattern. He simply looked out at all of us in silence for several moments, apparently checking the "vibe." Finally he spoke, in a measured, mellifluous voice that matched his beautiful moon of a face. I've long forgotten what he said, but I do remember the words entering me like soft bolts of energy. His charisma was indeed soft and essentially feminine, yet without a trace of effeminateness. Though his background was in Zen, he was by then eclectic and very much his own man. His dharma talks were uplifting and he made his points gently, slowly, carefully, always with a gaze that lingered lovingly on his audience. I don't remember his making a single stutter or slip of the tongue the entire weekend, even during the give-and-take of the question periods when many troubled students, including mental health professionals, would assail him with their most intimate psychological and spiritual problems. He handled all of it with grace and humor. My only complaint was that I was never able to find a seat close enough to the stage to see his face close-up. The veteran disciples were adept at arriving early enough for the first meeting to occupy the front rows of seats and then leaving coats, cameras and such on those seats during intermissions to retain occupancy for the entire retreat. I had to laugh to myself at the irony of such spiritual greed: "What? I should give up my seat here at the font of Enlightenment to some rank beginner? Never!"

By Sunday morning I was feeling some kind of inner opening, which I was able to trace back to an exercise Adya had led us through on Saturday afternoon. I don't remember the particulars of the exercise, but it had something to do with a simple technique for catching yourself in the act, so to speak, of using a defense mechanism, like bragging, or lying or any kind of reflex behavior. Somehow, during the exercise itself, I managed to catch myself in some such automatic thought, something like "You need to be smart to stay ahead, to survive." I actually saw the thought pop into my mind, make its statement, and scurry off the stage of consciousness like an exposed rat. That's when the opening occurred. I recognized it as such immediately, since I'd had many such experiences during my Zen years and knew their signs: a sudden surge of bliss, a sense of expansiveness, a whiff of the perfume of ego-less freedom.

Reinforced and enriched by Adya's charismatic presence, this little satori stayed with me for the rest of the retreat and for days thereafter. In fact, as I made the leisurely drive home on Sunday afternoon, it deepened into a kind of rarefied awareness of the transparency of everything. No matter what I focused my attention on, either inside or outside myself, it struck me as empty, in the sense of being no more than a shape of energy subject to momentary dissolution. Passing cars, the highway, cows, pastures, thoughts and feelings. And, of course, the emptiest thing of all: I myself! That meant I didn't exist; there simply was no "I" of any enduring substance. But if that was the case, I reasoned, then who was it that knew this? Such thoughts made me almost dizzy with delight, strangely the very opposite of the fear and horror a schizophrenic might experience on having the same realization. When I arrived home, even Dottie, who had always regarded my "exotic" spiritual interests with a cynical eye, remarked that I seemed to her somehow "different."

The trouble started when I went back to work the following week. Already on Tuesday I noticed a slight feeling of contraction in the expansiveness I'd been enjoying. It was still there but was beginning to be eroded by a tentative quality. Soon the tentative quality began to be accompanied by doubts and negative thoughts, at first occasional and fleeting but gradually increasing in frequency and finally also in their moroseness. Over a few days the thoughts traversed a descending trajectory from, say, "This high might not last" to "The more things change, the more they stay the same. Welcome back, neurosis!" to "My God, I'll take that abandoned child with me to the grave." There I was, incredibly, right back at square one,

Adya and Dr. P. and psychoanalysis be damned!

That was for starters. Then things got worse. As Thanksgiving approached, I felt my old obsessive demons growing in strength: "What you did is inexcusable … How can you live with yourself? … Analysis is bullshit; you'll never throw off this burden." The feelings of emotional pain and anguish that came with these thoughts were only intensified by my awareness that a decade of Zen meditation and four years of analysis hadn't done a damn thing to dilute their toxic nature. On the contrary, they had grown more monstrous than ever. I felt my psychic legs buckle as my thoughts turned to the final consolation of life's finitude. There would come a day when it would all, at last, be over. Yet on the worst days, even this balsam was taken from me by the demon of evil-magical thinking: "Death resolves nothing. Consciousness survives only to continue bearing the karmic burdens of life. And since what you've done cannot ever be undone, you're condemnation is eternal." As unbearable as such a consideration was for me during this vulnerable time, I still couldn't help smiling at its ironic similarity to the fear of eternal hellfire that had afflicted me in youth during my summer with Jennifer, with its acute sexual pressure and symptomatic nasal-phallic anxiety. My awareness of this linkage played no small part in helping me keep my balance during the most trying days. There was, somewhere in a sane corner of my psyche, the suspicion that this whole psychological inferno was somehow a hoax, and that analysis, my own skepticism notwithstanding, *was* working and would see me through it.

Another perspective that helped was my view of the spiritual opening that had occurred during the retreat with

Adya and directly preceded my depression. While my demons would have had me dismiss this epiphany as merely the high phase of a manic-depressive episode, I had become wise over the years to what William James called the reductionist fallacy of "medical materialism" in spiritual matters.[34] Even in my misery I knew that science, operating from the subject-object paradigm, simply did not, nor could it ever, understand what had happened to me *from the inside,* and without the awareness afforded by the inside view, must recuse itself from any final judgment on the matter. This left me with the hopeful view that my personal ego, having been threatened by a legitimate spiritual experience exposing its utter "unreality," so to speak, had called up its army of delusive demons to battle me into submission. This in turn gave me the strength of stubbornness and insolence towards ego and its minions. Let them drag me to the gates of hell itself; I would soldier on.

I had, of course, fully informed Dr. P. of these psycho-spiritual developments. Indeed, he was of enormous help to me in working towards this healthy point of view that gave me the strength to continue with analysis, which I was, about every other day during that period, sorely tempted to drop. His own view of the matter was, of course, analytical and centered on the notion that I was at a critical point in the analysis analogous to that of a fever, a point at which things could go either way, for good or ill. As terrifying as this thought was, it also gave me an odd sense of anticipation of some sort of relief, be *it* for good or ill. The issue would at least be decided. During one session in October, when I was feeling something close to desperation, I remember his saying to me, in an almost imploring tone, "Can you just put yourself entirely in my hands for now? Can you trust me?" The truth was, I didn't know whether I could trust anyone or anything. I felt like an idiot. But just the tone and sincerity of his request, its quality of heartfelt concern, gave me the courage to answer, "Yes, I'll do my best." And I *did* then feel I was in his hands, at least for a while, and glad to be out of my own.

By mid-December I was feeling rotten enough to think about going back on Paxil, which I had weaned myself off the previous Spring; and after talking it over with Dr. P., who agreed it was a good idea, I did so. I'd had, over the years, several heated discussions with him over the merits of anti-depressant drugs for an analysand. His position was straightforward: if they become necessary, use them. After all, it's fairly well established by now that, whatever else depression may be, it's certainly also an organic disease. You wouldn't withhold insulin from a diabetic, so how could you justify withholding an SSRI from a depressed person? My position, at first, was that Paxil introduced a variable into the analytic process that made it impossible to judge its progress objectively. He pooh-poohed this, arguing that, while Paxil might take the edge off psychic pain, it didn't resolve anything on the existential or human level. Only analysis or something like it could do that, and one would, over time, inevitably be able to discern whether such resolution had been brought about.

In time I came around to Dr. P.'s point of view, and I have never regretted it. For one thing, Paxil helped me out of a very dark place in which I could not have remained indefinitely. At their worst, the obsessive thoughts became scorchingly powerful, and no mental gymnastics I could devise availed against them. For another, some honest soul-searching on the matter revealed to me the extent to which my anti-drug stance was conditioned by my "macho" Zen attitude towards adversity in general: face things squarely, no matter what. Exemplars for this were those innumerable anecdotes from Zen lore (probably apocryphal but who could be sure?) telling of the fantastic spiritual exploits of the greatest masters: Master X offering his own body as food for some starving wolves; Master Y sitting *zazen* all night without stirring in the middle of a mosquito-infested swamp; the young so-and-so, in an effort to gain acceptance as a novice, cutting off his right arm to demonstrate his sincerity. What's a little depression next to that? Such attitudes were ubiquitous at the monastery I attended; they were a palpable vapor in the air we all breathed there, especially during the rigors of *sesshin.* I do believe many lay students (and probably monks and nuns as well) allowed this foolish Zen machismo to keep them from getting the medical help they legitimately needed.

There was also the fear among many, more understandable I think, that anti-depressants would either dull consciousness enough to attenuate, if not abort outright, effective meditation and its resulting insight, or somehow taint or invalidate such insight as did come. To this I can only say that I have not found it to be so in my own case. SSRIs are not sedative and in no way reduce alertness; on the contrary, taking the edge off depression as they do, they help to heighten it. I've experienced moments and periods of insight both on and off Paxil, and I find it impossible to discriminate between the two conditions whether the yardstick be depth, clarity, intensity, bliss or any other feature. In recent years I've noticed in my reading of American Buddhist books and magazines a slow but significant shift in attitudes among various Buddhist communities towards a more open, flexible view of anti-depressants, a shift aided in no small measure by the counsel of the many psychiatrists who nowadays also meditate. It's good to see American common sense prevail over Japanese extremism, or at least what Americans perceive as Japanese spiritual heroism, in this matter.

Be all that as it may, in the analytic hour that is our focus here with its two-dream harvest, Dr. P., who, as I've said, was fully aware of my depression, was kind enough to ignore my sarcasm and respond in a simple, inviting tone, "Well, we can go right to the more recent dream if you like and come back to this Manhattan dream later."

"I think you'll agree that the two dreams are related," I said, "so why don't I get the second one out there now and then we can discuss them together."

"Fine."

It's almost too simple, too naked, to even be *a dream. It's the middle of the night. I'm lying in bed on my back, just looking up into the darkness. The only thing at all unusual is that I have an odd sense of expectancy, as if something out of the ordinary is about to happen. And as if on cue, it does: I hear the following words spoken somewhere above me in an imposing voice: "You must shift your allegiance from the ego to the Self." At the same time, up there in the darkness, six or seven feet above me and in my direct line of sight, I see a square on the left and a circle on the right, as if these figures were a visual demonstration of the injunction expressed by the words.*

"That's it … As I said, I can't really say whether this experience even qualifies as a dream. I'm fairly sure I was awake for it, or at most half-asleep. Either way, I certainly was fully alert. It imprinted itself on me in a way I'll never forget. It had the authority of Truth like few other things I've been told in my life."

"It might have been a so-called hypnagogic moment," Dr. P. speculated, "occurring at that mysterious threshold between waking and sleeping when defenses are low. But no matter. It's not so much the genre or category of the experience that's of interest here but its quality and content—in a word, its meaning for you."

"Well, as I said, I can't help thinking it's very much tied up with the Manhattan dream which I had a night or two earlier. It strikes me that this—let's call it 'hypno-moment'—that this hypno-moment is a direct commentary on that dream, removing all ambiguity, as if my unconscious didn't trust me to get the message that the dream conveys visually, as if its thinking were, 'We can't trust this numbskull to negotiate the symbolism of the Manhattan traffic-circle mandala, so we'd better give it to him straight, in his own simple language.'"

"Now, now," the good doctor cautioned good-naturedly, "that's dangerously close to Jungian blasphemy. We'd better step back from that precipice a bit … Tell me more about the relationship between the two dreams, or the one dream and one whatever."

"I have no doubt whatever that the Manhattan dream is archetypal, almost a textbook example. It's Jung 101. (That's why I don't see the need for the literal translation into the hypno-moment.) It's clear to me that the circle is a mandala representing my journey, both in life and, in a heightened sense, here with you in analysis. My movement is from north to south, noon to six o'clock, which means I'm making my way down into the unconscious. But the progress isn't direct, rather it's along an arc that will confront me with obstacles. One of these is the black man I run into, whose property I'm 'trespassing' on. That's the domain of the shadow who 'owns,' so to speak, all the anger, fear and general nastiness—the 'property'—I've disowned. But he doesn't mind my trespassing because he knows that means I'm trying to connect with him. After all, he's been so lonely for so long. In fact, he shows his gratitude for my efforts by giving me some advice, warning me to take care on this journey, which is not without danger. You see, I'm crossing 'the biggest square in the world,' crowded with all manner of vehicular traffic, which can be lethal. I must take good care.

"The two vistas I see off in the East and West distance, sunny Long Island and dark, murky Hoboken, represent the two figures shown to me in the hypno-moment, the Self and the ego. In heading towards six o'clock, the bottom of the circle of conscious/unconscious, it seems I'm approaching a crossroads, a point at which I'll have to make a choice as to which way to go. Will I embrace my True Self, what Zen master Huineng calls 'one's True Nature,' pictured in the dream as the sunny expanse of Long Island, or will I falter and scurry back, tail between my legs, to the dreary city of the conditioned ego, Hoboken, where I grew up? What will I do? What *will* I do ..."

Having listened attentively to my facile interpretation, Dr. P. took a deep breath and held forth: "Look, I know you're really hurting right now, so please try not to be offended by what I'm about to say. I only say it because, well, for the sake of the analysis, you need to hear it. The truth is, I have no issue to take with your reading of the dream. None. It was as 'textbook' as the dream itself. What I *would* take issue with, however, is the attitude of offended arrogance that shaped the flippant tone in which you delivered it. Now, I'm sure that that's coming mainly out of the anger being fueled by your depression. But you need to appreciate the irony that it only demonstrates your failure to grasp the subtlety of the message contained in the hypno-moment, a message you snootily dismiss as superfluous. In translating the dream symbolism into simple words and figures, the unconscious isn't questioning your intellectual prowess, which is considerable, but your awareness, the deeper intelligence that alerts you to your own egoic blind spots, in this case, your insecurity over your intellect, a faculty to which you're too attached. The very simplicity of the message, in evoking your arrogance, exposes this insecurity, and that is just the point. Like most academics in my experience, you suffer from 'the imposter syndrome,' the fear that some superior mind will eventually expose you as an intellectual fraud, or what's worse, a mediocrity. If you want my advice, take the verbal message of the hypno-moment as a gift, and let this little rebuke of mine for your paranoid misreading of the motive behind it make you all the more grateful for it. Apparently it *is* a message you need to hear in plain words."

To say I felt chastened by a homily Dr. P. could not have enjoyed giving doesn't begin to express it. But that was just the amazing thing about it: I felt humbled by it, not humiliated; chastened, not shamed. It actually felt good to be humbled! It felt good to feel gratitude for this gift of humility. How utterly different from the humiliation I had always chafed under from any criticism coming my way. I could only laugh at such a rare moment, so saturated with irony, and at the refreshingly odd sense of emancipation from ego that came with it.

"You see," Dr. P. continued in a softer tone, "the issue raised by these dreams is just another permutation of your leitmotif, analytically speaking, which is one of wounded self-esteem, the initial wound inflicted in your earliest days with the feeding problem. The crowning irony here—it's almost dazzling, really—is that even the 'precisely correct' reading of the Manhattan-mandala dream you gave kept you—*kept you*—from appreciating the momentous nature of the crisis you're approaching, the crisis of the crucifixion of the ego that must go before self-realization, to put it in Jung's terms. Even in verbalizing the crisis so articulately, as you did, it remained for you essentially unconscious. This is a wonderful example of the fiendishly subtle nature of intellectualist defensive armoring. To echo your own words, this time leaving tongue out of cheek, "What *will* you do? …"

"By the way," Dr. P. said as I got up to leave, "there is one significant bit of dream material you apparently *did* overlook."

"Oh? What was that?"

"Instead of telling you, Herr Professor, I'll give you two little homework assignments for next time: first, reread the ending of one of your favorite Kafka stories, 'The Judgment,' a story you once talked about at length here. I believe it was in connection with a dream about a parking lot.[35] As you read, consider that *other* meaning of the German word for 'traffic.' The other assignment is just to sit still for a few minutes and contemplate the koan of fitting a square peg into a round hole."

"Thanks, Dr. P.," I laughed. "A house doesn't have to fall on me. But I'll do the assignment anyway."

(14) March 2006: The Guru Koanundrum

I'm relaxing in a park that seems familiar. It might be Lincoln Park in Jersey City where I played a fair amount of baseball as a teenager. But here I'm in the main sitting area with its walkways, trees and benches of wood and concrete. A young man on the nearby green is holding forth and attracting a lot of attention, so I walk over to join the listeners. He's some sort of leader of an exotic Eastern religious sect and is pitching his brand of meditation as "the Way to Enlightenment." He's American, thirty-fivish, with a big mop of curly reddish-brown hair, and, as he speaks, his devotees are passing out maps to his compound in Virginia. I try to read one of them but have trouble making out the route. One of the assistants tries to help me, with little success, and I'm feeling unease over the trouble I'd have finding the place, should I decide to go there for instruction.

Meanwhile the guru himself is saying disheartening things such as, "If you do this meditation, be prepared to accept ten years of inactivity and unproductivity. You'll see no results for ten years." Hearing that, I shout out fiercely to him, "I'm over sixty years old! I don't have *ten years to wait for results! I'm outta here!" Walking away, I half expect—hope—he'll come after me, tap me on the shoulder and tell me something mitigating, … something conciliatory. But as the dream ends, he hasn't."*

"He '*hasn't*?'"

"That's right. He hasn't come after me."

"Hmm … Interesting that you should put it that way," the good doctor mused.

“How is that interesting?”

“Well, ‘hasn’t’ implies something that other terms you could’ve used, like ‘doesn’t’ or ‘didn’t,’ don’t.”

“Oh, you mean … lack of finality?” I asked cautiously.

“Of course. You see it, don’t you?”

“Sure, sure I do … now that you point it out. ‘Hasn’t’ implies that the dream ends on a note of ambiguity for me. There’s an implied ‘yet’: I’m still waiting for the guru to come and tap me on the shoulder, aren’t I?”

“I would say so.”

I shifted uneasily on the couch, suddenly aware of the cold feel of the leather and the overall chill of the basement. Even the Buddha statuettes on the bookshelves seemed to shiver slightly, their legendary equanimity disturbed. It was a typical Syracuse mid-March deep freeze, heralding the annual Spring blizzard, and I was so wishing Dr. P. would turn up the thermostat. But I knew from years of chilly sessions that he loved cold and hated heat. I’d speculated this was because heat made him uncomfortable in that massive frame of his, but it was doubtless also a matter of a little cold keeping both of us tautly attentive to the process.

And these days I was, in fact, feeling better able to pay attention to the process, since my Fall-Winter depression seemed to have run its course. Not only was the depression over, but my agonizing doubts about the therapy that had plagued me for so long seemed to have vanished with it. Not that I had wrestled my way to any sort of intellectual conviction of the validity of the process. Rather, to my surprise, I simply no longer felt the need of such conviction. The rightness of what I was doing was becoming, all by itself with minimal interference on my part, something that felt intrinsic to the process, something answering a need of my heart, a need that, itself, beggared analysis and that I was content not to question.

"Actually, that doesn't surprise me at all," I said, nodding at the aptness of Dr. P.'s linguistic *aperçu*. "It points up an issue that has vexed me ever since I first got involved with the Zen establishment in '85—the issue of spiritual authority, or, to put it more personally, the guru koanundrum."

"Excuse me, what was that last word?"

"'Koanundrum,'" I laughed. "It's just my little pun for stating the problem of the spiritual master or teacher.

"I see. And just how is that a problem for you?"

"Well, the dream, as usual, states it with marvelous compactness, don't you think? … Oh, by the way, that reminds me, I've got a second dream, or dream fragment, for today that I think ties in, in a fascinating way, with this one. I musn't forget to bring that in at some point … But anyway, this dream seems to illustrate some very conflicted feelings I have about spiritual mentors. On the one hand, I'm tempted by this young guru's promises of Enlightenment: 'Give me ten years and I'll get you there!' But, you see, that's a tremendous conflict for me right there; my God, a ten-year commitment at my age … What if he's wrong? What if he can't deliver? What if *I* can't deliver? What if some other path, some 'Road Not Taken,' would've worked for me and I'd missed it frittering away my last chance with a charlatan or an incompetent? I can't afford to waste time."

"Why do you say that? Why would it be your 'last chance'?"

"Look, at my age I approach any time-commitment of

more than a few months with extreme care. The closer you get to the end, the more precious time becomes. At this point I need to make whatever I invest myself in really count."

"That sounds a little frantic."

"You think? … I suppose it does."

"That might be the issue here, at least as much as the guru."

"You mean, my own impatience might sabotage anything even the greatest guru could do for me?"

"Yes."

"That does resonate with me, I must admit. My wife's always telling me I'm impatient ... Kafka called impatience man's greatest—in fact, his *only*—sin. It's his version of Original Sin. We're born with its taint and it casts its shadow over everything we do, everything we try to enjoy. It's the worm at the core of even the shiniest apple. We want happiness and we want it now, yesterday even. I guess in the dream it makes me unable to really take in what the young man is saying. I'm too worried about whether I'll get something out of it."

"Exactly."

"But wait a minute, Dr. P., there's a maddening paradox simmering here: on the one hand, we can't help being impatient because we're built that way. On the other, if we weren't impatient, if we were truly able to appreciate the guru's words, it would necessarily be because we were already enlightened ourselves and didn't *need* to get anything out of them. I wouldn't need to be able to read his map to get to his compound in Virginia because, in a sense, I'd already be there."

At this the good man just smiled.

"This is a wonderful koan, isn't it?" I continued, enthused.

"We could frame it this way: 'You can't get enlightenment until you realize you already have it.' I like that. It makes the whole problem one of 'seeing' rather than 'doing,' a problem of consciousness and not behavior."

"I like that too."

"Again I'm reminded of Kafka, a wonderful Western-style Zen master. He has so many fragments, even drawings, that zero in on this. One drawing has a stick-figure man facing the middle side of a three-sided fence that encloses him. We, of course, can see that he's not really enclosed at all. All he has to do is turn around, in other words, change his point of view, to realize he's never been anything but free … Then there's a short text I love about the Second Coming which says the Messiah will come, not on the last day, but on the day after that! Scratch your head over that one, huh? It's a mind-blowing way of saying, once we get over our impatience, that is, give up waiting (even waiting being a subtle form of impatience), time will end, since time itself is something we all create through our deluded belief that things aren't all already perfect. Once time goes poof, we'll see that the Messiah has always been right here and never been anywhere else. In fact, *we* are *He*."

"I like that very much," Dr. P. nodded. "That way of viewing impatience, as a sort of baseline human condition, unconsciously self-created, over and over, moment by moment, is something I see all the time in my patients. In some instances it's undoubtedly a root cause of the failure of therapy and, in many others, I'm sure, a factor in 'therapy interminable.' But your ambivalent feelings towards the guru—this conflict between anger over a ten-year demand and hope that he'll somehow come through for you—that only views the guru issue from the subjective angle, from *your* end of it as spiritual 'customer,' so to speak. Isn't the dream also saying something about the issue from the other, objective, pole of the relationship, the guru himself? Isn't it saying something about all spiritual teachers, in the end, having feet of clay? The dream scenario does suggest something of the snake-oil salesman in the park, his pitch drawing a crowd of the curious: 'Step right up, folks, tell ya what I'm gonna do ..."

"Yes, I think you're right there, but my sense is that it's making this very point in a way opposite to the way it's usually made, which *is* objective. You know, scandals over male Zen masters who bed down their female students, rampant disillusionment among students after a few years over their failure to 'get anywhere' under Master so-and-so, and moving on to the next miracle worker, or feeling you just don't have the right 'fit' with a teacher in terms of personality. This critique of the guru culture that has become commonplace, especially in American Buddhist circles, in the wake of the honeymoon with Eastern spirituality we all enjoyed in the sixties and seventies—I think the dream is trying to tell me that we have indeed met the spiritual enemy, and it is not the guru but ourselves. The enemy is not the object but the subject. All our psychospiritual needs, desires, expectations, projected onto these displaced Eastern masters suffering culture shock, or onto their green American 'heirs,' are foredoomed to profound frustration. No one could possibly meet them, and not because they weren't 'adept enough' or 'enlightened enough,' but because, as my own Zen master once put it in a *teisho*,[36] 'I have nothing to teach.' We all heard him say that. He said it very clearly, slowly, emphatically: 'I ... have ... nothing ... to ... teach.' And you know what, not one of the sixty or so students sitting their listening, including yours truly, heard it. Not one of us. And you know why? Because we didn't *want* to hear it. We didn't want to be told that, at the end of the day, only I myself have the capacity to realize my own true nature. No teacher can teach it to me or give it to me or somehow deliver it to my spiritual doorstep. *Self*-delivery is the only way.

"Which, mind you, is not to say that gurus are useless." Just as "mind you" came out, I became aware that I was lapsing into didacticism, but at the same time it occurred to me that I was really saying these words more to myself than to Dr. P., that, especially in view of the dream, I needed to reabsorb their truth. He probably recognized this and was prepared to let me go on. "On the contrary, they are necessary as guides, especially in the early stages of the spiritual path, but once we begin, mostly unconsciously, to make them the agents of our deliverance—*you,* as an analyst, might say to make them into the ideal parents we missed in childhood—we're headed down the slippery slope to a painful disillusionment. When my teacher told us all, so emphatically, 'I have nothing to teach,' he was articulating exactly the same mystical truth as Kafka's three-sided fence or day-after Messiah. The truth is within us, and nowhere else. Again paradoxically, the only useful thing a guru has to teach us is his own uselessness. If he can do that, he's a true master."

"Nice *teisho,*" Dr. P. quipped, amiably. "Of course, its value, as you say, depends entirely on whether it helps me to realize its own uselessness, right?"

"... Right," I answered, bracing for the inevitable rapier of irony.

"And if it did," he continued, furrowing his brow, "then I'd see, would I not, that it wasn't necessary in the first place. And that this time could've been more profitably spent discussing other matters, ... right?"

This threw me for a few seconds, until I realized he was just using some good-natured teasing as an oblique way of nudging me back to the matter at hand, an occasional strategy of his which I actually enjoyed. "So what about the other dream you mentioned earlier, which you think relates to this one?"

"Yes, yes," I chirped, glad of the reminder.

As I said earlier, it's not a full-fledged dream with a narrative structure or anything like that, but more of a quick scene focused on an arresting image. The image is of an old-fashioned doorknocker, quite ornate, in the shape of a gargoyle head, set in the middle of the door of a house I'm supposed to enter for some important purpose, I know not what. The head is of a washed-out green color, like weathered bronze, and human, more or less, but bug-eyed and freakish looking like all those cathedral and castle gargoyles from centuries past. As I reach for the knocker to signal my arrival, it suddenly comes to life and begins squirming and making hideous faces at me, as if to tease or mock me. But just as it does this, in the very same instant, I realize I'm dreaming—which changes everything. Now I'm fully in charge and I know it. It's a glorious, heady feeling of omnipotence, since I'm aware that I'm making all this up. At first I just regard the gargoyle with perfect poise and equanimity, marveling at the wondrous creativity of my own imagination: "Look what I'm capable of making, with no effort whatsoever!" Then I zoom in very close to it with my face, to appreciate some of the detail work of this, my 'art,' without a care as to whether it might not lunge and bite me on the nose. After all, why would I bite myself? Finally, I take the little fellow in my left hand and squeeze a bit, the way, as a kid, I used to love squeezing those pink rubber balls we used for playing stickball in the street. It feels good. Then I let go, pat it on the head—where else could I pat it?—and enter the house.

"That's a fascinating dream," Dr. P. granted, "though I fail to see any connection to the first one about the guru."

"Nor could you," I smiled. "You see, the connection lies in the association that shot into my mind—literally—upon waking, an association only I would recognize ... It all has to do with my very favorite German story, called "The Golden Pot," which is a romantic fairy tale penned by E.T.A. Hoffmann, the gothic novelist and short-story writer, around 1814. You've probably heard of Hoffmann; his strange stories influenced writers all over the post-romantic West, from Poe to de Maupassant to Gogol and Dostoevsky. He and his tales have also been immortalized in several musical works—Meyerbeer's opera, *Tales of Hoffmann,* and Tchaikovsky's *Nutcracker* ballet come to mind. Also, believe it or not, many films of the great gothic director, Alfred Hitchcock, show Hoffmann's profound stamp: his masterpiece, *Vertigo,* borrows a great deal from another of Hoffmann's dark fairy tales, *The Sandman,* and the earlier film, *Strangers on a Train,* uses the double or doppelganger motif from Hoffmann's story of the same name. So does Dostoevsky's first novel, *The Double.*

"Anyway, I must've taught this fabulous tale of his, *The Golden Pot,* which many consider his greatest, some twenty times over the years in my lit. classes, both in German and English—each time an adventure. The students always loved it."

"Again, very interesting, Herr Professor, but I still don't see—"

"—Stay with me, we're almost there," I encouraged. "I need to tell you a little about this 'Fairy Tale for Modern Times,' as Hoffmann himself subtitled it, to make the connection between the dreams clear … "*The Golden Pot*" is modern in the sense that it takes place in the German city of Dresden where Hoffmann lived for a time. So you've got these two levels of reality, the socio-historical and the fantastic, that collide in the destiny of the hero, a young theology student named Anselmus. One day, he starts having visions of green female snakes with beautiful blue eyes slithering through elderberry bushes. He falls in love with one of them, Serpentina, who turns out to be the daughter of the local eccentric archivist, Lindhorst, who is also a fire-breathing salamander in his spare time. You see where I'm going with this: several of the tale's characters have dual identities, one in the 'real' and one in the magical world. It's Anselmus' destiny to bridge the two worlds and ultimately bring them together within himself, which is to say, within the spirit of poetry, since this is what a poet did, in the eyes of the German romantics. In a word, Anselmus is to undergo all the trials on the spiritual journey leading, ultimately, to Enlightenment or Illumination. It was the poet, not the saint or the priest, who was the romantics' archetype of the spiritual hero. It didn't even matter, really, whether a poet actually wrote any verse, because he was defined by his consciousness, his awareness, rather than his pen.

"So, anyway, the story reaches its climax in the battle royal that erupts between the forces of bourgeois society and those of the mythical world of the salamander for possession of Anselmus' soul, so to speak. The conflict rages fiercely and, at the critical point, the hero is sorely tempted to give up and become a conventional bourgeois housekeeper. However, strengthened by his love for Serpentina, who can manifest as a beautiful princess, he perseveres and finally emerges triumphant from his ordeal, which, as Hoffmann makes metaphorically clear, amounts to undergoing that transformation of consciousness which is a *sine qua non* of the poet, a transformation signaling the total conflation of the bourgeois and mythic worlds. This, for me, is no different than Jung's ideal of individuation, or Zen's goal of Enlightenment. Novalis calls it 'romanticization,' defining it as the ability to see 'the extraordinary within the ordinary and the ordinary within the extraordinary.'

"To me, this story—fabulous in every sense—is a perfect template for the psychospiritual journey, the journey to the Self, as Jung understands it. Its rich fabric of metaphor and allegory contains everything important that Jung writes about: archetypes (Lindhorst as the Wise Old Man), the collective unconscious (the mythical world), transformational symbols (the golden pot itself, for one), living in a utopian Atlantis (the self-realized condition), and so on. It's also full of arcane alchemical images of transformation like the ancient manuscripts Anselmus copies for Lindhorst with their strange signs and squiggles, as if he were helping his mentor to preserve the Emerald Tablet itself. Then there are all these exotic potions and elixirs and smoky concoctions, mostly made by Lindhorst to induce some altered state in his disciple Anselmus, drinks right out of some medieval alchemist's 'bartender's manual.' The atmosphere of alchemy pervading the tale is a constant reminder of Jung, who, as you know, sort of rehabilitated that old, discredited para-science for use as an elaborate symbology for charting the individuation process. That's one of the reasons I love the story so much; it's also one of the reasons I love talking to you here in this 'underground,' surrounded as we are by all your alchemical bric-a-brac, the retorts and the old books and so forth."

As he nodded I also caught Dr. P. glancing over my shoulder at the clock on the bookshelf behind me and knew I'd better come to the point, which, happily, I was ready to do. "There's a moment in the story that has Anselmus standing in front of the bell rope affixed to the huge main entrance door to Lindhorst's mansion. He is reporting for his first day of work there as a copyist of manuscripts, which means, allegorically, the first day of his apprenticeship to Wisdom. Naturally, all the dark forces of ignorance are arrayed against him in an effort to keep him out of the house, totally unbeknownst to the green novice himself. All he knows is that when he yanks on the rope, it makes a tremendous cacophonous clatter and turns into a basilisk, an enormous mythical serpent that immediately entwines the poor, hapless Anselmus in its deadly grip and squeezes him into unconsciousness. So, round one goes to Evil."

At this point the expression on Dr. P's face had entirely lost its preoccupation with "getting to it" and become all attention. I felt he was now with me for this ride. "So you're saying the dream borrows from that threshold moment in Anselmus' journey to show you something about your own—a sort of comparison?"

"I have no doubt whatever about it. What's more, I'm encouraged by what I see here, because it's clear I get through this initial crisis in much better shape than the ultimately victorious Anselmus does, just as I seem to have come through the depression of recent months. That light switch of awareness that suddenly goes on in the dream, turning what begins as an ordinary dream into the lucid kind, where you know you're dreaming, tells me that my consciousness has deepened, at least to the point where I'm now able to control some of the gargoyles of delusion that have afflicted me for so long. Something in me is beginning to sense that all those monsters are really of my own making, and, wonder of wonders, knowing that makes me feel a little freer of them."

"That's wonderful and I congratulate you, Herr Professor. Moreover, I think I can—at last—infer, at least in a general way, the connection you have in mind between this dream and the earlier one. Nevertheless, I'd much rather hear it from you."

"Glad to oblige," I said, feeling I was hitting my stride. "Actually, this is where the whole thing becomes fascinating. The element common to both dreams is the guru figure, although I doubt Hoffmann knew that term. In the first dream I walk away from the young guru in the park and what I consider his excessive demands, though clearly I retain an emotional attachment to him, as evidenced by my hope that he'll come after me. That dream shows a certain spiritual immaturity, an unreadiness to walk the path on my own. Now, in the second dream I overcome the gargoyle demon through my awakened consciousness, the leap to lucidity, so to speak, and am able to enter the house—"

"—Yes, but only to apprentice yourself to another guru,

the old archivist," Dr. P. objected. "There's still this lingering dependency on the Other for spiritual guidance, wouldn't you say?"

"I certainly would, except for one thing ..."

"And that would be? ..."

"Just this: You see, I've always understood this tale, and have taught it to my students, as a psychospiritual allegory. This means that, after all is said and done, the entire narrative is to be regarded as an externalization of the internal process of individuation. What I mean is that everything that happens to Anselmus is to be understood as, essentially, an inner psychological event. But you can't really narrate a character's psychological experiences in strictly internal terms, as bio-psychic processes, without turning an exciting story into a tedious science textbook. So what the storyteller does is use the external world as a metaphorical field of inner action: Serpentina is Anselmus' anima function, the elixirs he drinks are his own inner inspiration, and Archivist Lindhorst is his own deepest wisdom, guiding him past the dangerous pitfalls on the Path.[37] And that's just my point: since Lindhorst *is,* ultimately, an aspect of Anselmus himself, a facet of his psyche, this means Anselmus is indeed following his own inner light. And, by analogy, so am I in my dream when I enter the House of Wisdom. I'm not signing up with another guru—another Zen master, another Adya, or even another *you*—at all; I'm committing myself to my own inner resources. I'm finally entering my own house. The two dreams, as a sequence, seem to be depicting a transition I'm making from a lingering, ambivalent dependence on the Other for my own growth to the place where I truly have to be for genuine growth to happen: in my own house. That's precisely what growth is, isn't it, movement from the inn of the Other to the home of Self."

"It is, indeed," Dr. P. agreed, giving me a little Zen gassho[38] by way of acknowledgement. "But please don't check out of this particular inn just yet, all right?"

"Well, as tempting as that is, I'll probably show up for next time," I said.

(15) July 2006: Beach Blanket Buddha

I'm plodding northward through the hot sand of a Cape Cod beach, probably Nausset Light or Marconi, in Eastham. Out of the corner of my left eye, I see a solitary figure seated on a blanket, laid over the sand and set back a ways towards the base of the rising dunes. Instinctively turning towards it, I approach the figure and suddenly recognize, to my utter astonishment, none other than the Buddha himself, catching a few late-afternoon rays. He smiles at me as I come near and motions for me to join him. Instinctively I avoid sharing his blanket—that would be presumptuous—and simply drop down onto the sand on my knees about two feet in front of him, facing him—just as I used to do before the roshi in the old days of dokusan.[39] *He faces the sea and I face him.*

I gaze at him, intoxicated by this big, bald, spherical figure of a man, as he sits there clutching his shawl to his chest lest the strong sea breeze blow it away. There's something slightly comical about him, and this arouses in me a kind of insouciance that allows me to ask the impertinent question, "So, when do you think you'll get Enlightenment?" He answers simply and without guile, "Oh, that happened a long time ago." Then I move in close and embrace him, catching the scent of fresh lotus petals as I do. Retreating to my haunches, I ask, "What must I *do to get Enlightenment?" He answers, "You can do it in three months if you just drink three liters of __________ per day." (In the dream I hear clearly the liquid he names, but now, in the telling, it eludes me.) I say, "That's it? That's all?" He answers, "That's all there is to it."*

"Fascinating."

"Isn't it though? … I've had other dreams involving the Buddha, particularly during my Zen years when I was sort of infatuated with this new spiritual hero from the East, but never one as intense as this, never a one-on-one encounter, and, of all places, on an East Coast beach."

"Yes, and, interestingly, it's been—how long now?—a good dozen years since you last sat *zazen,* hasn't it?"

"That's right, the obvious irony being that, as I drift further and further away from Zen, the Buddha seems to be gravitating closer and closer. It raises the question, Was the Buddha himself a Buddhist?"

"Blasphemy, Oriental style!" the good doctor quipped. "But it also strikes me that the encounter takes place on a beach on the Cape, from which you've just returned from your annual holiday. Did anything happen during your two weeks there that might have led to such a dream?"

"Certainly nothing leaps to mind … I mean, after all, the whole point of going there is to unwind for two blissfully uneventful weeks; you take your watch off, pull the plug on the TV and only read newspapers on Sunday. So if anything 'happened,' it must've been subtle."

"I'll take 'subtle.' 'Subtle' is good."

"Well, as always, we rented a Cape Codder in Eastham for the first week and stayed with my sister, who now lives there, for the second. Dottie and I took the usual day trips to our favorite haunts: Hyannis for prowling the old book shops; Chatham, which is right at the Cape's elbow, for the awesome ocean view from the bluff and the great clam chowder—at the Squire Inn, by the way; and Provincetown for its rustic, faintly grubby seaport charm. (By now we've collected a handful of restaurants in P'town that are happy to serve straights.) Other than that we spent time, as always, with our old friends from New Jersey, the Klinks, an extended family teeming with siblings and children now living on the Cape. They're part of a small German-American community that has sort of dug in there since after World War II. American children of European immigrants tend to continue many of the Old World cultural patterns of their forebears. So, many New Yorkers and Jersey-ites of German descent go north to the beach—to the Cape or to Maine—just as their German parents went north to Sylt or St. Peter-Ording on the North Sea. As a native American, that struck me as so oddly counterintuitive when I first learned of it in the 80's: if you have a choice, you don't go north to the beach, obviously you go south!"

"But *you're* going north on the beach yourself, in the dream, aren't you?" Dr. P. asked, obviously very pleased with himself.

"Yes, ... so?" I asked with a slightly annoyed edge in my voice.

"Nothing, nothing at all. Just an observation," he answered, holding his hands up, palms out, to affect innocence.

"Anyway," I continued, "as I said, nothing much happened. I immersed myself in two books, *The Kite Runner,* a novel by an Afgani-American doctor that's all the rage these days, and Thomas Mann's *Der Zauberberg* (*The Magic Mountain*), which I cheated on by reading it in English translation as a graduate student. Now, at the end of my career, I wanted to 'make amends' by rereading it in the original German. I got about halfway through it and put it aside, vowing to get back to it soon.

"The only ripple in this placid pool was a visit by my daughter, Denise, who came up from New York City with her fiancée, Josh, for a few days. I think I've mentioned here that they've been living together in an apartment in Lower Manhattan for the last few years. They both work in computers and are doing very well for themselves. Dottie and I were delighted to have them with us, what with both our kids living so far away and visits limited to three or four a year. I enjoyed watching Denise and Josh interact with each other, so playful and full of fun, all the seriousness of the daily grind falling away from them in the healing tranquility of the Cape, as it already had for us. Afternoons at the bay were especially pleasant, watching them frolic in the warm low tide, dunking and splashing water on each other, giggling and exploding in laughter. They're both large-bodied young adults, Josh about six-five and Denise five-eight or nine, so it was like watching Godzilla and Gwangi tangle in the Sea-of-Japan surf."

Dr. P. chuckled at my reference to Japan's favorite atomic-age nightmare and waited for me to continue.

"I think it's in such 'little' moments as these that a parent realizes how much, how madly in love he is with his children. I don't think I could ever love Denise more than I did that afternoon in the sheer enjoyment of seeing her in grown-up play ... You know, it's funny, Dr. P., as I tell you this, I'm getting the same feeling of a welling-up of an abundance of love that I felt on that afternoon, ... the same feeling I felt ... in the dream ... yes, in the Buddha dream. *That's* what ties it all together, isn't it? The feeling! I said before that the stimulus for the dream must've been something subtle, and it was, wasn't it? It was the infinitely subtle, but also infinitely powerful feeling of compassion … And, you know, just as I say that, an old memory of my daughter pops into my mind."

"Go on."

"It's amazing how nimbly the mind moves … Let's see, it had to be when she was about twelve, so let's put it at 1990 or thereabouts. It was late on a Spring morning and I was down in the basement doing a twenty-minute workout on my stationary bike—God, how tedious those workouts were, especially considering the bike I was using was a piece of junk I'd picked up at some garage sale for a song and hardly had enough stability to keep me from toppling over. Anyway, maybe halfway through my workout, my mind a blank, I somehow caught the flesh of my lower leg on a nasty tooth on the chain wheel and saw stars. But almost instantaneously, and completely anaesthetizing me to the pain, something awesome, slightly to my right and halfway down towards the floor, exploded into visibility, utterly transfixing me. It was—how can I put this without sounding mad—it was a fiery vortex of intense orange, gold, and yellow coloration, just hanging there in the air, yet not at all still. It writhed, sort of like a corkscrew cloud, turning in on itself with a profound intensity, and this writhing was somehow, in a way I can't explain, the visible expression of a boundless compassion. But not just compassion either; there was more. The compassion was wrapped around an equally boundless source of pain and suffering, as if the one couldn't exist without the other. The two were literally interblended, like the dark, rain-pregnant area within an otherwise fluffy cirrus cloud—just writhing around each other right there in mid-air off to my right.

"But there was one other thing about this event that was equally self-evident to me, though, again, I couldn't say how or why. It was—now hold onto your hat—it was that I knew beyond any doubt that I was looking into the vortex of my daughter's karma, not just her personal karma, mind you—that was just the outside tip of the writhing vortex—but the karma of the entire human race, maybe even the entire cosmos—I don't know—stretching back beyond the mists of time itself. But as mesmerizing as this visual aspect of the experience was, it was really that utter intensity of compassion that went deepest, as if the cosmos were embracing itself in the throes of its own boundless suffering, the whole thing surfacing in consciousness as it came to a head, so to speak, in the person of my daughter Denise. I remember looking at her that evening, still bathed in the afterglow of the experience as I was, and feeling the most intense stabs of love I had ever known. I think this registered with her unconsciously too, since I caught her occasionally returning my glances with a relaxed smile, an unusual mood for her at that time as she was already well into the 'terrible teens.' I never said a word to her about the experience, but I remember thinking then, and I still do think, that a person could almost wish to know such pain for the chance to also know the love that hides within it … As Nietzsche put it, 'Freude—tiefer noch als Herzensleid.'"

"I'm sorry, my German … ?"

"'Joy—deeper yet than agony.' … Needless to say, I didn't even begin to process the experience for weeks after it happened. I kept it to myself until I got into *dokusan* with Eido Roshi during Memorial Day *sesshin* at DBZ and told him about it. When I finished my account, I put a question to him; I asked, "Roshi, is it possible for one person to experience the karma of another, as seems to have happened to me?"

"And what did he say?"

"Nothing, nothing at all—he just looked at me for a long moment with that steady Zen gaze and finally rang the bell for me to leave. I left thinking I'd asked a stupid question and put the whole thing out of my mind. That evening after dinner, during the relaxation hour before evening sitting, I was lounging on my floor mattress casually paging through a copy of the *Mumonkan* or *Gateless Gate,* the signature Rinzai Zen koan collection. As I turned the page to koan number 35 and absently perused, I suddenly sat bolt upright; right there on the page in front of me, in a textbook example of synchronicity, was the clearest answer to my question I could've hoped for."

"In the koan itself?"

"Yes. I'll never forget the words: Title: 'A Woman's Split Soul.' Text: 'Wuzu asked a monk, "A woman split her soul; which was the real one?"' Then Master Wumen's comment: 'If you can understand the real one here, you will know that leaving a shell and entering a shell is like lodging at an inn.'[40] Isn't that fantastic!"

"If you say so," the good doctor responded with a shrug, "but it's not entirely clear to me what—"

"Forgive me. Zen metaphors can be bewildering to us Westerners at first. It's really just saying that, from the enlightened point of view, personal identities are as superficial as shells or clothes we put on and take off without a thought. Questions about 'the real identity,' 'the true self' and such are wrongheaded. They come out of our inability, or unwillingness, to see that it's all One, that *all* karma is cosmic karma, even if the tip of the vortex is something that looks like a separate person. It's the same fiery vortex that issues, so to speak, in, now 'me,' now 'you,' now 'my daughter Denise.' My question to the Roshi *was* a stupid one and I'm lucky he didn't whack me a few times with the *kyosaku*.[41] The next time I got into *dokusan*, a day or two after that, I told him of my serendipitous discovery and, again, he said nary a word. He just sat there with a Cheshire cat grin. Now how's that for economy of teaching? Question put; answer delivered; not a word spoken."

"I guess you can't beat it for efficiency," Dr. P. conceded. "We here, on the other hand, are forced to plod along with 'the talking cure.'"

"That's all right," I said, "I'm just pulling your chain a little. Obviously speech and silence go hand in hand, just like compassion and suffering in my 'vision.' … But I want to get back to the dream before I lose the thread. When I first brought all this up earlier, you'll recall I prefaced it by saying that it was the *feeling* in the dream, that overwhelming compassion, that tied it all together: the dream itself, my delight in watching my daughter frolic in the bay and now this 'vortex vision' I've just related. It's as if the Buddha-on-the-beach dream is the efflorescense, the coming of age of that loving vortex of long ago. I mean, that feeling literally apes the organic growth of a plant, wouldn't you say?"

The doctor nodded, closing his eyes.

"And one more thing. Since this hour's been all about how, in the depths of consciousness (or whatever it is), opposites blend—speech and silence, compassion and suffering—let's add the dream to the list. After all, if the vision is telling me I shouldn't wish for a pie-in-the-sky world of all compassion and no pain, isn't the dream telling me I shouldn't seek Enlightenment or Wisdom that exists apart from Ignorance, apart from my own stupidity?"

"I'm not sure I follow ..."

"What I'm saying is that my question to the Buddha in the dream is just as benighted as my question to the Roshi in *dokusan*. Denise's karma and my own: a distinction without a difference; the Enlightened versus the ignorant condition: ditto. That's how I read the Buddha's crazy answer to my question anyway. He tells me to drink three liters a day, over three months, of a liquid the identity of which the dream deletes from my recall. The 'blank' in the Buddha's answer is identical to the Roshi's silence in *dokusan*. There obviously *is* no such liquid, anymore than there ever was an *aqua vitae* made with a pinch of the *prima materia* sliced off the Philosopher's Stone in all those zillions of medieval alchemical experiments. The Buddha—or my unconscious, take your choice—is just yanking *my* chain here, using a sort of practical joke to snap me into the awareness that this very moment, right here, right now, with all the mess of my own distemper, is Enlightenment itself. If I were to go off racking my brain to try to fill in the blank with the name of the magic elixir, I'm sure he would just sit there on that beach blanket laughing his ass off.

"Another way of seeing the Buddha's little joke is to focus on the time element in it," I continued after we'd both shifted positions. "I'm to drink a liquid, I know not what, for three months. That'll do it, he says, tongue firmly in cheek. This is to disabuse me of another wrongheaded idea, that Enlightenment is somehow the last step in an incremental series, in other words, a matter of time. Of course, it isn't, any more than the relation between conscious and unconscious minds is temporal, that is, the problem of a putative past separated from a putative present. All these categories exist in the mind only and have nothing to do with 'the way things are,' as they say in Zen. There's a wonderful Zen anecdote that brings this point home. A novice approaches the master with a question (half of Zen is hilarious Q and A): 'Master,' he says, 'how long will it take me to gain Enlightenment if I give up my comfortable householder lifestyle and check in here at the monastery, devoting myself to *zazen* with great intensity?' The master pretends to think it over for a moment and finally answers 'ten years.' Crestfallen over such a long haul, the student then says, 'But Master, what if I wear a hair shirt and sleep on a bed of nails and take only one meal a day of rice-gruel slop and do *zazen* for twenty hours a day?' Again, the master pretends to ponder the question, this time even more deeply, and finally comes out with 'twenty years!' This is certainly about the folly of regarding effort by itself as a guarantee of spiritual 'success,' but it's just as much about the folly of regarding the connection between time invested and Enlightenment as a causal one. There is no 'cause' of Enlightenment; that would be a case of the tail wagging the dog."

"Still, you must admit," the good doctor ventured, "three months is a lot better than ten years."

"But I just explained that it's not a matter of time—"

"—I'm not talking about time, appearances notwithstanding," Dr. P. smiled. "I'm talking about the difference between the guru in the park whom you told about in a dream some months ago, with his requirement of a ten-year commitment on your part, and the Buddha in this one who's reduced that to 'three months.' It may not be temporal in its deepest reaches, but it's clear to me that *some* kind of movement is going on in you that is availing itself of metaphors of time to convey a sense of its imminence. You're approaching something, or it's approaching you, and, judging by the feeling-tone of the beach-Buddha dream, it's quite wonderful … Let me just speculate a bit here: inasmuch as this is just as much a human as a cosmic matter, one having to do with the profundity of parental love, I suspect you may finally be experiencing the flipside of the parental guilt that has oppressed you for so long, and that we might look forward to a coming-to-terms with your life koan, as it were, a final, and happy, balancing of psychological accounts." With this I felt an enormous surge of gratitude and hope.

As we got up together a moment later, it occurred to me that that last comment of Dr. P.'s was probably the only one of any substance he'd offered in the entire hour, that I had done almost all the talking myself. "You know," I said to him as I started up the stairs, "I'm beginning to think you're just about half a Zen master yourself."

"Is that right?" he parried, without missing a beat. "And pray tell, what would the other half be … Cape Cod beachcomber southward bound, perchance?"

(16) October 2006: "I am Tony Soprano!"

He pulls his toll ticket out of the dispenser on a summer afternoon as he enters the Jersey Turnpike, heading south towards Newark, just west of the Lincoln Tunnel. He's got a big, fat Vegas Classic panatella jutting out of his mouth, which he inhales deeply as he steps on the gas. Coming from the car radio is the primitive staccato beat of a tune being sung, or rather growled, by a basso with a Jersey accent: "I woke up this morning and got myself a gun, / Mom always said I'd be the … chosen one." Suddenly I realize I'm not just dreaming about *Tony Soprano … I'm dreaming that I* am *Tony Soprano! In fact, in the instant of this realization I swipe the cigar from my mouth and roar those very words in dark exultation: "I …* am *… Tony … Soprano!" And the strangest thing: just as I roar, my point of view in the dream shifts like lightning from outside Tony to inside. I'm suddenly looking out through* his *eyes, only now they're mine. Then the thought occurs, "I can live with this guilt. No problem."*

"So," the doctor began, "do I need to start coming to these sessions with a bullet-proof vest on?"

"Nah, not if you stay in line. Tony's a social animal, gregarious even."

"Actually, I don't get HBO, so I've only seen a couple episodes of the show on other TVs."

"You're kidding—you don't have HBO? Outside of sports and old movies, HBO's the only thing worth watching on television. *The Sopranos* alone is worth the price of admission."

"You're probably right. The ones I have seen were riveting."

"I'm sure they would be, to an analyst. After all, you've got the oxymoronic situation of a cold-blooded killer in therapy for panic attacks. Ain't that a hoot?" And just as I said that, I felt a pang of embarrassed self-reference, exacerbated by my awareness that Dr. P. was on to me. But he didn't say anything; he knew by now it was enough to wait for me to pursue the matter on my own. "My oh my! How the truth just dribbles out, huh?"

"Yes, and thank God for it. It moves things along."

"Well, I guess, then, that I'm also speaking the truth in the dream: I *am* Tony Soprano, or at least that's the way I see myself, a cold-blooded child-denier in therapy for anxiety stemming from guilt. Although, I'm more of a phobic type than a victim of panic attacks. I at least can avoid situations that trigger anxiety, unlike Tony who lives under the sword of Damocles. Also, my guilt is at least partially conscious; I never go anywhere without my sidekick of a conscience. Tony's conscience, on the other hand, is that of a sociopath, deeply repressed and out of the way—except, of course, for those inconvenient panic attacks. And those appalling nightmares about Pussy, the brother he had whacked for flipping—he was shot on a yacht and dumped in the Atlantic—and who now haunts his dreams in the guise of a dead mackerel on ice in the local fish store with Pussy's bloated face and thick lips … Pussy sleeps with the fishes."

"So, what else do you make of your own dream?" the good doctor asked, nudging me back on course.

"There's no question it's an encounter with the shadow,"

I said without hesitation, "but it's certainly not a simple encounter, despite the dream's suggestion of a mindless barbarism."

"Please elaborate."

"Well, here again as in earlier dreams the shift in point of view strikes me as key. In other words, the dream's form or structure is at least as important as its content."

He nodded thoughtfully, implying I should go on.

"To me this means that what the dream is saying about my relationship to the shadow, and a possible change in that relationship, is more important than the shadow figure in itself."

"I'm not sure that's not a truism, but go on anyway," the doctor reflected.

"Come again?"

"Well, I just mean that dreams of the shadow are *always* about the dreamer's relationship to it, the status and permutations of that relationship, and so on. There's no such thing as the shadow 'in itself.'"

"Ah, I see. I guess I'm not putting this clearly. What am I trying to say? Let's see … It seems to me the dream is reflecting not just a change, but a significant change, maybe a profound change, in my relationship to the shadow. Yes, that's it—it's the fact that the change itself is important enough for the dream to do a big presto-change-o manipulation of its own ontological structure, in having me actually morph from an observer of Tony *into* the man himself. I'd say that's a pretty big deal, wouldn't you?"

"Possibly. Let's hear more."

"Well, look, we've spent a lot of time here discussing

the gradual process of getting to know the shadow in the course of analysis, the pitfalls and problems of that evolving acquaintance, such as avoidance and identification, the delicacy of steering a middle course and so forth—you know what I mean … Well, I think this dream marks a big shift in the direction of my identification with the shadow—now hold on, let me explain," I urged, as the doctor opened his mouth as if in protest. "I'm not using the term 'identification' in the way you might think … This is a terribly subtle point; I only hope I have the power to get it across … Let's put it this way: If I say to you, 'I *am* Tony Soprano!', which amounts to saying, 'I *am* evil!', there are two profoundly different ways to intend that statement, one in which the word 'evil' is an adjective and one in which it's a noun … Are you with me?" I felt he was, but only tentatively, with thinning patience. I felt I'd better get to it and fast. "Well, I'm using 'evil' as a noun, that is, I'm saying that, in *becoming* the evil that Tony is, in making it my very being (hence: ontological), which happens, as it were, magically through the dream's shift of viewpoint, I in fact overcome that evil—I vanquish it totally, turning it into its own opposite: good—this on the mystical principle of the meeting of opposites in the deepest depths of the mind … Please stay with me a bit longer; this is *not* just some trivial exercise in grammar … Whereas if I had intended 'evil' as an adjective, I would've been saying no more than that I was adding the quality of evil to the mix of character traits that make up my personal identity—which is the sense in which such a statement would normally be used and understood. For example, we say that, in committing murder, John X has turned evil, that is to say, he's now a being with a loathsome quality, among others, that we term 'evil.' You see, it's the difference between what Zen calls the delusive mind of dualism (A *has* B), our usual condition, and that Oneness that has nothing to do with number, wherein existence, 'is-ness,' is at last fully present to and identical with itself (A *is* B *is* me). Here the difference, or *différance*, between 'being' and 'having' has completely fallen away. That's why a certain Zen master, back in the 60's era of nuclear anxiety, could say with utter placidity, 'If somebody drops a bomb on me, no problem. I'll just become the bomb.' A sword cannot cut itself. Anything you become you redeem ... That's why the dream, the instant I shift into Tony's persona, has me emphasize the word 'am'; it's not a perfunctory introductory, 'Hi, I'm Tony Soprano!', but a majesterial 'I *AM* Tony Soprano!' ... God, not to be blasphemous or offend your delicate Catholic sensibilities, but it almost carries the awe of the Old Testament Yahweh's 'I am who am,' where 'am-ness' (a better word then 'is-ness') is revealed to be the very seat of Divinity.

"Is this making any sense at all?" I asked, cringing just a little.

"I think so," Dr. P. said tentatively. "My but you certainly are full of philosophical piss and vinegar today, aren't you? You're going to make me earn the check ... Seriously though, what I think you're saying sounds very much like philosopher of religion Franklin Merrell-Wolff's notion of the superior mode of knowledge that comes with 'the Recognition,' which is his term for Enlightenment. He even calls it 'knowledge through identity,' a condition in which the knower, the thing known and the act of knowing are all one and the same. Here in analysis that would mean knowing the shadow from the inside, as it were, by actually *being* it.[42]

"I must say I'm not quite sure, as an analyst, what to make of this idea of knowledge of an archetype through identity with it. Jung insists, of course, that the archetypes can never be directly known or experienced, being as they are part of the objective psyche, that is, the collective unconscious. But I don't think he has in mind the kind of knowing—intuitive mystical knowing—that I believe you're referring to; it's more of a labored, emotional-analytical awareness of the reflected images of the archetypes as we experience them in dreams. In becoming known and understood through analysis, these images are said to be integrated into, or coordinated with, consciousness; and this enrichment of consciousness is the individuation process. What you're getting at strikes me as something entirely different. Whether at some point it tallies with individuation remains to be seen, in my view; Jung himself is not always so clear on what it is that constitutes the psychic *summum bonum.* So let's just say that, for now, I'm willing to suspend judgment on this question of mastering the shadow by 'becoming' it, in other words, the matter of your dream interpretation, at least in the context of a discussion of the mystical consciousness with its 'altered states,' especially in view of the fact that our Western psychology simply does not yet know enough about them."

"I couldn't agree more," I seconded heartily. "And what makes the whole business even harder to sort out—fiendishly hard really—is that, with Enlightenment, the so-called signifier and signified, or concepts and their referents (another pair of opposites), are also revealed to be One, in the sense of an ontological continuum, which means for all intents and purposes the collapse of the signifying images of the archetypes into the archetypes themselves. This makes Jung right in an odd sort of way since, in one's coming to 'know' the shadow through such identity with it, as happens in Enlightenment, the shadow as such must cease to exist, and there would then be … nothing to know, at least from an intellectual point of view. This implies that, once something is completely liberated, even from the depths of the transpersonal or collective unconscious, assuming that to be possible at least in theory, it ceases to exist as such in the sense that it is revealed never to have existed at all. It was merely formed and held in a kind of pseudo-existence by the binarizing mind. This is only one or two steps away from the Buddhist notion of *sunyata,* the fundamental emptiness of all things, don't you think?"

"I'm not sure what I think at this point," the good doctor said, shaking his head. "You've probably heard the Zen story about the two monks who have taken their intellectual dissection of the dharma about as far as it will go, at which point one of them says, in effect, 'Oh, screw it. Let's have a beer.' Well, we can't have a beer here—alas!—but we can at least take another sip from the refreshing font of your Soprano dream."

Far be it from me to resist such a graceful segue, I thought. "You should know," I continued, "the return of the tollbooth image did not escape me."

"Good," he smiled.

"Nor did the vast difference in the image's function here from what it was in that early Keystone Kops/Lincoln Tunnel dream. There I'm being pursued for not paying my toll. Here I swipe the ticket without a thought as to any toll, as I chomp on a six-inch phallitela."

"Phalli- what?"

"Phallitela. Tony's phallic panatela. A marvelous expression of the shadow's attitude of fucking anything it pleases and damn the consequences—"

"—I'm sure you're not announcing that as your new 'liberated' attitude towards sexual behavior," the doctor queried, apparently needing reassurance.

"Of course not. That would be 'evil' as adjective rather than as noun, a mere affectation as opposed to transformation. Where *were* you ten minutes ago?"

"Now, now," he said, raising a cautionary finger, "no need for smart-ass remarks. Don't forget, I can always have one of the boys turn you into a soprano of a quite different sort."

We laughed, and it felt good. This delightfully dark kibitzing, I thought, is just the sort of fun you can have with the shadow when you get to know it a little. "You know," I said, resuming my associations, "although I was born and raised mostly in Hoboken, New Jersey, a concrete jungle that had no shortage of 'wise guys,'[43] I don't remember ever laying eyes on anyone I knew to be one. Oh, they were around all right; I know that they controlled the numbers racket in the various candy and newspaper stores around the city in the 50's and 60's. People would pick up the evening edition of the *New York Daily News* and turn immediately to the sports section in the back to locate the last three digits in the number for the "Total Mutual Handle" at some racetrack that day. That would be the winning number. Of course, over the years you'd spend thousands to win hundreds.

"Still, I couldn't tell you who belonged to what gang. It wasn't until I met my wife, who is of Italian-ethnic extraction, that I had my first 'close encounter' with a wise guy. It must've been in the mid 70's, after we'd been married a couple of years and we were in Brooklyn visiting Dottie's mother, sister and brother for a few days. They lived in an Italian-American neighborhood in the Red Hook section of Brooklyn, literally a stone's throw from the East River piers with their corrupt mob-ruled unions. (In fact, I might mention as an aside that the great film, *On the Waterfront,* which is about just this union corruption on the Brooklyn piers, was actually filmed mostly in Hoboken. So Dottie and I have always had this weird bond of a film masterpiece about mob violence in the neighborhood *she* grew up in that was made in the neighborhood *I* grew up in!—But I actually watched some of the filming myself; it must've been in 1952 or 53 when I was in grammar school. Anyway, one day around noon when I was in a small crowd watching them shoot from off to the side, the crew broke for lunch and I actually saw the great Marlon Brando, who was eating his sandwich on some nearby tenement stoop, get shoed away by an irate landlady for loitering on her property. Of course, he was dressed in character and obviously looked to her like a bum, so who could've blamed the woman? The kicker is, he simply got up without protest and shuffled off to finish his sandwich elsewhere.)

"... But back to my close encounter. It was a hot evening in July or August and we'd just finished dinner. Strains of Neapolitan trumpets wafted in from the street below through the open windows of my mother-in-law's flat. It was one of those great street festivals being celebrated in honor of the Blessed Virgin. You could almost smell the *zeppole* and the Italian sausage sizzling in their grease. My mother-in-law and I were at the window overlooking all the revelry, just leaning on the sill watching in silence. The feast was set up on the far side of the street intersection that lay just to the right of our house as you looked out, so, let's say, no more than a hundred-thirty or so feet from our vantage point. So Mom and I had the equivalent of upper-box-seats at a Mets game. As was the custom, a life-sized statue of the Virgin had been set on a pedestal right there in front of the church that stood on the intersection. Looking closely at the statue, you could see the traditional ribbons of paper money, doubtless mostly ones and fives, hanging down along the pedestal's base from the Virgin's feet, sincere donations of a community that hadn't much to spare.

"Anyway, as we watched from our private box, we observed a short, swarthy man dressed in a polo shirt and slacks as he approached the statue and pinned, not a bill, but a roll of bills to one of the dangling ribbons. Once satisfied his gift was secure, he just stood there with hands clasped together at his belt and head slightly bowed, apparently in silent prayer. Noticing my interest in this quiet little vignette amidst all the raucous celebrating, my mother-in-law, a streetwise lady, 'born and bred' as they say, who had taken upon herself the role of informal neighborhood sentinel, turns to me and says, 'You see that guy standing in front of the Virgin over there? That's Joey Bananas [excuse the alias]. They say he's whacked at least ten men … But he always gives to the Church.'

"And that, Dr. P., was my close encounter—as close as I ever want to get, anyway—with a wise guy."

"And from it you learned? …"

"… that even Tony Soprano has some good in him—no, no, it's more than that. It's that good and evil, Saints and Shadows, are at bottom just further empty categories, polarized mental constructs that actually tend to create the very divisions they're meant only to reflect. "

"I see. So you'd be willing to overlook, even tolerate, the brutality, the violence, of a man like Joey Bananas?"

"No, of course not. I'm no libertine. Once the cosmos has come asunder, we have no choice but to play by *some* rules of law and order to protect ourselves. We've made our bed, as they say. But for a human being, mere law and order can never be enough. We must, at the same time, find some way to re-member, to reattach, the 'things that have fallen apart,' to paraphrase Yeats, to restore 'the center that could not hold.' … I suppose that's as good a way as any to explain why I'm here doing this with you."

We both just sat quietly and relaxed for a moment. A brief time-out seemed in order. Then a happy thought popped and I chirped up: "My favorite holiday, Thanksgiving, is not far off. That means a horde of relatives will be descending on the McCort compound for a few days of wine, wom- … er, wine and song. Among them will be my brother-in-law, Rick, who's driving up from Staten Island with his son, my nephew, Joseph. Now there's a guy—Rick, I mean—who's almost a dead ringer for Tony Soprano's nephew, Christopher: same slim build, same shock of chestnut hair, same 'fuhgeddaboudit' Brooklynese, same coarse charm, same broad humor, even the same aquiline beak. And yet, five minutes' chatting with Rick will show you that, for all their superficial resemblance, he is the flipside of Christopher, a coke addict who has his own fiancée rubbed out for talking to the Feds; whereas Rick, an ex-Marine Vietnam vet who is no stranger to violence and can handle himself, is a deacon in the local Catholic church and ministers to shut-ins after Sunday Mass.

“And yet, just how thin and porous, how subject to temporary erasure, the line between ‘Rick’ and ‘Christopher’ is in any of us, was brought home to me in chilling fashion one evening in Staten Island some years ago on an errand Rick and I were running to the corner grocery. We were walking up to the entrance to this Mom-and-Pop store to pick up bagels or something when a young neighborhood tough, who was standing in the doorway leaning against the doorpost, raised his leg and braced it against the opposite post, effectively barring us from entrance. Accentuating his insolence with a defiant silence, he just glowered at us, challenging us to a response. Now, whereas *my* instinct was to back off and head over to another grocery across the street, an intention I signaled to Rick by protectively extending my arm diagonally down and in front of him, he just gently pushed my arm aside, walked right up to the youth, who had a good four or five inches on him, as casually as you please, looked him straight in the eye and bellowed, in his boldest drill-sergeant bass, ‘MOVE OR DIE!’ Everyone in the parking lot within earshot of the confrontation stopped and looked, as the young man meekly removed his leg to let us pass.

“Now, if you ask me whether Rick, a Catholic deacon, meant what he said, I can only answer that you had to be there, because then you would know, as I knew, and as our young thug certainly knew, that the situation was, as they say, a no-brainer … Oh yes, it occurs to me that Rick and Christopher share yet another element of differential symmetry: Rick, I’m afraid, can only rarely find it in himself to pick up the phone and share the bounty of his Christian ministry with his own brother Andy, who is schizophrenic and lives alone with few friends and little social support; and Christopher's very Christian last name is 'Moltisanti'—'many saints.' Wonderful imbroglio, no?!"

"See you next week," Dr. P. said, rising. "I'm off to the medicine chest."

(17) January 2007: Judge Loophole, and a Little Help from My Friends

I'm in court to answer for a traffic violation. I have the ticket with me. Dottie is sitting next to me. I stand to face the judge who says: "You know, Mr. McCort, I could use a loophole in the law to sentence you to death. I'll make my decision tomorrow when we reconvene." The scene shifts: I'm outside the courthouse with Dottie and a few friends who showed up for moral support. They play down the judge's threat, reassuring me, "Don't worry, it's only a traffic ticket. He'd never do that." They take it very lightly.

"Stuck in traffic again, are we?"

"I know you well enough by now to feel sure you'd never allow yourself such a cutting pun if you believed the dream reflected any real inner threat," I said smiling.

"You know me well, indeed, Herr Professor" Dr. P. replied, brushing some imaginary lint from his pant leg. "But what about you? Do *you* feel that way about it?"

"Yes, I do; and I'm sure you could tell me why I do," I answered, as we went back and forth in this manner, each telling the other what was on the other's mind. This is not to say we enjoyed such easy interpsychic *Verkehr* all the time these days, or even as a rule; to be sure, we continued to disagree occasionally on this or that point of the meaning of a dream image or intent, and at times one of us would be nonplussed by some subtle distinction made by the other on a question arising, usually, from the spiritual end of the psychospiritual continuum (such as his or my 'definition' of Enlightenment, as if there could be such a thing). But on the whole I would say that Dr. P. and I had forged for ourselves a relationship which, from my side at least, could be described as enjoyable, harmonious and efficient. It was, furthermore, a relationship nourished in no small part by a deepening bond of what I felt to be mutual affection. Over our years together, I had come to feel I cared as deeply about the doctor's well being as he, the "official" caregiver, did about mine. To some extent this was a paternal affection on my part, which, in an odd and fascinating way, fitted in seamlessly with the filial feeling I'd long had for my younger therapist-father.

I suppose a natural consequence of all this was that I actually began to look forward to our sessions, no longer simply going to them out of some perfunctory sense of discipline or routine. Moreover, insatiably curious sort that I am, once I became aware of this, shall we say, happy change of attitude in myself, I tried to reason out what other, more objective, factors, quite apart from this bond of affection, might account for it, which meant, in effect, taking stock of where I, as an analysand, stood in the analytic process. I felt, after some six years, that I'd bared much, perhaps most, of what needed to be bared and, with the help of Dr. P.'s unfailing attentiveness and keen insight, had worked through a good deal of the pain that came with it, and not just once but over and over again, dream by persistent dream, to the point where I could actually feel the lifelong brunt of conflict deep within me grow thin and porous, as if it were an ancient knot about the thickness of a ship's rope that had at last begun to fray. There would likely be no further stinging revelations to endure, and, even if there were, I knew I could count on the "rhythm" of the analysis to carry me through them. This brightened my outlook and moved me to take life less "seriously." No longer need my sessions, nor life itself, I felt, be so grim. This, in turn, allowed me to take a more relaxed and creative approach to the sessions, which had the paradoxical effect of making them even more productive than they had been: the less need I felt to get something out of them, the more they yielded, and the more clearly I came to understand the Zen wisdom that there is a sense in which less effort is, indeed, more. Only, the price in great effort had first to be paid (over six years, in my case) before it could finally begin to be let go of.

Then there was one other factor—I'll call it "contextual"—that tended to undergird my growing sense of optimism. It's simply that, more and more, I found I was losing my preoccupation with, and even interest in, the whole idea of a "cure." It seemed to me it was quite enough to be doing this work, which I found so enriching in and of itself, apart from any psychological "pay-off." The work, after all, had a direct, compelling appeal to my deepest emotional and intellectual values, values I had myself spent decades promulgating to others in the classroom and in my writing. Such an intimate nexus between therapy and my own heart's delight was, as the proverb says of virtue, "its own reward." I found I no longer much cared whether I was still "neurotic" or which diagnostic category I fitted into. And this very indifference to matters that once sorely vexed me, doubtless a combined product of the therapy itself and advancing age, seemed to be itself "curative." For all I knew, such indifference was what was meant by "cure." It got harder and harder to keep notions of health and pathology apart. Was there, at least with respect to the mind, any line between them not drawn in the sand by the intellect? And then, I thought, didn't the same dialectical idea, the same looking-glass logic, also apply to those other sacred cows of mine, Ignorance and Enlightenment. Would I ever outgrow my knee-jerk reflex to separate them? Ah, the perfidy of the dichotomizing intellect, this inner thinking machine of ours, in the service of the ego, I reflected. And all this led further to thinking about thinking and about the nature of the act, or should I say "event," of thinking, and finally to the conviction, which for me personally is now beyond dispute, that all thought thinks itself, since, after all, what could any so-called "thinker" possibly be other than a product of thought. "Thought there is, but none who think it," as the Buddha might have said.

This was all well and good, but it is not to say that I now regarded myself as some shining paragon of mental health—far from it. I was still subject to occasional bouts of depression, but they were shorter now and seemed to be diminishing in frequency. Yet when they did come, they always showed up wrapped around my life koan, "the Problem," which seemed to contain within itself, like some psychic microcosm, all the debilitating emotions, obsessions and moods that had ever afflicted me. I mean, of course, the "abandoned child" and my own implacable martinet of a conscience. What was the status of *that* issue at this point, for certainly it alone was the standard against which the success or failure of my analysis was to be measured. In a strange way, I thought, this made my "case" an easy one to judge. Had I come to terms with this weighty matter, or had I not? If I had not, then this new hard-won, carefree attitude of mine towards life could be no more than a temporary self-deception. On balance, I did think the sensation of granite-like "hardness" the problem always presented when it took over the inner space of my consciousness had softened somewhat, but that did not give me confidence enough to feel I could do without Dr. P.'s assurances that I was "getting there."

So when I came in on this frigid January afternoon with my dream about "Judge Loophole," it was, as I told him, at the tail end of one of these occasional spikes of depression that continued to assail me; and it was, by now, no longer a matter of determining which problem, but which aspect of "*the* Problem," the dream was about.

" … No, but seriously," I continued, "the dream doesn't really scare me, even though it looks scary on the surface with its threat of execution."

"Are you sure? I mean, this is *execution,* and for something as minor as a traffic violation, say, speeding or driving the wrong way on a one-way street. Sounds pretty scary to me," the doctor said, in a mildly ironic tone I felt was intended to goad me gently towards considering a certain point of view. But, alert to his opening pun as I had been, I already knew where he was headed. And, of course, he knew I knew.

"My dear Doctor," I said drolly, "we both know only too well that the word 'traffic' in my dream lexicon is a code word used by my unconscious for 'intercourse,' this via the German word *Verkehr,* which, conveniently, translates as both vehicular and sexual 'traffic', i.e., 'intercourse.' This pun has come up here at least one other time—I think it was in our discussion of that parking-lot dream years ago, and my associations to Kafka's story, 'The Judgment,' which, you'll remember, ends with that ambiguous image of bridge 'traffic' that accompanies the hero's self-execution. And, of course, we also know there's nothing 'minor' about that kind of 'traffic violation' in the court of my conscience ... Still, at this stage of the game I regard the dream as nothing more than a further phase in the slow working-out of 'the Problem,' just the next in a series of the egoic demon's last gasps before he expires ... It's not unlike the finale of Tchaikovsky's *Pathetique Symphony,* the most profound music of longing ever written: again and again the heartrending waves of the strings rise up, each time crying out a more desperate demand for fulfillment—to no avail. Destiny remains unmoved, and, at last surrendering to exhaustion, the cellos wither and shrink down into a succession of pathetic whimpers, fading finally into the silence of death ... This is the music Stravinsky is said to have listened to on his own deathbed—Stravinsky, mind you, that primitive modernist who loathed all things romantic!"

Narrowing his gaze ever so slightly to a squint, Dr. P. exhaled audibly through his nostrils and urged, "Herr Professor, could we please get back to court—I mean, with all due respect to Tchaikovsky, Stravinsky, Rimsky-Korsakov and the entire litany of musical '–sky's' immortalized by Danny Kaye?"[44]

Taken aback by this vulgar reduction of my little peroration to farce, I eyed the Doctor in mock-horror, feigning speechless incredulity in the face of such abject philistinism. "Okay, pal, let's bring it down ta yewer level," I snarled in my best Damon-Runyon-ese, having decided to avenge myself by indulging one of my favorite pastimes, the Joisey wise-guy tease: "Look, dis here fuckin' dibble wut's in my noggin, see, da one wut wants an eye fuh 'n eye—nuttin' less—and don't show no moicy, see—anyway, dis here dibble—I gottim on da ropes, see, and e's goin' down fudda count … See?!"

"I see," said Dr. P., rolling his eyes. "Nevertheless, just for the hell of it, the dream … *See?*"

Loathe as I was to leave off kibitzing—I was having too much fun—I could tell the bit was wearing thin and so reluctantly turned my attention to the dream. "All right, back to court we go. Or should I say, 'back to *Mc*Court.' … That's me all right, 'Dennis Son o' the Court,' to invoke the meaning of the old Gaelic prefix. That's just what I am, a true son of the court. I've often wondered what nefarious influence my legalistic surname might've had on the formation of this draconian conscience of mine. It's hard to believe your own name, your lifelong 'badge,' so to speak, doesn't have some impact on the way you view yourself and the world. Some people pay a lot of money to change a name they're unhappy with."

"That's an interesting point you bring up, and I don't doubt there's some truth to it. My own name, 'Purper,' as you would know, is a corruption, linguistically speaking, of the German word for 'purple': *Purpur.* I consider myself to have lucked out on that score: most English speakers' associations to 'Purper,' like my own, would include such happy things as 'royal purple,' 'porpoises' and 'purpose,' as in 'purposeful' or one's 'life purpose.' All wholesome signifiers. Your name could, of course, go in the same affirmative direction, suggesting as it does the bedrock value of justice; a 'son of the court' is a 'son of justice.' The problem here is the age-old one of the mind's tendency to take a good thing too far, turning a virtue into its own vice. Wise King Salomon becomes hanging Judge Roy Bean. Justice becomes vindictiveness."

"Yes," I agreed, "and yet it's this same faculty of reason, the tool of intellect, that operates in both. Reason and its m.o., logic, can usually find a way to give the grasping ego what it wants; it acts only too often in the service of the personal or collective will. And it serves as well as a cover for that will, giving it the appearance of fairness and balance. I'd go so far as to say your own profession, psychoanalysis, is based on that consideration: conscious reason as a mask for forbidden motive and peremptory affect. The great social theorist, Theodor Adorno, wrote a brilliant study called *The Dialectic of Enlightenment,* which lays out in a profoundly penetrating analysis just how that noble Age of Reason itself, the Enlightenment of the eighteenth century, has warped into the highly organized technological capitalism that rules us all with an iron fist in our own time. He calls our culture an 'industry,' 'the culture industry,' to convey the idea that every aspect of our lives today, including even such traditional bastions of creative freedom as art, music and literature, is rigidly controlled and manipulated by the plutocrats of industry—the corporate moguls and financiers and bankers—who bend none other than this quasi divine power of ours, *reason,* to their own rapacious wills. What was, a little over two hundred years ago, humanity's best hope for freedom and equality has, for us, morphed into a grotesque caricature of itself.

"This very fact, that even the most benign power is subject to the law of dialectical transformation, this bipolarity that is of the nature of all power, rendering it intrinsically unstable and vulnerable to corruption, could—I say *could*—cause me some anxiety as I regard the dream character of Judge Loophole. This, especially considering how very much at home dialectical swings are in dreams: light becomes dark, inside outside, smiles leers, and so on."

"You stress 'could,' implying, I take it, that it doesn't?" Dr. P. interrupted.

"That's right, it doesn't, as I said earlier. I doubt very much that Judge Loophole will turn into Judge Bean, say, in a future dream, despite even the dream's own suggestion that he easily could—you know, by invoking that 'loophole' in the law in order to find me guilty, a loophole he even appears to taunt me with simply by mentioning it."

"So where is this confidence coming from that you're safe from this potential tyrant's abuse of power? How can you be sure he won't sentence you to death when court reconvenes?" the doctor asked with some insistence, though I knew from his even tone that that insistence was affected, that it was his, by now familiar, way of getting me to articulate what he had already clearly seen from the beginning. He wanted to assure himself I saw what he saw.

"Simple," I said, "I have friends here, people who are on my side. When court adjourns and we all meet outside, they assure me that the judge would never pull such an outrageous stunt, that I really have nothing to worry about, and this does reassure me. You'll recall, one actually says to me, 'Don't worry, it's only a traffic ticket. He'd never do that.' This is a long way from the cobra under the bridge—no mitigating presence there!"

"Fine," Dr. P. said, "I'm with you, but still, they're merely expressing an opinion; maybe they're just trying to be optimistic, for your sake—you know, helping you to keep your spirits up." He was playing devil's advocate, a strategy he employed now and then to help me clarify, and thereby reinforce, my own point of view. I appreciated this because it usually worked.

"Ah, but you're judging the logic of the dream by the same criteria you'd apply to an actual social situation in waking life; and we both know that 'dream society' has an entirely different ontology."

"Do tell," he perked up, as if this were news to him.

"I've long been convinced that every single element in a dream represents—no, *is*—some aspect of the dreamer, everything right down to the carpet the dream characters are standing on. (I'll put aside for now the psychospiritual conclusion I think follows from this, that dreams are much closer to the way things really are than is waking life.) This means that my friends are decidedly *not* expressing a mere opinion but are actually mitigating, as the opposite pole of a dialectical dynamic, the judge's potential harshness. Despite appearances, the two exist interdependently (as, in myriad ways gross and subtle, all things in a dream exist interdependently with all other things): at this point in my process, I would say that there can no longer be a 'hanging judge' conscience all by itself, without a differentially symmetric group of friends—compassionate friends—to balance it out. The dream is a gauge of the shift of the psychic balance of power. And while I have to be careful to avoid my tendency towards literalistic interpretations in these matters, I don't expect to have many more—oh, to hell with it: caution to the winds—*any* more dreams of the cobra sort."

"Excellent!" the doctor beamed. "But say more about these supportive friends of yours in the dream. Are they actual friends in life; do they remind you of anyone you know?"

"Hmm, I'm not sure … There are maybe three of them, all male I think, and they surround me and Dottie, who's by my side and is, I suppose, 'friend number 1.' None of the three resembles anyone I know, so I suppose they're just the 'idea' of friends, 'generic friends,' you might say—just as Judge Loophole is probably an allegorical image, to the point of caricature, of 'an-eye-for-an-eye' Old Testament justice. Actually this very feel I get from them of generality convinces me even more of their essentially dialectical relationship. There's nothing from my personal history here to complicate things. Even Dottie, who is, of course, at the center of my personal history, is, in this dream, really just another supporter. There's little sense of her as an individual."

"I see, so no relation to personal history, right?" he asked, in a way that unmistakably conveyed the sense of, "Think again, buster!" Getting the message, I immediately began to reconsider and needed about two seconds to catch up: the first to remember that this kind of question almost always meant: "Notice what's right here in front of your nose," and the second to actually notice him. "Ah, of course," I said with some embarrassment, " … a friend by my side, huh? So it's you on the other side of the dialectical seesaw, balancing out the judge with your compassion and moral support?"

"And why not? Is that so far-fetched?"

"No, it's not; but it's a group of men, three of them …"

"So? … You've never dreamt of me in the form of a group before? If memory serves, you once dreamt of me as your little female cousin—wasn't it way back in the Frankenstein-in-the-forest dream early on?"

This was not the first time the good doctor had astonished me with his uncanny ability to recall dreams from years earlier and then proceed to make telling connections between them and a current dream. But the link he was about to forge here and now convinced me he carried around some kind of dream roledex in his head: "So a small 'support group' would certainly be no more outlandish a symbol for me than a little-girl companion, don't you agree?"

I just nodded. When he was right, he was right.

"Case in point," he went on. "A few years ago, I appeared in a dream—or so we agreed at the time—as a small group of psychospiritual masters—what was the name of the organization ... oh yes, Avatar. I was 'cloned' into this cadre of Avatar masters whose offer of support you were resisting at that time, so much so that you actually left the group's inner sanctum—for you a claustrum, a hellhole of anxiety—and stepped outside, only to face a seedy neighborhood, with your car—i.e., your direction in life—nowhere in sight. In our discussion we decided that, on balance, the claustrum was a better deal than the 'seedy' unexamined life ... Remember?"

I could only shake my head in admiration. "I must say I'm impressed ... ; and as someone whose job it is to interpret literary texts to students and others, I must also admit that in this moment I feel just like a text myself, one you've just read with great precision ... So you're saying the dream is showing me my present-day self as a sort of field of more or less balanced tension between the poles of justice and mercy, or conscience and heart, with you as an image of the latter?"

"That's a good way of putting it."

"This idea of balanced tension ... dialectically opposite poles held in equipoise," I went on, "I see another way in which that might apply to this dream."

"Oh? Please, go on," he said, this time genuinely curious.

"Well, it has to do with the pun, you know, the verbal ambiguity in the charge against me: 'traffic violation.'" As I said this, I could see immediate recognition in Dr. P.'s expression. "In terms of the spectrum of violations from trivial to serious, this whole trial depends on one's interpretation of the term 'traffic,' doesn't it? Is the 'trafficking' I'm charged with vehicular or sexual? Or, getting a bit subtler, is the very ambiguity of it meant to undermine the distinction itself between trivial and serious; psychologically speaking, to inject a much-needed sense of doubt into the lopsidedly condemnatory attitude I've always had towards myself? Is my unconscious saying to me, in effect, "Look, it is possible, you know, to regard the thing for which you've so long crucified yourself far less seriously. Your culpability in the sexual act at issue here may be no more serious than that attached to an ordinary traffic ticket." And as so often with the magic of the unconscious, no sooner is something suggested than it is so—in the psychic economy; and all I need do is let it be so."

"And can you let it be so? Will you?" he asked. It was a serious question.

"Yes, I can, and I certainly intend to," I answered, with all the sincerity I could muster. "I think I'm finally ready to let Judge Loophole clone into the Keystone Kops."

"I believe you," he nodded. "Just stay between the pairs of opposites and all will be well. Be wary of your tendency to search out loopholes to unsettle things that have been settled."

"Of course ... *loopholes*!" I cried out in amazement, "the most striking word/image in the dream and we've hardly even considered it!"

"So consider already."

"Well, you brought it up, so how about taking the lead here, especially since I've got nothing."

"Fair enough," the good doctor conceded. "My first thought goes to the original meaning of the term which was used to describe a small hole or slit in the wall of a fortress or castle through which to shoot. The legal sense of it, as a means of escaping or evading the enforcement of a law, came, I think, much later. Today it's what a shifty lawyer might use to get a guilty client off. But interestingly, the way the term is used in your dream, legalistic though it be, also strikes me as a throwback, metaphorically, to the older physical sense of 'loophole.'"

Intrigued, I was all ears.

"Consider, now, that it's the judge himself who threatens to use it—as the 'small hole' in the bulwark of the law through which to fire an offensive weapon at you—and not a shyster lawyer looking for a way out for his client. To me, this shabby maneuvering on the judge's part undermines respect for his authority, in fact, it makes him into a silly, even an absurd, figure. How can you take seriously any judge who'd be willing to resort to a loophole, a defect in the law, to condemn someone to death? This is the objective psyche pointing out to you the absurdly extremist tendencies in your superego. 'Judge Loophole,' as you've aptly named him, turns out to be an oxymoron … So this is yet another irony generated by the tension of opposites in the dream: justice comically half-masking vindictiveness."

"I guess," I said, spinning out the thread, "it's comic in the way most attitudes and behavior strike us as comic when taken to an extreme—you know, Moliere's hypochondriac or Scrooge's miserliness. But when the trait is in yourself, as this vindictiveness towards self is in me—it's like being trapped with a … well, what else, a cobra in your head, poised to strike at its own sadistic pleasure, and that's anything but funny. Also, in my case the dark humor of it includes the transformation of the initially objective scales of justice—there it is again: reason—into the endless obsessive concern with details, details being another way of viewing 'loopholes,' so that these are now the hair-splitting legalistic form the cobra strikes take: 'Did I do the right thing in that last phone conversation with Nicole? Did I say the right thing? What did I mean by each particular thing I said? Could I have intended something else by those words, something culpable? Let's go over it all again and try to pin it down.' Each act, each word, each thought, each intent … ad nauseam and beyond, until what had been a sharp, incisive, healthy mind has turned to mush. I think this nightmarish potential transformation of true justice, which normally has humane term limits built into it, into endless legalistic obsession is the real threat Judge Loophole poses to me. A never-ending turning-over in the mind of loopholes in the moral law is the execution I really dread—a kind of death in life. Thank God for a little help from my friends.

"Another friend of mine, Kafka—a friend in misery—knew exactly what I'm talking about here. I believe he had every neurotic trait I have, and what's more, he grew up, like me, in a religious tradition—in his case, Judaism—that nourished them like poison mushrooms. In fact, Kafka's most famous piece, after *The Metamorphosis,* is precisely about this problem of the tendency of the reasoned consideration of an issue to turn into appalling hair-splitting obsession. Even the title of the piece, 'Vor dem Gesetz' or 'Before the Law,' suggests its neurotic grimness."

"'Before the Law' … 'Before the Law' … Oh sure," the good doctor affirmed in recollection. "That's the tale about the guy who just sits and waits outside and never does get admitted to the Law, isn't it?"

"That's the one," I said. "Kafka calls him 'ein Mann vom Lande,' 'a man from the country.' He comes to town to gain an audience with the Law—it's a parable—but the doorkeeper tells him maybe later but 'not now.' So he takes a seat and waits … and waits … and waits … his whole life. Nobody else ever shows up seeking admission. Just before he closes his eyes in death the doorkeeper tells him the reason no one else ever came was that this particular entrance was reserved for him alone."

"Your friend's gallows humor is on full display here, I see," Dr. P. chuckled.

"You haven't heard the half of it," I said. "Most readers think that little story is all there is to it because it usually appears in anthologies all by itself. (And it certainly can stand alone.) But the fact is, Kafka tucked it into his unfinished novel, *The Trial,* itself a gallows tale about a man executed for crimes never specified to him. Anyway, there's a scene in the novel that takes place in a cathedral, in which a priest preaches the parable to an empty house, so to speak, and afterwards falls into conversation with the antihero about the meaning of it. Now, get this: whereas the parable itself occupies a mere two pages of text, the debate between Joseph K., the antihero, and the priest over its interpretation occupies eight. Eight! They argue and haggle with each other, affirming, doubting, challenging, examining and reexamining every nuance of the story, as if they were trying mightily to push a helium-filled balloon under water, only to have it pop back up to the surface the instant they let go: 'the return of the interpreted.' The Law or the Scripture may be clear in itself and to itself, but the instant man begins to try to clarify it for *him*self, it 'pops back up' and all neurotic hell breaks loose and you have to start all over again and you wind up with eight pages of commentary on two pages of original text.

"Of course, those eight pages are only literally 'eight.' They end—or rather *don't* end—with … dot … dot … dot, suggesting, for man, a kind of eternal damnation to interpretation … Will we ever know with finality why the man from the country fails to attain the Law? Kafka's genius gives us room to read the scene as a whole, that is, in its cathedral-debate setting, in myriad ways. Many see it as his riff on the centuries-old tradition of hair-splitting rabbinical commentary on the *Talmud*, the original Jewish scriptures, while others, like me, prefer the more individual-psychological approach I've sketched here. Frankly, I think both takes on it are fundamentally the same. Whether you call it religious dogmatism or neurotic perfectionism, it's the same hell. You cannot wrestle, that is, debate, with the shadow side of Scripture, i.e., its Meaning, or with its spawn, the draconian conscience, without going to hell; and in hell you'll stay until you wise up and give up the struggle."

"That's well put," Dr. P. said thoughtfully after a moment. "On the other hand …" Oh God, no, I shuddered inwardly. "… on the other hand, aren't the rabbinical way of viewing the world—the ceaseless struggle to match text to meaning—and the … oh, let's call it the 'romantic' or 'poetic' way, which reads the text, or anything else for that matter, *forward* in a bliss of interpretation for its own sake, with no concern for match-ups—aren't these two modes *themselves* just another permutation of that dialectical rhythm that makes the world go round?"

Mouth agape, I could only stammer, "Thanks, … I needed that."

(18) June 2007: Lust Encumbered

It's night. I'm lying on my back on a bed in a hotel room in some European city, maybe Prague. The room is all but dark, the only illumination coming from a tiny lamp on a nightstand and a weak plane of light cast by a streetlamp against the room's ceiling from the street below. There are several people in the room around the bed, but they're no more than indistinct shadows shifting vaguely in the murk. On the bed next to me is a young, raven-haired beauty, with full red lips, passionate piercing eyes and unblemished skin as smooth as caramel. Suddenly she asks me, "What do you want?" Lifting her and holding her directly above me on the bed with the boundless strength of desire, I answer, in a virile voice matching that strength, "I want YOU!" The boldness with which I assert my desire for her surprises me. Slowly, gently, I lower her onto me and start to garland her face with soft kisses. After a moment she pulls back a bit, perhaps aware of the others in the room. I feel some uncertainty as to whether she really wants me. She seems to, and yet ...

The scene shifts: I'm walking the nocturnal streets of the same city, several blocks from the hotel. It feels like the maze of narrow streets that make up the Old Town section of Prague. Suddenly realizing I've lost my way, I try to use my usually reliable sense of direction to regain orientation. Approaching the nearest street sign, I read "Manhattan Ave.," which should reassure me with its familiar name but somehow doesn't. My sense of urgency mounts: I need to get back to the hotel to catch the limo ride to the airport for the flight home. There's not much time left.

"So?"

"Well, the dream has the usual imaginal trappings of the unconscious: the light above, the dark below, the—"

"—Excuse me, Herr Professor," the doctor remonstrated, "but you know better than that by now. Be very careful of using words like 'usual' or 'typical' when talking about your dreams here. Such terms often reflect, as in this instance, the scholar's attitude of 'I already know all this,' which cuts off discovery. If you already know something, what's the point of discussing it? It's already socked away in your inner vault of knowledge where it lies useless. We operate in present time here, which is not to say we don't note similarities among dreams, recurring themes and so forth; it's just that, when you tell a dream, you should always let everything you say express an attitude of first encounter, no matter how many variations on the dream you think you've had before."

"Sincere apologies!" I blurted out, and meant it. "You couldn't be more right. It's a lesson I thought I'd learned well in my Zen years: There really is no such thing as perfect repetition—better yet, 'repetition' *period.* Every sitting, every greeting, every cup of coffee happens for the first time. How much more so every dream. That sense of 'here we go again' is a delusive attitude of mind cast upon experience to deaden it … I think a good form of spiritual practice might be to eat the same food for breakfast every day for a year—make it something you like to begin with, since the challenge would be to continue liking it by experiencing it each morning, as it were, anew: 'Hmm, I've never tasted *these particular eggs* before.'"

My sincere apology to Dr. P. and enthusiastic support

of his plea for mindfulness were inspired, at least in part, by a milestone I had recently reached in my own life, one that, ironically, had brought this very lesson home to me in a once-in-a-lifetime way. It was one of those strange synchronicities in which life prefigures therapy: I had retired a month earlier after thirty-nine years as a professor of German language and literature at Syracuse University. This is to say, through no virtue or effort of my own, sheerly by dint of circumstance, I had shuffled off a thick cast of routine in which I'd wrapped my mind over nearly four decades in a plaster of Paris of internal sentences such as: 'fifteen weeks to go,' 'two more tests to correct,' 'oh no, not German 101 again,' 'that makes seventy-five semesters, or is it seventy-six.' During my working years even the mindfulness enjoined on me by Zen practice couldn't spring me from this prison of routine. Occasionally, to be sure, there would be glimmers of freedom: a literature course, maybe on Kafka or Zen or both, that would grab the students, and me along with them, and keep us enthralled all the way through; or the book I wrote in the late 90's which summed up what I had learned from study and spiritual practice and seen reflected in my favorite writers. But such oases would always eventually disappear back into the fog of dreary routine. I felt powerless to sustain them.

All that changed with my retirement. Suddenly, on that first Monday morning in June 2007, I awoke to see, stretched out before my mind's eye, nothing but empty space. I had no routine, none at all. What I had, for the first time since infancy, was a blank slate of 24/7, to be filled in by … my own interests and preferences. It felt exquisite: I could do, or not do, whatever I damn well pleased—*for the rest of my life!*

How I savored, giddy with delight, that first breakfast, with its two cups of coffee and thoroughly read newspaper. I listened to NPR radio till noon, no longer frazzled by the clock and the need to rush off to meet a 9:30 class. That was for my younger peon colleagues, whom I'd left behind to toil and moil in the vineyards of knowledge.

The stereotype of the new retiree, of course, is that of a man who finds this sudden freedom daunting, even frightening. He is warned by seniors and psychologists to prepare himself an elaborate schedule of activities, associations and hobbies well in advance of the big day so as to avoid the pitfall of depression that awaits him as a result of having had his identity, fashioned through his job, stripped from him. You need something to get you out of bed in the morning, went the conventional wisdom, something other than the double-shot of schnapps recommended by the philosopher Schopenhauer. Though unsure, I bet the opposite way on myself and seem to have won my bet. I prepared nothing. I phoned no one. I took full advantage of sleeping in on weekday mornings and loved it. Strangely I did not waste away into a drooling, senile cast-off of academic capitalism (despite what my wife may tell you). I found it wonderful at last to have the time to savor all the little pleasures of life I had allowed the press of work to bulldoze out of my days: staying up late to read, long naps whenever I felt like it, the aforementioned leisurely breakfasts. And in allowing myself to slow down and breathe in this way, I soon found myself itching to get back to more "serious" pursuits such as research and writing, literary translating, or maybe even nonfiction or creative writing of some sort.

One thing that helped me decide to take this unstructured—some might call it "lazy"—approach to retirement was a dream I reported to Dr. P. a few weeks earlier, during the period of the final days of my last semester when I'd already begun to clean out my office. I told him of a dream of the night before in which I found myself in some sort of large barracks-type building, near the head of a long line of inmates waiting for release that wrapped itself around the building's floor several times and completely filled its space. A few uniformed soldiers with rifles patrolled the inside, keeping a sharp eye on us. I was lucky enough to be near the head of the line; in fact I was the next to be released but one, so I felt confident, however tentatively, that freedom was near. A turnstile released the man in front of me, and he walked directly over to the nearby single glass door, the sort of door through which you'd exit a drug or small grocery store. It was the building's only exit. My sense was that, in heading for the door, the fellow had to make an effort to restrain his pace, lest one of the armed guards take a dim view of his rush to freedom.

The dream's reflection of my attitude towards retirement, with its unflattering image of the university as a prison camp, was so unmistakable, so blatant, that Dr. P. allowed himself to begin chuckling over it well before I could finish my report; and of course his chuckling was immediately infectious, so that I was barely able to get the final words of my narrative out of my mouth before we both decompensated into hysterics. "That … bad, … huh?" was all he could get out between paroxysms of laughter. Upon subsequent discussion we agreed that my life till then had had quite enough of schedule, routine and regimentation, thank you, and that it was worth a try to commence retirement without any artificial structure at all just to see if an organic one might evolve on its own. To date, I've had no second thoughts about it.

To be sure, discussions of retirement with Dr. P. had their serious side too, one of them in connection with the dream of desire I reported at the top of this particular session. After some preliminary work of association to the dream on my part, I suddenly asked, "Listen, do you think my 'liberation' from the university might also signal a parallel liberation from sexual guilt? I mean, considering my recent dream of getting sprung from the prison camp of academe—you know, 'free at last, free at last!' and all that; and now, a few weeks later, I dream of this sultry liaison with a dark-haired beauty in some exotic European hotel. Maybe sudden freedom in one area will spread its 'contagion' to others, right?"

Dr. P. smiled wanly as if to convey caution. "There's no way to predict such things. There could be such a bourgeoning effect of liberation: sometimes major transitions, 'passages,' from one stage of life to the next work that way; on the other hand, there might also be a lapse into a deeper entanglement in old problems; or, a third possibility, there might be no significant effect of retirement on sexual disposition. I would be remiss, though, if I didn't mention the caution that, often, when a man withdraws from the daily grind he's known for so long, he finds himself facing his demons without distraction—"

"—But that's a big reason why I come here every week, isn't it?" I interrupted, with just a smidge of accusation, "to head all that off at the pass."

"Quite so," he affirmed, "quite so. So we'll just keep our fingers crossed and see what happens."

I wasn't exactly thrilled at the good doctor's invocation of luck in the matter; at the same time, I knew he was no prophet and could offer no guarantees. Moreover, I had by now a deep trust in the process we were doing together and knew my best hedge against the vagaries of retirement was to dig into the work and keep at it. Somehow retirement would take care of itself.

"So, let's get back to that Prague hotel room, shall we?" he smiled, gently nudging the discussion back on track.

As I turned my thoughts to the darkened room, a curious association suddenly popped: "You know, it's the strangest thing—and yet I'm not at all surprised, since the hotel room does feel as if it's in Prague and Kafka's ghost does often seem to be sitting here next to me on the couch. (It's as if I'm doing analysis for both of us.) The minimal light in that room, with only the ceiling being dimly illuminated through a window by a streetlight from down below—it's taken directly from a striking image that occurs at the beginning of the second, middle, section of *The Metamorphosis.* It's the evening of the same day, the day of Gregor's change, and he's just resting in the middle of the floor on all … eights, or all tens—it's hard to pin down—in the wake of the catastrophic exposure of his hideous insect body to the family. It's dark because the light hasn't been turned on; he can't reach the switch (would it have been a switch by 1912—probably not), nor has any family member had the guts to enter the room and flip it on for him. So the only light he's got is from the street, and even that is high above him, leaving him only the feeblest visibility down there on the floor."

"And yet the two rooms, yours in the dream and Gregor's,

are not entirely parallel with respect to light, are they?" Dr. P. suggested, encouraging me to compare closely and carefully.

"No, they're not," I agreed, feeling the momentum of interpretation gathering. "In my dream there's the tiny lamp on the nightstand. It's not much but it's more than poor Gregor has."

"More for what purpose? Why do you think light is an issue in either scenario?"

"That's easy—well, I say 'easy' only because it's part of a detailed interpretation of the story I've worked out over some twenty years—"

"—Which means, let it be noted, that the light image has sunk deep down into your unconscious and has profound significance for you."

"No doubt. But, you know, it's not just the light but its complement, the darkness. It's the whole chiaroscuro effect; after all, what pair of opposites shows more clearly than light and darkness the total interdependence of terms. You can't have one without the other; they're ontologically joined at the hip. Likewise, I'm sure, what they stand for in both my dream and Kafka's story—the symbiosis of conscious and unconscious. Some Kafka critics like Emrich[45] deny that Kafka ever uses symbols or metaphors, unlike most writers, but don't you believe it. He was just better than most at hiding them, like here with the dim light in Gregor's room. Lying there in the darkness on the floor of his own bedroom, Gregor is plunged deep down into the hell of his own unconscious; the murky floor is his 'rock bottom,' so to speak. The comforting light of consciousness, what there is of it at least, is up on the ceiling, way above him, far out of reach. It's so different—and yet maybe not so different—from the man in 'The Cell,' that parable we talked about here some years ago, in which the poor bastard, having fully identified with the bland electric light of the room he's in, the light of consciousness, finally realizes that even that comfortable room is a trap, and now begins to peer into the other room, the room of dreams, wondering if *it* might not have an exit. That guy could be Gregor the evening before his metamorphosis."

"So you're saying Kafka's tale is about the nightmare of Gregor facing his own unconscious 'full throttle,' so to speak—a sort of psychotic break?"

"That's more or less the way I tend to read it, and explain it to my students, though I generally do without the lexicon of psychopathology," I said. "You have to remember, my dear doctor," I quipped, "poor Gregor didn't have *you,* or someone like you, to accompany him on the perilous journey down onto the floor of his own being. I, of course, do, and your indispensable company on my descent is represented in the dream by that little, yet vital, lamp sitting on the night table, the lamp of insight, enabling me to see and, in some necessary sense, appreciate and assimilate the dark forms I encounter down there on the floor—or, more precisely, on the bed. Currently sinister though they be, those forms are aspects of my self, or Self, capital 'S.'"

"Yes, let's get back to that bed."

"Would that I could, believe me! … At any rate, what's clear to me is that the modest lamp enabling me to see what I'm involved in on the bed symbolizes you as an enabler or instrument of some nascent insight on my part into my own sexual make-up, with all the—forgive the metaphor—warts included. Lust there is on this bed for sure, but just as surely it's lust encumbered."

"Encumbered how?"

"Well, that brings us right back to all that darkness: It's not only the sort of global darkness comprehending the unconscious domain totally and uniformly, but also patches of deeper darkness within the darkness, so to speak, … discrete, particular dark forces lurking within it … forces that are, shall we say, tainting the erotic atmosphere with nasty things like guilt and aggression. That's how I read those vague forms shifting back and forth around the bed. What scares me is that they *don't* scare me in the dream; it's as if they belong there, restlessly hovering around me, as if they're a necessary, and therefore oddly comfortable, accompaniment to any sexual experience I would have."

"They would be the 'warts,' the rough equivalent of Gregor's vile insect body, wouldn't you say?" Dr. P. asked softly, clearly intending to keep the question as unobtrusive as possible.

"I'm afraid so," I had to admit, feeling an inner repugnance even as I did so.

"All the guilt about sex," he began, "and the instinctual anger in reaction to that conditioned guilt—after all, how many men in this society don't ache to destroy the forces of authority that have robbed them of the profound pleasures of the body almost from day one—all this encumbrance of conflict reducing what should be an explosive release into freedom to a tiny firecracker painfully going off, usually in one's own hand [he couldn't help adding] … Feel it, feel the pain, the age-old ache, the profound deprivation of it. You know how the paradox works: as with any other straitjacket, the one on your genitals is its own principle of emancipation. As long as you don't flinch from the misery of it and allow yourself to slither back into resistance. You're ready to face and bear the misery; you now have the capacity to bear, and, through bearing, to transcend it … Transcendence just means the misery of conflict dissipates since there's no longer any attitude of attachment in you, with which you're identified, to keep it intact."

Leaning on the familiar strength of his fatherly tone, even more than on the words themselves, I did my best to let it all marinate within and around me; and, as so often in such moments of openness, a memory dropped into consciousness, almost like a coin into an old-fashioned pay phone. It was something I hadn't thought about in many years: "Would you believe I've only been to Harlem once in my life? … Weird, isn't it, for someone who grew up right across the river?"

Dr. P. just cocked his head quizzically in response, as if to say, "Yes, and the reason you bring this up now, pray tell, is? … "

"It was near the end of December, 1972. By then I'd been seeing Dottie for several months, so this would be two Christmases after my fateful final phone conversation with Nicole. I mention the link because the guilt over the child that had plagued me after the break-up with Nicole, having subsided somewhat over the intervening few years, came roaring back once I realized I was falling in love with Dottie. The likelihood that this 'monkey' would be on my back every time I got into bed with a woman dawned on me with a sickening shudder. It was weighing especially heavily that Friday evening after Christmas when we went to a holiday party in Harlem at the invitation of a good friend of Dottie's—her name was Sandy and she was black. They'd met in some science course at LIU and become fast friends; both were pre-med. Anyway, Sandy lived by herself in a high-rise apartment building in Harlem … I still remember driving north that evening up the FDR Drive along the East River heading for … a Harlem address, of all destinations! I was feeling, quite apart from the odd mixture of guilt and sexual heat I'd grown used to in Dottie's proximity, also this vague uneasiness combined with a sort of snooper's delight in having access to a social event at which 'Whitey' was generally not welcome. My girlfriend, who, though of Italian ancestry, could've passed for black herself, was my ticket of admission.

"Up in the elevator we went to, maybe, the fifteenth floor; we got out and turned right, down a short, dimly lit corridor to the apartment door. Dottie pressed the bell and, within seconds, the door swung open … I'll never forget the charge of excitement I felt as I looked in on a roiling sea of blackness—a few candles providing a modicum of light for a mass of shifting black forms, the dancing figures of some twenty-five or thirty friends of the hostess, who greeted us with a squeal of delight—"

"—Excuse me," Dr. P. broke in, "you describe the dancers as 'shifting black forms …'"

"Yes, I know what you're getting at: the shadows 'shifting vaguely in the darkness' around the bed in my dream—I'm sure that image is what sparked my memory just now, and that that night at Sandy's party is the key to this dream … and to a diagnosis, for good or ill, of the state of my libido … Just moments later, as we were slow-dancing and I was savoring the subtly perfumed warmth of Dottie's body pressed against mine, I looked up to find us totally surrounded by those shadowy forms. Without realizing it, we had literally danced ourselves out to the middle of the floor. As far as I could tell from a cursory glance around the room, I was the only white person there! Despite my immediate self-censure, I couldn't help feeling a twinge of claustrophobia as I involuntarily turned my head to locate the door. The darkened living room seemed quite large and fully occupied; the furniture had either been moved out or, more likely, pushed back against the walls to provide the maximum area for dancing. There would be no quick bolting from there.

"But as the moments passed, I found myself relaxing, letting the music and the atmosphere of intimacy pervade my body and finally also my mind. Slowly it became clear that I had no cause for anxiety: the young couples dancing around us seemed oblivious to my presence among them. I even began to feel an odd sense of gratitude to them for accepting me—but then I thought, no, no, that's not it, 'acceptance' makes too much of it; that's my own ego making me the center of attention; it was simply that I was being ignored, absorbed as they all were in one another, and somehow I found this much more comfortable than any sort of acceptance would have been. And with that I felt free to enjoy the sensual intoxication of the first slow dancing I had done in years. Dottie was especially fetching that evening in her snug red wranglers and a lightly scented neckerchief that set off her dark hair. For a few moments at least, I was lost in her beauty. It was only when the self-congratulatory thought suddenly occurred to me that I was still capable of enjoying the pleasures of eros without guilt that, of course, the sense of guilt returned, and I could only inwardly curse my seeming powerlessness within my own emotional house ..."

"... Still, there *was* that small oasis of forgetfulness, wasn't there?" Dr. P. asked in a coaxing tone.

"Sure, but what's the good of it if the sense of self-awareness must inevitably return to destroy it?" I asked with bitterness.

"But you see," Dr. P. retorted eagerly, "that's precisely what analysis is for: gradually to dismantle the wall between these two compartmentalized states of consciousness, the simple, naïve level of the oasis and the mature level of the self—in Blake's terms, the song of innocence and the song of experience. That's what the transcendence implied by Jung's ideal of individuation means: what we transcend is the infernal conflict between innocence and experience, or, more narrowly in your case, innocence and guilt. We reach a condition in which even these polar opposites are revealed as inseparable, and, once thus revealed, begin to flow happily into and out of each other. This is freedom."

"But do you see me as anywhere near such a condition? I certainly can't say *I* do."

"I do indeed," the doctor answered consolingly. "I would ask you to look at the dream in the context of the Harlem memory you just related. Earlier you complained that what upset you about the dream was the fact that the shifting shadows around the bed, the shadows of 'guilt and aggression' as you called them, didn't particularly scare you; in other words, you were afraid you might be about to surrender to depravity, to your own dark nature, perhaps in some private sadomasochistic orgy of lust there on the bed. You were appalled by your own apparent indifference to that possibility. But here again I must point out to you this stubborn tendency of yours to deny yourself the benefit of interpretive doubt. To me this relaxation you feel within the circle of your own shadow projections indicates, not indifference, but ease, … comfort, … a growing acceptance of those dark urges. Don't you see, you're not surrendering *to* them, you're surrendering your disowning *of* them as necessary parts of your psychic make-up; and, of course, to the extent you manage that, you gain mastery over them."

As I listened to Dr. P.'s corrective take on the dream, weighing and pondering it, even rooting for it, some unexpected support suddenly showed up: "Wait a minute, … of course! Your reading is spot-on. How could I forget the Tony Soprano dream we looked at not so long ago? As I recall, I read that dream myself pretty much the way you just read this one—a lessening of the distance, the alienation, between me and the Shadow … I don't get it, Dr. P. How could I see it so clearly there and be so blind to it here? I must be regressing."

"*Au contraire,* Herr Professor—if you'll pardon the clash of languages," the good man chuckled. "The process itself is a *pro*gression, objectively so, and, as such, remains relatively unaffected by the vagaries of the interpreting subject. Besides, that's what you have me for, to keep you on the interpretive straight and narrow. That being so, let me just put the period to this sentence by adding that the progressive, unfolding nature of analysis is also indicated in your dream by the street sign you come to on your anxious wanderings through the maze of Old Town Prague: 'Manhattan Ave.'"

"How so?"

"Prague is Harlem, and both are for you exotic 'foreign' domains of the shadow. Manhattan, or, more precisely, the avenue running through it, is an intermediate zone between Prague/Harlem and home, the home of the Self, analysis being the journey to one's true home. Bearing in mind that the dream is depicting this essentially circular—better yet, spiral—process with linear imagery, I would say it's telling you you're well on your way."

"Hmm ... so you say—but if that's the case, why am I not reassured by the street sign?"

"How should I know?" he answered with a shrug and a sudden Yiddish inflection. "Maybe because, if you take Manhattan, you get 'the Bronx and Staten Island too,' as it says in the song."

As I glowered at him, he laughed and got up saying, "Lighten up already, Herr Professor, or you'll wind up fretting all reassurance right out of the dream."

PART THREE: TRANSFORMATION

(19) September 2007: Gregor (the Musical?)

A beautiful woman with flowing dark hair is sitting next to me on a bench—I think it's the organ bench—in a church choir loft. I'm explaining to her with great pleasure how medieval choirs of monks sang their chants, how they stood, maybe a dozen of them, in a semicircle and followed the manual direction of the choirmaster who stood in the center before them—all of which is very curious since, in waking life, I know almost nothing about such matters. Yet, as I explain it to her, I have in my imagination a vivid picture of just such a choir of monks, standing in semicircle, singing to my own direction: each monk is chanting a different tone and I can actually "see" a golden beam of tonal energy coming from the mouth of each, from all twelve of them, all tonal lines converging in ... me, their leader. (It's as if I were the hub of an arc sending twelve spokes of music into me.) Somehow I am the meeting point for all twelve notes, which together form a grand chordal harmony. I note how beneficial the semicircle formation is since it allows the monks to see not only me but each other as well.

"Sounds like you missed your calling."

"Not a chance. Don't you remember how I dismissed Father York's advice to 'teach in black'?"

"Not the priesthood; I meant music."

"Ah, well, you may have something there. In the immortal words of Walter Pater, 'All art aspires to the condition of music.' She is the queen of the arts, and I her devoted subject."

"So what happened—how did you miss the bandwagon?" Dr. P. asked, mixing the metaphor as he shifted his weight to settle in comfortably for the session.

"Oh, I don't know," I mused. "Both my parents liked music well enough, but neither played an instrument so there was no hands-on influence of the sort you usually hear about in musical families. None of the kids in the neighborhood, which was working and lower-middle class, took lessons and I don't think it ever actually occurred to me to ask for music lessons of any kind. I did, however, take *art* lessons, drawing and painting, in seventh and eighth grades—I'd shown some small talent in copying as a boy—but, ironically, as I matured my interest in music deepened at about the same pace my interest in art declined … At any rate, by sophomore year high school the workload had gotten very heavy and there was no time for anything but listening to the stereo … uh, hi-fi. Actually, it was the old hi-fi phonograph we had that helped me discover the fabulous world of sound we stodgily call 'classical music,' a world I've lived in with awe ever since. A friend of mine from school lent me an LP of Dvorak's *New World Symphony.* I'd mentioned to him in passing that I loved the background music of some popular adventure series on TV—I think it was *Don Winslow of the Coast Guard.* He said he had that very music on record. "No way!" I scoffed. Next day he handed me the record. One play-through and I was hooked. You know, in that mid-fifties period of late radio/early TV, many kids developed a lifelong love of classical music from shows that used spirited passages from the 19th-century romantic-symphonic repertory to underscore the hero's derring-do; for a child's imagination there was something deeply magical in discovering, on the old 78 LP's, the musical source of his hero's courage: the Lone Ranger rode Silver to the majestic strains of Liszt and the breathtaking excitement of Rossini;[46] even Bugs Bunny and friends staged a cartoon production of Wagner's *Ring* cycle! Would you believe, Bugs as Siegmund, munching on a carrot and greeting Hunding with 'What's up, Doc?'"

"Yes, it's a classic! I've seen it many times," Dr. P. enthused.

"All my life, it seems, music has been a kind of spiritual food for me, filling a need religion had failed—and failed miserably—to fill. My doctoral dissertation, which later became my first book, was about relations between music and literature. The literary period I wound up specializing in, German romanticism, was almost as much about music as literature; the romantic poets even held music above their own verbal art, mythicizing it with such epithets as 'the music of the spheres' and 'fluid architecture.' I remember my astonishment when I read that Schopenhauer virtually equated music with his philosophical first principle, the World Will; and I was even more dumbfounded when I came across Nietzsche's stunning assertion, 'Without music life would be a mistake.' During my graduate school years especially, the German soul in this Irish-Italian-American body of mine resonated like wind chimes to all this rhapsodizing about the art that was supremely sufficient unto itself and needed no earthly models. At the same time, I remember being taken aback by Thomas Mann's critique of music and the German national character in his last novel, *Doctor Faustus,* a post-war book treating Germany's passion for music as a kind of Faustian bargain culminating ultimately in the catastrophe of the Nazis ... But you know, Dr. P., I think Mann's pessimism had, in the aftermath of my reading, an unintended paradoxical effect on me: all it did was deepen my awe of the demonic power of music, particularly German music: Beethoven, Schumann, Brahms, Wagner! … I'm sure I should never be allowed to hold any political office."

"Don't worry," he said, tongue firmly in cheek—still, just a little too fast for my liking.

"Through college and grad school and even in my early years at S.U., I sang tenor in several first-rate choral groups. Singing was the one way open to me of being actively involved in the music I loved; my last year in Baltimore at Hopkins, I was a member of the Baltimore Choral Arts Society and had the unforgettable experience of participating in a performance of the Brahm's *Requiem.* This was a massive chorus of about eighty voices, supported by the Baltimore Symphony Orchestra. That event was the closest I ever came, before Zen at least, to what you, as a psychologist, might call 'a peak experience.'"

"And with that recollection," the doctor smartly interpolated, "it seems you've found your way back to your dream, which is all about choral singing, isn't it?"

"Yes. It was dazzling, … uplifting—the dream, I mean—full of magic, and awe. I don't think I've ever dreamt a more profound affirmation of life. I only wish my actual life reflected the dream more closely."

"Maybe it does, only in some mysterious way you can't see, not yet anyway. Maybe at some point you will see it. It sounds like an archetypal dream, and you know they can be prophetic … But please go on."

"Well, the choral image is certainly mandala-like: the monks in a semicircle all singing to me as if to a center; each note is a grace note—I swear that just came out of me; I don't even know what a grace note is," I said laughingly.

"I think it means 'gratuitous,' in the sense of not being essential to the melody, a note just added on for ornamental purposes," the doctor said with satisfaction. "Here, of course, I would take it as a clear pun from the unconscious—"

"—Sure," I said, right with him on point, "all twelve sung notes are grace notes in the sense of being a gift … a gift to me, something gratuitous, something I could never secure on my own."

"That's right."

"Sounds as if it might be the fruit of the unconscious process we're doing here, the fruit of individuation: doing these sessions is like planting seeds, and at some point the harvest is there; but you can't 'make' the seeds grow, can you?"

"Quite right—'grow' is, strictly speaking, an intransitive verb."

"But thinking about this music of the monks, this chanting: I don't think I actually *heard* anything in the dream, the dream had no sound at all. Rather, the sound was translated into the numinous visual imagery, into those twelve beams of light that came into me from each mouth … That's almost sexual, isn't it? I was penetrated, ravished, you might say, by twelve grace notes simultaneously, all of them together composing some sort of angelic 'visual' chord."

"The mystical literature is replete with descriptions by men of being, as you put it, 'ravished' by grace, or the Godhead, or the experience of the *unio mystica*. It's as if the human soul were essentially the feminine principle, prior to any gender distinction … It certainly all sounds like a wonderful experience of celestial harmony."

"Yes," I agreed, "but, curiously, it's a harmony expressed by music that's *seen* rather than heard, as if the tonal or auditory experience itself were too sublime for human ears, even in a dream. It's almost as if it had to be deflected to the eye."

"That would be in line with the romantic notion you mentioned earlier of music as a quasi transcendental art form, not bound by earthly models … So I take it you can't say anything about the music *qua* music?" the doctor probed.

I shrugged as if to agree, but in that instant a thought popped: "Well, hold on a minute now. There's certainly one thing I can say about it: it's that these monks are decidedly *not* singing Gregorian chant."

"How do you know that?"

"Simple," I said. "Though there's no sound, it's clear to me that each monk is singing a different note; each beam of light has a slightly different hue, as if to indicate a spectrum of tones, all of them blending to make up this grand chord. That would indicate they're singing the kind of harmony-based music we moderns are accustomed to, made up basically of chordal progressions. Historically that developed well after the plainsong of Gregorian chant, so it couldn't be Gregorian … Do I have that right or am I just blowing smoke here?"

"No, not at all," Dr. P. agreed, then summarizing my point with slow, gentle emphasis: "Over time, the Gregorian developed, … metamorphosed, you might say … into the harmonic—"

"Come again?"

"I say, Gregorian metamorphosed into harmonic …"

At first I couldn't believe he meant what I took him to be saying. But his Cheshire Cat grin immediately gave the lie to that. “You son of a -----,” I just managed to catch myself. “How the hell do you come up with these things?” I demanded to know.

“That’s easy,” he answered, “I don’t—*you* do; more precisely, your unconscious does. I’m just here to notice it … So tell me again about Gregory, or, in its Czech form, Gregor.”

Still a bit numb from the verbal shock, I nevertheless felt my mind abuzz with all sorts of associations, as if the Gregorian pun had cracked a dam. But they were whirring by so fast I was afraid I wouldn’t be able to catch any of them. Grabbing onto one, I said, “Actually, there are two metamorphoses in Kafka’s story, in my view at least. The first one is the horrific one announced in the opening sentence: poor Gregor wakes up one morning to find himself transformed into an insect in his own bed. Thus begins his season in hell. But the second metamorphosis, which few have noticed and which your pun just thrust before my mind’s eye, is far more important than the first and has to do with the meaning of Gregor’s death, which occurs near the end of the story. Death too is a metamorphosis; what is born must die, which for Gregor means that life as an insect must come to an end. The problem is that the story right up to Gregor’s death has been told from *his* point of view as a character: the third-person narrator, relinquishing his omniscience, has limited his own vision to that of Gregor from the get-go, never letting himself see, feel or experience anything Gregor doesn’t see, feel or experience. So when Gregor dies, who is there to tell of that death or of the family’s grief, future prospects, and so forth—in other words, who is there to narrate the final four or five pages of the story?

“Kafka’s answer is that Gregor himself, through his death, makes the leap from character *in* his own story to narrator *of* that story. The truth is, he’s *always* been the narrator of his own story (just as each of *us* is of our own), only he didn’t realize it. This explains the oddly close proximity of the presumably omniscient narrator to Gregor’s viewpoint right up to his death. To die to one’s role as a mere player in one’s own life is to be reborn as the author, the creator, of that life. This is freedom, this is Enlightenment: a glorious metamorphosis! Read this way, the story ends in spiritual triumph, but few, I’m afraid, are ready to concede such affirmation to the dour Kafka. I personally have no trouble doing so because I’ve collected a number of other parables and short texts of his that I can cite in support of this optimistic view—”

“—All well and good, Herr Professor,” the good doctor interrupted, “but the dream?”

“Well, I would say you’ve pretty much done my work for me there with your deft sleight-of-word,” I chortled. “You’ve somehow managed to read the whole dream for me as a pun expressing this analytical process we’re doing here in terms of a metamorphosis of yours truly from a Gregor-ian insect (my self-loathing tendencies) to the liberated author of my own life (I make my own music): from Gregor-ian to harmonic … I mean, come on, the dream has everything to persuade me it’s worthwhile coming here: the issue of identity (what are we *really* now?), ontological shift (are we really only a single thing or essence?), transparency (both semantic and visual), economy (you reduced it to a pun), … above all, that spiritual affirmation that means ultimate freedom from all these vexing issues in a vision of unity: the one and the many; the monks and I are One. The music is all there really is; what else matters? … I'm telling you, Dr. P., I had this dream a few nights back but I still feel bathed in its afterglow."

"Yes, and I congratulate you; it's a marvelous dream, literally so," the good man nodded deeply, but then raised his head and cocked it ever so slightly, which I knew well was prelude to a "but": "There are, however, one or two elements in it I'd like to take up with you further: going back for a moment to the absence of audible music, its having been replaced by a visual symbol, those multi-hued rays of energy emitted from the monks' mouths—your use of a romantic aesthetic principle to interpret that, namely the transcendent nature of music, and so forth. And, of course, you cite Schopenhauer and other thinkers of the period to support this reading. My problem with that is it's too abstract, too intellectualized; it's something you've probably told your literature students umpteen times [I nodded agreement], but it opens no window onto your personal psychology. What is the *psychological* function of the shift of the monks' singing from ear to eye in the dream? What does it mean in terms of your own psychic economy? What does it mean to *you*, as opposed to Schopenhauer? … I don't feel we've uncovered that yet."

We just looked at one another for a moment, both pondering his question. I felt, though only darkly and intuitively, there was something to it, and I thought I even sensed a wisp of an inkling of what it might be, but I could not bring it into focus, could not articulate it. "I don't know; nothing's popping," I said. "I would've thought the sort of archetypal-symbolic way I viewed it, in the style of the German romantics who themselves were fascinated by dreams, would be self-sufficient. I mean, it's a dream percolating up from the depths of spirit, you know, *de profundis*. Wouldn't that stand on its own? Why do you think there's more to find there?"

"Because there usually is: don't forget the profound compactness, the layered nature of dreams. Levels of meaning bourgeon, proliferate, even though occupying the same symbolic space. Generally it's unwise to bypass the personal unconscious on a beeline for the archetypal, a charge that has been leveled against those Jungians of a Hillmanian persuasion.[47] It leaves too much unexamined psychological baggage behind, baggage that *will* at some point return to weigh you down. It's akin to my reservations about Rinzai koan Zen with its battering-ram attack on the fortress of Enlightenment. Sure, you may muscle your way past your defenses to some kind of breakthrough, some flash of satori, but, since you haven't done enough personal psychological processing to prepare for it, you'll soon find yourself back at square one, with the added burden of having to cope with the desolation of loss. Better to treat the personal with the same careful attention, the same reverence, if you will, as the archetypal. After all, the realm of the psychospiritual is fundamentally democratic … Anyway, don't get your shorts in a knot over this, just talk and see what happens."

"Well, as you know, when I get stuck, I find visualizing the dream and just describing some arresting visual feature in it sometimes gets me off the dime."

"Fine."

"Actually, in this case it's ironic, don't you think," I laughed, "since 'vision' or 'visuality'—visualized music—is itself the issue … all those wonderful rays of 'silent sound' meeting and blending at some midpoint on the front of my body, at my heart, I guess … and those twelve monks arcing around me, all directing their spiritual energy at me … You know, it does remind me of … something … the arc and the spokes homing in on me … Where have I seen that before? … Wait a minute, wait a minute. That's just the point, isn't it? It's *seeing* we're talking about here, not listening. The monks are all *looking* at me, … and I at them. It's a mutual regard with the eyes, and the music is really secondary, which is probably why it's silent, as if the volume were turned down or muted to minimize distraction. And I'll bet that's why my associations were blocked: without quite realizing it I was looking for some monolithic aural connection, a musical connection; after all, the dream does have all these trappings of religious music. Yet it's really a visual thing that's going on here, isn't it? It's not that music is irrelevant either—no, not at all—it's just that its meaning is subsumed by the visual metaphor, which, as usual, stands for consciousness, the ultimate seeing. For me anything, including music, has meaning only insofar as it deepens consciousness in some way. Even music, this divine gift to the human ear, must find its ultimate fulfillment in seeing.

"I can see you're wondering, my good doctor, what's gotten me all wound up on this point, and I'm going to tell you. In the instant, a moment ago, I made that observation about the irony of 'visualizing' a dream about 'vision,' it came to me: Some years ago, when I was researching my last book,[48] I came across a fascinating anecdote about the late-medieval Rhineland mystic and cardinal, Nicholas of Cusa or Cusanus. It was in a wonderful book on the Trinity by my colleague in the Religion Department at S.U., David Miller (he's come up more than once in our sessions), a book called *Three Faces of God.* Miller tells of a picture of Jesus that Cusanus sent to some young monks in a Benedictine abbey at Tegernsee. It was intended as an aid to their meditation and was one of those images whose eyes follow you as you move about the room. The monks were instructed to post it on a wall, about eye high, and then stand around it in a semicircle regarding it regarding them, so to speak. They were to 'see,' and in seeing to appreciate, the miracle of Jesus's omniscience, shown here in his ability to put his complete attention on each one of them simultaneously—an obvious impossibility for the fragmented human mind. Yet with the God-man it was so. The thing is that it required the monks' awareness of this miracle, through their visual contemplation, for it to be actualized, to exert its spiritual power, the idea being that God needs man's cooperation. What good is the infinite without an open, receptive finite for it to shine through?

"Anyway, this idea of a *coincidentia oppositorum*—Cusanus' expression—of a power transcending even the logical principle of non-contradiction, grabbed hold of me then and, as you well know, has yet to let go. To me it's as close as our thinking can come to the ideal of self-realization—a Self that is realized as the connection between things, as opposed to being any particular thing itself. I'm not at all surprised I dreamt about it."

"Nor am I," said Dr. P., seeming still preoccupied. "Tell me," he continued, "is David Miller a friend of yours?"

"No, I can't say he is," I answered, a tad disconcerted by the abrupt shift in focus. "But he's certainly a terrific colleague, one whose scholarship has been of enormous help to me in my own work … I do wish he *were* a friend."

"So why isn't he?"

"In other words, why haven't I seen to it is what you're asking."

"That's right."

"That's a good question, one I have asked myself. I suppose the superficial reason is that he's a bit shy and standoffish and so am I, a situation not conducive to easy interaction."

"As you say, it's superficial. The sublime interests you two share should've easily lifted you over such social speed bumps. Besides, I know you and you're definitely not shy and standoffish."

"Yeah, but the point is, I am with *him*."

"Which brings us back to my original question, 'why.'"

"I don't know," I stammered, feeling all of a sudden on the defensive, not to mention resentful of Dr. P.'s pulling me down from the empyrean heights where I love to linger. "There's just something about him I guess I find off-putting, enough at least to keep me from pursuing contact …"

"Go on."

"Well, it's just that … Oh God, how do I put this?" I was finding it painful. "It's just that his capacities, his accomplishments, make me feel small. They dwarf my own. I mean, he's written so much more than I have … He's got command of all the ancient languages, not just Latin and Greek but Hebrew, Farsi and God knows what else, not to mention a reading knowledge of the modern European tongues which I'm sure he takes for granted as prerequisites for scholarship … I know, I know," I interrupted myself, raising a hand, "I'm sure

I'm idolizing the man. I've made him into some paragon of scholarship I can invoke as an inspiration but no longer relate to as a man … a friend."

"Why do you think you've allowed him, albeit unconsciously, to make you feel small, to 'dwarf' you, as you put it?"

And there it was. Something in the way the good doctor enunciated the verb 'dwarf,' adding just the barest extra stress to it, opened it all up. "Ah! … Gregor is a kind of dwarf, isn't he?" I snickered, shaking my head in amazement. "In fact, I *have* always thought of him as an obscenely large insect about the height of a dwarf because he can only open his bedroom door by turning the door handle with his toothless jaws, which would make him between three and four feet tall when standing on two, or three, legs. That, of course, brings my father into it: one of the reasons I've always identified with Gregor, as has already come to light here, is his deeply troubled relationship with his father, who, the story slowly reveals, has gradually withdrawn affection from him over the five years he's been out of work. Hideous, unloved Gregor is at least in part a reflection of his father's unconscious resentment of him for his superior earning power, which for a man means superior worth. The father's withdrawal of love becomes a successful strategy for deflating the son's sense of self-worth. My own father's problems with self-esteem over a work life spent in repetitious drudgery, that misery of his spilling over into a compulsive and constant needling of me at lunch, at times making me feel like something subhuman—I'm sure I've projected that sense of being made to feel like vermin onto many other men I've met in life, especially older colleagues with whom I've felt myself to be in competition, like David … And with him it's been even more pronounced, I think, because he bears a certain physical resemblance to my Dad: same medium stature, same style and cut of hair …"

"Having now seen, and seen clearly," Dr. P. began, in that soothing fatherly tone of his I'd come to love, "how you've been unconsciously turning David Miller into a foil for working out these deep emotional issues with your father, you can now begin to withdraw that projection, and see David as just … David."

I smiled agreement and, getting up to leave, was waylaid with, "One more thing: note here how the chain of your associations led down from the celestial choirs of angels, from whom I had to pull you away, to Cusanus to David Miller to father, ending up back on the dusty floor with Gregor. From the archetypal to the 'earthly, all too earthly,' you might say. Each so-called level contains all the others, like a hologram or like Whitehead's sense of 'process,' if I catch his drift. It's a very good lesson for you with your Germanic predilection for things metaphysical."

"Thanks, I'll keep it in mind," I responded somewhat snappishly, heading out.

"Careful, Herr Professor," he said airily, reaching for a sheaf of nearby papers, "or I'll be forced to disclose the meaning of the *other* pun in your dream."

"What *other* pun?" I demanded.

"Oh, the one you dropped well before 'Gregor-ian,'" he sniffed, "the one in the dream's frame that has you sitting at the organ high up in the choir loft, next to that stunning brunette … As below, so aloft—now there's a coincidence of opposites you can really sink your toothless jaws into."

(20) February 2008: Doughnuts for the S.U. Ladies

Some ladies from the university are paying me a visit at my basement flat in Hoboken. They seem to be a mix of administrators and faculty, four or five in all. They're seated together on the living room sofa behind the coffee table, which is bare. It appears I'm out of snacks to serve them so I ask their leave to run out to the local bakery for some doughnuts. However, just outside my house I see this massive sea of cars filling the entire area—curbs, street, sidewalks—everywhere. You literally can't cross the street without climbing over six or seven cars to get there. Even my own car has been crowded out into the middle of the street about four cars away from me. To reach it I begin climbing over the hoods of the cars in between, and, just as I'm about to slide off the second hood onto a thin patch of open street, I note that the next vehicle before me is a big, black SUV occupied by two additional ladies, apparently late-arriving members of the visiting party. I climb onto their hood, still on my way to my own car, saying as I do, "Excuse me, I just need to …", but before I can even finish my sentence, they begin backing up their SUV with me still on the hood. I scream at them, "Listen to me! You don't listen to me! You've got to listen! Nobody listens!" I'm furious with them.

"I'm listening."

"Hey, isn't that the signature greeting of that radio call-in shrink on the TV sitcom?" I asked cheerily.

"I wouldn't know," the good doctor scowled. "I studiously

avoid all portrayals of the profession in the media. Too depressing."

"Depressing for you, hilarious for me," I chortled. "Maybe you need to lighten up a little." Of course, no sooner were the words out of my mouth than I rued their utterance. I'd allowed my high spirits to seduce me into a thoughtless comment bordering on disrespect. But then, who could blame me; the last few months had been brimming with the sweet ghee of unalloyed joys and pleasures: I was still giddy with the freedom of retirement and I'd finally gotten to see my beloved Cape Cod in the exquisite Fall season, blissfully free of all the congestion of summer vacationers. I'd even found myself a retirement "job" that was a pure delight: I'd been hired by a former colleague in the German Department at S.U. to translate his autobiography (life as a half-Jew growing up in war-torn Berlin), already published in German, into English for publication in the States. Finally I knew the joy of work that pulled those rare happy souls I'd always envied out of bed in the morning, without so much as a snifter of Schopenhauer's schnapps.

I looked back over recent months, taking stock in an effort to divine the causes of my current sunny outlook. (Being unused to such optimism, I was no doubt also looking over my shoulder, scanning my rear, in the words of the immortal Satchel Paige, for whatever was "gaining on me.") Certainly retirement with its bracing emancipation from the drudgery of routine had played an important role. The very idea of spending the twenty-four hours "my way" was still intoxicating, and I came to realize the immense psychological toll even rewarding work took on one when performed under compulsion. Still, even the welcome milestone of retirement was not enough to explain the day-to-day buoyancy I was feeling. It seemed to me that, if I was not already changed in some significant way within, then all that free time on my hands would have been rather a curse than a boon. I knew the work of self-inquiry I'd been doing with Dr. P. for some seven years by then was bearing fruit, that at some fundamental level I now felt much more at home in my own skin than I had before analysis. I pondered whether this inner shift was attributable to something intrinsic to the analytic process or simply to the "therapeutic" effect of my relationship with Dr. P., or, what seemed most likely, to some combination of subjective and objective factors. There seemed to me no way to come to intellectual certainty on the matter, but I also felt grateful that it was, in the end, unnecessary to do so, and again grateful that I was comfortable with that state of affairs, which, ironically, I felt certain I would not have been without the analysis.

What clarity my review of recent months did bring had to do with a marked shift in the themes, imagery, and intensity of my dreams, a shift unmistakably paralleling the pleasant euphoria I was enjoying in waking life. (This quickening of my dream life had come in the wake of a fairly long period of dreams characterized by emotional flatness and atmospheric dreariness.) Here again, I had no way of knowing which was cause and which effect in the matter. I only knew that it all started late the previous year around the time I had the dream of the musical monks. That dream, with its vivid, numinous imagery of wholeness, seemed to open up a rich vein of psychospiritual energy infusing new delight into every aspect of my life and activity. It struck me as the spiritual equivalent of stem cells, whose undifferentiated purity enable them to promote growth in any area where growth is needed. It also "fathered" a sequence of similar, and similarly energizing, "Enlightenment dreams" in the weeks that followed, which, of course, I promptly took up with Dr. P.

One of these concerned the mythical figure of Ganymede, the quasi divine cupbearer to the gods and "patron saint" of those, such as waiters and waitresses, who serve others. I'm in a restaurant being served by Ganymede himself, resplendent in his short white coat. As I sit there feasting my eyes on his beauty and grace of movement, it occurs to me with delight that he embodies the secret of Enlightenment, but what is that secret and, even if I should divine it, would I be able to hold onto it? Associating to the dream with Dr. P.'s help, I connected it to one of my favorite German novellas, Thomas Mann's "Mario and the Magician" (1929), an enthralling allegory foretelling the violent overthrow of the Fascist conjuror, Mussolini. In it the Mario of the title, a young, naïve waiter living in a southern Italian village, murders a magician visiting the town out of humiliation over the latter's exposure of him during a public performance as a victim of unrequited love. The humiliation had included the audience's laughter over the magician's mocking reference to Mario as "our Ganymede." This is a case of a basically good-natured but gullible young fellow driven to an "evil" act by his own inexperience. We read the dream's Ganymede symbol as an expression of the mystery of what lies "before or beyond good and evil," for which "Enlightenment" is as good a name as any. Naturally I appreciated the dream's implicit reference to the superficial nature of my own harsh moral censure of self, and, beyond that, to the facile nature of moral condemnation generally that only too often becomes part of the evil it presumes to condemn.

Another, equally fascinating, dream in this series had me climbing a wide spiral staircase in some grand cathedral. I was going slowly up the steps with Eido Roshi, my old Zen master. Brilliant light streamed in through the high Gothic stained-glass windows that rose along the curved stairway wall. We were both dressed in our appropriate ceremonial garb, he in his Rinzai Zen vestments and I in the Catholic black cassock and white surplice I'd worn for years as a boy acolyte. As our feet touch each of three successive steps, one above the other, three increasingly intense flashes of blinding (though painless) light occur: boom, boom, boom! With the third flash, Eido Roshi says, in a voice the hypnotic solemnity of which I knew well, "This very moment of climbing the stairs is It!" With this I'm filled with bliss and light. This dream needed little discussion to reveal itself as an inner-alchemical syncretism of, on the one hand, spiritual path and goal, and, on the other, Eastern and Western views of that path.

My point is that I began allowing myself to think I was finally learning to live life to the full, the way it was meant to be lived—and this well into my sixties! Could this be the "something wonderful" Dr. P. thought I might be approaching way back in our session on the "Beach Buddha" dream of the previous year? I had no wish to deny it. Then again, might not all of it—the prediction of wonders, the Enlightenment dreams, the deepening joy in waking life—be pointing to the occasional, completely random, yet sublime, moments of Emptiness I'd begun to experience during this same period? These I recognized to be openings onto the freedom known in Zen as *sunyata,* that ultimate cosmic principle of emptiness that pervades all things. Though sharing them with Dr. P., I'd otherwise kept these moments to myself, aware from experience of most Westerners' suspicion of esoteric Eastern notions of emptiness, wrongly equating them as they did with nihilism and vacuity.

Such moments are very hard to talk or write about. Though their power, being spiritual, negates even the coarsest field of consciousness at the time of their occurrence, yet they are of a gossamer delicacy that vaporizes in the straitjacket of words. Still, I cannot resist the lure to convey some sense of one of the most vivid of them. While watching, and only half-listening to, a Saturday-afternoon college football game on TV during that time, I happened to overhear the announcer refer to "the Notre Dame tradition." In the very instant he dropped that tired, old, shopworn phrase, I suddenly experienced his words as, not merely pointing to, but actually *embodying, being,* the tradition itself. Word and thing were in that moment identical. There was nothing in back of the words that could be identified as "the Notre Dame tradition" in and of itself. There simply *was* no such thing outside the verbal construct, never had been, never would be. And, of course, as with this one thing, so too with everything else. Words, thoughts, images, sensations, even so-called hard-and-fast things "out there in the world," were, in that pristine moment, all just so much wondrous smoke and mirrors being conjured up, over and over again, by some supremely mysterious matrix that eludes all naming.

Persuaded, if not quite convinced, that I was now on the fast track to Nirvana, I felt confident enough to broach the subject of termination with Dr. P. "So what do you think?" I said to him at the top of a session a few weeks before this one. "Things are going swimmingly. My neurotic symptoms are no longer an issue—not that they're entirely gone, just become ineffectual, irrelevant, and that's good enough for me," I beamed. "Eventually I'm sure they'll just wither and die; and even if they don't, who cares? They'll just become the harmless oddball uncle who lives in the attic … I know there's no end to true self-inquiry, that it's a lifelong business. There'll always be the next dream to learn from. Which all just means that, at some point, we need to draw an arbitrary line that says, 'This much analysis and no more,' don't you think? I'd say I'm about ready at least to consider drawing such a line, for a time in the not too distant future, but, of course, I'm eager to know your feelings on the matter …"

I said this, trying to seem as casual and nonchalant about it as possible, a posture I immediately recognized as silly in view of my effort over the years to conduct myself in the analysis with as much honesty as I could muster. I laughed in the realization there was no need for such posturing and had, as I did so, the distinct impression that Dr. P. had followed this inner mini-drama of mine like some soap opera on afternoon TV. His response convinced me of this even further. While lauding my initiative in raising the issue, and agreeing that I had worked myself into "a good place," that, in fact, I had gone further and deeper into the process than most analysands he'd had, there was nevertheless "unfinished business" we would do well to take up before seriously considering the matter of termination. He pointed out that I continued to experience psychological lows or depressive "crashes" on the heels of many of those flashes of satori, that I had not yet learned how to "rest" in that pristine condition. (Does anyone ever, I remember wondering.) Then too, there were still spikes of unresolved anger occasionally manifesting in dreams, like the one I'd brought on this day.

"So what's going on here between you and the fair sex from the Hill,"[49] asked Dr. P., generously ignoring my boorish remark about "lightening up."

"It seems my unconscious is doing some much-needed ventilation of frustrations built up over a long career," I answered. "The formality of my relationship with those ladies in the dream: The visit is more like one of those old-fashioned, constipated faculty teas than a fun get-together with friends and colleagues. It's all so cold and perfunctory," I shivered with distaste, "pretty much like most social functions I ever attended on the hill over the years … The tea image cinches it … I *hate* tea! It's the last thing I'd serve anyone, particularly at a friendly gathering … But the situation is literally 'distasteful,' so naturally I'm not serving anything that tastes good."

"What makes it so distasteful?"

"Several things, I think: the fact that there are no men there, for one. Normally, on those rare occasions when I find myself the only man in a circle of women, I enjoy the pleasant, almost subliminal sexual tension pervading the room. But here, the absence of men is definitely oppressive, which means I'm not enjoying this particular female company. This tea party is a drag … I'm sure this has to do with what many male professors at S.U. privately—and disparagingly—refer to as the 'feminization' of the university in recent years. Women are now running the joint, and the men have gotten the subliminal but unmistakable message to stand aside and salute 'Yes, ma'am' to the various officers comprising the new matriarchy. I mean, come on now, in my last years there the four people in the hierarchy of my 'superiors' extending right to the top were women: Department Chair, Dean of Arts and Sciences, Vice Chancellor and Chancellor! Now, the two of these four women I know personally, I happen to like, but the entire line-up of four somehow becomes oppressive. It's a kind of gender overcompensation that leaves us men feeling like supernumeraries, … like excess baggage."

"Tell me, why do you think you find having four women over you oppressive?"

"Would you mind rephrasing that?"

"Come on, you know what I mean."

I shrugged, affecting innocence, and asked, "You mean, apart from the fact that too many of the New Wave of S.U. women, both administrators and faculty, are insufferably self-important stuffed shirts, that the university's commitment to gender equality comes mainly out of shallow ideological conditioning and an egoistical need to appear politically correct, to appear 'with it,' that keeps the place mired in intellectual mediocrity, and that our administrators of the feminine persuasion, many of them technocrats or scientists, haven't the slightest appreciation of the critical importance of the humanities to a liberal arts education? … You mean, apart from that?"

"Yes, apart from that."

Having, with that rhetorical flourish, exorcized what was doubtless a demon of residual dream anger from my system, I inhaled deeply and set myself to ponder the deeper implications of the doctor's question. "In theory," I began, "I don't mind the idea of a matriarchy, and I even have a sort of romantic, nostalgic sympathy for those nineteenth-century reconstructions by anthropologists[50] of an ancient pre-Greek matriarchal society presumably overthrown by the male barbarism that, now thinly veiled, continues to rule the West today. And … frankly, I just love women; they're my preferred sex—by far! … But, deep down, I have to admit there's something about female authority that makes me bristle. When my wife acts all bossy and points out in that edgy tone of hers something stupid I've done or something obvious I've forgotten (obvious to *her*), I feel my hackles rising. When a female superior at work appeals to my male vanity to get me to do something I'd rather not—a ploy most men would be too embarrassed to try—I can feel the bile rising over such manipulation—"

"—And why do you think that is?" the doctor persisted.

"Yeah, I know, I know" I said with exaggerated weariness. "My mother made me do it, or, in this case, feel it. It's always one or the other of them, isn't it?"

"Come now, Herr Professor, you're too far along in this process to fall prey to such blatant deflection of the issue."

"Yes, you're right, of course … I still, even after all this time, resist putting the blame on her for so much of my conditioned behavior."

"Of course you do; that's part of the conditioned behavior. And let me remind you, we don't say 'blame,' but rather 'responsibility.' Using the non-judgmental term minimizes resistance and keeps us clearheaded."

Nodding agreement, I suddenly recalled an incident from childhood: "I remember once taking a pretty good licking from some tough older kid who lived around the corner from us in Hoboken. I couldn't have been more than twelve … Anyway, I ran into the house, saw my Mom in the kitchen and, in tears, rushed into her arms. She consoled me for a moment while teasing the story out of me. After things cooled down, she stepped back from me and said, somewhat sternly, 'You know, I think you ought to go over to the YMCA and sign up for some boxing lessons. We can afford them.' I know she meant well, and I couldn't argue with the advice—still can't really—but just those few words of hers, intended to help, awakened in me a consciousness of stereotypical masculinity that's been a burden ever since … I don't *want* to be able to beat the crap out of another man, and yet there's this conditioned part of me, possibly formed that very day, that does! The ideal of masculine courage, and its flipside, shame, is a curse to me. It's poisoned far too much of my inner life, and was obviously a major dynamic in the 'abandoned child' scenario that drove me here … I'd be so much happier if I only had the courage to embrace the coward I am! But, you see, the culture, probably for sound evolutionary reasons, simply provides no models to support such a radical move. The only way to do it would be to abandon the support of cultural images entirely. That's why Enlightenment fascinates me … You know, beyond the pair, courage and cowardice."

Dr. P. sat thoughtfully for a moment, then picked up the thread: "Getting back to the dream, it's not obvious to me that the university ladies are trying to manipulate you. In what way do you find that situation manipulative?"

"I don't think they're manipulating me here so much as reaping the benefit, so to speak, of the conditioning already long since done," I answered, as much to myself as to him.

"The excessive politeness on both sides, my own obeisance, the quasi militarist line-up of female soldiers on the sofa—"

"And you're off to pick up dessert for your superior officers, reduced to the lowly status of a go-fer. Is that it?"

"Yeah, I suppose so."

"It recalls your dream of some months ago about impending retirement—release from a prison camp of armed guards."

"I'm afraid it does … But, you know, come to think of it, there is one element in this dream, at least, that contradicts abjection, and that's my anger—righteous anger, I'm tempted to call it—when the two latecomers back up their SUV with me on the hood."

"Ah yes," Dr. P. recalled, "Let's pursue that."

"That anger is the one thing in the dream I feel good about, so it must've been some sort of emotional release, maybe a catharsis … And the words I shout at those women—they're from the depths. They carry a torrent of frustration over the bitter vetch of being ignored—as a man, as an individual, as a member of an academic department the university barely tolerates: 'Listen! You never listen! Listen, damn you all!' I'm shouting at the top of my lungs … But, you know, Dr. P., I think there's an even deeper 'ignoring' going on here that the dream dramatizes, and that has to do with my—for lack of a better term—message, with what my teaching presence at S.U. has been about. Basically, I think it's fair to say my 'professing,' that is, what I've been at pains to 'profess' since around the mid-eighties, is precisely the important kind of self-inquiry you and I do here. Self-knowledge, and the profound adventure of the path to it as portrayed in literature—

Kafka, Hesse, Mann, the German romantics and Idealist philosophers, moderns like Rilke and J.D. Salinger—this is what I've been about in the second half of my career, since around the time I discovered Zen, the Eastern path that opened my eyes to the true meaning of my own discipline.

"My anger and frustration in the dream are, I believe at bottom, directed at my female superiors who seem not to have taken the slightest notice of the actual content of my work, neither in its classroom-pedagogical nor published form … And women are supposed to be the more empathic gender, generally more sensitive and open than men to the values embodied in the study of humane letters. But here they're just clones of their male associates, concerned only that our books and articles and teaching continue to burnish the institution's image. 'What have you done for our collective ego lately?' Oh, sure, my publications received the requisite polite applause and miniscule raises in salary that are built into the 'just noticeable difference' system of rewards at S.U., but, with the exception of some students who still have ears, no one on the hill is really listening to what I'm saying. No one has come up to me and said, 'You know, I think you're onto something there. I'm going to look into it for my own life.' Hence, 'Listen, ladies, listen, damn you! Why won't you listen?' I mean, is the record of all our teaching just something to be boxed and stuffed away in the university archives when we retire? Are our thinking and writing as professors really pushing back the boundaries of human ignorance or have they rather become part of a system designed, consciously or not, to keep those boundaries intact? If the latter, then we have the ultimate irony: ignorance in the guise of its own antithesis.

"My first thought was that the huge jam-up of cars outside my apartment in the dream stood for the glut of students forever being 'processed' in a chaotic system of mass education. This, I suppose, would make the students mere 'vehicles' of our professional self-aggrandizement, so many cars we 'climb over' to get what we want or cars we 'drive' to distraction—that would be yours truly on the hood and the two ladies in the SUV, respectively. But now I'm not so sure—another image comes to mind ..."

"No need to choose between interpretations," Dr. P. hastened to remind me. "Remember, dreams are overdetermined."

"Right, ..." I said absently, now totally in thrall to the chain of associations.

"I'm seeing the grand display case of faculty books just outside the Dean's office on the third floor of the Hall of Languages ... My God, it's the perfect symbol for what I'm ranting about! That case must be about twenty feet long by five feet wide. It contains, I suppose, most or all of the recent books published by Arts and Sciences faculty. And, would you believe, mine is right there in the middle of that massive book jam-up, just like my car in the dream in the middle of that glut of cars in the street ... I'm not kidding! I'll take you over to H.L. right now and show it to you," I said laughing as Dr. P. politely but firmly declined the offer and smiled. "Now there's the real chaos," I continued, "a massive traffic jam of knowledge. A sea of knowledge obliterating a drop of wisdom. How can any one book, even a book about the 'necessity to change your life,' to speak with Rilke, expect to be heard in this cacophony of scholarly voices? How many of the ladies have read any of the books in the case, I wonder."

"Are you presuming to single out your own book as a unique font of wisdom?" asked the good doctor.

"Not a 'font,' just a 'drop,'" I answered raising a cautionary finger. "The word was 'drop.' And besides, I'm taking my lead here from the dream itself, which, as you well know, speaks from a place beyond ego. What's more, the other arresting image in it, the doughnuts, tells me I'm not deluding myself here."

"Oh? How's that?"

"Those doughnuts, I'm absolutely sure, stand for *mu*, the signature koan of Rinzai Zen," I said, tickled at the thought of it.[51]

For a moment he looked nonplussed, but then he suddenly grinned and said, "Wait … I think I actually get this … The doughnuts are zeroes, right, and *mu* is the ultimate zero, the zero of *sunyata*?"

"Bingo! Through the 'vehicle' of my book (my jammed-up car), I'm trying to bring the 'good news' of *sunyata*—Enlightenment—to the S.U. ladies and am having a devil of a time doing it."

"Well," he said skeptically, "that's clever but it may be a bit of a stretch …"

"Allow me to change your mind, good sir," I answered smartly, now sure of my ground. "The connection that clinches it is Salinger's *Catcher in the Rye,* just about my favorite novel of all time. You'll recall how the adolescent hero, Holden Caulfield, is caught up in his own existential crisis on that fateful weekend as he wanders up and down the canyons of Manhattan, after being expelled from yet another school. He can't bring himself to go home and tell his parents. Sick with worry, he goes into some uptown greasy spoon and orders coffee and doughnuts. The first doughnut sticks in his throat; he literally can't swallow it. I wrote an article[52] in the 90's showing Salinger's source for the image of the 'doughnut-stuck-in-the-throat' in an old Zen koan collection brought out by Paul Reps in an edition Salinger is known to have read.[53] Anyway, the point is that *mu,* like any good koan, gets 'stuck in your throat,' which is Zen's way of saying that the quest for Enlightenment is fraught with difficulty and danger. There will be suffering. You may hit an impasse and feel trapped, unable either to move ahead or back out. You're stuck and it sucks. You can't swallow that miserable *mu* doughnut, nor can you spit it out. All you can do is 'keep on keepin' on.' *Mu* stands for both the hardships of the spiritual path and the glorious ground zero of freedom that may be your reward if you persevere on that path."

"I see," said Dr. P. "Well, I'm convinced, but apparently those ladies from S.U. aren't," he quipped. "My sympathies."

"Resistance is fierce," I said. "When I try to get to my 'vehicle,' the book-as-car that is to take me to the bakery, the place where *mu* gets baked, which is deep in the mind and heart of each of us, so that I can bring some *mu* doughnuts back to them, they literally 'back away' in their SUV, almost jostling me off their hood, at which point I begin to harangue them for their obliviousness … I'm struggling, in vain it seems, to use the vehicle of my scholarship to bring the communion doughnuts of *mu* to my sisters—and brothers—in this ostensible community of learning."

"It seems an almost Kafkaesque quest," reflected Dr.P., bringing my literary soulmate into it.

"What '*almost*'?" I fired back. "You should've known better … But now that you mention it, naturally there's a short parable that fits right in here," I said, summoning up the narrative line.[54] "It seems the emperor, on his deathbed, has whispered a message in the ear of a messenger who is to deliver it to … *you,* the reader. But the obstacles between the royal chamber and 'you' are more than formidable: great throngs of mourners in and around the palace, and filling the courtyard, the outer palace, and further courtyards, then still another palace, at last the outermost gate, that leading to the imperial capital, and finally beyond that numberless open fields, and on and on. 'Mission impossible,' literally. At one point the narrator describes the capital as 'crammed to bursting with its own refuse' [not unlike our car-packed dream street]. Then he ends with, 'Nobody could fight his way through here, least of all one with a message from a dead man.—But you sit at your window when evening falls and dream it to yourself'… Kafka tells the tale in the rare second person: It's a 'dream' that you or I or any other reader is having right now, the dream, unconscious of course, of rescue, … the dream of redemption. And since it *is* a dream, it is 'you' who are playing all the parts: your waiting self, the messenger, even the emperor, and everything in between. It's a perfect narrative circle, all neatly closed in on itself … a *mu* doughnut baked to perfection."

Dr. P. just sat there, looking past me. Finally, he got up and chirped breezily, "Well, guess I'll head up to the kitchen and check the breadbox … A doughnut sounds nice."

(21) May 2008: Eye Trouble

I'm in a beautiful, old, well-appointed house in North Baltimore with family and friends. Apparently we all live there together. It's late afternoon on a fair spring day and the golden light of the setting sun is streaming through several high windows into the living room where we're all gathered. For some reason I need to go around the block we're living on, but North Baltimore is a complicated section of the city and I don't know my way around. Lucky for me, the TV-sitcom psychiatrist Frasier Crane is with us. He's sitting on a cushion in the middle of the living room floor facing the light. Just in front of him, set up on a low easel or stand of some kind, is a big map of the city, and Frazier is pointing out with his forefinger, for my benefit, how to circle the block. But I'm standing off to the side and can't follow his finger very clearly. I move in closer but still have trouble seeing. The map is too big, too detailed, blocks and street names look microscopic, and besides, my eyes are giving me trouble. They just won't focus, no matter how hard I try. There's something wrong with them; it's almost as if they're paralyzed. As if that were not enough, Frasier has now finished circling the "map block" with his finger and doesn't seem inclined to repeat the gesture. If I didn't get it the first time, tough luck, I guess. He just sits there smiling like a Buddha.

"The Buddha is back."

"Yes, he is, once again in the guise of a moon-faced man, this time Frasier Crane," I elaborated.

"Yes. Do you want to fill me in on him?"

"Sure. Actually, you may recall he came up briefly in a session a few months back. It's the name of a TV-sitcom character who is a radio psychiatrist. People call in with their problems and something usually goes awry as he tries to 'solve' everything in two minutes … You know, Therapy Lite."

"Ah yes, I remember now. One of those farcical pop depictions of analysts, so near and dear to my heart," Dr. P. said, slapping that vital organ with his right hand in a mock gesture.

"You should give it a chance," I teased. "It's very clever, brilliantly written and extremely funny."

"Forget it. The last lampooning of the profession, or fictional treatment of any kind for that matter, I thought was any good was Mel Brooks's movie, *High Anxiety*, which must go back a good thirty years. And even that was inspired by a shrink movie I always considered highly overrated—Hitchcock's *Spellbound*, which simplistically equates 'cure' with the recovery of a single repressed memory."

Little "extraneous" exchanges like this were quite common for us now, especially at the start of a session as we eased into the work. I might mention to him a book I'd picked up at Barnes and Noble which I knew would interest him, or a "must-see" video I'd rented, or a good Italian restaurant I'd been to. (Both married to women from Italian-American families, we shared a partiality to Italian cuisine.) Occasionally he would suggest a book for me to check out on Amazon.com, one elaborating some subtle point or complex point of view he had expressed in a previous session, say, in the area of psychology or philosophy or even history. For instance, he was a devoted student of the philosopher, Alfred North Whitehead, who had collaborated with Bertrand Russell to produce the mighty *Principia Mathematica,* perhaps the most important work on the logical foundations of mathematics since Aristotle. Dr. P. was enamored of Whitehead's philosophy of process, a microanalysis of the fluent nature of all phenomena leading to all sorts of fascinating paradoxical and quasi-mystical insights into the nature of time and space. I found it admirable that no text in philosophy or theology or even mathematics seemed too daunting for his insatiable intellectual curiosity. On any given Thursday afternoon, on my way to the couch for a session, I, incurably nosey as I am about other peoples' reading habits, might notice, lying open on a desk or a table or a stack of books, an edition of the *I Ching,* or a book by the Catholic mystic, Thomas Keating, or an abstruse analysis of consciousness by idealist philosopher David Chalmers, this last next to an equally abstruse materialist analysis by a philosophical opponent, say, Daniel Dennett. If he needed to brush up, or even learn for the first time, an area of math prerequisite to reading some technical study in logic, he would do so, and enjoy the process. He urged me to look into some of these esoteric matters for myself, particularly those of theological or religious import, but usually I would beg off, protesting that ten minutes of thought per day on such a rarefied level of abstraction was my absolute limit.

All this was a natural outgrowth of the bond that had formed between us over seven years of weekly meetings. Forcing ourselves to maintain some artificial rule of business-only protocol, especially in this latter phase, would have been as futile as trying to keep school kids quiet during recess. These days our weekly meetings felt more like visits between friends, one of whom happened to be an analyst, than formal analytic sessions. In all that time together it was inevitable that I would form some picture of the man's private life, yet his discretion, both natural and cultivated, kept this from ever becoming more than an adumbration, the broadest of sketches. My relationship to Dr. P. was of the oddly inverted sort unique to analysis in which the patient comes to know the doctor "deeply" before knowing him superficially. There was, of course, his early Catholic Jesuit training that came up in our very first session, a developmental course we shared and the revelation of which disarmed my outermost defenses against the analysis. He was, as mentioned, married, to a woman who was also a psychotherapist. They had no children, a deliberate decision arising from a mutual recognition that their analytic work was a calling demanding a near-total investment of self, and not merely a profession or an occupation. As if in consolation for this sacrifice, they were blessed with a bevy of step-grandchildren on whom Dr. P. doted, to the extent of donning a Santa suit every Christmas on their behalf and doing the honors to their piercing squeals of delight. By now his ample girth made him a "natural" for the role and he no longer needed the artificial silvery whiskers.

He was by nature a gregarious man, who, apart from reading, enjoyed nothing more than the pleasures of good conversation. So thoroughly well-read as he was in his own field of psychology and in such adjacent fields as social science, philosophy, religion and literature, he had aspirations of establishing some kind of institute for applied psychoanalysis in greater Syracuse that would bring together experts and students in these various areas to share ideas and reflections, stimulate one another with thoughtful questions and inspire mutual insight.

Though as liberal and non-dogmatic a man as one could imagine in matters of religion, he still managed to keep himself solidly grounded in the Catholic faith of his upbringing. In this we parted company as I no longer felt any personal affinity to the Church, though I certainly shared his recognition of the universal psychospiritual value of some of its symbols, above all the cross and crucifixion as an image of every man's spiritual charge to bring the warring opposites within his own nature together in unity. I also shared his profound lament over the increasing "tone-deafness"[55] of our literalist technological era to symbols of any kind and their numinous power to open us up to the deeper strata of consciousness wherein lie true peace and a palpable awareness of our solidarity with all of creation.

One such symbol was sitting right in the middle of the dream I had just told—right there on the living room floor of "my Baltimore home," lit up by the sunbeams that shone through the windows.

"So what do you think is up with this embodiment of the Buddha in a TV-sitcom character?" the doctor asked, getting back to the matter at hand.

"Oh, I don't know, but it certainly is a rare blend of the sublime and the ridiculous, don't you think—" I said smiling.

"—Hold it right there!" he interjected, sitting up. "Toss-off remarks like that can be very telling, and my analytic nose is telling me this one is telling us something … The sublime and the ridiculous. The ridiculous and the sublime. The ridiculous Frasier and the sublime Buddha … Try running with that."

He was right. It was a provocative conjunction, one that stirred the inner embers: "Well, let's see, … Frasier has this round moon face and could certainly pass for a moon-faced Buddha, but only in appearance, since he's basically a buffoon, despite—or rather because of—his highbrow pretensions to good taste and intellectual refinement. In the end the joke is always on him: the rare wine goes sour, the precious painting is a fake, a pet theory of his is contradicted by experience at every turn … On the surface, it's not obvious to me why my unconscious would choose to manifest the Buddha's wisdom and compassion in the guise of a boob."

"That's why we go beneath the surface. Is that all there is to the character: one-dimensional fecklessness?"

"No. To be fair, Frasier's got other qualities that round him out, even Buddha-like qualities, come to think of it: compassion for others, a sense of social justice, a playful sense of humor … In one episode he tries to deflate his brother's insufferable sartorial effeteness by wearing sweats and sneakers to a performance of *Die Walküre.*[56]"

"Now that's my kind of opera buff, or *buffo*, or buffoon," he deadpanned. Clearly he was free-associating right alongside me. "But, I'm thinking," he continued, turning serious, "maybe if we turn the screw on this comic character just a little bit, say, from buffoon to … *trickster*. What do you think?"

"Trickster," I repeated. "Hmm, you mean in Jung's archetypal sense of a fool or clown figure who's really wiser than his social betters, like, say, Charlie Chaplain's tramp or Bugs Bunny?"

"That's right."

"I don't know, I'm not sure that computes. As I just said, Frazier is a stuffed shirt himself; that self-important persona is the whole basis for the show's comedy. He's more likely to be the target of a trickster than a trickster himself, I would think."

"Ah yes, but you see, what you're saying applies only to the logic of human relationships as mirrored in the 'realistic' sitcom's ensemble, whereas your dream is another matter entirely: the limits placed on ordinary relationships don't apply to dreams, especially archetypal ones in which all elements are aspects of the dreamer. Frasier can personify both the trickster in you *and* its target, say, the aloof professor who too often leads with his intellect. He's obviously a complex projection of many parts of your psyche, a projection which you, as the observer-persona with whom you identify in the dream, are having trouble grasping … But just think about it for a moment: If we regard Frasier as a trickster figure, then the connection to the Buddha isn't hard to figure since tricksters in many mythologies are gods or demigods or quasi-divine figures of one kind or another. Hermes, for instance, is the messenger of the gods in Greek mythology and a god himself, but in his function as messenger he's a trickster, often crossing boundaries and violating prohibitions that mere mortals are compelled to uphold. In the case of this archetypal dream of yours, however, it seems clear the trickster has rather an inner psychological than an outer social function, or, to put it the other way around, the 'society' the trickster in your dream is tweaking is that of your psyche with its conflicting forces all jockeying for dominance. The question then becomes, what precisely is this clownish shrink, Frasier, trying to accomplish? What tricksteresque 'therapy' is he administering? I'm assuming, of course, and I think with good reason, that this particular trickster, inasmuch as he reminds you of the Buddha, embodies the benign, or helpful, or light side of the shadow archetype of which he is, according to Jung, a subtype.

Still, if he's a trickster, benign or no, the key to understanding him must have to do with trickery, or cunning, or even deception, of some kind."

"I see," I said, searching my mind, into which a question suddenly dropped: "By the way, whatever else this character may mean, he's also got to be my own private inner 'Dr. P.,' doesn't he? I mean, come on, he's a therapist!"

"Well," Dr. P. began, choosing his words carefully, "he could be my therapist's dark side, which you may be unconsciously picking up on, by which I mean the dark 'manipulative' side of the Light Trickster—if that's not too convoluted. A sort of Milton Erickson[57] Svengali type who was not above using subtle hypnotic devices—tricks of the trade, you might say—in ways his patients were hardly aware of to change them 'for the better.' That, of course, becomes a very tricky ethical issue. It's not something I would ever do, consciously at least."

"No," I agreed emphatically, my eyes suddenly widening as it came to me, "but we can't say it isn't something a trickster-esque Buddha might do, or, more precisely, my inner Buddha or Self, which we know works in very mysterious ways ... In fact," I said, assuming a cryptic tone, "I think I can say with confidence that he's *already done it* at least once before!"

"Has he now?" the doctor said, himself now wide-eyed. "Do tell."

"It just hit me that, when I finished telling this dream earlier, you kicked off the discussion with the seemingly innocent remark, 'The Buddha is back,' which I even seconded with 'Yes he is' or 'That's right' or some such, but then immediately went off on a tangent about Frasier and the sitcom, completely ignoring the signal contained in your word 'back,' which, of course, alludes to my Buddha-on-the-beach dream of so many moons ago."

"You didn't ignore it," he said smiling, "you just put it on the back burner, for now, when we need it. That's why you recalled it when you did—a very smart thing to do … Carry on."

Who was I to disagree? Thus encouraged, I forged ahead: "All of a sudden it's obvious to me that my earlier Buddha-dream is the code or text to be used in interpreting this one—better yet, each dream interprets the other. They're like mirrors facing each other with me in the middle—it's a slightly giddy feeling, not at all unpleasant."

He simply nodded, giving me free rein.

"Based on these two dreams, I would say my inner Buddha is definitely a trickster, or at least has strong tricksteresque features. Probably because, in order to break through the intellectual fortress that is my defense system, a rule-breaker, even a paradigm-buster, is called for—an 'outside' or 'marginalized' or 'renegade' force from within that will undermine my over-reliance on the dualizing tools of reason and logic, tools I use relentlessly, like an obsessed sculptor working a block of granite, to construct my world: If 'A' is true, 'B' must be false. If 'A' is good, 'B' must be evil, and on and on.

"Anyway, just look at the earlier dream: 'Beach Buddha' tells me the 'Answer' to my quest for Enlightenment lies in some magic potion I need to take every day for three months—three liters a day, as I recall. The problem is, my recollection of the dream upon waking strangely deletes the name of the liquid. That's the trickster at work for sure, an editorial gremlin erasing 'the key dream word,' the 'Answer to it all,' and sending me off on some wild goose chase—at least, that's the way we read it then, and *this* dream certainly confirms that reading for me. Here, as Frasier, the Buddha again seems to be sending me off on a wild goose chase, showing me on a map of Baltimore I can't see clearly how to get around the block … It's the same deal, isn't it? In the first instance I can't *hear* the answer; in the second I can't *see* it. That map would test even a cartographer's patience, with its sea of microscopic lines and signs and squiggles. And besides, I seem unable to focus my eyes—"

"—Yes," Dr. P. interjected, "that's you in the persona of the 'optically challenged observer,' to put it in politically correct terms. Tell me about that."

"My eyes just won't focus the way they should … I rub them and rub them and blink a dozen times and still … They feel strained to the breaking point, or to the point of paralysis, as if they're being used to …"

"To do something unnatural?"

"Exactly! Something unnatural, something they're just not made to do."

"Well, then they pair up perversely with the map, don't they? Defective eyes straining to read an illegible map!"

"Buddha's the dream-maker here, isn't he," I said, feeling myself relax deeply. "Not just the Frasier character but the trickster-creator of the entire dream as it becomes the koan: How do you get there from here if you can't get there from here? How do you navigate the unnavigable? … A man like me, committed to the limited resources of the mind alone, cannot get there. My consciousness, intellectually driven steel trap that it is, is not equipped to 'catch' it, and could not take it in even if it somehow did. The 'eyes' of this consciousness exhaust themselves, grind down to paralysis, in their futile efforts to reduce the infinite to terms of ordinary visibility. As long as I go on clutching my inner maps of the world—my pet ideas, theories, beliefs—as if they were some elite means to an end and not *themselves* part of the world they seek to explain, seamlessly continuous with it, just so long will my eyes remain exhausted and out of focus … I can't get there from here because there's nowhere to get. I'm already there, aren't I?" I asked rhetorically and with a sudden upsurge of joy, needing no response yet nonetheless inviting one. "That's the reason the Buddha is smiling his trickster's smile as he gives me directions for 'getting around the block' by rotating his finger around that tiny area on the map: What he's really doing is showing me how I'm running around in circles … In truth, I am always already my own elixir, my own destination. I am the circle, circumference and center, and the space in between. I see that I am … He."

I took a deep breath, exhaling fully. It was the kind of total release, from the solar plexus, that feels like the end of a long trial, in this instance a trial leaving me brimful of the knowledge that I was perfectly fine just where I was. So many dreams I'd had over the years about trouble with seeing, many of them scrutinized in analytic sessions—maps, clocks, street signs, writing on blackboards, final exam questions, arcane script on parchment—and so much frustration. It turns out they had all been messages from my inner Buddha, with his panoptic vision, his ability to see in all of the "ten thousand directions"[58] at once, using a bit of benign trickery to get "myopic me" to step back behind my own eyeballs and study their diseased ways of seeing the world. I was to watch my own mind, not so much its content (content was being handled by analysis) as its habitual mode of functioning, its mechanics, so to speak; not the "what" but the "how."

"How wonderful," I exulted, "to see a long-vexing dream problem vaporized by simply seeing how I see. No longer need I be like Kafka's man hemmed in by a three-sided fence.[59] Maybe now whatever I thought I was looking for can rest easy, at least for a while."

"And how are the eyes now?"

"All's clear."

(22) August 2008:
Close Encounters at the Women's Building

I'm on the S.U. campus heading swiftly up the paved path towards the south entrance to the Women's Building. There's a big academic conference being held there and I don't want to be late for one of the lectures. Suddenly I'm confronted by these four or five women, primly dressed like academics, who form this tight little phalanx in front of and around me and begin pushing me backwards, in a southerly direction away from the entrance. I protest, "Ladies, I want to go north!" and try to push back, whereupon a sort of gentle, and not unpleasant, back-and-forth tussle ensues.

Next, I find myself in the lobby of the building, just outside the conference auditorium, involved with an extremely seductive young black woman who's coming on to me no holds barred. She's dressed in a tight sweater and jeans and, before I know it, we're knotted together in this passionate embrace. I pull back just enough to ask her, "Can I have your e-mail address?" to which she answers, "Yes, of course."

Fade out, fade in: the lecture's letting out, we're all moving through the lobby towards the exits. Suddenly a uniformed security guard grabs me by the left arm. I bellow at him, "Take your hands off me! I'm a professor here, a respected member of this academic community!" as I yank my arm away. A second guard comes running up to aid the first. Him I also dispatch verbally, then proceeding on my way with a swagger and an imperious reproach to both guards: "How dare you approach me this way!"

Epilog: I'm back at home, the place abuzz with family

and students. I call for their attention and tell them all about the little contretemps with the guards at the conference. They seem either incredulous or unimpressed, I can't tell which. I think to myself, "How odd that they don't find this incident interesting."

"Go ahead, say it."

"Say *what*?" he protested, as if he hadn't a clue.

"Oh, I don't know, maybe … 'The S.U. ladies are back!' or 'The cops are after you again!' or …"

"Well, are they?"

"To which group do you refer, good sir, ladies or cops?" I asked, playing the pedant.

"Take your pick."

"Well, there's no denying those ladies are of the S.U. variety. Whether they're the same ones from that dream of several months back—the ones I tried to serve doughnuts to—is hard to say. Then again, does it really matter? Since they're a group, they probably stand for an idea or attitude of mine rather than a specific person or persons."

"And what idea or attitude do you think that might be?" he asked as he nestled into his chair, resting chin on palm.

"It's hard to say … That odd little dance we all do, all of us in a bunch like that, them wrapped around me so snugly, jostling each other back and … Oh my God!" I suddenly shouted, "I don't believe it!"

"Believe it."

"It sure fits in thematically with the scene after it, doesn't it? … That sexy black girl and I going at it in the lounge. And of course, where does it all take place? Where else but in the Women's Building, the one place on campus set aside for female physical activity, 'indoor sports,' as it were. Yeah, the Women's Building: That's a pretty thinly veiled euphemism for 'the woman's body,' wouldn't you say, … you know, the place I'm trying to enter—and *do* enter, as it turns out, since the next scene has me leaving the building/body. I guess that's me pulling out. Unfortunately, the main event, the 'lecture' (how's that for another euphemism?), is edited out. How do you like that? I get all the foreplay, the thrusting back and forth inside the vaginal 'pouch' of women and the 'darkly' lustful embrace in the 'lounge,' just outside the inner sanctum of the lecture hall/room/womb, and I get to make my exit afterwards, but it's all anticlimactic—or should I say 'pre- and post-climactic?' The climax itself, the pay-off, the orgasm, intellectual though it be, is deleted … Maybe I just go unconscious during it. You know, now that I think of it, I've often imagined the perfect lecture as having the rhythm of a perfect orgasm: a gradual build-up to a sudden and complete loss of consciousness, a sublime if brief death of self-awareness, all trace of the onerous 'me' drowned in the bliss of communion, be it with another mind or another body … But then, I don't even get the bliss here, do I, just the unconsciousness—"

"—And not only that," Dr. P. chimed in, "but you're nabbed for the 'illicit' pleasure you don't even get to enjoy, aren't you?"

"Ah yes, the security guards, the guardians of the security of the Women's Building a.k.a. woman's body. God forbid I should have an erotic dream without the minions of conscience! My unconscious seems to have an inexhaustible supply of visual puns for my particular intrapsychic version of the eternal battle between *Neigung* and *Pflicht*. (Those are

Schiller's moral-aesthetic terms for the antinomy, 'inclination' and 'obligation.') Here it's in the specific terms of instinct versus inhibition (or prohibition), or, in the broadest view, nature versus culture. Even in my dreams there's no such thing as a 'pure' experience, is there, an unconflicted, integral event not tainted, not compromised in some measure, by the *Wächter?*"

"The *what*?"

"'The Watchman'—it's the title of the briefest of abstract parables by Kafka, running hardly more than five sentences: The I-persona tells of slipping past 'the first watchman' while the latter is distracted, then realizing what he's done, running back to apologize and offer excuses and getting no response whatever from the watchman. It ends with the fellow asking, 'Does your silence indicate permission to pass? …' This is a little riff of Kafka's on the wound of human consciousness, or self-consciousness, a wound that refuses to close. It sometimes seems we can't do anything without running it by 'the Watchman'—least of all, the sex act. Even if we occasionally manage to get halfway through a spontaneous act of any kind—say, for some reason the inner filter is momentarily 'off-line'—it will inevitably pop back up and bring all innocent joy to an abrupt end. Everything reverts to its quotidian sluggishness, weighed down by the divided energy of calculation … The infuriating obsequiousness of that final question, 'Does your silence indicate permission to pass?' … Maybe I'm a little ahead of Kafka's I-persona here, a tad more evolved, since I at least stand up to the watchmen, the security guards, who catch me as I'm 'pulling out' of the 'Woman's Building.' Maybe I can't keep them from showing up, even in my dreams, but I think I'm at a point now where I can at least challenge them. I don't think that would've happened a few years ago."

"I agree," Dr. P. said, "and yet, in the dream's closing scene, which is a sort of review of the preceding ones, you *do* appear to be running those earlier events past another 'seat of judgment,' so to speak—I mean the people at home, family and others. Don't they compose another 'watchman,' with the authority to give or withhold approval? Isn't the 'wound of consciousness,' as you so poetically put it a moment ago, still open?"

"Yes, but I think not as wide: You'll note that I'm more amused than bothered by their indifference to my report of events at the Women's Building. Actually, their indifference and my amusement over that indifference, taken together, strike me as something akin to a leveling blow to the Watchman within, an attenuation of conscience, a softening of its old brutality that gives me hope for a balance—who knows, maybe even a harmonization—of these hoary old psychic enemies to come."

"Tell me," asked Dr. P., "how do you imagine such a harmonization? To put it in terms of a metaphor I know you're familiar with, would it be in the sense of Nietzsche's lion or his rolling wheel?"[60]

"Ah, I see. Great question, wonderful distinction: you're asking, would it be the kind of uneasy peace maintained by a leonine dictator, a psychic tyrant ruling with an iron fist, or the 'peace beyond understanding' promised by St. Paul, a spiritual peace that would be absolute."

"More or less."

After taking a moment for reflection, I ventured, "Well, I certainly must concede the dream doesn't get beyond

Nietzsche's second stage, the rule of the lion, but that's certainly light years ahead of the lowly camel status I was mired in when I first came here—you remember, the pathetically mewling professor who tortured himself over fairness in grading students' tests and papers, terrified of King Cobra Conscience. At least now I'm enough my own man to shake off the clutches of the security guards, even after blowing off a major taboo with my invasion of the sacred temple of womanhood."

"No question," Dr. P. agreed with an emphatic nod, "but are you sure there aren't in the dream at least some tracks left by the self-rolling wheel, if not the wheel itself?"

I laughed. "Wheel tracks, Derridean traces, traces of a Presence now absent, *always* absent. Zen would call them 'the tracks of the ox', the hoof prints left by the untamed Mind of Enlightenment. 'Look!' the roshi says. 'There's the ox's tail, sticking out from behind that boulder over there. Run and see if you can grab it!' … I don't know, Dr. P., I've been around the spiritual block enough times by now to be wise to certain things, such as the fact that the wild ox or the self-rolling wheel (choose your own metaphor) cannot be chased and thereby overtaken. Its very nature is to remain a step ahead of us. So it seems there *is* a God, there *is* the 'peace that passeth understanding,' only, as Kafka laments, 'not for us.' So I don't expect ever to dream of myself as a self-rolling wheel," I concluded glumly.

"Poor man," the good doctor whined in mock-consolation. "Even in dreams no billows of beatitude; how much less in dreary waking life. Must that accursed serpent rear its venomous head every time you enter the Garden of Eden?" he cried out in thespian bathos, raising the back of his thick, lilting hand to his forehead.

"All right, knock it off," I smirked. "There's no call for that."

"Look," he continued, ignoring my words, "you just cited Kafka to me, the Kafka of despair, sounding for all the world as if that were some sort of final pronouncement on the subject. You seem to have utterly forgotten the other pole of the dialectic. I mean the lesson taught by Gregor Samsa, a lesson *you* taught *me*, Herr Professor, not so long ago."

"Sorry, I don't ..."

"No, apparently you don't. What did you tell me about Gregor's death?"

"Well, that it's really not hopelessly tragic since it marks a passage to ... Oh, I think I see ... Wait, are you saying that the dream is like Kafka's ... ah ..."

"I'm not saying anything; I'm just trying to refresh your memory of what *you* said, and said with the power of heartfelt conviction, I might add."

"Yes, yes, of course," I brightened. "Gregor's death as insect-character is his awakening to his true nature as narrator, as storyteller ... By analogy, that would mean there's a chance for me somehow to transform from a character in my own dream into the aware dreamer himself, to go up a dimension in consciousness. It's like Pirandello's *Six Characters in Search of an Author.* It's only the author who can see that his story is something made up, a fabrication, an illusion. From the characters' point of view it's all very real, full of sound and fury. In a sense just waking up from any normal dream is enough to let you see that 'it was just a dream,' and, if the dream happened to be a nightmare, to bring great relief from suffering. But that relief passes quickly and it's back to business as usual. On the other hand, when you dream lucidly and actually wake up *within* the dream, it gives you an astonishing sense of mastery over the life being dreamt in that moment; you can levitate, fly and do any number of other wondrous things. What I think you're saying is that the phenomenon of lucid dreaming, or aware dreaming, is a kind of trace or track of the self-rolling wheel that's rolling not too far 'up ahead.' … You know, just considering that, just turning it over in my mind, is enough to stir in me a sense of being on the track of lucidity, which of course is light, the light of Enlightenment. It occurs to me that once you discover yourself as the author of your own dream, the one who's making it all up, 'bad' as well as 'good,' you might as well take the next step and discover that there *is* no such 'one.' There *is* no author, no storyteller, only story; no dreamer, only dreaming. As Yeats asks, "How can you tell the dancer from the dance?" Life is just a dream, and that very dream is what I truly am; that's my true nature. And that makes my true nature the 'peace that passeth understanding.' The put-upon professor I seem to be in my dream is not an autonomous entity at all but only an entity *being dreamt* … by me-as-dream-machine, me as the pure activity of dreaming. How free that makes me feel! In being everything in general, in being the entire fabric of the dream—professor, women, guards, building, the whole story— I find myself freed of the burden of being any one thing in particular. I discover the dream's essential emptiness; it's a phantasm as empty of substance as a murder in a movie. I'm like the spirit that 'moveth as it listeth,' a self-rolling wheel at last taking flight, now banking into and out of this cloud and that and the other. What's become of the conflict, the suffering it all began with in this dream called life? … Left far behind on the ground below."

I stopped, just looking at the man in gratitude for yet another precise turn of the inner screw to this joyful deepening of consciousness. He smiled back. There was no need to say anything.

But of course there always is the next thing to say, the next moment of the dream, and for me then and there this was a labor of love: "I want to tell you now the most exquisite dream I've ever had. How is it possible that I should have come so far with you without ever mentioning this dream? Astonishing! And yet maybe not so astonishing when I consider your oft-repeated maxim that things tend to come up here as they're needed … Actually, you know what, I'm not going to tell you the dream at all—I'm going to *read* it to you, or at least my written record of it, right out of that copy of my book[61] lying next to your desk over there, the one I gave you way back when and which I can see from here is bookmarked at about the middle, which means you've already read my account, so this'll be a refresher for both of us."

With the dream on my mind as I walked over to Dr. P's desk to get the book, I mentioned in passing, "Let's see, it was back in the nineties, the early nineties I think, when I had it. I'd been practicing Zen for about five years, going on faith and promise more than anything else. This dream was my first real breakthrough, the first parting of the curtain, revealing in radiant clarity what all the fuss and nonsense were about. I can still recall, from the period when I wrote my book a few years later, the pleasure I took in introducing the dream with the vertiginous paradoxical question, 'If during a dream the idea occurs to one with overwhelming conviction that life is just a dream, is that a dream?' ..."

Sitting back down, I cast a quick sidelong glance at my mentor who just sat there with folded hands, looking straight ahead. I opened to page one and began: *The car rolls down the parking lot ramp at twilight, hitting bottom with a bit of a jolt. From there it circles the crowded lot tentatively, looking for a space. I feel a little better the instant I realize I am driving, better still on noticing my dad sitting next to me. He's been dead for only about four years and so still has some of that vigorous "just-been-living" look of the recently departed. Wife and children are seated in back, but they are only vaguely there, functioning as mere "accompaniment." This is clearly going to be a "front-seat" episode between Dad and me.*

The lot is full, so I head back up the ramp. As I do, he reaches behind his lower back with closed fist and begins massaging. "Hurt?" I ask. He nods yes, continuing to rub. As we approach the top of the ramp, he leans toward me slightly and says sotto voce, *as if to prevent their hearing but without their noticing, "I have to leave," by "leave" clearly meaning "die again, this time on* this *level." Overcome with sadness, I reply, "You don't have to do this, you know." But he insists, "Yes, I do," and I say, "Okay, Dad, you're the boss. Whatever you say."*

We embrace each other (who's driving?), twice it seems, which adds a curious element of ceremony to the profoundly sad leave-taking, sadness and ceremony blending in a kind of mutual benediction. By now we are at the apex of the exit, atop not only the lot but, it seems, the dark-and-crowded-lot-become-world. From this sudden horizon I look away and up into the early evening sky, now in its most intensely ambiguous twilight, and behold a darkening dome pregnant with awe—vast, mysterious, inviting, writhing in ecstasy. Transfixed, I know I am gazing into the Source and realize instantly that everything, absolutely everything, is part and parcel of this Womb, shaped by It, born of It, kept by It, and dissolved back into It. It goes through all, permeating all with Its orgasmically free flow. It is what everything is and what anything means.

Dizzy with delight, I convey the glad tidings to my father. "Life is just a dream, Dad! It's all just a dream!" I chortle, still hugging him and acutely aware as I speak the words that I am speaking them from within a "dream." At the same time, the words also seem to issue from the writhing vortex of twilit Sky. But, most strange, they issue forth both audibly and visibly, as if the Sky has become a kind of articulate cosmic mouth whose speech is its writing and whose writing is its speech. As I continue to gaze upward, I revel in my inability to tell one of us from the other.

Heading up the stairs a moment later, my feet, as it seemed, barely touching the steps, I heard and felt the words assail me from behind, so casually dropped though they were: "'e' is for 'ebony,' making 'e-mail address,' if you drop the 'ad,' dream code for 'black body armor,' wouldn't you agree?"

(23) November 2008: The General Was a Slacker

I'm a soldier standing in formation on the grounds of base camp and find I have to pee. I break ranks, run into the nearby barracks and head downstairs to the latrine. Just as I'm finishing my business, my sergeant bursts into the privy and barks at me that officer so-and-so wants to see me on the double. I rush back upstairs where the officer is waiting, fists on hips, to dress me down for leaving the line. Just as his tongue-lashing reaches fever pitch, the general happens to walk by. He stops and asks, "What's going on here?" The officer explains the situation to him as I stand by listening, till suddenly the general waves him off saying, "Well, I think we have to cut this man some slack here."

"'Slack' is good, isn't it?"

"You bet it is, especially for someone at the mercy of military authority," the doctor answered, briskly rubbing his palms together to fend off the November chill. As usual, the portable space heater was off.

"There's an interesting 'back story' to this dream I must tell you," I said, ignoring my own discomfort with the chill. "You'll recall our conversation of last week, on the threshold of the election, and my qualms about voting for Obama on account of his pro-choice position on abortion?"

"As if it were yesterday," he said, cocking his head to attention. "You were, shall we say, a little frustrated over your inability to cast a 95% vote for the man, while officially abstaining on the abortion issue. It had to be either all or nothing."

"Right, yet it wasn't as if I were a confirmed pro-lifer either. The thing is, as you well know, I don't really *have* a position on abortion, one way or the other. It's just too much of a hot-button issue for me."

"Yes, and last week we followed the thread holding that button in place back to your guilt over the 'abandoned child' and that problem's oversensitizing, metastatic spread to other issues having to do with the welfare of children. As I reminded you then, it's what analysis calls a 'complex', a number of highly charged ideas and feelings, largely unconscious, clustered around a particular traumatic object or experience. Your difficulty in sustaining an objective consideration of the abortion issue is, as we've seen, part of your guilt complex, which, in *its* turn, is rooted in early repressive attitudes surrounding sex and the body. You know very well, of course, that you're far from alone in being troubled by abortion. Few other issues in this society have caused such radical polarization … red states and blue, demonization of pro-choice physicians, and so on—"

"—Sad but true," I interrupted, "but that brings us back to my story, because I'm here to tell you I *did* go ahead and vote for Obama, despite my inner unease; I *did* break ranks with the Church Militant, or the hierarchy of conscience, or whatever label we want to pin on that brutish authoritarian force within me that for so long has cramped my spontaneity, … lamed my ability to act decisively in so many areas of my life … The election was Tuesday and I had the dream Sunday night. As soon as I woke up Monday morning, I knew I was free to vote as I wished. I can't really tell you *how* I knew this, just that I woke up feeling the freedom, the inner 'slack,' as a kind of thick, palpable openness or spaciousness. Whatever forces had been blocking my view of the horizon—the horizon of this election, at least—were just not there anymore. And they haven't come back since. I'm fine with my vote."

"Well, that certainly is good news," Dr. P. beamed. "You see, you've discovered you can support a candidate, even vote for him, without feeling that every abortion performed as of his swearing-in is on your head. Your conscience is no longer the hangman's noose it once was; the noose now has some 'slack.' You've found within yourself the flexibility to weigh Obama's virtues, those qualities that attract you to him—openness to financial reform, cooperative foreign policy, unflappable demeanor, and so forth—over against the one issue that, not so long ago, would've made that noose uncomfortably tight, and come out on his side. The general still has the authority, no question, but he carries it more lightly than he used to. I guess you could say he's become a bit of a slacker. (Pun fully intended …) He's now authoritative rather than authoritarian."

"That's it exactly, and what feels so good is that, for me, that distinction is no longer just one of vocabulary. I can feel that it's seeped deep down into my gut … You know, it's astonishing to me how infantilized my conscience has kept me for most of my adult life. I wonder if that's the reason the dream cast me as an 'infantryman,' a man who has remained utterly infantile or childish on so many levels, standing in line like a dutiful soldier, probably waiting to have my tin plate filled with some mess mush. Of course, soldiers are well named 'infantry' since they're utterly dependent on military authority for their very survival, as are priests in that other 'army,' the church militant, come to think of it … Which means, I suppose, that the whole military symbology of the dream is not just about the strictness of my conscience—and its slackening, let's not forget—but the institutional roots of that strictness in a religious authoritarianism I took with lethal seriousness as a boy when my conscience was forming … eternal hellfire being the ultimate stockade for conviction by an ecclesiastical court-martial—or should I call it 'General Ecclesiatical Court Martial,' better yet 'General Ecclesiastical Mc-Court Martial.' Yeah, that's the one.

"God, that image takes me back … I must've been about ten or eleven and I was serving as an altar boy in my parish church, Our Lady of Grace, in Hoboken. It was a huge Gothic church, more like a cathedral really with its tremendous vaulted arches, always so high and gloomy during the week with most of the lights out when the nuns would take us over there from class for morning Mass or Thursday confession … Anyway, during one particular week I was serving at the altar for an early Mass, probably the six-thirty, kneeling there on the bottom altar step in my black cassock and white surplice. The sleep was still in my eyes and I was performing all the ritual moves 'on automatic.' Finally it came time, just before the offertory, to fetch the wine and water and bring them to the priest at the top of the altar who, as always, poured from each into the chalice. On this particular morning the priest was a sandy-haired young man I'd never seen before, who happened to be visiting the parish that day, so I was totally unfamiliar with his style as a celebrant, which, as it turned out, was unique. He took the wine cruet from my hand and emptied it completely into the chalice—*drained it!* From the water cruet he carefully let just a single drop, no more, fall into the wine. Innocent though I was, I instantly recognized this as a most unusual ratio of the one to the other. Then, looking up at me from the cup, he said, 'Go back to the sacristy and refill the wine cruet … Go ahead, I'll wait.' Naturally I did as ordered, but, still a little sleepy as I was and somewhat thrown 'off rhythm' by the unusual request, after refilling the wine cruet at the sacristy sink where the wine bottle stood, I also absently took a few sips of water to relieve my dryness of mouth, totally forgetting about my communion fast, which in those days prohibited any intake of food or water from the preceding midnight till after communion.

"The rest of the Mass proceeded without incident, but, on my way home afterwards for breakfast, it suddenly hit me that I'd taken communion after breaking my fast. Now, my first, or gut, reaction, which I remember clearly to this day, was an intoxicating mixture of awe and excitement: awe over the Brave New World I had stumbled into, a world of commandment tablets smashed and taboos spit upon, and the excitement of doing just whatever the hell I felt like doing. Please don't misunderstand, I made no immediate plans to rob a bank or rape the girl next door (I wouldn't have known how anyway); I had no agenda at all. What I had was a ten-year-old's version of a brief taste of freedom, a whiff of the heavenly perfume of personal autonomy. It was a very small window that closed after a moment or two: even before reaching home I was already thumbing through the Baltimore catechism in my head to find out how I should think about the 'problem.' When I brought it up to my mother a bit later during breakfast, she went ballistic. You'd think I had slit the throat of Jesus Christ himself; after all, how much worse would that be than defiling a consecrated communion host? On and on she ranted, shrieking rhetorical questions hysterically into the air: "What do we do?! What *can* we do?! Nothing! The deed is already done! Oh my God!" and such. She even went so far as to call the rectory in crazed quest of absolution over the phone. I remember feeling my little window of autonomy sliding shut as I sat there hunched over my Cheerios listening to her; I guess I just couldn't stand the tension of two contradictory worlds opened up before me at once. One had to go, and I guess it had to be the New World, which hadn't had time to take root ... You might say that was my first encounter with the C.O.,[62] the world of light and the world of darkness in collision. It certainly was an abortive one."

"Now don't go getting down on yourself over that," the good doctor cautioned. "As you pointed out a moment ago, you were just a child, nowhere near ready to appreciate, much less embrace, the dangerous dynamics of dialectical transformation. It's hard enough to do it here and now with me, under so-called ideal conditions. There is, however, something else I believe to be significant about this event and that would be the seed it planted in you, the seed of an understanding—no, an *insight*, a direct experiential insight—into the fundamental bipolarity of life, of nature, of the universe itself. A seed that would lie dormant for decades until a critical event in your life—the 'rejected child'—would activate it, setting off in its turn a decades-long inquiry into the meaning of this demon of contradiction that seems to drive us all. Look at all that inquiry has produced, for yourself and for others, among whom I include myself: a long and fruitful affair with Zen, a strong body of scholarship, all the books and articles examining the demon from various angles, all the reading, studying and thinking, and, modesty aside, the courageous inner journey you've taken here with me ..."

I was grateful for the gilded frame he had just placed around my personal history, within which even my profoundest lapses were made to appear somehow noble, perhaps even necessary. And it felt almost like an expression of this gratitude from the unconscious depths when I then presented him with a reading, suddenly become clear, of another part of the dream: "You know, Dr. P., it occurs to me that when I break ranks in the dream to go downstairs to the latrine, that descent is really the 'disobedient' one down into the unconscious I've made with you. Down into the 'toilet' of sex we go, into all these deeply embedded attitudes of the body's unwholesomeness, to examine them, and once examined, to cast them aside. Each steady gaze at an old memory, at a moment of early life whether internal or external, reopens that childhood window onto an awesome, enlarged world, the window that was slammed shut so long ago ... When I think about it, I suppose any authentic psychoanalysis is a breaking of ranks in a societal sense, since it's this very split-level mind itself which each of us is that gives society its foundation. As Freud said, 'Repression is the price man pays for civilization.' In a sense analysis, in promising a 'dangerous' autonomy, is the enemy of society, which is ironic because I know Freud didn't envision it that way, at least in the early years. As I recall, even after his one pilgrimage to the States, to Clark University in Massachusetts with Jung around 1911, he remained decidedly pessimistic about the importing of psychoanalysis to America, a society he continued to view as an appalling hotbed of anarchists who were bound to misuse its therapeutic benefits ... I don't think Freud would've had much use for my slacker of a general either; for all I know, he might've held some such stereotyped Bolshevik image of the American military."

"On the other hand, Herr Professor," the doctor crowed, "you and I, red-blooded Yankees that we are, have no trouble at all rejoicing in this fine figure of a general who sees no particular harm in a soldier's occasionally breaking ranks to exercise his penis, and even living to tell the tale in analysis … By the way, I'm sure I needn't point out that the exercise on the dream's manifest level, urination, is a sort of inverse euphemism for intercourse, with the urinal as vaginal receptacle. There can be little doubt of this, especially in view of your strong urophiliac tendencies. (We've been over this ground more than once.) Then too, in the context of this dream, and some others I can recall, I now feel inclined to view your urophilia as, among other things, an aspect of the infantilism we discussed earlier. It's all rooted in the earliest diaper-changing and toilet-training behaviors performed and attitudes conveyed by mother and father. This is where the alienation from the body, particularly from the private parts with their 'vulgar' excretory functions, really begins. Maybe you were toilet-trained too young, or too fast; very early training was the accepted wisdom back in the 1940's. Your urophilia could be an unconscious form of protest against this. The literature does associate urethral eroticism with aggressive, even sadistic, phantasies in children. It may be your way, unconscious to be sure, of rebelling against society's premature attempts to civilize you. You are, literally, 'pissed off' at being 'regimented,' forced to stay in line and hold your urine, when you really need to let it go."

"Yes, but let's not forget," I countered, "the whole point here is that I *do* let it go—and without consequence. Society's ultimate arbiter, conscience, in the person of my generous general, undermines the hard-ass line taken by his own underlings, the two officers, with a dismissive wave of the hand. That general—let's call him 'General Slacker'—feels like some sort of newborn presence within me, like a freshly minted self into which my old adversary, Judge Loophole, has morphed. If memory serves, in the Loophole dream the quality of mercy was evident only in my friends outside the courtroom, and after the proceeding; here it's been blended within the principle of authority itself, and I feel I *am* both of these at once … At the same time, Dr. P., there is one thing about General Slacker that bothers me."

"Oh? And that would be? …"

"Well, I'm afraid he bears an uncanny resemblance to Sterling Hayden," I said sheepishly.

"Sterling *who*?"

"Hayden … Sterling Hayden, the actor who played General Jack D. Ripper in that dark-comic masterpiece of Stanley Kubrick's, *Dr. Strangelove*. You must've seen it. It dates from the mid-sixties: an anti-war film that virtually launched the counterculture era."

Dr. P., movie buff that he was, indicated immediate recognition with copious nods of the head.

"I'm sure you can see why this would bother me a little … I mean, come on, the man is a sociopath! He wants to blow the Russian 'Commies' to kingdom come and, as I recall, actually pulls it off: That closing scene with Slim Pickens riding the nuke accidently released from his bomber like a rodeo cowboy, 'Yahoos!' and all, still gives me chills whenever I think of it. Now why on earth would my unconscious want to clothe this shining new spirit of liberalism within me in the figure of a madman?"

He just sat there for a while without expression, pondering the question, perhaps waiting for me to come up with something on my own. But I was drawing a blank, so, after a while, he turned to his tried-and-true strategy of dropping hints, which consisted in feeding me clues to a possible answer until that answer suddenly popped into my head. (I always wondered, facetiously, whether the therapeutic benefit to me was inversely proportionate to the number of clues I needed to "get it." If I needed more than three, game over!)

"Well," he began, "General Ripper, as I recall, is a farcical character drawn in the broadest strokes—grotesquely so; still, there is at least a little more to him than his military-satirical 'nuke 'em' mentality, don't you think?"

"There is?" I answered, at a loss.

"Sure there is. I'm thinking of a particular scene which has him sitting at his desk, totally absorbed in his own paranoid ramblings. If memory serves, the camera eyes him from in front of the desk at about chest level, looking up a bit—it's not quite a close-up but almost …"

"Say no more," I broke in, lighting up. "You're inching towards the infamous cigar, the pana—er, 'phallitella!'"

"Ah yes, there's that devilish coinage of yours again," he laughed. "Where have we seen that before, let me see …"

"Don't trouble yourself," I said, suddenly deflated. "It was the Tony Soprano dream from about two years ago: another dream of mine picturing phallic overcompensation in a violent psychopath. I must say, this is getting depressing."

"Easy now," he cautioned. "Remember, everything depended then, as it does now, on how the dream is read; so let's proceed slowly … For one thing, why must it be '*over*compensation,' or compensation at all, for that matter?"

"What do you mean; that's standard psychoanalytic—"

"—Exactly, it's standard, it's boilerplate, it's even clichéd. What's it got to do with us, with you and your unique dream? Do you think your unconscious consults a psychoanalytic handbook before spinning a dream?"

"Point well taken. Still …"

"No, no, stay with me here. We've already established General Slacker's baseline profile as that of a reasonable, even a generous, man. I see no reason to chuck that because he happens to remind you of General Ripper. The question we need to ask is, what particular aspect of General Ripper is the dream incorporating in General Slacker and why."

"Yes, that's right, and that brings us back to the phallitella—"

"Right," he smiled, "and to my question as to its meaning."

"Well, if not compensation, what else could it be but … Oh, of course, expression, self-expression, no? That would mean the long cigar, in the case of *my* general at least, General Slacker, doesn't compensate for potency, or lack thereof, but rather expresses that potency, even celebrates it—a sort of swaggering, devil-may-care *joie de vivre* over it."

"Now you're onto it," he smiled. "All of which makes your general a fusion of superego and id, authority and instinct. *That's* what your dream takes from General Ripper, not his farcical, limp-dick sociopathy."

"You know, that actually rings true to me because the Sterling Hayden screen persona always impressed me with its strong masculine charisma; that charisma was always there no matter what role he played, comic or dramatic. I would even say it made him a sort of one-note actor."

I let myself breathe and just relax into this more edifying, creative reading of the dream, until the usual noxious thought presented itself, threatening to spoil it: "There's only one problem with this interpretation."

"What's that?"

"The general in my dream doesn't have a cigar."

"Maybe that's because your unconscious knows that *you* know that, quite often, a cigar is so much more than a cigar."

"I see," was all I could summon up. Mortally stung by this latest thrust of wit, I was unable to let the matter rest but cast about the room for a rejoinder—*any* rejoinder. Spotting the pack of Marlboros lying open on his desk, I said, "So tell me, what's a cigarette?"

"*Touché!*" he roared.

(24) January 2009: Bringing Up Mom and Dad

I'm sitting on a Persian rug in the middle of some ornate room at the feet of my mother, who is reclining in an easy chair, giving off a—for her—oddly regal air. I complain to her that I have a two-week trip to Prague coming up which I'm not looking forward to because I have to go alone. The prospect of such a lonely sojourn depresses me, I tell her. She gazes at me with serene eyes and says in a most soothing voice, "I'll take care of it; I'll fix it." And she does*—immediately! Don't ask me how, but even while I'm still seated there on the floor, she somehow manages to pull a few strings (with whom, I wonder), and it turns out that Dottie now has permission to go with me.*

"Uh-huh ... So?"

"I don't know—I have mixed feelings about this one."

"How so?"

"Well, on the one hand, it's nice to have my Mom on my side in a dream for a change. Usually she's a noxious presence in one way or another: angry or depressed over something I've done or not done, or even just some way I happen to *be*. On the other hand, *look at me!* There I am down on the floor groveling at her feet, still the pathetically subservient son, as if she were some high-and-mighty queen lounging on her throne ... You know the story."

And indeed he did know the story. Dr. P. and I had by now reached a point of what one might call "historical familiarity" in the analysis, that is to say, a point at which I could simply allude to one or another of the fundamental scenarios of my early life, without necessarily rehearsing it in depth: "You know the story," "We've certainly been over that often enough," "Need I say more?", or some such referential expression on my part, would sometimes be enough to evoke for both of us a vast terrain of my personal history which would then link itself up, almost automatically, with some new point I was trying to make in that moment.

Of course, Dr. P. was always the final judge of the suitability of such "shorthand communication," or, in Stephen King's apt abbreviation, SSDD,[63] to a given situation, for, although the *psycho*analytic or Freudian phase of my analysis, concerned primarily with the earliest memories and experiences, was substantially finished, the phases were discrete much more in concept than in fact, so that, if he thought it necessary or worthwhile to sift through the early memories yet again, even this late in the process, I would always do so, to be sure with sulking reluctance at times, feeling put out by the tedium of yet another "re-run." Yet on days when I was smart, it would occur to me that, from his own personal point of view, Dr. P. had even less cause to look forward to such re-runs than I, so that if he was pressing me for one, he must have a damned good reason. And, so far as I can tell, I must say that, almost without exception, his instincts served him well.

A good case in point would be the "abandoned child" scenario, which, the reader will not be surprised to learn, turned out to be the toughest, most tenacious, most intractable problem to come up in my analysis. Not to be flippant about it, because it almost destroyed me, but this was my Wagnerian leitmotif, the doleful melody that announced itself, directly or indirectly, in almost every session, particularly during the late-early and middle years. This was the magnet that drew all my other issues to itself and seemed to shape my psychopathology into a perverse whole. Whether we'd be talking about my early life, my current home life, my job, or even some neutral philosophical or religious matter, sooner or later some element of the discussion would cue the 'abandonment' leitmotif, and Dr. P. would, more often than not, have me sing that old tune one more time, each time painstakingly reviewing the same cluster of obsessions and feelings that clung to the pain like barnacles to a ship's underbelly. Sometimes I would cry out, "Enough! What's the point? Nothing ever changes! I'm sick and tired of talking about it! Talk is useless!" Yet calmly he would beg to differ, gently he would insist on the importance of reviewing the matter as often and as long as it took to work through it.

Dr. P. is the only therapist of the three I've been with who was more interested in talking about my symptoms than I was. No amount of repetitious complaining ever seemed to faze him; never once did I detect the slightest trace of the therapist's eye-rolling, oh-no-not-that-again expression. On the contrary, whenever I would confess my own embarrassment over the intractability of the problem, its refusal to just "fold up and blow away," and my need to bitch and moan about it again and again without surcease, he would say things like, "Why *shouldn't* you complain about your symptoms? After all, that's where all the pain is" or "Jung always stressed the centrality of symptoms to the analytic process; in fact, he believed that the key to their resolution lay in careful attention to them, which naturally includes discussing them. Symptoms contain their own solutions within themselves." (From my vantage point, the tendency of many therapists to discourage their patients' going-on about symptoms is terribly misguided. It seems to come out of a fear that the floodgates of complaint, once opened, will lead to the engulfment of the therapy by an endless river of whining. I have strong doubts about this. In my experience, a few minutes spent venting about symptoms at the top of an hour always brought relief and a willingness on my part to use that relief for productive work. By the same token, the disapproval of discussion of symptoms by my other therapists, whether overt or covert, always intensified them, turning them into the gorilla in the consulting room, this on the principle that anything suppressed becomes stronger.)

Through all this Dr. P. never tired of reminding me that the most difficult problems needed to be "processed" or "worked through," that is, reviewed as often as necessary to alleviate the pain that suffused them. In effect, through sheer analytic repetition, they were to be reduced to mental-emotional puree, made as innocuous as the contents of a jar of Gerber's baby food. It was almost as if the true active ingredient in the cure was this very relentlessness of repetition, the unremitting exposure of a problem to the glare of consciousness, the patient confronting of it over and over again, until finally, slowly, reluctantly, yet inevitably, it gave up all its bugaboo aspects, one by one, and melted down into a vaporous puddle like the wicked witch of the West. This, at least, is how I experienced it. This is not to devalue the roll of insight in the process. The seeing of connections between *now* and *then*, the spontaneous linking-up of, say, a dream image or phrase or mood with a relationship or experience in life, the being-taken-aback by the sudden noticing of a 'rationale' for some irrational act or habit: in a word, the "aha" experience; this too has its indispensable role to play. Indeed, I would say the synergy generated by these two interactive factors, persevering repetition over time punctuated by the essentially sudden, timeless seeing of connections, is the essence of that power that forges healing. But we must all be disabused of the stereotype of therapeutic insight, nurtured by Hollywood, as some one-time-only, grandly exploding Roman candle within, lighting the way to "happily ever after." That only happens in *Spellbound*.

From the standpoint of analysis, my mother was one of those archaic psychic realities which, it seemed, could not be "processed" too often. So, on this occasion, when I invoked the shorthand "You know the story," Dr. P. blinked twice and begged to differ: "One thing I know about 'the story,' as you put it, is that it's never-ending. As long as you live it goes on and on. That means it continues to be written here and now even as we speak; and not only that: Knowing as we do from analysis that the past has no independent existence of its own but is always an aspect of the present, we can say that what you dream and think and feel about mother today, in being raised to consciousness through our work here, acts retroactively on the oldest, most calcified emotional structures deep inside you, raising them from the 'living death' of unconsciousness, quickening them, making them malleable as new energies for use in fashioning the work of art that is your life. It is in this psychic sense, contrary to all *common* sense, that analysis claims the past can be changed."

For some reason on this day I was more irritated than uplifted by Dr. P.'s admirable idealism, so I took the low road, belittling his lofty rhetoric with a dismissive retort, and enjoying doing so: "That's all well and good, but what's it got to do with me, with this dream?"

"You tell me. You're still running the show."

"I don't see any connection. To me this dream is just the latest episode in my personal soap opera … If it were on afternoon TV, we could title it, *As the Stomach Churns: The Dysadventures of Dennis, the Pathetic Son*."

Fully aware as he was that my venomous tongue was one of my preferred ways of whining, Dr. P. held his own, content simply to meet me eye to eye for a moment, before continuing matter-of-factly: "Oh, I don't agree, Herr Professor. I don't agree at all. I think you're selling this dream way too short. It's begging you to take another, closer look. Only this time you must look, not just from the neck up, but with your whole being—toenails, sinews and heart."

At this advanced stage of the game, it was a rare occasion indeed that would find me impervious to this sort of exhortation coming from the man who had become my cherished mentor, but I guess I was just in a contrarian mood that day, and besides, I simply couldn't see any hopeful sign in the dream of a shift in my relationship with Mom. And I told him so: "Look, you know I'm in tune with your holistic way of viewing dreams, but I don't see it yielding anything new here. This dream takes its place in the long procession of depressing Mom dreams stretching back ad nauseam, to the misty beginnings of my analysis; and it's basically no different from others I've reported here recently—what was that one about a month ago—oh yeah, she slaps me and I shout, 'Go ahead, do it again! Take your best shot!' Or the one in which I hug her and tell her I love her, to which she reacts with a look of profound mistrust."

"But, Herr Professor," he hastened to remind me, "have you entirely forgotten the subtle signs of change we detected in those recent dreams: your standing up to that slap—literally, from the table—and how we equated the act of standing up with the German *Aufstand,* which means 'rebellion' or 'uprising.' You're asserting your independence. And in the other one, how you just turn and walk away from that look of mistrust, again a strong gesture of emotional autonomy."

And it was true. I had allowed my gloomy reading of this day's dream to cast a pall over those two recent, more hopeful ones, thereby effectively sweeping all three into the dustbin of 'disappointment dreams' I'd been filling since Mom's death. How powerful the force of habit, how essential the corrective viewpoint of the analyst. Nevertheless, in that moment I was still at odds with the doctor over the merit of the current dream: "Yes, quite right, and thank you for refreshing my memory, but this one strikes me as a relapse into the miasma of all those doom-and-gloom dream-encounters with Mom. Just look at it: the subservient position I'm in down there on the rug, looking up at her, needing her to solve my problems for me, which she does, apparently with a snap of the fingers ... No gesture of independence there, wouldn't you agree?" I asked facetiously, all but challenging Dr. P. to persuade me otherwise.

Which he proceeded to do: "When I asked you just now to regard this dream with your whole being, from the depths of instinct as well as through the laser of intellect, I was, to be sure, reminding you of something you already well know from our years of work here, but it was also more than that: I was trying to get you to step back and broaden your scope, to take a fresh look at mother, noticing perhaps the somewhat novel surroundings in which she appears and even the rather novel air or attitude she sports here. I believe this dream is presenting mother in a new light. Consider the Persian rug you're on with its intricate symmetrical pattern; the classical pose assumed by mother in her regal chair, tantamount to a throne; above all, the serene voice of reassurance—I believe you called it 'soothing' … These are numinous images, images of radiant power, which mark this dream as the first, or at least the first you've reported, in which your mother appears as an archetype: Mother is here … Mother, writ large, so to speak. This puts your position of subservience to her in an entirely different light and makes any comparison with earlier dreams in which she shows antipathy or disappointment or—how shall I put it—a condescending solicitude towards you beside the point. This, I believe, is an entirely different order of dream, one arising from the collective unconscious and inaugurating—no, that's not too ceremonious a term to use here—I say 'inaugurating' a new order of relations with a new and nurturing Mother. If you're subservient here, prostrate before the 'Queen Mother,' well, that's precisely the proper attitude to assume before an archetype, one of deep reverence and respect, because, as you know, what you're revering is an aspect of your own inner divinity. It's the only form of self-esteem—or rather Self-esteem, capital 'S'—worth a damn … Actually, those recent dreams of mother you mentioned a moment ago with their subtle permutations alerted me that a dream like this one might be in the offing, and voila, here it is."

"I can't believe how obtuse I was," I muttered to myself, sobered though happily so. This was one occasion on which I was delighted to be persuaded I was wrong. And now that Dr. P. had helped me change my perspective, associations began to light up in me, a spontaneously creative phenomenon I'd come to regard as confirmation of the rightness of an insight or point of view. The most significant of these revolved around the first mature novel by one of my favorite modern German writers, Hermann Hesse, who wrote *Demian*[64] in 1917, during the First World War, just after he had himself undergone an analysis in Zurich with a student of Jung's. "You know, in *Demian,*" I said, as Dr. P., who I knew had read the book, gave a nod, "the hero, Sinclair, joins the elite group of seekers who gather around Demian's mother, the charismatic matriarch, Frau Eva; she gives psychological and spiritual succor to all of them. She seems to be an inexhaustible font of refreshment. Hesse skillfully blurs the borderline in this character between the individual woman, the ordinary mother, and the goddess who is Mother to all. When I see my dream from the point of view you've just put to me, it becomes obvious that my Mom has several features recalling Frau Eva in the book. The biblical Eva or Eve is, after all, the universal Mother, the Earth Mother, and my mother here seems so much more, so much grander than … well, than my mother as I knew her in life. Her … uh … I want to say 'aloofness,' but that's not quite it. Her … serenity, which suffuses that regal posture and the voice emanating from it, gives her a transcendental aura that leaves no room for doubt or resistance on my part. I'm sure my commitment to her *during* the dream was total, and I can see now that it was only on waking and thereafter that that sacred symbiosis became obscured in the fog of old mental habits."

The good doctor nodded slowly and with a certain solemnity, eyes all but closed, as if to give formal sanction to my words, then adding, "So you see, while your mother may have fallen short in some ways on the personal level, yet on the level of myth and archetype, to which our work here has given you access, she is more than making up for it."

"No question. But then, it *is* reciprocal, isn't it? You could just as well say that *I've* managed to bring *her* up well over the past eight-plus years," I said, savoring the irony of it.

"Quite right," Dr. P. responded. "In analysis the child gives birth to the parent … But getting back to the dream, I would ask you to have another look at the image of yourself there on the rug, which I would say you interpreted with only partial accuracy: prostration before mother, yes certainly, but this is the great Earth Mother before whom prostration is called for. Moreover, you saw your humbled self only in relation to the image above, the Mother, ignoring the equally important image beneath, the rug—indeed, the Persian rug with its elaborate and colorful mandala design, an obvious manifestation of the Self archetype. The fact that you are 'down on' that rug, solidly planted on it, says that you are becoming firmly 'grounded' in the Self. Remember, the psyche or Self is one, and the archetypes, while being discrete forces, are nevertheless not separate, so that any change or movement in one has a ripple effect throughout the system. So it's not surprising that the 'elevation' of mother to the stature of an archetype should be pictured in a dream that also has you reclining on the foundation of Self."

"Yes, and now, as I think about the specific help Mom gives, it all falls into place. I'm facing a two-week trip to Prague, an exotic, 'foreign' city my unconscious likes to use as an image of itself, the deep, dark place where instinct, particularly sexual instinct, is at home. (We analyzed one, quite erotic, Prague dream in some depth a year or two ago.) But I'm unhappy about the trip because I have to go alone. I complain to her, she tells me she'll fix it and she does—instantly: She gives me my own wife as a traveling companion. Well, what has she fixed? I would say, neither more nor less than my entire relationship to my unconscious, in particular the anima, and she's done this simply by manifesting herself, by being there. That's why the 'fix' is instantaneous, done with a mere snap of the divine fingers, so to speak! ... I'd even go so far as to say that, in 'graduating' to universal archetypal status as she does in this dream, my Mom is transformed within me from an age-old impediment to my marriage, particularly its sexual dynamic, into a kind of priestess presiding over it, blessing it, consecrating it—in all its raw sensuality ... This is true mothering ... Earth Mothering ..."

After a moment of reflection, Dr. P. extended my idea: "And why shouldn't we broaden the sense, the significance, of marriage intended by the dream to include the analysis itself, this quest of ours to 'marry' conscious and unconscious phases of the Self. After all, from a psychic point of view any true marriage, any coincidence of opposites, is ultimately a facet of Selfhood."

These were all weighty matters, and I knew I would need time to assimilate their sweep. As if to relieve me of the temptation of attempting to do so right then and there, my unconscious provided me with a sudden distraction, in the form of a memory of an event of long ago that seemed trivial at the time of its occurrence: “My God, how things do come full circle! … It was around four in the afternoon on the day of my wedding, August 5, 1973, a perfect sunny Sunday. We were all in the Baroque reception room of an exclusive French restaurant in uptown Manhattan, waiting for the minister we’d hired to show up and perform the ceremony. We were a modest group: Dottie and I, parents on both sides, siblings and a few close friends. We’d already had a few glasses of complementary champagne by the time the minister, Wild Bill Kelly (don’t ask!), pulled up on his Harley, came in and put on his surplice for business. It seems we were just one of several couples on his busy agenda of weddings for the day. After asking us how we’d feel about the mentioning of Jesus’s name in the ceremony and being told ‘No, thank you,’ we all assembled before him, Dottie and I closest, as he set himself to read the rites. Just then, in that briefest of intervals before he began to speak, I heard my Mom, who was standing right behind me, say to me in a low voice, ‘You know, you can still come home if you want to,’ and my best man, Jerry—he of the acid tongue—snap at her in an audible whisper, ‘Yeah, he can go home and play with his trains!’”

Laughing again now in the recounting of the incident just as I had thirty-five years earlier when it happened, I shook my head in amazement at the symmetry of it: “What my mother couldn’t give me then, her heart’s unreserved blessing, she gives me now in full measure, and then some. Dottie and I can go to Prague together—a delayed honeymoon!”

It was, of course, only natural that I would think of my

father in that moment. Where was *he* in this joyful "family reunion," I wondered. I had only the vaguest memory even of his presence at my wedding. How completely obscured in her thick shadow he stood on that day. Noticing my preoccupation, Dr. P. asked, "What is it?" When I told him, he was, as so often, right there with the relevant connection: "Do you remember that dream you reported a few months ago of your father sitting in the darkened movie theater, looking like a Rastafarian, black face, dreadlocks and all?"

"How could I forget it?"

"It occurs to me now, in light of this discussion, that there's a lot more to it than we were able to appreciate then. For one thing, when you step out into the lobby for popcorn, only to return to find him gone, his seat empty, and your little daughter sitting in the next seat crying that 'Baba' won't be around anymore to give her hugs and kisses, do you remember what you say to her to soothe her?"

"Sure. I say, 'Don't worry, *I* can give you those now.'"

"That sure looks to me now like a changing of the guard. Doesn't it to you? Once years ago father appeared to you in a dream in the guise of another, quite different, black man: Snoop Dogg, or Snoop Dad, as you called him, a ruthless drug dealer ready to ship you off to the cemetery. Here he's evolved into a Rastafarian, an empathic, perhaps even messianic, shadow figure, able not only to give affection himself, but, more importantly, to empower *you* to give affection to your daughter. He disappears when his work is done.

"*You* are his work."

(25) May 2009: Prisoner of Love

"Don't let the stars get in your eyes / Don't let the moon break your hearrrrt." It's the velvet tenor of Perry Como, my Mom's favorite crooner during the 50's and 60's. He's squeezing out the tune with as little effort as possible, as usual, though the sound does somehow fill the spacious, well-lit venue—some sort of gymnasium, it seems. Perry's singing at a mic. set up under one of the basketball hoops of the main court. As he stands there facing out to the court, only his mouth is moving. I sit on the gym floor with crossed legs, somewhere near the top of the key, watching and listening to him. There are others scattered around the floor behind me, to about mid-court, maybe seven or eight, all sitting and listening like me. Together we make a sparse audience. One of these, positioned maybe a dozen feet behind me and visible if I turn my head sharply right, is a young black man of twenty or so. I notice he's laughing at the performance in a ridiculing way, not even trying to suppress it. Of course, this is contagious and I start to guffaw myself. There we sit on the hardwood floor, laughing at Perry together in this odd, conspiratorial, wink-and-nod relationship. Every time I turn my head to see what my co-conspirator is up to, the laughter starts up again.

And it did right then and there as well, as if we too were co-conspirators. I really don't know which one of us started it. Maybe we just fell into it together, but almost immediately we caught ourselves up and Dr. P. just sat there eyeing me with that cat-who-ate-the-canary grin, provoking me to begin with "What? What are you grinning about? Come on, out with it!"

Shifting in his chair and allowing only the slightest apologetic bow of the head, he said, "For now, I'll say only that it's interesting that, in telling the dream, you introduce Perry as 'Mom's favorite crooner.'"

"Well, he was."

"I'm sure he was. What I'm getting at is that your very first identification of him—clearly spontaneous and thus revealingly truthful—is with reference to *her*—not yourself or pop culture in general. I mean, you could've said something like … 'the voice of Perry Como, big-time 50's crooner.'"

I was piqued by the aptness of his point and, seeing no way of countering it, I thought I might at least dim its luster a bit by viewing it as superfluous: "Even if I had, it wouldn't have taken me long to get around to her. She's all over this dream—implicitly."

"Tell me about it."

"It all ties in with the fact that Perry Como was, far and away, my Mom's favorite crooner. She definitely had some sort of middle-age housewife's crush on him. She loved that pleasant, saccharine singing style he had, avoiding all emotional extremes, all fortissimo high notes, one cloying ballad sounding pretty much like another; and the bland, inoffensive wardrobe, always either a blue serge suit and tie or a light buttoned-down cashmere sweater—and tie. But it went further than that; it was the whole Como persona: the Italian heritage—although, curiously, the same heritage failed to endear Sinatra to her; the humble craftsman roots, starting out as a barber; the faithful clinging to one non-celebrity woman during a long, happy marriage; the Catholicism; the whole narcotizing, white-bread modesty of the man …"

"Sounds like you've given this some thought."

"Not really, at least not since the days of my youth when I'd occasionally tease Mom over her little infatuation. We would be watching his old variety show on TV and I'd drop remarks like 'Frankie wouldn't go near that dog of a song,' or 'Is that a different tie he's got on tonight,' or I'd just start snoring during the 'dramatic' climax of a torch song like 'Prisoner of Love,' and of course she'd glare at me and give me an annoyed tsk. … Actually, it's just the sort of behavior the young black man in the dream and I engage in, making fun of the lethally bland Mr. C. …"

"Shadowy tweaking of mother's overly correct, conservative taste, huh?"

"Without question. It was then and it is now. But it goes deeper, much deeper, than that even. It's not just her bland taste in music; it's her profound attachment to a certain image of innocuous masculinity that I guess I found constricting, … neutering, even emasculating, on some deep level at least. Although I probably couldn't have put it this way then, I think I found Perry Como an affront to my libido, my animal nature, which of course I was steeped in at that time, notwithstanding the Catholic straitjacket. That such a milquetoast, who I felt had absolutely nothing to do with me, with my instinctual life, with my oversexed blood, should capture her admiration and affection …"

"And she didn't care for Sinatra, you say?"

"Surely this doesn't surprise you; Sinatra was almost an alter ego of Perry. She said it was Frank's 'sleazy' voice she didn't like, but it was a lot more than that: the jazzy, finger-snapping style, with dangling cigarette and cocked fedora; the bad-boy image with all those marriages and divorces (for a *Catholic* no less!); the constant insinuations of mob connections; the torrid, and very public, love affairs with high-profile Hollywood *femmes fatales* like Ava Gardner, all of it splashed all over the tabloids … Did Perry ever make the tabloids, even once? … An irony here is that my mother grew up with little Frankie on the very same block in Hoboken, on 3rd and Jefferson Streets. They knew each other as young children; in fact, my mother claims she delivered bags of groceries to the Sinatra flat now and then."

"Interesting. Of course, it's much easier to idealize someone you don't know personally."

"Even apart from that, there's no way my Mom could ever have favored any crooner over Perry. Despite his good looks, or rather *because* of his Catholic choirboy's good looks, he presented precisely the image of polite masculinity, erased below the navel, that my mother needed in order to feel safe enough to give her heart."

"Is the Perry Como in your dream 'erased below the navel,' as you put it?"

"'Erased below?' … let me think … certainly not literally, but … ah, I see where you're heading here: In reporting the dream, I described him as moving 'only his mouth' as he sings. The rest of him is as still as a statue, almost like a cheaply drawn cartoon in which the character's mouth is the only moving part in an entire scene. Is that it?"

He nodded, implying I should continue in that vein.

"Well sure, that's the functional equivalent of an erasure,

wouldn't you say? Erased or immobilized, either way we've got repression. Here it's repression twice over, I guess: my mother's repression of the body erotic reflected in my own frozen-statue—or 'statuesque'—version of Perry Como ... It reminds me of one of the funniest parodies I've ever seen on TV. Back in the 70's there was this late-night comedy ensemble show called 'SCTV' ('Second City TV,' I believe), a sort of predecessor of 'Saturday Night Live,' that did these spot-on impressions of TV celebrities and their programs, people like Bob Hope and Walter Cronkite. Anyway, one show had Eugene Levy, a comic actor, doing Perry, presumably coming out on stage to begin his variety revue; only 'Perry' didn't walk out, rather he was rolled out on stage lying in bed, with the covers all the way up to his neck and tightly tucked in under the mattress—a hilarious caricature of Perry's relaxed, laid-back style. And he came out singing! Lying in bed, softly crooning to the audience, his eyelids drooping on the verge of sleep, his mouth his only moving part, almost his only *visible* part ... I don't think I ever laughed harder in my life; and even then the irony was not lost on me that Perry was *in bed*, the last place my mother would ever have wanted to see him."

"Did mother watch that program with you?"

"Oh no, it was on much too late for her, but I remember wishing she were there to see it. I'm sure that spoof would've pricked even as hagiographical an image of Perry as hers ... But I always felt that for her the male body basically didn't exist below the neck—nor did the female body, for that matter: In the late sixties, during the interim between graduate school and my first year at Syracuse, I was still seeing Susan, the blonde girl from Iowa whom I'd met at Hopkins. [Dr. P.

nodded in recognition.] It must've been in June or July and Susan called me one morning at Mom's from Long Island, where she was staying with a friend, to ask me to ask my Mom for advice about a tampon that was stuck inside her, the string for easy removal having come loose. So I did. Mom, of course, got on the phone and gave Susan what advice she could, but, boy, did I catch it after she hung up. Assuming the darkest of her Frankenstinian masks, she asked me in a withering tone, 'What were you doing talking with her about *down there*?' … '*Down there,*' Dr. P., '*down there!*' I was twenty-seven years old at the time!"

"Standard geographical euphemism for the sexually nervous," he said in summary, "the lost continent of Australia, down there … down under. You can't see it from 'up here' because it's tucked in 'down there.'"

"Yeah, an entirely private part of the planet's body, you might say … Speaking of private parts and their relative anaesthesia resulting from our own confused feelings about the body, feelings we inherit from the culture through Mom and Dad, as usual it's my invisible partner here on the couch, Kafka, who most intimately corroborates my own experience. He was a lapsed Jew who lived in Prague, but his aware sense of his own conflicted, even contradictory, attitudes towards the body differs little from that of a lapsed Catholic like me brought up near New York City. His whole adult life Kafka was obsessed with health regimens and dietary prophylaxis, yet he frequented so-called houses of ill repute. How's that for a mind-body split? In a letter he once referred to his own body of which he took such meticulous care as 'an alien obscenity.'[65] Again and again he confessed to friends his inability to distinguish love from lust, even filth.[66] For me this explains those most peculiar love scenes at the inn in *The Castle*, in which we see the antihero K. rolling around with Frieda in beer puddles … But I think Kafka captures the anguish of our Western alienation from the body most devastatingly in his brief parable, 'The Green Dragon,' a piece that, whenever we took it up in class, never failed to stun my undergraduate students into embarrassed silence. I took that as a culturally conditioned reaction demonstrating to me the importance of teaching it as often as possible … You know, instead of paraphrasing the piece for you off the cuff, if you don't mind I'll just read it to you quickly from your copy of *Parables and Paradoxes* sitting on the literature shelf over there."

Getting up to fetch the book, I began reading on my way back to the couch:

> The Green Dragon: The door opened and what entered the room, fat and succulent, its sides voluptuously swelling, footless, pushing itself along on its entire underside, was the green dragon. Formal salutation. I asked him to come right in. He regretted that he could not do that, as he was too long. This meant that the door had to remain open, which was rather awkward. He smiled half in embarrassment, half cunningly, and began:
>
> "Drawn hither by your longing, I come pushing myself along from afar off, and underneath am now scraped quite sore. But I am glad to do it. Gladly do I come, gladly do I offer myself to you."[67]

Dr. P. gave a wry smile; clearly the piece needed little interpretation for him. But since this was an analytic session and not a literature tutorial, I felt a strong need to express to him at least a few of my thoughts and feelings about it, and these in a style and tone I would never have permitted myself with my undergraduate students: "There you have it," I said, "in a few short strokes of the pen a reality check from the master on the myth of male-female sexual bliss, supposedly the peak human experience short of seeing the face of God himself. And what do we have here: the man and the woman reduced to their symbolic genitals. Wonderful synecdoche, the whole contained in the private part of each: The male organ is the standard repulsive reptilian, here, to be sure, not the snake but a hideous wounded dragon—not quite castrated, mind you, which might be more merciful (in the way sudden death is preferable to slow torture), just scraped sore … castration by centimeters, no doubt over a lifetime of painful close encounters. Still, the old boy remains fat and succulent, meaning all juiced up and ready for action; nothing but nothing will kill that urge … And just look at *her*! … What? You say, except for her voice as narrator, she's not there? *Au contraire, mon cher.* You're forgetting the synecdoche: She's the room! Get it? Room equals womb. She's telling us how it was the last time that dragon/drag-on/dragged-on penis entered her roomy, womby vagina … Of course, it helps to know that Kafka was well aware of that antiquated German word for woman: *Frauenzimmer*, literally 'woman's room or apartment.' That's right, that's what women used to be called by German men: wombs or "baby ovens." Not that the word is unique to German; in *The Interpretation of Dreams* Freud says it exists in one form or another in many European languages … But you know what really gets me here, Dr. P., the detail in the piece that just breaks your heart: it's the dragon's inability to accept her invitation to 'come right in.' He's just 'too long,' so that 'the door had to remain open, which was rather awkward.' … No, no, it has nothing to do with the size of the organ because, remember, the dragon also represents the *whole* male body; it's both a phallic synecdoche *and* the whole body, both part and whole, at the same time. (Kafka likes to conflate these opposites.[68]) When the dragon says he's sorry he can't come all the way in, he speaks every man's unconscious anguish at his inability to crawl back up into that womb from which he was once so rudely expelled, to return to that original Eden, that *Urgarten* of female embrace he never ceases to yearn for, however vaguely and dimly. Even in this most primordial of unions, it seems, there always lingers a tiny open sore in the middle of the wound of self-consciousness. A scrape, an oozing scab of alienation, from self and from the woman, that never quite heals. The tragedy of sexual alienation is the purest romanticism, understood as man's perennial state of divorce from nature. Perry's love song, sung from a mouth in a head sitting atop a paralyzed body, is just my Mom's and my own little contemporary pop incarnation of it."

Dr. P. sat still for a while, apparently considering my little peroration. I must confess I was a little embarrassed over it, probably fearing he would think it a bit excessive, even though analytic protocol said there was no such thing and my years with him had all but inured me to such self-consciousness. What he said, however, only disposed me to a deeper intimacy: "You know, Herr Professor, you're a lucky man to have found such a literary soul mate as Kafka. You've used him here as a lens through which to focus so much of your own analytic material. For you he's been like that wonderful metaphor of Freud's for psychopathology, the crystal vase lying smashed on the floor, the shards of which, though now separate, nevertheless retain a symmetrical pattern indicating its lost wholeness. You read Kafka's shards, these little parables, as clues to your own lost wholeness, and in the very reading of them, act to restore that wholeness, now on a level of awareness immune to breakage."

"Thank you for that," I answered. "It's true, I've always tried to erase the line between my life, my work and whatever form of psychospiritual practice I happened to be doing at a given time. I did it with Primal Therapy in the 70's, with Zen in the 80's and 90's, and, of late, with you here. Of course, what *I* call commitment, those around me might call obsession. It hasn't always been a walk in the park for them, especially Dottie. But for me, I guess it's the only way ... But listen, your kind words give me courage to take a further step, a step towards more intimate personal revelation in these ruminations of mine over the body and its longings. What I'm about to say, though framed by the generalized 'we' because I do think it has widespread application, applies very much to myself, to my own sexual experience and to an almost lifelong process of thought about my own lust: ... Kafka is saying, to me at least, that even our most intoxicating paroxysms of desire, our very lust, merely exposes our estrangement from the body. This is because lust is the body's only—and barely—adequate response to the profound frustration over the loss of that original oneness with the sexual other, that primordial androgynous condition pined after by the romantics.

Now I'm not saying there aren't acts of intercourse that go beyond lust to something deeper (call it 'love')—I know there are, I've even been blessed with a few—just that lust and its occasional relief through orgasm are the best we can usually do. Now, if we observe lust closely (*after* the fact, of course) and try to determine just what it is that gives it its power, we discover that it always contains an element of degradation, whether of self, or other, or both. This degradation gives pleasure. The reason it gives pleasure is that, as a near-total rejection of the will to a corporeal solidarity with the other deemed unattainable, it becomes, by virtue of this very negation, a paradoxical echo of that solidarity, which was unalloyed infinite bliss, much as we retain a powerful retinal afterimage of the sun after turning our eyes away from it ('rejecting' it). The unconscious reasoning goes like this: 'If I can't become one with her body, which is my only way of becoming one with my own, I can at least become one with my hatred of this body for betraying me as it has, for becoming this fleshy "green dragon" that can never come all the way in.' This pleasurable hatred, in all its degrading power, is what we call lust. It's our consolation prize.

"Now don't get me wrong. I think lust is a terrific consolation prize, but let's face it, it's an itch that can never finally be scratched (the fact that for some it can become an addiction is proof of that), which means, alas, that, as a solution to the problem of the lost oneness that gave rise to it, it only compounds the alienation it seeks to overcome … Maybe an analogy from a standard textbook on abnormal psychology will serve to illustrate: We all know about phobias, how irrational yet powerful they can be: fear of water, closed spaces, public speaking, and so on. Fewer people know about the phenomenon of counterphobia, which involves dealing with a phobia, not by the usual avoidance of the object or situation that evokes anxiety, but doing the very opposite: inviting that object or situation, courting it, mastering it by sheer dint of will. The problem is, however, that since the countering behavior is unconscious, it becomes a problem in itself in the form of an addiction. One feels compelled to master the phobia over and over again. That feeling of mastery becomes a kind of rush (the parallel to lust begins to emerge): So Evel Knieval makes a lethally dangerous career of jumping over the Grand Canyon on his motorcycle, never quite overcoming his unconscious fear of heights, or Steve Irwin becomes a handler of dangerous animals, eventually losing his life to a stingray.[69] Many people with a high threshold of danger—mountain climbers or auto racers, for example—are said to 'get off' on their own exploits. Like most of us with respect to lust, the counterphobic is attempting to solve a 'deep' problem, one of fundamental alienation, with an addictive behavior that only drives the problem deeper into unconsciousness. An acrophobic who boards an airplane and suffers is more conscious, hence closer to individuation, than a confident counterphobic pilot. I'm not saying lust is an addiction per se; on the other hand, to me it doesn't seem that far from one either … As I think about it, Perry Como in my dream strikes me almost as a kind of comic counterphobic, his underlying phobic anxiety a reaction to his own lust. He attempts to master his fear of his own powerful libido by attacking it with saccharine love ballads: He will 'love-sing' his fear into submission. Unfortunately, as with any counterphobic maneuver, it doesn't get him ahead; here, in fact, it *turns him into one*: he *has* a body all right, it's the animal he sits on top of as if it were a horse (an all but *dead* horse beaten into catatonia with love songs), but he'll never *be* that body ... Maybe that's what's tickling my funny bone here, and that of my shadowy black friend."

Careful listener that he was, Dr. P. allowed himself a moment of reflection before responding. "Those are fascinating observations you make on the phenomenology of lust," he began finally. "I would say they belong as much to 19th-century German *Naturphilosophie*, the vitalism of Carus, von Hartmann, Nordau[70] and others, as to the more modern depth psychology on which analysis rests—bearing in mind, however, that the latter did evolve out of the former. Still, either way, knowing you as well as I do, they tell me a good deal about your sexual mode of being-in-the-world. So let me just zero in on the speculation with which you concluded your remarks and ask you to take another, closer look at what's going on between you and the black youth."

"Well, as I mentioned, we have this bond of shared awareness of the utter silliness of Perry's performance, leading to this mutual laughter we can't suppress—no, no, the fact is, we don't *want* to suppress it. It's too much fun."

"Yes, I believe you referred to the two of you earlier as 'co-conspirators,' a couple of, shall we say, restrained iconoclasts poking fun at Perry's, and through him mother's, repressed sexuality ... You see, this is the kind of measured, balanced relationship with the shadow one hopes to establish in analysis: no violent overthrow of the *ancien regime*; by the same token, no capitulation to sterile, sexless, white-bread romanticism (the Hollywood kind). Either of these would be lopsided—gross violations of the dialectical spirit on which the psyche thrives. And I wonder if you can detect another image in the dream that supports this reading."

I thought for a moment but drew a blank, indicating this with a shrug.

"Interesting," he said. "You overlooked a very similar image in a dream from a few months back that had you sitting on a rug—"

"Oh, of course," I broke in, "the dream about Queen Mom on her archetypal throne! I'm prostrate before her on that Persian rug with the mandala design, which we read as 'being grounded in the Self.' Here I'm down on the floor again, but … in this instance there's no rug, we're on a hardwood surface … Oh, yes, yes, I see, a hard surface but not a bare one: I'm sitting in the circular part of the key, which is a kind of mandala in black paint. Players on offense are only allowed three seconds in that area at a time before committing a violation. You might call it a sacred space, one not to be entered into by the profane; yet there I am, sitting right in the middle of it, enjoying myself with my shadow compadre, laughing at taboos surrounding the body I once took much too seriously …

"… Hey, wait a minute, wait just one minute," I abruptly interrupted myself, raising a hand to my forehead. "You don't know anything about basketball. You're the anomalous American male with no interest in American sports. How could you possibly pick up on the image of the key, which I think I mentioned only briefly in telling the dream? Are you some kind of closet fan?"

"Not guilty," he answered. "But I did go to high school and I did take gym class, so a basketball court is not totally alien territory to me. As a matter of fact, if your high school was anything like mine—and I know it was since we both come from the Jebbies[71]—you went to many dances in your gym, dances for which the music was provided by a hi-fi record player and a stack of records, a few of which, in *your* day at least, were made by … none other than that clean-cut singing barber. And you know what, I'll just bet that, on at least one occasion, you were out there on that strobe-lit court, probably somewhere near but not quite inside the top of the key, slow-dancing with some cutie from St. Al's or Holy Family to the rueful strains of 'Prisoner of Love.' … Ah, such delicious irony."

I bathed in the nostalgia conjured up by the good doctor's mood picture. His point about irony, however, went right by me until later that evening when I had a chance to reflect, because the only thing it occurred to me to say at the moment was, "What do you mean, 'in *your* day'?"

(26) July 2009: A Breakfast Gathering

I clap my hands three times: "Let's go, people. The flapjacks are getting cold!" I'm waiting for family and friends to gather around me there at the bottom of the stairs just inside the entrance to my house, so we can all go out together for breakfast on this sunny Sunday morning. "Two minutes!" I shout, feeling I need to take command. Denise, still upstairs, complains in that petulant teen tone of hers of needing more time, whereas my good friend Leonard Gerber and his two little boys are right there with me ready to go. Dottie and one or two others come running up and are also ready. People seem to be responding and I'm confident we'll all be on our way together in a moment. Denise finally comes down the stairs towards me; she's wearing the purest white communion dress, decorated with a simple red sash. I compliment her on her appearance and she smiles. This is a tough and delicate negotiation, I think to myself, getting all these different people to cooperate in a common undertaking. Meanwhile one straggler, in an adjoining room, apparently needs a little more time; whoever it is won't be ready in two minutes.

"Breakfast, my favorite meal."

"Mine too," I said, "especially when you're surrounded by friends and family, and somebody else is doing the cooking."

"That's right. In the dream you're all going out—leave the cooking to Denny's or I-HOP, right?"

"Well, I don't know if we're headed for either of those places. The dream doesn't get that far. Actually, I hope it's a little more upscale, say, the Waffle House or … what's that new spot on Onondaga Hill people have been raving about? …"

"Oh sure, that's, ah … yeah, 'The Egg and I.' I was there with Susan and the grandchildren not long ago. First rate! I'm telling you, they do things there with eggs you wouldn't believe. One of the kids had them with mint jelly, no less. I tasted them and, you know, they weren't bad, not bad at all."

"You're a much more adventurous gourmand than I am. I'm not much for jelly to begin with, *mint* least of all, and just the thought of putting it on eggs … ugh!"

It was this sort of informal exchange, often trivial yet always enjoyable, that had come, after almost nine years, to typify the first few minutes of our sessions, and at times more than that. Yet often as well, the subjects we'd wander onto would be more intellectually substantive, though seemingly no less irrelevant to the analysis than the trivial ones. Dr. P. might offer a thumbnail comparison of the deep similarities he saw between Thomas Keating's "centering prayer" form of meditation[72] and the Eastern styles of Indian vipassana or Tibetan vajrayana or Japanese shikantaza. I recall on one occasion arguing with him over St. Thomas Aquinas' five proofs for the existence of God in the *Summa Theologica*; the question, as I recall, was whether the argument "by design" trumped the argument from "first cause." Of course, I was way out of my depth here, but, having come through the Jesuit educational mill, which rests philosophically on the Aristotle-Aquinas axis, I knew just enough about the *Summa* at least to give the man a run for his money.

An outsider might question whether all this wasn't a waste of valuable session time. Indeed, I did myself more than once during the middle years when such tête-à-têtes became more frequent. To be sure, I enjoyed stimulating conversation as much as the next man and more than most, but wasn't I cheating myself by copping out with "small talk," however high-flown? The answer, in a word, is no. The reason is that what might seem at first blush like small talk turned out to be more often than not a chain of associations that eventually led to an important analytical insight. An "innocent" discussion of food or restaurants might lead to reminiscences about the old Sunday dinner ritual at home and how Mom would try to guilt-trip me into not going out with my friends, particularly those of the female persuasion, if Aunt X and Uncle Y were expected. I recall once reciting to Dr. P. the shortlist of my favorite classical composers, which of course I embellished with paroxysms of enthusiasm for the particular virtues of each—"Ah, the tragic depth of Chopin … the grandeur of Wagner … the fierce independence of Beethoven," and so on. Without in the least attempting to invalidate the intellectual and spiritual value these artists had for me, he nevertheless managed with consummate skill to shift tracks in the discussion for the purpose of showing me the extent to which I was using music as a substitute for the "meaning" or fulfillment I had failed to experience in early life. (To this day, I'm not sure whether, or, if so, to what extent Dr. P. is right in this, but his delicate handling of the matter disposed me to remain open to the possibility.)

This was one of the subtlest and most important lessons about "correct" analysis I learned from Dr. P.: that, as a matter of fact, *nothing* was, nor could anything ever be, irrelevant to the process because, at bottom, there simply was no boundary between the so-called process and "real life." Ultimately, life itself and the process were identical. Another way of putting this would be to say that the analytical mindset trumps all others except the authentically spiritual, that is, that, except for spiritual Enlightenment, analysis is the most comprehensive standpoint one can take vis-à-vis a given moment of consciousness. It yields the deepest truth about the phenomenal field at hand. No matter what point of view one takes toward anything—intellectual, emotional, moral, aesthetic, even philosophical—that point of view is necessarily undergirded, informed, by the personal psychology of the one holding it. Nietzsche recognized this clearly and came, rightly, to be called "the philosopher with the hammer," which is to say, the philosopher who smashed the eternal verities with the hammer of his psychology. Like it or not, man is basically *homo psychologicus*. This is a sobering truth the analysis imposed on me only slowly over time, one that forced me to let go of my humanist's belief in man's fundamental autonomy or free will, a posture I ardently held to, though admittedly not without bouts of profound doubt, when I met Dr. P. and that initially caused much friction between us. On the other hand, my confidence in the reality of the spiritual, in the sense of a fundamental consciousness ontologically prior to the individual, as ultimately trumping even the psychological dimension remained intact during the long analytical process, and continues to do so, and this is the final fact that balances the scales for me. Complicating, or, depending on one's point of view, simplifying the matter, was my deeper awareness, gained from years of Zen practice, that authentic spiritual truth could never be eclipsed even by the truth yielded to psychological inquiry because psychology, to the extent it is a systematic discipline, is based on the paradigmatic split between subject and object, between the one observing and the thing observed, whereas spiritual truth is precisely that which is revealed when this tragic split is healed—or, better yet, is shown never to have existed in the first place.

Of course, I was helped enormously in making this profound shift in my outlook to *homo psychologicus* by my gradual realization that Dr. P.'s spiritual sensibility was akin to my own. Somehow I could accept the bleak truth of the unconscious determinism revealed to me by analysis so long as I could remain confident that the ultimate freedom, which was spiritual, remained immune to that truth, a beacon from beyond it, yet somehow also co-extensive with it, pure and shining. I could see that it did so for him, so I had, so to speak, a kindred spirit waiting to receive me at the threshold of this new world view. It seemed only natural, then, that the spiritual tenor of my dreams should become more pronounced as the analysis moved into its terminal hours.

Case in point: my breakfast dream. Steering back to it, Dr. P. observed, "Well, this certainly seems like a happy family picture. Is it?"

"Yes it is. In this case appearances are not deceiving: *Schein* is *Sein*," I quipped, alluding to one of my favorite German rhyme-puns.[73] "And don't worry, I know exactly where you expect me to take this dream—"

"—Excuse me, where I expect? ..."

"Oh, don't pretend we can't read each other like books at this point. We're getting to be like an old married couple: I know what you're going to ask before you ask it, and you know the answers, most of them anyway, before I open my mouth ... Of course, that doesn't obviate the need to state things anyway, to make them explicit; there's a subtle level of validation on which most things "register" only if they're spoken … So let's see … oh yes, your expression 'happy family picture' told me you had picked up on my daughter's pristine white communion dress, the symbolically appropriate garment for the morning meal that 'breaks the fast' extending from yesterday's supper. (No, there are no munchies, no late-night snacks, in archetypal dreams!) What's more delightful than a family being a family, a family in joyous 'communion'? Isn't this mutual delight in one another the very essence of the Eucharistic sacrament, the *κοινωνια* or fellowship? Maybe Denise's 'first communion' is *my* 'first communion' … communion with the members of my inner family, my archetypal family, the family of my soul: There's Mother and Father—no, not featured here by any means but there by implication, by 'feel,' by a certain warm and protective ambiance; there's the Innocent Child in the communion dress who, in a symbolic sense, shows the way; there's the anima in Dottie who comes running to me when I summon her; even the shadow is here, about to break bread with us: he's the one who's not quite ready to join in, who'll need a few more minutes to get ready … Why? Because that's his place in the family, to be the black sheep, the 'odd man out,' the one who fits in by not quite fitting in … I guess with all this communion symbolism the dream is showing me how much Catholic there still is in me, huh?"

I could see that Dr. P. instantly sensed this as a question with some charge for me, raising as it did the issue of my deeply ambivalent feelings towards the Catholic church. I can't count the number of dreams we'd been over reflecting this ambivalence. So, with his exquisite sense of tact, he gave an answer that, while confirming the obvious, at the same time grounded the Catholic symbolism in my dream in the broader spiritual-historical vision of Jung, which he knew would sit well with me. He knew I wouldn't mind having Catholic symbols in my dream as long as they weren't *just* Catholic: "Well, sure, those are your roots, and Jung does indeed consider breakfast and communion in the Catholic liturgy to be virtually synonymous. At the same time, genius in the history of Western symbology that he was, Jung clearly saw the roots of the Eucharistic sacrament, and even of the Mass itself, in the ancient, archaic transformation rituals of alchemy,[74] which in the early Christian centuries was all bound up with the Gnostic religions, the origins of which are themselves shrouded in the mists of the richly syncretistic pre-Christian religions of the Persian Middle East, such as Zoroastrianism ... It's one hell of a knot of historical strands!"

I didn't even pretend to get all of that, mainly because my mind, for reasons of its own, had latched onto one particular word in the good doctor's little lesson in religious history, "alchemy," and, for the moment at least, refused to go any further: "Hold on a moment," I interrupted. "... Are you saying that the ceremonial transformation—actually, I think the proper liturgical term is 'transubstantiation'—of the bread and wine into the body and blood of Christ during the Mass actually derives from the attempts of the ancient alchemists to transmute base metals into gold?"

"*I'm* not saying it," Dr. P. corrected, "Jung is; and who am I to question him?"

"This is fantastic," I mused, suddenly feeling filled with awe. "My mind is abuzz with connections ... I just hope I can slow it down enough to look at one or two of the more electrifying ones … Ah, … yes, yes, *Schein* and *sein, Schein* and *sein*, appearance and reality, the Germans' love of metaphysics, hell, *my* love of metaphysics, of first principles! I mentioned the distinction earlier in response to your question about the dream's happy-looking family: 'Yeah, we're happy,' I said, '*Schein* is *sein*,' the appearance is the reality, what you see is what you get. But in the Mass, of course, it's just the opposite; you get what you *don't* see: the body and blood of Christ, which looks for all the world like plain old bread and wine. But the liturgy insists the reality, the substance here, absolutely contradicts the appearance … You won't believe this, my friend, but the instant you uttered the word 'alchemy' a moment ago, into my mind popped that incident from childhood I told you about recently in which my mother got hysterical when I told her how, as an altar boy, I took communion at Mass after forgetting that I'd broken my fast with a sip of water. I think in a sense that debacle finished the Eucharist for me as a meaningful spiritual event; it became just another thing to feel guilty about. But now, with this dream it strikes me that a kind of transubstantiation of base metals into gold may have taken place: the abased experience of childhood is here redeemed, transformed into the gold of a fun family gathering—for breaking the fast, no less, for communion. This happy breaking of the fast with loved ones transubstantiates that fateful sip of water of so long ago. What *looked* base then is, in the dream reality of this moment, radiant … My dream, it seems, is not only *about* transubstantiation, it is *itself* an event of transubstantiation: it *is* what it is about. It closes the illusory gap between the dream picture and what the picture is *of*.

My Zen intuition tells me this fire of enthusiasm coursing through me right now is saying that when one thing, just a single thing, gets transubstantiated, the entire universe gets transubstantiated. Solve one koan, one mystery, and you've solved them all. Now *that's* communion!"

The dream's radiance seemed to emit a gossamer shimmer that filled the room, softening the hard edges of the furniture, swirling around and through both analyst and analysand. It was almost too much for me, too rich. I needed something earthy, something ordinary, to tamp it down. No sooner sought than found. Before my mind's eye it was as if a curtain suddenly parted, revealing an atmosphere redolent of the inviting aromas of good cooking and a large, round kitchen table covered with a white satin cloth on top of which sat the trappings of breakfast in progress: plates, some with eggs and hash browns, others with pancakes and sausages, whether links or patties; creamers of maple syrup and molasses; half empty juice glasses; cups and decanters of coffee; the odd cup of tea; three sets of salt and pepper shakers strategically placed; saucers of jam, marmalade and whipped butter; cut-glass dishes of nuts, cashews and hazel; three toweled baskets piled high with fresh bread: wedges of crisp Italian (from Gustoso's), sliced pumpernickel, rye and semolina; each item being used, each food consumed as it was meant to be. Slowly raising my inner eye from the table to those seated around it, I went on to describe the scene to my dear listener with relish. I told him how we were all seated, with Aunt Alma directly across from me, shooting me that devilish little smile of hers every so often; next to her Uncle Ben, busy as usual with the more piquant foods he preferred, the salami, the hot peppers and the stale Italian biscuits;

he was, also as usual, arguing politics with Uncle Duke, the brother he cherished who sometimes lost his temper over a dissenting opinion but who also laughed easily and loudly. Every few minutes that explosive cackle of his would pierce the air, blotting out the hum of conversation. The others would all suddenly stop, look at him, and laugh themselves without knowing the reason. Then a few seconds later the hum would resume. My Dad sat between my uncles, appropriately, since he tended anyway to play the role of arbiter in their political debates, as in the other "hot" issues to which they usually gravitated, such as public policy, education, and the workplace. My sister Iris was on my left; finished with her eggs, she was cracking hazel nuts for one of the several cakes my Mom would bake for the gala Thanksgiving dinner that evening. Iris didn't have much to say at the table, for her voice, soft as chiffon, was no match for the foghorns of the men. To me she spoke with her eyes, her face or the occasional soft elbow to the ribs whenever someone said something amusing or silly. To her left sat Annie, spinsterish life-companion of my Mom, who had 'been in the family' as far back as my memory stretched, my first and only babysitter, without whom such gatherings as this would have been unthinkable. And finally, next to her, Uncle Ben and Aunt Alma's three little daughters, Lonnie, Jackie and Gussie, who formed a sort of subset at the table, all three squeezed together on two chairs and totally absorbed in coloring within the lines in the Crayola coloring books my mother brought out for them to keep them amused while forced to sit among all the "boring grown-ups." My Mom, needing to jump up every few minutes to keep everyone sated and content, had no particular seat but would occupy whatever chair happened to be vacant until suddenly pressed into service again. Having for the moment extricated myself from any particular conversation, I just leaned back in my chair and let it all impinge on me, sights, sounds, smells, the overlapping and crisscrossing of the buzz, the whole mood of hearty togetherness: "I'm telling you, it's a fact: Nine out of ten people get all their news from TV ... I got it in that little shop on 1st and Washington, you know, right next to Woolworth's ... The schools aren't what they used to be, even Catholic schools. I was beaten by the nuns once a week at least ... Lonnie got almost all 90's on her report card, only one 85 in arithmetic, right Hon'? ... Yeah, that's Mrs. Elrich. She's tough ... The Republicans are all in it for themselves, the little man be damned ... Anybody up for a little game of Scrabble later? ... I dunno, Annie, you whupped us pretty good last time with that triple word score on ... what was it, 'quiz?' ... Pro football will never make it big on TV—you can't really see the action ... Benny, toss me a slice of that semolina, will you? ... Sure, here you go ..."

As my little vignette, half memory, half reverie, faded out, Dr. P.'s big, round face came smartly into focus, triggering in its turn perhaps the most moving recollection of all, which I promptly added as a tag: "Sitting there at the grand round table, taking it all in, perfectly content to be one among this family of affectionate revelers, I knew somehow that one day in the distant future, a day like today, I would look back upon this sublime moment with an ache of nostalgia that could ravish the heart of an executioner ..."

I looked raptly at Dr. P., who sat there with just the barest trace of a smile, eyes closed, head resting on palm. Obviously still caught up in the spirit of domesticity, he smiled more broadly and said, "You know, Herr Professor, there's a nostalgia that is so poignant, so sweetly sad, that it turns missing into having, absence into presence, desire into fulfillment … Another Buddha, another face of communion. Congratulations, and thank you for sharing that."

"Believe me, Dr. P., just at the moment I can't find any 'me' who's doing the sharing. I must've lost it at the table."

"Well, you see, that's the roundtable of the Self. When there's no longer a 'me' at the table because it's disappeared into the bodies and minds—better yet, into the body and blood—of those around you, then you've really become master of your own house."

(27) September 2009:
A Diamond ’neath the Sole of My Shoe

A eulogy is being given for a friend from my old Zen group who has just passed away. The venue is the Little League baseball field of my boyhood on 4th and Hudson Sts., located on a bluff overlooking the Hudson in Hoboken. The Zen officialdom conducting the eulogy are all assembled on the platform that has been set up between 3rd base and home plate, facing out towards right field, maybe a hundred fifty feet away, where the congregation sits on outfield bleachers set against the right field wall, some four feet high, and rimming the bluff. As I approach the bleachers from the first-base area to take a seat, I’m carrying in my right hand my old "Jesuit" book bag of shiny black leather; it’s the kind of bag the Jebby[75] professors toted around campus in my undergraduate days at St. Peter’s, typically packed with the works of Thomas Aquinas and Aristotle that formed the core of their compulsory philosophy curriculum. Climbing the bleachers to the rear- and uppermost tier, I set the bag down on the bench and myself beside it.

The eulogy is given, the accompanying ceremonies performed, and we all stand to leave, heading in the general direction of center field. Moving along with the crowd, I suddenly realize I’ve left my bag behind and turn to go back to retrieve it, but now find moving against the crowd too difficult, and so decide to circle around the crowd back to the first-base area and return to my seat from there. I’m relieved to find the bag sitting on the bench where I left it, but, when I open it to check the contents, I’m amazed to discover all the books inside covered over with something like a half-inch-thick coat of wet white paint. It may be whitewash.

"Fascinating."

"The Jebbies have invaded the zendo!" I shouted in mock-horror.[76]

"Yes, they have, but then, it's not the first time, is it?" countered Dr. P.

"That eludes me. What do you mean?"

"Remember your history: imperial Spain, late sixteenth century, the period called 'the Counterreformation.'"

"Ah, of course," I smiled in recognition, delighted by this agile link of Dr. P.'s to Jesuit origins. "St. Francis Xavier and company … the Spanish and Portuguese Jesuit missionaries in the Far East and all their aggressive proselytizing, saving all those coarse heathen souls *ad majorem Dei gloriam*."[77]

"You know, Father York might not appreciate your cynical way of characterizing the early missionary work of the order," Dr. P. ventured with a sly smile, gently wagging an index finger.

"Oh, I'm sure he'd have a good belly laugh over it. It's my old retreat master, Father Callahan—remember him?—and his twisted ilk around whom I'd be much more likely to hold my glib tongue. I'm afraid that even in God's work, as in any other line, there are Jesuits and then there are Jesuits … Actually, come to think of it, I can think of *three* Jesuit invasions of the zendo in pursuit of God's work, that is, if you'll allow me to count myself, toting my black Jebby book bag in the dream, as the third wave: The first was Francis Xavier and the second Heinrich Dumoulin, the great German scholar of

Japanese religion, particularly Zen Buddhism, in the middle decades of the twentieth century. Father Dumoulin wrote a two-volume history of Zen that's still the standard reference work in the West; but what originally drew me to him was his translation, circa 1943, of the great Chinese koan collection, *Wu-men-kuan* or *Gateless Gate*, into German.[78] This was a wonderful gift of which I made copious use in my undergraduate German lit. courses featuring Zen as a theme. It's brilliant and it saved me a mountain of translation work from English back into German … Now, if you consider the three waves of the Jesuit invasion of the zendo in succession, the first, under Francis in the mid-sixteenth century, was narrowly militant: There was, in the beginning at least, little awareness of or concern for Japanese language, customs or native religion. The Jebbies naively thought they could just march in there and wave the sword of conversion over everyone. Of course, it didn't work out that way. The second wave, made up of Dumoulin all by himself, was curious, sympathetic and intellectually receptive: Dumoulin was the Western counterpart of D.T. Suzuki, the prodigious scholar at Columbia who served as a bridge between East and West. Both men helped introduce us to the history, the lore, the mystical style and substance of Zen. Now, in September 2009, here comes yours truly, a product of eight years of Jesuit indoctrination, to mark the third in this three-wave invasion by the Society of Jesus, and I can't think of a better term to describe this wave than 'surrender.' I came to Zen literally carrying Jesuit weapons of theological and philosophical dialectic, symbolized by the bag full of Aquinas and Aristotle, and promptly surrendered them; which is to say, the moment I began sitting *zazen*, I did all I could to leave my Catholic worldview behind and become a vessel of satori, a channel of enlightened wisdom.

"So you might say the three waves, viewed in sequence, trace an interesting trajectory of Jesuit-Zen relations moving from an attitude of conquest through one of mediation to my own attitude of surrender. When I commenced practice in the mid-eighties, I wanted nothing more than to become a blank slate on which Zen could inscribe its most profound lessons. Based on my own experience growing up trapped inside the draconian nightmare of Catholic doctrine, particularly with respect to matters of conscience and sexual morality, I was convinced by the time I hit my majority that Christianity had nothing to offer—and everything to sabotage—anyone in serious quest of self-realization, or individuation, or Enlightenment, or whatever you want to call it. Zen was tailor-made for me. Despite its rigors—and let's face it, they are severe—it fit me like a pair of comfortable slippers right from the get-go. It had a self-punishing grit, a toughness, an exotic flavor, and a generically Buddhist psychology and epistemology informing it that strongly attracted me. As you know, I'm referring here specifically to the doctrine of *anatma* or no-self, the Buddhist denial of the existence of a discrete center of consciousness called 'I.' I loved finding out that, underneath it all, I didn't exist as a separate self in the way I'd always believed. If Enlightenment meant coming to see this truth beyond all doubt, which of course implied unloading all that guilt for my 'individual' sexual sin, well then, that was something worth giving my all to attain. Certainly that was what 'the end of suffering' of which the Buddha spoke would mean for me ..."

Dr. P. took the opportunity afforded by my pause to ask, “And now, in light of the work we've done here, would you say your Zen experience matched your hopes and expectations? Did you succeed in surrendering the black bag containing your Jesuit Catholicism to Zen?”

“Let's put it this way,” I answered, feeling a strong need to hit just the right note, since the matter was subtle and important. “I think I did surrender to the extent I was able, but it wasn't profound, or at least not profound enough to bring about the necessary shift in my center of gravity from subject to master of my own mind. Oh, to be sure, I had more than my share of satori or kensho experiences, moments of piercing through the veil of *mayā*[79] to the astonishing and exhilarating emptiness of it all, but, alas, all of it left my neurotic character structure, with all its attendant misery, firmly in tact. These illuminations, genuine though they were, and *are*, in my own estimation, merely bypassed my problems, momentarily slipping through my defenses to give me a sip of the elixir, a whiff of the perfume, as it were … Actually, that was the rap against the Rinzai style of Zen, that it used koans to ‘muscle’ you through your own resistance to some sort of breakthrough, only to drop you back in your old loony bin a few days later. I would go so far as to say this sort of practice can be dangerous for many Zen students who are psychologically fragile to begin with: To see ‘the face of God’ before you're ready to see it can be devastating; it can cause a big spike in symptoms of anxiety and depression once the ecstasy wanes (after all, look at what you think you've lost!), and in some instances can even lead to a psychotic breakdown. Koan meditation is not something to approach lightly.”

"So where does all this leave you?" the good doctor queried. "Would you say the dream is vouchsafing you the rare privilege of attending your own eulogy, your own Zen funeral?"

"I have no doubt whatsoever it is, especially since the dream doesn't make clear who my deceased 'friend' is," I replied without hesitation, "but at the same time, it's by no means an occasion for sadness; devotees of dialectics that we are, we know there can be no death without life, no ending without a beginning. The end of my life in Zen in the dream is at once the beginning of a deeper life—you could even say, paradoxically, it's the beginning of true Zen, for Zen is only true Zen when it entirely forgets itself and ceases to 'stink of itself,' as the masters are wont to say."

"That's a tad esoteric, a tad 'inside.' Would you mind humoring us barbarians at the temple gate with a bit of elaboration?"

"Oh my God," I hooted in good-natured scorn, "as a Jesuit product yourself, you must see the irony in your own metaphor: It would seem you've traded places with the 'barbarians' encountered by Xavier and company when they hit Japanese soil! … But, irony aside (if that's even possible), I'll bet my honorary membership in the Society of Jesus that it's all in the dream. Let's see if we can work it out … Ah, let me think, … I would say it's fairly clear that my getting up and leaving the eulogy at its end means walking away from Zen, which I did in the mid-nineties. I stopped doing *zazen*, and so also stopped going to the Zen center, which effectively meant breaking with that whole community, even on a social level … It was a difficult period for me emotionally. There were wrenching feelings of doubt and failure to cope with, yet on a deeper level I felt I was doing what was necessary for myself, for my spiritual health, even if the reasons weren't clear at the time."

"Are they any clearer now?"

"Much. Without belaboring it, I'll just mention two of the big ones: First, around the time I left it, the Syracuse Zen Center was rapidly transitioning from a small, intimate group of sincere students who wanted nothing more than to sit *zazen* together in a dusty attic into some kind of behemoth conglomerate with its own landed estate, hundreds of members and a busy agenda of community-involvement programs and/or quasi religious and social services. Nothing wrong with any of that, mind you; it just wasn't what I wanted or needed at the time. Then too, there was this incessant preoccupation of the Zen establishment with dates and anniversaries, which came to grate on me: all the puffed up pride of the first this or the tenth that or the hundredth other, whether it was the hoopla surrounding the centennial of the 1893 World's Parliament of Religions in Chicago or the founding of the third American Zen monastery in the state of New York or so-and-so Roshi's twentieth anniversary of being off saké. It was the beautiful simplicity of Zen, its uncluttered style, that originally attracted me, and I guess I felt this was being seriously compromised by its 'success.' It was, horror of horrors, starting to feel like the Catholic Church!

"The other factor, much more important, was a growing dissatisfaction with the heart of the religion, *zazen* meditation. In Rinzai Zen you're either doing *zazen* or you're fully enlightened and no longer need to do it; it's either practice or Enlightenment, there's no middle ground. Anyway, around year five of the nine-plus years I practiced *zazen*, it began to give me headaches, especially when I did it intensively for days at a time such as during retreats. Slowly I lost faith in its effectiveness or utility for me as a spiritual tool. This gradual disillusionment, over years, was accompanied by a growing depression, possibly caused by my helpless sense of loss of a way of life that had meant everything to me, or perhaps by the effort of concentration required for *zazen* itself, which no longer agreed with me, or both. (I think it was both.) Also, I can't discount the possibility that daily *zazen* was causing some de-repression of my deeper personal issues, particularly my guilt over the 'abandoned child,' but without providing any means of working through the painful feelings that were surfacing. (Eventually that's what drove me here to you.) The few Zen veterans whom I told of my trouble commiserated with me, but could offer little help. One suggested I see a therapist who was also a Zen adept, which I did; after listening to me, he suggested I might have lost the capacity to do the practice, which amounted to telling me what I already half-believed but wasn't quite ready to accept. But soon the time came when denial no longer made any sense, and I walked away from Zen, just as in the dream … I became a dharma drop-out."

"But, of course, in the dream you walk away only to turn around and walk right back, don't you?" the doctor astutely pointed out.

"Yes," I said pensively, "I'm sure the heart of the dream lies right in that return walk to the bleachers to retrieve my book bag. I want to go over that part slowly—"

"—Excuse me, did you say '*go over*'?"

"Yes, you know, go back over that segment of the dream carefully."

"Interesting turn of phrase."

"Come again?"

"It's interesting to me that you use the expression 'go back over' to convey your intention to examine a part of the dream that has you 'going back over' to the bleachers to fetch your book bag. You could say you're going back over your 'going-back-over.'"

"Sorry, Dr. P., that's linguistically amusing, but I don't see—"

"—Herr Professor, you know very well I have no interest in amusing you, at least not during session. I'm trying to—"

"—Wait! Wait a minute!" I loudly interrupted, surprising even myself. "I know exactly what you're trying to do, and please forgive my obtuseness. You're trying to get me to focus on the sense of going over something, of reviewing it, rehashing it, and, linking the two 'goings-over,' to ask whether the going back over to the bleachers in the dream isn't perhaps itself a kind of review ..."

Watching the relaxed smile etch itself on the good doctor's face was all the confirmation I needed. The curtain was parting: "And what other kind of review would I be dreaming about but the review, the going back over my life, that we do here?"

The twinkle in his eye intensified as I continued: "That makes this dream a kind of stocktaking of three long segments of my life: my years with the Jesuits, my years in Zen and now my years here with you, the years of analysis. That's a long odyssey for one short dream to encompass; it gives new meaning to the analytic term 'condensation.' It occurs to me that each of the three periods lasted just about nine years, if you view my first year out of college as a gradual weaning-off the Jebbies …"

"Yes, but what is the dream telling you about the relations between the three phases; let's call it the 'status' of each phase, its valence or importance in your life vis-à-vis the other two?"

"Well, they're certainly not just a chronological succession, not just one following on the heels of another over my mature decades. You know, try this, try that, try something else."

"How do you know that?"

"Because of the way the third phase, which is our work here—you know, the analytical 'going-back-over' things—comprehends the first two. It enfolds them."

"Could you explain further?"

"I'll try; I may need your help."

"That's what you pay me for."

"Hmm, … let's see … I'm cutting back across the baseball field—"

"Yes, across your 'Field of Dreams,' so to speak."

"Yes, of course, that's got to be the analytical dream work, a nine-inning/nine-year field of dreams we've covered together, you might say … And in doing this, I at first encounter resistance, the crowd heading home. That's me in the first year or two battling my own anger towards you, the scapegoat therapist, everything within me pushing me away from what I thought I detested. But finally, I wise up and find a way past my resistance, giving it a wide berth as I circle back around first base towards the book bag. I suppose you could call it 'getting to first base.' Then the long years of cooperation, collaboration … And finally, the relief of finding the bag still sitting there on the bench."

"Yes, and now, finally, the denouement: What is it you find when you open the bag?"

"Yeah, that's the crux of it all right … Whatever it is, I have to remember that it's contained within the field, that is, the scope, of the analysis, this going-back-over the field of dreams we've done. So it's as if the dream is pointing out to me what analysis has revealed about my life with the Jesuits and my subsequent life in Zen … So, I open the bag to find my Jesuit books covered with thick white paint. How did the paint get in there? … Hmm, someone must've surreptitiously poured it in during the few minutes I was walking away, having left it behind. It must've been someone from the Zen group gathered there. Who else would've bothered? But why? What motive? … My only clue here is my feeling that the paint might actually be whitewash, which is a different substance than paint. You'll recall I speculated it might be whitewash when I told the dream earlier. Of course, to an old lit. professor like me, the idea of whitewash immediately raises the 'metaphor flag': To whitewash something is to cover it over, to hide something unsightly, say, a stain or smudge, from view with a veneer of purity …"

"Is this what Zen did? You said the culprit must've been someone from the Zen group."

"I'm afraid so. Whoever it was tried to exorcize my Catholic demons with the power of Zen, but all he really succeeded in doing was 'whitewashing' the Church within (the books in the bag), covering it over with a veneer of 'Eastern purity,' 'Eastern simplicity.' When I look at it this way, I can only conclude that *I'm* the culprit here, albeit an unconscious one, just as I'm the one whose eulogy is being given. That's why both culprit and deceased are anonymous. As in any archetypal dream, the dreamer is both the doer and the done-to of anything that happens … Make no mistake now, I'm still convinced that Enlightenment is the true purity, the true simplicity, and that Zen is *one way* of finding it; but I suspect that most of us who venture into Zen manage little more than a psychological whitewash job."

"Well," the doctor sighed, "It's certainly a sad tale your dream tells. My condolences."

The ever so slightly upturned corners of his mouth gave the lie to his words of commiseration. He knew, and knew that I knew, that the dream was a pure delight. He was merely waiting for me to lay the final interpretive stone, to attach the last Lego piece.

Which I was now proud and happy to do: "No need to be coy, my friend. We both know this dream is a joyous event, a virtual fanfare trumpeting the wonder of what you and I have accomplished here."

"Oh? Do tell!" he said, continuing the perfectly transparent pretense.

"I said before that the dream shows the two earlier phases of my life, the Church and Zen, to be *contained within* the 'field' of the analysis. This idea of containment is crucial because it says something about levels of comprehension of truth. It means that, when I open that bag, what I see, through the clear, transcendent eye of analysis, is the psychological truth of my earlier identifications with Catholicism and Zen, which is that basically I used one layer of repression, Zen, to 'whitewash' the earlier repressive layer of the Church, with its awesome power to alienate us from the body and its instincts. But, you see, the analysis, by virtue of its transcendent vantage point, ultimately reveals these two to be empty attachments, prisons without a prisoner, which means transparent, … just nothing at all. Analysis has done what it can to give me steady access to the vision of *sunyata* that Zen had promised but, in my case at least, couldn't deliver. To see the emptiness of one thing, and in so seeing to realize you're already free of it, is to see the emptiness of everything, without lifting a finger. Once free, you're 'condemned' to this freedom, as it were, 'condemned' to enjoy everything just as it arises, good, bad or indifferent. You can never go back to your old neurotic prison for long; it just won't have you. It's like my friend Kafka's three-sided fence: Whether you're hemmed in or not depends entirely on your point of view. Once you see there's no fourth side, you're out, even if you're still in! … Oh, by the way, one final association to the dream while I'm waxing here: Baseball is played on a diamond, and the 'jewel of Zen' is 'The Diamond Sutra of Perfect Wisdom,' the longest sutra by far of those that are chanted during retreat and one that never failed to move me deeply. Like all sutras, its subject is Enlightenment, that exquisite freedom that comes with clarity of vision of which I just spoke. When in the dream I 'go back over' the field to retrieve my book bag, I cross second base, which is the apex of the baseball diamond. That suggests that maybe, just maybe, this analytic going-back-over the field of my life has enabled me to touch the tip of the 'Diamond of Perfect Wisdom.' If it has, then you as my guide through this long process must be playing second, huh?"

As I spoke this little quip to my mentor of so long with the deepest affection, those sublime verses of the Buddha that end the "Diamond Sutra" floated through my mind, bringing tears of happiness to these tired old eyes. I couldn't help but recite them to him: "Like clouds, a flash of lightning, or a dream / So is all conditioned existence to be seen."

"Dr. P.," I said after a moment, ever so slightly clearing my throat, trying, unsuccessfully, I think, not to sound as if I were bringing up a momentous issue, "... I know our time is about up but there's one other thing I wanted to mention today—again."

"Again?"

"Yes. It's a matter I raised some time ago, maybe a year and a half back, but, as it turned out, prematurely."

He just sat waiting. He knew.

"It's about termination. I'm thinking maybe it's time ..."

"... I see. And why do you bring this up just now. What makes you think it's time?"

"Very simple," I replied, brimming with profound gratitude and respect for the gift of this man sitting in front of me. "I don't need you anymore."

He just looked at me steadily for a moment, which in my uncertain state seemed like an eternity, and finally burst into a huge smile, replying, "I see," and, feigning insult, added huffily, "Well, if I'm not needed ..."

"I'm afraid you're not. I think I can take it from here. Let's face it, when our sessions become the highlight event of my week, the thing I look forward to most, it's probably time to call it a day, wouldn't you agree?"

"I would, indeed, Herr Professor, except for the 'probably.' Let's say today's session marks the end of the analysis proper. Next week we begin the termination phase."

"Oh? There's a *phase* for termination? It needs a whole phase?"

"Absolutely, though it needn't be long, a few weeks, a month or two. It depends. It's to consolidate the gains you've made and make sure there's no backsliding into symptoms, which can happen if therapy is ended precipitously; patients who after years suddenly one day just get up and say, 'See you around, pal,' and disappear don't realize how important it is to wean carefully off a relationship that has sustained them emotionally for so long. Only a fool would toss his Prozac vial in the trash one morning and say, 'I'm done.' Same here … So, see you at the usual time next week?"

"Sure … It's funny; now that I'm done, I can't say I feel any exuberance over it, any particular need to end it … But then, by the same token, let me ask you: If I should run into trouble in the future and feel the need for your services again, could we 'reverse' the termination, so to speak, and work together again?"

"Herr Professor, my door is always open to you … But let me ask *you* a question: What do you think you'll do with the extra Thursday afternoon hours coming to you?"

"Oh, that's easy: I'll be spending them on the book I'm writing about us."

"Hmm … Be gentle with me, will you?"

Conclusion

As I write this, it has been about a month since the termination phase of my analysis ended, and with it the nine-year ritual of my Thursday afternoon visits to Dr. P.'s basement, the "underground unconscious." As I take stock, I can say that I've had no significant withdrawal pains of which to complain. However, that may be because we are still in close touch busily fine-tuning this very book the reader holds in his hands. As for termination itself, it's not as if we did anything particularly new or different in those sessions, at least not that I'm aware of. It was pretty much business as usual, but—and this is the difference—our business was conducted in an atmosphere of awareness that the end was close at hand. Gone was the open-endedness of the analysis, gone the quasi delusion that this protective cocoon would or could nestle me forever. So the feeling I had of being in a sort of halfway house during termination became, in effect, a safe way to wean off the process.

And yet, in the broadest sense, it strikes me that there really is no reason for analysis, or at least the analytic cast of mind, ever to end. After all, what could possibly be a sufficient reason for someone to resume the habit of relative unconsciousness, the condition that made formal analysis necessary in the first place? It's not as if you've been riding a train that brings you to a certain station at which you get off and "stay put" for the rest of your life, whatever that would mean. On the contrary, once you board this train, "the self-realization express," you'll never get off, nor will you ever want to, even when the formal part is done.

However wise men may define self-realization, or individuation, or enlightenment—and the definitions are as legion as the name itself—the one thing they all agree on is that it has no end. It's infinitely perfectible. Which is wonderful because, if it had an end, it wouldn't be a mystery. Anything we could "get to the bottom of" would hardly be worth the effort. So, there will continue to be dreams, the veiled meanings of which I will continue to ponder; there will continue to be meditation, though for me at this point meditation is more a state I find myself to be in now and then than a technique for training the mind I deliberately practice. Certainly there will continue to be problems, probably even patches of depression, but these no longer threaten me, as I know I'm in command of inner resources capable of vaporizing them when they come. For me, continuing to deepen consciousness, literally ad infinitum, is now the way I choose to live, and is as well the way par excellence I would heartily recommend to others, not only those like me who struggle with lifelong emotional entanglements, with or without "symptoms," but also, perhaps even especially, those in mid-life who find themselves asking the question, "Is this all there is?" Analysis and its aftermath have become my version of what Aristotle called "the good life."

This raises the interesting question of the specific kind of analysis I underwent with Dr. P. The reader will have noticed that I give relatively little attention to this matter in the book. While it's true that Freud and Jung are frequently mentioned, particularly the latter, in our exchanges, yet I never go so far as to identify the analysis as "Jungian," which, if one must label it, is probably as good a label as any. There are a few reasons for this. One is that Jung himself disavowed the term

"Jungian analysis," on the grounds that it implied a protocol, a formal set of rules and procedures to be followed by the analyst, which he insisted was not the case; rather, he claimed, each case, within the framework of certain broad parameters or phases, dictated its own unique path as it unfolded, a perspective which puts a high premium on the intelligence, imagination and flexibility of the analyst. By the same token, my long conversation with Dr. P. was made up of so many different strains, psychological, spiritual and artistic, that to classify it in my narrative as "Jungian" would have struck me as an impoverishment. Jung certainly provided the framework, but, as I see it, even his illustrious name cannot bear the full weight of this narrative.

More important, however, for present purposes, is that, above all else, I wanted this book to be *my* story as an analysand, necessarily told from my own analysand's point of view—the point of view of the one on the receiving end—not Jung's or even Dr. P.'s (though, of course, it can't help being partly his story too). This meant that Jungian protocol or theory *per se* had only tangential relevance to the book; much more important was how I, as a patient, understood or misunderstood such theory and what role my own complex relationship to depth psychology, evolved over decades of study and teaching, played in the analysis as it progressed. This is where the drama lay, in the twists and turns of my rich relationship with Dr. P. As a seasoned professor of German literature and various modes of literary criticism, my own understanding of Freud and Jung is perhaps adequate to a stimulating argument over the pro's and con's of depth psychology in general—in other words, good enough, one would hope, to make the heated exchanges between Dr. P. and myself, and the psychodynamic subtext underlying these, compelling reading, but that understanding is certainly nowhere near that of a trained analyst. So I would caution the reader not to regard my tale as in any sense a textbook of analytic procedure or even a summary of its worldview. There are plenty of analyst-authored books that offer that.

A word about the term "analysis" seems in order here, this being the one I use through most of the book, in contradistinction to the perhaps more commonly known "*psycho*-analysis." Jungians explain that, generally speaking, an "analysis" unfolds in four successive phases: confession, interpretation, education and transformation. (In the book I have, for narrative purposes, condensed the two middle phases into "education.") Needless to say, in practice these are not nearly a neatly discrete chronological sequence but evidence considerable overlapping and a fair amount of unpredictable falling back and jumping ahead. Reality, alas, is always messier than our paradigms of it. Nevertheless, beneath the surface chaos the contours of this four-phased sequence can be discerned. Jungians identify the first two phases, confession and interpretation, with the sort of "psychoanalysis" developed and practiced by Freud, one involving mainly the de-repression of personal experiences and their interpretation. An analysand may "get off the train" with their conclusion, so to speak, relatively free of symptoms and fit for life in the way a post-surgical patient returns to life in a condition of biological homeostasis: back up to zero. But Freud himself lamented such a sad state of affairs in which the gains offered by even the most successful psychoanalysis merely freed the patient of his own personal suffering in order, as he said, to "open him up to the general suffering of the world." Was that all there was?

Always the visionary, Jung insisted there was more, much, much more, and devoted himself to shaping what he called "analysis" as an organic extension and development of Freud's psychoanalysis, literally, ad infinitum. Anything having to do with "the Infinite" had, of course, to entail a parting of ways, which happened in 1913. Jung's addition of the "education" and "transformation" phases meant, in effect, the opening-up of psychoanalysis to a future-oriented, palpably religious dimension which he sometimes called "individuation" and sometimes "self-realization." Freud, bent on defending the scientific credibility of what many critics derided as his "Jewish science," would have none of it and dismissed Jung's initiative as dangerous "mysticism."

But for me phases three and four of "analysis" are as necessary to one and two as exhaling is to inhaling, and, not unlike the rhythm of breathing which has no discernible horizon or endpoint, they expand one's vision of life's possibilities "oceanically."[80] The exhilaration of this expansiveness and the sense of rich, creative possibility that comes with it are what I hope to have conveyed, however modestly, in the third part of the book, entitled "Transformation." Although so-called "deep" or archetypal dreams had a part even in the Freudian beginnings of my analysis, they became much more frequent, intense and awe-full in the later years, especially the last two. The dreams recorded in part three, though among the most important and interesting, are only a small sample of those I reported to Dr. P. Their numinous quality, the commingling energies of their vibrant images, began in time to seep into my waking consciousness, giving me a sense of what the German romantic poet Novalis called "the extraordinary within the ordinary." I know of no better capsule description of the religious sense than this: one's openness to the extraordinary right in the middle of old, humdrum, everyday routine. The great romantic theologian Friedrich Schleiermacher had a very simple definition of religion quite close to this: He called it "the experience of the Infinite within the finite." My point is that this delightful sense of having one foot in each of two commingling worlds, for me the most desirable of lifestyles, is nonetheless one I might well have missed had I gotten off the train at the end of my psychoanalysis.

Trains move horizontally. Another way of imagining the "two-worlds" consciousness opened up by analysis is in terms of Jung's own "vertical" distinction between the personal and the collective unconscious. Phases one and two come under "personal," three and four under "collective," the latter comprising a mysterious abyss beneath and beyond the limited threshold of individual experience. This is the realm of the spiritual: bottomless, inexhaustible, it is, in its deepest depths, where what we call "God" is to be found. Everything common, discrete and familiar to us, our ordinary everyday world, notwithstanding its appearance of solid stability, "hovers," "vibrates," in the cosmic palm of this abyss. It is the land of deep dreams where my adult daughter may appear to me one night as an eight-year-old in a resplendent taffeta communion dress set off by a wine-red sash or where I may come upon my mother lolling like Cleopatra on a throne of polished ivory. You don't need Jung to tell you these images are communicating something of great moment about your life; you just need him, or his surrogate, to help you figure out what it is, so that you can enjoy and appreciate it without the frustration of puzzlement.

My life's work, which has consisted in trying to figure out what those waking dreams we call works of literature "mean," and then sharing whatever I come up with with others, may have given me a leg up, so to speak, in the work of analysis. I was used to interpreting texts of stories, plays and poems, accustomed to looking at and beneath their verbal surfaces for clues to messages and meanings from the Abyss. My love of literature and the work—correction, *play*—of interpreting it has led to my forging, over the years, deep bonds with two stories in particular, E.T.A. Hoffmann's "The Golden Pot" and Franz Kafka's *The Metamorphosis*, both of which are taken up in detail here in chapters 14 and 6, 18 and 19, respectively. These two works, along with one or two others not mentioned in the book, have become for me master narratives, life narratives, virtual blueprints of what Joseph Campbell called "the Hero's Journey"; from first reading (the first of scores of readings), I identified with their spirit of inner adventure, their courageous exploration of that final frontier of the Self. This vibrant personal bond made the many classes in which I taught these tales to students some of the most memorable events of my life. There is no way I could ever have endured the ordeal of analysis without the support, the virtual friendship, of Anselmus and Gregor Samsa.

It is, I think, important to emphasize, with respect to these, my two "literary brothers," that I took an active hand in transforming them into what they became for me. Reading is never a merely passive exercise; it is active, shaping, creative, whether we're aware of it as such or not. It is better to be aware of it and use it to one's advantage. While remaining "objective," i.e., "professional," in my reading of these two tales, in the sense of basing my interpretations on the "factual" evidence of the texts and peripheral documents, there nevertheless came a point, as there must, when I had to use the evidence I had marshaled to opt for one interpretation or another. Early on in my career I chose to see "The Golden Pot" and *The Metamorphosis* as hopeful tales, indeed as grand epiphanies, narratives of the heroes' personal crises issuing in spiritual triumph. In the case of Kafka, this went against the grain of much critical opinion, which saw little that was humanistically or spiritually redeeming about Gregor Samsa. With respect to Hoffmann's tale, too, there were commentators, including even one of Jung's most illustrious students, who analyzed Anselmus in a tone of moral disdain as a "romantic escapist" whose delicate artistic-spiritual sensibilities were too fragile for the philistine society of early nineteenth-century Dresden.[81] But this weight of critical opinion went against *my* grain, moving me early on to take these two literary brothers to my bosom as proto-Jungian heroes and keep them there as constant reminders of the poet Rilke's charge to each of us that "you must change your life."[82] For me this is what Anselmus and Gregor did, in the process giving me a kind of spiritual blueprint for my own ordeal to come.

I belabor this matter of interpretation, whether of stories or dreams, only to help allay any anxieties on the part of the reader who may be considering undergoing analysis. One need not be an expert in literature or alchemy or ancient, arcane religions or have highly developed interpretive skills to take this dream trip of interpretation; one needs only good will, a normal intelligence and a spirit of adventure. The analyst will provide all necessary expertise. Also—and this, I admit, is a bit tricky—it is important for an analysand to learn to be less concerned with getting the interpretation of a dream, or symptom, or behavior, "right" than with getting it "vibrant." Another way to put this is that, if it "feels right," it probably *is* right. If it quickens you, enlivens you, causes chills to run up and down your spine, go with it, even if cold logic, strictly speaking, offers a "more convincing" point of view that, however, leaves you indifferent or antipathetic. Just as I created Anselmus and Gregor out of my own deepest psychospiritual need, even against the weight of critical opinion, so too should an analysand create for herself enriching readings of her own dreams that move her along in the direction of her true Self. If you travel far enough on the self-realization express, you will reach a point at which it becomes obvious that discovering the Truth and creating the Truth are indistinguishable.

In closing, I feel it incumbent on me to make it clear that, while my story may be one that shows analysis in an unequivocally favorable light, it should in no sense be taken as a dogmatic endorsement. What's good for me may not be good for another.[83] I've had too much disappointment in my life with paths that led nowhere, or simply led to other paths, to tout any one way as *the* Way. There are many ways to "the good life," and many more to come, I'm sure. For all I know, there's a reader out there somewhere who has been touched by psychospiritual genius—another Rinzai or Meister Eckhart or Jung—and is on the verge of blazing an entirely new trail to the Self, a trail wide enough to accommodate numberless wayfarers for ages to come. But if you're like me, your best bet will be to scout the shifting contours of the Western psycho-spiritual terrain slowly, carefully, and discerningly, until you come upon a path and a guide traveling it that move you to sign on. That's your "Dr. P."

Endnotes

1 See Gerd K. Schneider, *Es hätte alles bedeutend schlimmer kommen können; die Erlebnisse eines deutsch-amerikanischen Bauchnabeljuden Berliner Herkunft [Things Could've Been a Lot Worse: The Experiences of a German-American Bellybutton Jew of Berlin Origins]* (Vienna: Praesens, 2008).

2 This last-mentioned Flaubert's *Temptation of St. Anthony*, not a personal "Confessions," to be sure, but certainly a classic tale concerning the inner life.

3 In his memoir, *Angela's Ashes*. See the obituary, "Frank McCourt and the American Memoir," in *The New York Times*, July 25, 2009, edition.

4 Defined by Jung as "an acausal connecting principle," at work, for example, when it rains while the medicine man is doing his rain dance.

5 *The Razor 's Edge* (New York: Vintage, 2003), 4.

6 "Sitting" is an expression commonly used by American Zen students to refer to meditation. In doing *zazen* meditation, one sits still with folded hands and back upright on a black cushion or *zafu,* the legs crossed, typically, in the quarter-lotus position.

7 Northrup Frye, *The Great Code: The Bible and Literature* (New York: Harcourt Brace Jovanovich, 1981).

8 The koan is the principal form of meditation practiced by the Rinzai sect. Philip Kapleau (*The Three Pillars of Zen: Teaching, Practice, and Enlightenment,* rev. ed. [Garden City, NY: Anchor Doubleday, 1980]) defines it as "a formulation, in baffling language, pointing to ultimate truth. Koans cannot be solved by recourse to logical reasoning but only by awakening [through *zazen* meditation] a deeper level of the mind beyond the discursive intellect" (369; see n. 21). An example of a Rinzai koan well known to Westerners would be the question, "What is the sound of one hand clapping?" The koan alluded to here may be formulated thus: "Show me your face before your parents were born."

9 In his essay, *Dissemination,* trans. Barbara Johnson (London: The Athlone Press, 1981).

10 Actually, the experiment is called "the reversible goblet" (sometimes "the face-goblet illusion") and was introduced in 1915 by the Danish psychologist Edgar Rubin (1886-1951). It has become the classic demonstration of figure-ground reversal.

11 The archetype is a fundamental concept in the psychology of C. G. Jung and may, for our purposes, be defined as a psychic force lying in the deepest region of the unconscious, "beneath" the personal unconscious of Freud. Archetypes are impersonal and inherited, containing the accumulated wisdom of the human race over eons, and thus are said to reside in the collective unconscious. Archetypes and the collective unconscious are basically what separateJungian "analysis" from Freudian "psychoanalysis," Freud having rejected them as "mysticism." So Jungian analysis more or less parallels psychoanalysis to the "bottom" of the personal unconscious but then goes on to this deeper collective region of the psyche. Archetypes take on powerful imagistic forms as they manifest in deep or "archetypal" dreams, which they often do in times of crisis when the individual is driven to summon his own inner resources. They can point the way to the solution of conflicts, provided they are read by the

conscious mind carefully and wisely. Examples of archetypes would be the anima (mentioned in the text here), the shadow (one's dark, hence disowned or repressed impulses), the persona (the masks of the social self displayed to others), and the Self (at once the center and circumference of the psyche). Though archetypes are discrete forces, yet they are interwoven in the psyche's complex economy. In addition to dreams, archetypes often manifest in the artistic-cultural products of the dreaming imagination, such as the famous rose window of Notre Dame Cathedral (Self), the Mona Lisa (anima), the phantom of the opera (female anima, called "animus"), or Mr. Hyde (Dr. Jekyll's shadow)

12 See his masterful study, *Orientalism.*

13 See Sartre's magnum opus, *Being and Nothingness* (1943).

14 In *Dissemination,* trans. Barbara Johnson (Chicago: U of Chicago P, 1981).

15 "DBZ" refers to *Dai Bosatsu Zendo,* the Rinzai Zen Buddhist monastery founded in the Catskill Mountain region of Central New York State in the 1970's by my former teacher, Eido Tai Shimano Roshi.

16 See "Kafka Koans," *Religion and Literature* 23 (1991): 51-74.

17 For a good edition, see *The Metamorphosis,* trans. and ed. Stanley Corngold (New York: Norton, 1996).

18 In the closing lines of his sublime epic poem, *Faust.*

19 In chap. 24, "In the Happy Isles," of *Thus Spake Zarathustra,* trans. Thomas Common (New York: The Modern Library, 1954).

20 See Chögyam Trungpa, *Cutting through Spiritual Materialism,* ed. John Baker and Marvin Casper (Berkeley: Shambhala, 1973).

21 Kapleau 279.

22 See *The Spectrum of Consciousness* (Wheaton, Ill.: The Theosophical Publishing House, 1977), esp. chap. 6.

23 See Robert Langs, *Technique of Psychoanalytic Psychotherapy* (Lanham, Md.: Jason Aronson, 1989) and Mark Epstein, *Thoughts without a Thinker: Psychotherapy from a Buddhist Perspective* (New York: Basic books, 1995). The other three names on the list were Wilma Bucci, Peter Fonagy and Roger N. Walsh.

24 See *The Uses of Enchantment: The Meaning and Importance of Fairy tales.* (New York: Knopf, 1976).

25 Franz Kafka, *The Metamorphosis, The Penal Colony and Other Stories,* trans. Willa and Edwin Muir (New York: Schocken, 1961)

26 See, e.g., *The Metamorphosis,* which can be read as Gregor's ascent from the level of protagonist to that of author-narrator of the story as of the moment of his death; see also the parable, "The Spring."

27 Most of them have to do with such obvious matters as: set time and place, fair fee, privacy, monitoring the ground rules, proper dress and reasonable vacation interruptions. For further detail, see Robert Langs, *Ground Rules in Psychotherapy and Counselling* (London: Karnac, 1998).

28 Alas, the significance of baseball, and of C.F. Meyer's connection to that sport, never came to clear light in our discussion of the dream. It has, however, occurred to me since

then that my unconscious, in its infinite wisdom, was using the dream as a forum to tell me something profound about the—to put it kindly—esoteric nature of much contemporary scholarship in the humanities. To wit, in Goethe scholarship, which I know something about: "Goethe and the Yoyo"; "Goethe and Ice-skating"; and "Goethe and the Threnody." This is to pass over in silence much poststructuralist scholarship in vogue in literary studies since the late 1960's. It can speak for itself. (Or can it?)

29 This alludes to the philosopher's notion of *Geworfenheit* or "thrownness," i.e., the arbitrary life circumstances into which all human beings are "thrown" simply by virtue of being born.

30 Interestingly, to test for accuracy shortly after writing this chapter, I phoned Dr. P. himself to run my recollection of our discussion of this dream by him. He said that as far as memory served, it was accurate, and that, in any case, he agreed with the written reconstruction.

31 See note 21.

32 *Dokusan,* in Rinzai Zen, is the private interview between roshi and student in which the student is tested for insight into his koan. It is a way of keeping track of the student's maturation in his spiritual practice.

33 The *mu* koan recalls an exchange between Master Joshu (9th century) and a monk wherein the monk asks Joshu, "Does a dog have the Buddha nature?", and the latter answers, "mu!" (no) (Kapleau 76). The novice meditates upon this "mu" until the Zen master is satisfied that he has sufficiently discerned its spiritual significance.

34 In his introduction to the classic *Varieties of Religious Experience.*

35 Dr. P. is referring here to the dream discussed in chapter 8.

36 The Japanese word means basically "sermon," but one delivered by an enlightened master.

37 Like members of the earlier circle of German romantic writers based in Jena, e.g., Ludwig Tieck, Hoffmann was well aware of this allegorical technique of externalization for representing interior psychic processes. What is more interesting is that he may also have been aware of the use of the technique in such ancient Indian epics as the *Bhagavad Gita,* which is mentioned by name in *The Golden Pot.* Arjuna, the hero in that epic, and Anselmus in Hoffmann's tale both suffer inner trials by fire that are portrayed as external social events. This adds a touch of Eastern spice to Anselmus' spiritual adventures paralleling my own foray into Zen Buddhism. An adequate, if not entirely felicitous, translation of "The Golden Pot" can be found in Leonard J. Kent and Elizabeth C. Knight, eds., *Tales of E.T.A. Hoffmann* (Chicago: U of Chicago P, 1972) 14-92.

38 The Japanese term, *gassho,* designates, in Kapleau's definition, "the gesture [in Zen practice] of raising the hands palm to palm to indicate respect, gratitude, or humility, or all three" (365).

39 See note 32.

40 The koan as paraphrased here is taken from Thomas Cleary's translation, *No Barrier: Unlocking the Zen Koan* (New York: Bantam, 1993), p. 161.

41 The *kyosaku* is the traditional flat-edged stick used in Rinzai Zen monasteries

during *sesshin* (retreat) to strike meditators from behind on the fleshy part of the shoulders near the neck. Appearances to the contrary notwithstanding, it is not intended to punish the student, say, for laxity but to spur her to greater effort, which it does, when applied correctly, by arousing energy.

42 Merrell-Wolff's mystical philosophy of mind is set out in his study, *The Philosophy of Consciousness without an Object: Reflections on the Nature of Transcendental Consciousness* (New York: Julian, 1973).

43 A euphemism for members of organized-crime families.

44 The singer-comedian (1913-87) is forever linked with one of the most popular patter songs of all time, "Tchaikovsky (and Other Russians)."

45 See Wilhelm Emrich, *Franz Kafka,* 4th ed. (Frankfurt a.M.: Athenäum, 1965) 74-91. More recently, Stanley Corngold has argued subtly, brilliantly and convincingly that Gregor is not a symbol or metaphor of any kind, but, on the contrary, is intended by Kafka as the enactment of a strategy of figurative reversal: the "metamorphosis of the metaphor" back into literal representation; i.e., Gregor "really is" to be seen precisely as a human being who finds himself in the body of an insect. (See "Kafka's *The Metamorphosis:* Metamorphosis of the Metaphor," in Franz Kafka, *The Metamorphosis,* trans. and ed. Stanley Corngold [New York: Norton, 1996] 79-107.) Interesting as all this may be, it does not particularly concern us here since, throughout this book, I am presenting personal, and not scholarly, commentary on Kafka.

46 The works alluded to are, respectively, the tone poem, *Les Preludes,* and the overture to the opera, *William Tell.*

47 The reference is to James Hillman, an American psychologist who studied at the C.G. Jung Institute in Zurich and is credited with the development of archetypal psychology. His magnum opus is *Re-visioning Psychology* (1975).

48 *Going beyond the Pairs: The Coincidence of Opposites in German Romanticism, Zen and Deconstruction* (Albany, N.Y.: SUNY Press, 2001).

49 "The hill" is a traditional epithet for Syracuse University, which sits on one.

50 One of the most prominent of these was the Swiss jurist and scholar, Johann Jakob Bachofen (1815-87), whose work I came across in the 1980's while doing research on his contemporary and compatriot, C.F. Meyer, a writer discussed here in an entirely different context in chapter 11. Bachofen is the author of *Mother Right* (1861), an early anthropological study postulating a prehistoric "gynecocracy."

51 See notes 8 and 33.

52 See "Hyakujo's Geese, Amban's Doughnuts and Rilke's Carrousel: Sources East and West for Salinger's *Catcher,*" *Comparative Literature Studies* 34.3 (1997): 260-78.

53 See Paul Reps, ed. *Zen Flesh, Zen Bones: A Collection of Zen and Pre-Zen Writings* (New York: Anchor-Doubleday, n.d.).

54 It's called "An Imperial Message."

55 For this apt term as a description of our society's current obliviousness to the spiritual power of symbols, I am indebted to a letter written by religion scholar Harvey Cox and published on p. 6 of *The New York Times Book Review* for October 18, 2009.

56 Wagner's music drama (opera), *The Valkyrie,* the second of four comprising the

mythic cycle, *The Ring of the Nibelung.*
57 Milton H. Erickson (1901-80), American psychiatrist and psychologist, generally regarded as the foremost practitioner of hypnotherapy of the 20th century.
58 Traditional Buddhist metaphor for the mysterious sort of omniscience that comes with Enlightenment.
59 See p. 262.
60 In *Thus Spake Zarathustra* the philosopher envisions human evolution in terms of the successive stages of camel, lion and self-rolling wheel, that is to say, respectively, tamed beast carrying society's burden, ferocious beast that casts off that burden in rebellion, and the free, spontaneous wheel rolling effortlessly down the hill.
61 See note 48.
62 The coincidence of opposites.
63 Same shit, different day.
64 *Demian* is a *Bildungsroman* or novel of inner development tracing the growth of the hero, Emil Sinclair, from earliest school years to young manhood and breaking off at the beginning of World War I. Sinclair comes under the influence of a series of mentor figures, the most significant of these being the titular character who teaches him psychological self-reliance and whose mother, Frau Eva, welcomes him into their circle of spiritual adepts.
65 See *Briefe [Letters], 1902-1924* (New York: Schocken, 1958), 131.
66 See Gustav Janouch, *Gespräche mit Kafka: Aufzeichnungen und Erinnerungen [Conversations with Kafka: Notes and Recollections]*, 2nd rev. ed. (Frankfurt a.M.: S. Fischer, 1968), 239 and 242.
67 The book I read from here is: Franz Kafka, *Parables and Paradoxes. In German and English* (New York: Schocken, 1961), 151.
68 See, e.g., the parable, "The Spring," in *Parables and Paradoxes*, 185.
69 I use both Knieval and Irwin as generic hypotheticals for illustrative purposes only and intend no assertions about their personal psychodynamics.
70 Carl Gustav Carus wrote *Psyche* in 1846, Eduard von Hartmann wrote his 3-volume *Philosophy of the Unconscious* in 1869 and Max Nordau wrote *The Conventional Lies of Our Civilization* in 1883, each work an important philosophical forerunner of the individual-psychological edifice of psychoanalysis that Freud would construct at the end of the 19th century.
71 An inside nickname for the Jesuits.
72 Father Keating sets forth the rationale and technique for centering prayer in his book, *Open Mind, Open Heart: The Contemplative Dimension of the Gospel*, 20th anniversary edition (New York: Continuum, 2006). This is a book highly praised by Dr. P. who, let it be noted, has, among his other qualifications, a doctorate in theology, which, of course, gives his opinion on such matters considerable heft.
73 *Schein* (pronounced "shine") means "surface appearance," the "shiny outside" of a hing; *sein* (pronounced "zine") means literally "to be," hence, the being, essence or inner core of something. Germans love indulging in verbal play with this rhyming pair of opposites.

74 See his study, *Transformation Symbolism in the Mass* (1944-45).
75 See note 71.
76 A zendo is a large hall or room within a Zen monastary where meditation (*zazen*) is practiced.
77 This, the Latin motto of the Jesuit order, translates as "for the greater glory of God."
78 The two works by Dumoulin mentioned here are *Zen Buddhism: A History*, trans. James W. Heisig and Paul Knitter, 2 vols. (New York: Macmillan, 1988-90); and *Wu-men-kuan [Der Pass ohne Tor]*, Monumenta Nipponica 13 (Tokyo: Sophia UP, 1953). *Wu-men-kuan* is the original Chinese title of *The Gateless Gate* (Jap. *Mumonkan*), the early 13th-century Chinese koan collection still in use today in Rinzai Zen practice and previously mentioned here on p. 279 and p. 442.
79 This is a Sanskrit word referring to the illusory world, i.e., the phenomenal world or the world as perceived through the senses, which we generally mistake to be a more or less fixed entity.
80 In a response to his friend, the novelist Romain Rolland, at the beginning of *Civilization and its Discontents* (1930), Freud claimed to have none of the former's religious sensibility, which Rolland had described to him in a letter of 1927 as "an oceanic feeling."
81 The student alluded to is Aniela Jaffé, in her book, *"Was C.G. Jung a Mystic?" and Other Essays*, trans. Diana Dachler and Fiona Cairns, ed. Robert Hinshaw (Einsiedeln, Switzerland: Daimon, 1989).
82 The final line of his poem, "Archaic Torso of Apollo."
83 That said, I would caution against the serious pursuit of any path that failed to take repressed feelings and experiences into account. If I've learned anything from my own inner odyssey, it's that this accumulated baggage of life cannot be left at the station. It boards the self-realization express with you "regardless."

Selected Books from PalmArtPress

Michael Keith
Perspective Drifts Like a Log on a River
ISBN: 978-3-941524-387-3 (EN) *
200 Pages, Pensees, Softcover, English

Carmen-Francesca Banciu
Light Breeze in Paradise
ISBN: 978-3-941524-95-8
ca 360 Pages, English/Greek

John Berger / Liane Birnberg
garden on my cheek
ISBN: 978-3-941524-77-4
60 Pages, Poetry/Art, Softcover/flaps, English

Carmen-Francesca Banciu
Berlin Is My Paris- *Stories from the Capital*
ISBN: 978-3-941524-66-8 *
204 Pages, English

Michael Lederer
In the Widdle Wat of Time
ISBN: 978-3-941524-70-5 *
150 Pages, poetry and very short stories, Hardcover, English

Dorothea Flechsig
NightSwim
ISBN: 978-3-941524-72-9
60 Pages, Poetry, Hardcover, English/German

Manfred Giesler
The Yellow Wallpaper *Ein Monologue*
ISBN: 978-3-941524-75-0 *
68 Pages, Theatre, open-thread cover, English/German

Carmen-Francesca Banciu
Mother's Day - *Song of a Sad Mother*
ISBN: 978-3-941524-47-7 *
244 Pages, English

Jörg Rubbert
Paris-New York-Berlin - *Streetphotography 1978 - 2010*
ISBN: 978-3-941524-58-3
260 Pages, Photo Retrospective, Softcover/flaps, English/German

Runhild Wirth
Come Here, I Want to Ruin You!
Palast der Republik - Analysis of Dissolution
ISBN: 978-3-941524-52-1
120 Pages, Poetry/Art, Hardcover, English/German

Alexander de Cadenet
Afterbirth - *Poems & Inversions*
ISBN: 978-3-941524-59-0
64Pages, Poetry/Art, Softcover/flaps, English

Wolfgang Nieblich
Distant Yet so Near or **The Currywurst**
ISBN: 978-3-941524-49-1 (EN) *
64 Pages, 18 Coloured Fotos, Engliish

Michael Lederer
The Great Game - ***Berlin-Warschau Express and Other Stories***
ISBN: 978-3-941524-12-5 (EN) *
242 Pages, 18 Short Stories, Softcover, English

Maria Reinecke
La Rambla - *Barcelona Story*
ISBN: 978-3-941524-20-0 (EN) *
91 Pages, Short Story, English

* Also available as E-Book